STONE SOULS

A Dystopian Novel

Doug,
Enjoy the
book like
you
enjoy the
beaches
in!
ct.

James Rourke

Printed in the United States of America

ISBN: 978-1-956019-74-2 (paperback)
ISBN: 978-1-956019-75-9 (ebook)

**Canoe Tree
Press**

4697 Main Street
Manchester Center, VT 05255

Canoe Tree Press is a division of DartFrog Books

Dedicated to
Juliette Juber
May your world be infinitely brighter
than the one in these pages

CHAPTER 1

FACING THE DAY

Human beings are the root of every meaningful problem on Earth. No other creature causes individual and group disharmony like "Homo sapiens." Thousands of transgressions reveal the horror people often are to themselves. Every scar on history. Every tear pulled from children's eyes by underdeveloped adults. Fools oblivious of their own bias smugly present theory upon theory designed to elevate the lot of humankind. These efforts ultimately fail because of each theorist's faulty vision. Thankfully, there is no problem that cannot be solved by the deaths of the "Homo sapiens" most responsible.

Kurt Adams chuckled as he constructed the final draft of his message for Omega and Alpha-level officers. These words, which he hoped would galvanize the purifiers, were the driving force of his life. The evidence of their veracity was all around him in the glorious vistas offered by the Common States of America. So much blood spilt — the blood of the unworthy, the uninspired, the unwilling — and the unimaginative - to create the vibrant society that he safeguarded. Another ocean's worth would be gladly shed to maintain his beloved home.

He smiled as he drew a deep breath and exhaled slowly, serenely embracing his present moment. Wearing a simple black tee shirt and gray gym shorts, he began the process of brewing his habitual morning cup of coffee. The automatic coffee brewer hissed to life as he stepped back from the glossy, marbled island in his open kitchen. Thoughts of the coming mission and the bloodletting he organized contributed to his peaceful demeanor. How he loved what he did and his place in the Common States of America. His world was, in many ways, brutal. Some might say ugly. The fact his joy was incomprehensible to some meant nothing.

The coffee brewer paused, still a good minute from completion, which allowed him to gaze, as he often did in the morning, at the unobstructed view of Chicago from his penthouse apartment. The towering complex, erected a mere ten blocks from Forbearance University and one mile from the Museum of Fine Art, allowed him to admire the beauty of the city, transformed by the will and vision of the C.S.A. Every street was pristine, landscaped medians and immaculate sidewalks running as veins through the city. Forbearance University, with its polished stone buildings and marbled arched entrances, glistened in the morning sun, a vison of transcendence in the heart of the city.

It took less than twenty-five years to make the city a marvel, as opposed to the three hundred years of stagnation, excuses, and delusion that the city had to bear when it was a part of the decrepit United States of America. It was little wonder that, despite the lamentations of lesser people, another initiation was primed to unfold.

"Kurt?" A woman's sleepy voice drifted from the bedroom, cutting into his meditations. He did not answer, though his smile did fade. "Kurt? Come back to bed. It's early."

"No," Kurt said in a voice unblemished by emotion. Back to bed? Bed was for fucking and sleeping, not lazy lingering and mindless chatter. He had fucked and slept enough the previous night. There was no need to be abed. "Do feel free to join me in the kitchen, Laura. I know you love the view."

"That I do," Laura marveled, striding into the open space. She wore a pristine white bathrobe, opened to showcase a curve-hugging purple teddy. "Sure you don't want to come back to bed?"

Kurt responded abruptly, looking at her and nodding. "Positive."

He circled the island and moved to a black leather couch situated before the massive windows in the living space. The panoramic windows allowed Laura to enjoy the view of Lake Michigan from the rarified air of Kurt's home. He motioned Laura to join him. As always, she did. Kurt rubbed her leg as she sat, causing a beaming smile to burst onto her face as she fell into her nook on the sofa. Tranquility combined with radiance as she nuzzled, eyes closed, and sighed. After a second sigh, Laura returned her attention to Kurt, who was enjoying the quiet. He gently played with her hair as he smiled upon her. She paused between the seconds before speaking.

"This moment can't last much longer, can it?"

"Such is the nature of moments," Kurt replied, looking at a black clock with silver Roman numerals situated on the wall high above the floor.

"Gotta get to work?" Laura asked the question with full knowledge of the answer.

"I do," Kurt said. "There is still much to prepare before the seventh."

Laura stopped talking as Kurt's head tilted toward her, ice replacing the previous warmth of his gaze. She knew the answer to her unspoken question would be no. Always no. "I'm sorry. I know you can't disclose your work to anyone without clearance, let alone me."

"It is not personal," Kurt responded in what he surmised was a reassuring tone. "Do not take it that way."

"I know. I just...." Laura looked at Kurt's face and recognized the necessity of changing the topic. "So, um, do you want me to...?" Laura stammered as she considered her question. She quickly settled on what she hoped carried the best chance for a positive response. "Be here when you get back tonight?"

"I will not be back tonight. Or the next. In fact, I likely won't see you until we cross paths in Room two seventeen on the seventh."

"Wow!" Her surprise overrode her disappointment. "You're going to make an appearance in two seventeen? I'm shocked."

"It is necessary," Kurt said.

"I see. 'It is necessary.'" Laura echoed, mocking Kurt's serious tone. "How do you know I'll be there?"

Laura's bravado caused him to smile. "You will."

"And I will be there for you?"

"You will," Kurt boasted, leaning in to kiss Laura. She playfully pulled back for an instant before grabbing his head and dragging him in.

The kiss ended because Kurt stood up, pulling himself away from Laura's loving vise grip.

"That is one thing I do...admire...about you," Kurt said with cautious sincerity.

"What's that?" Laura asked, now sprawling on the couch.

A wry smile appeared on his face. "You may well be stronger than some of the Alpha's I work with."

"Am I?"

"Don't let it go to your head. I work with some surprisingly weak people. Would you like some breakfast before I go?"

Stretching her arms above her head, Laura cooed, "That would be lovely." Head settled into a pillow, she prepared for a lazy morning.

"Excellent!" Kurt turned on his heel and snapped an order. "498! Breakfast!"

"No, Kurt. I didn't..." Laura groaned, and her face contorted as if she just smelled something rancid.

Model Life Being #498-Active Model, a slender android standing about six feet tall, entered the room. It was graceful and almost completely silent, as if walking on a cushion of air. The height and the silver and black hues interwoven throughout its torso and limbs were not standard to the Active model but Kurt had made some alterations to his personal attaché. A translucent, ceramic faceplate had facial features moving in a constant flux of programmed emotions. Simulated polite tones came forth with the being's metallic voice.

"Good morning, Commander Adams. Ms. Laura. What may I do for you this morning?"

Laura nodded at the android as she quickly walked to Kurt's side. She placed a hand on his shoulder and rose to her toes so she could whisper, sharper than intended, into his ear. "I didn't want an MLB. I thought..."

"I know what you thought," Kurt said dismissively, stepping away. "That's not what it is."

"Everything copacetic, Commander?" the MLB asked. Neither the android or Kurt revealed if they noticed Laura's sigh, delivered with a far different tone than earlier, accompanied by rolling eyes.

"Indeed, 498. Indeed. I will be leaving in twenty minutes to continue preparations for the initiation protocols. Please make Ms. Laura whatever she desires for breakfast."

"It will be a pleasure, sir."

"Outstanding," Kurt blurted with fierce formality. He continued to deliver orders with the full expectation they would be followed. "Then proceed to Forbearance University for the gala tonight. Laura, I will see you on the seventh." Kurt exited to the bedroom without waiting for a response from either Laura or 498-A. Which being was more important to him was up for debate.

"What shall I make for you, Ms. Laura?"

The fact the MLB seemed oblivious to her frustration fueled Laura's anger. She glared at her android host; a dozen sharp quips accompanied by flippant requests raged across her mind. In the end, however, she requested a spinach and mushroom omelet, home fries, a side of bacon, a cup of tea, and freshly squeezed orange juice. If one is allowed to enjoy the luxuries afforded an Omega-level officer, then it is best to enjoy the perks.

CHAPTER 2

CARRYING A LEGACY

Erin McGreggor, chancellor of the Common States of America, writhed at a desk. She was granted full access to the president of Forbearance University's office to prepare for the fiftieth anniversary celebration. All was in readiness for the evening. Almost all. Hanging over Erin's head was the task of submitting the final edits of her opening remarks. How she hated preparing speeches; more, she believed, than giving them. She was a workhorse, satisfied to work tirelessly behind the scenes rather than a show horse stepping forth for public consumption. Years of on-the-job training had not altered this fundamental trait. She knew deep in her core that the event being marked was worthy of celebration. That she, as chancellor, should usher in the evening was completely understandable and, in the end, an honor. Personal discomfort was a small price for the good of all.

A glance at the digital wall clock informed her that the final draft was due in fifty-seven minutes. Plenty of time to deliberate, brood, and ultimately make very few changes as the speech had already endured multiple drafts and edits.

"Madam Chancellor," a robotic voice spoke through the communication link Erin wore as an earring, "you asked me to...sir...please wait...."

A second voice, agitated and terse, was picked up by the comlink. "Just let me by, you glorified can opener."

Erin's door was pushed open, and Ryan Vancese stormed into the room with all the vigor his eighty-eight years of life allowed him to muster. Cane in hand, he started to speak — only to be interrupted by the dutiful MLB.

"Prime Minister Vancese has arrived, Madam. Shall I...."

"We're fine, 1-E. Thank you."

"Very good," stated the dutiful MLB.

"Very good," mocked Ryan Vancese. "Damn android insisted I wait in that room like some child waiting for a pediatrician. I'm not having it."

"Very mature. You do realize I could program 1-E to physically restrain you if I so choose?"

Ryan grunted, "You do realize I know you would never do that."

"No," admitted Erin, smiling at the elder statesman, "I would not. What brings you around, Ryan? I am not changing my decision about you sitting on the dais with me tonight."

"Oh, that I know," Ryan conceded. He circled the desk as he shuffled with his cane. Leaning back, Erin wondered what her ever sharp-witted mentor was plotting. "I learned long ago how to recognize when a McGreggor made up their mind because, once that happens —"

"— we become immovable. So you've told me. Often."

"The truth bears repeating," Ryan declared, now standing behind Erin. Whatever combination of past memories and present moments brought a glint to his eye would never be known. His hand almost fell on Erin's back but, at the final moment, it found her chair. "What are you doing here? Still uselessly agonizing over your little speech?"

"While I would not categorize it that way, yes, I am." Erin leaned forward, resting her chin in the palm of her hand. She was doing little more than pretending to read at this point, as she found it difficult to concentrate with Ryan leaning over her left shoulder.

"May I take a closer look?" Ryan asked. "Perhaps a second reader could allay your fears?"

Sighing, Erin rose from her chair. "By all means."

Ryan groaned as he settled into the black mesh office chair. He snapped a pair of readers onto his nose and leaned toward the screen. Head cocked to the side, Ryan mumbled as he read the first line. Halfway through the second sentence, he smacked his lips as if enjoying a fine meal. An approving grunt rose from him just before he hit 'send'. Erin's shocked gasp only caused him to smile.

"There you go," the octogenarian laughed, quite pleased with his action.

"Ryan! I wasn't —"

"The speech is ready," interrupted Ryan confidently as he pulled himself to his feet, "and so are you."

Erin folded her arms and unfolded them. Eventually, after shifting her weight from her left leg to the right, she opted to fold them again.

"I'm supposed to be grateful?"

Ryan shrugged. "I have no idea. I just know you're ready."

"Thank you." Erin fumed. She settled back into her chair as Ryan circled to the front of the desk and took a seat. After a brief struggle with her face, Erin smiled and shook her head, shaking off the shock of Ryan's action. "You must have been quite a character in your youth, Ryan."

"I was what I was. You know most of that history. The real force was your grandfather. None of this would have happened without Daniel's vision and tenacity. He was a prodigious man. And you are a worthy heir to his legacy. Don't forget that."

Wistfully, Erin said, "I won't. Of course, you were instrumental in that revolutionary process. History will remember you as one of the architects of this society. You were, and still are, a force yourself."

"Those were some extraordinary days," Ryan responded, losing himself momentarily in memories. Returning to the present, he spoke forcefully. "And we have extraordinary days before us. The initiation of Louisiana looms not long after tonight's festivities."

"That it does. You're not here to make a last plea for a change of plans, are you? Seeking an audience for the ole soft sell?"

"No." Ryan rebuked the insinuation with a disgruntled tone, accompanied by the waving of his hand. "You and Special Agent Adams seem to have a vision for the unfolding of the initiation protocols. Which, you remember, I helped write some fifty years ago."

"This I know," Erin admitted even as she reworded her earlier question. "Are you sure this isn't a final sales pitch?"

"Definitely not. Just an old man feeling nostalgic. Proud of our past and looking forward to your future."

Erin blushed despite herself. Content with his visit, Ryan pushed himself to his feet. Erin rose with him, despite his insistence she remain seated.

"Stubborn," Ryan groused.

"Determined," Erin corrected before turning more serious. "I feel like we should toast your previous thought."

"Perhaps we will tonight, Chancellor," Ryan said as he reached into his jacket pocket. He produced a folded piece of paper, which he handed to Erin. "For now I offer you this, written by your grandfather's own hand."

Erin's heart pounded with increasing force as she unfolded the document to see a draft of her nation's Declaration of Independence. The words pulsated with life. Hope, purpose, and courage could be gained by simply holding the relic in the hand of your heart. The lined paper, slightly stained in the upper right corner by what appeared to be coffee, seemed impervious to time. It was a mystical scroll carrying the truths that set a nation free. That other nations, due to their crippling stupidity, could not comprehend its glory was unimportant. Perhaps even tragic.

"My...how long have you...?"

"He handed it to me on April third, two thousand forty-eight." Ryan stared into the past as he spoke. His pride in his friend and their accomplishments filled the room. "The next day, April fourth, he sent the final copy to the president of the United States. It is time for it to be in the hands of the right person."

Erin put the paper on her desk and bent over it. She gazed, bathing in the document that carried her grandfather's spirit and her father's hopes. Thirty seconds ticked away before she looked up at Ryan, body still bent over her inheritance. "This is my grandfather's writing," she whispered. "This is amazing. I don't...thank...."

"It is indeed amazing. It is the final draft written by the hand of Daniel McGreggor before he took to the keyboard. He was rather old fashioned in his approach to writing. But effective, I think."

"Indeed," Erin echoed, watching Ryan amble to the door. As was his manner, he did not say goodbye but just left when he felt there was nothing else to say. She touched a broach on her jacket and whispered. MLB 1-E, having received her signal, opened the door, only to be verbally assaulted by the prime minister as he pushed by. The commotion caused by Ryan's exit completed, Erin returned to the historic document in her hands.

A Declaration of Independence from the
Common States of America

When in the course of human events it becomes necessary for a people to recognize the bonds of national unity are merely aged chains forged of archaic philosophies and a faulty concept of human nature, and that these chains only tether them to an already failed experiment, then liberating people of reason and breaking all bonds with a hollow and decrepit nation becomes the worthiest of goals; but a decent respect for a shared past requires that they should declare the causes that demand the severing of all ties.

We hold these truths to be self-evident, that Homo sapiens are creatures of a certain kind and are not, nor ever have been, conceived as equal. No sociocultural theory, no government program, no shallow philosophy, or earnest and unrealistic religious hopes can alter this fact. Attempts to deny the reality of human nature only leads to the stunting of promise, the praising of mediocrity, the dampening of creativity, the creation of a pathologically immature nation, and a dishonorable citizenry that is increasingly dependent on a labyrinth of lies and self-deceptions in order to maintain fidelity to a patently false ideal.

Governments are instituted among people to guarantee the skilled, intelligent, and motivated have the resources and freedom to develop, with steadfast resolution, their best faculties. These efforts are validated by the ongoing dedication of the good citizen to his or her essential duty: the improvement of the nation. The goal of the good citizen is to enhance society and the goal of society must be to prepare their citizenry for this purpose. There is no greater good. Stable societies cannot be based on abstractions which are naught but pillars built on sand. Government, therefore, must promote, protect, and ensure the symbiotic relationship between citizen and state. The good of the many must outweigh the good of the few and, particularly, the one.

The efforts of the good citizen must not to be hindered by the lazy, the slovenly, the uninspired, the delusional, the unimportant, the bitter, or any member or faction of the egocentric masses interested completely in themselves, incapable and unwilling to work to any fruitful and collective end.

The role of government is not to fund foolishness, save those unwilling to work on their own salvation or funnel valuable resources to the perpetually needy, but should, by any means necessary, annihilate the existence of these destructive attributes and the people who worship dysfunction.

The manner in which a government directs a nation's wealth and resources forecasts that nation's destiny. Therefore, the Common States of America establishes itself out of an authentic desire to do that which the United States of America so often promises and, with stunning regularity, fails to do.

The United States cannot keep its cities clean and accepts crime as an inescapable part of the human condition.

The United States cannot keep its children safe, as all forms of child abuse is rampant and punishment is meek.

The United States, embracing a dogma of unthinking and reckless parent worship, allows children to suffer because of spineless institutions that prevent the immediate removal of children from the hands of derelict adults.

The United States cannot properly educate their citizens because the inept, disinterested, and slothful are allowed to occupy space in the classroom, protected by the law, while the taxpayer investment of $200,000 per child over a preliminary academic career is wasted.

The United States tolerates thoughtless, vulgar, uninformed, and destructive speech because it is a nation of cowards afraid to declare some thoughts are not worth sharing. Sanctifying free speech over intelligent thought is the sign of a nation deserving of desertion, if not death.

The United States spends billions on prisons, rehabilitation centers, homeless shelters, and welfare. This investment bears no fruit and prevents progress in more productive arenas.

The United States worships poverty for it allows unenlightened leaders to appear magnanimous while they privately detest the poor but use them as political props.

The United States worships greed and materialism even as they decry these traits in individuals they loathe.

The United States has promulgated a myth of equality and a delusion of freedom to maintain the allegiance of a people who can never be equal and lack the gravitas to even comprehend the meaning and value of freedom.

The United States has failed to grasp the evidence of history that trumpets the simple truth that humanity and dignity is earned through consistent effort, be it individual or collective.

The United States has continued to promote the false idea that mere birth into the genus Homo sapiens carries with it a mark of intrinsic value.

The United States has allowed the lie of intrinsic value to create an inescapable cult of narcissism that harms the population more grievously than any pollutant possibly could. Its growth continues unchecked and unchallenged.

The United States has allowed this cult of narcissism to metastasize into a media that merely serves its own myopia.

The United States, in its media, politics, and sociocultural fabric, is a nation of factions fanatically dedicated to false narratives rather than the search for truth.

The United States has embraced an apologetic doctrine where there can be crime with no criminals.

The United States has become completely unworthy of its historic exemplars. Monuments to such people are a sham and an insult.

The United States has descended into an intellectual and ethical nadir, thereby permitting infantile projections, unsubstantiated accusations, shallow reasoning, and petty cleverness to be mistaken for high wisdom.

The United States publicly lauds industriousness as a virtue but only rewards such effort in certain arenas.

The United States publicly laud productiveness but routinely coddles and excuses lethargy and indolence.

The United States has created an economic system that does not reward excellence so much as ownership and the navigation of legalities.

The United States allows the false idol of discrimination to trump reasoned analysis and to excuse lowly character.

The United States has allowed itself, because of the aforementioned transgressions, to settle on a national ethos that is repugnant and unworthy of loyalty.

It is for these reasons that we, the representatives of the Common States of America, inform the government of the United States of America that it is our intention to extricate ourselves from this wretched union. Whatever blood is spilt will be on your hands, as you could allow a peaceful exodus. Regardless of your actions, the inevitable will occur. A nation will be founded that rewards excellence, promotes growth, dismantles crime, and allows human beings — creatures of a most particular kind — to flourish.

CHAPTER 3

OUT OF THE BROKEN PAST

Faculty and alumni of Forbearance University in Chicago, Illinois, moved hastily alongside honored guests as the hour approached. Some settled into the seating arrangements established in the various courtyards on campus while others sought their assigned halls where the evening's greeting would be broadcast. In a mere fifteen minutes, Erin McGreggor would be delivering a short address to usher in an evening of celebration. Of course, it was not merely Forbearance University that was electric. The citizens of the Common States of America whether in larger cities, suburban dwellings, or rural hamlets, were united in their love of country and dedication to its purpose. They worked hard and reaped the benefits of their fortitude. Through their combined efforts, their new nation delivered on the failed promises of the United States.

People gathered in city squares and open fields to watch Erin's address on Megatron screens provided by the government to enhance the local celebrations. The sounds emanating from house and block parties dwindled, swallowed by the clock as eight p.m. approached. From Cedar Rapids, Iowa, to Detroit, Michigan, faces beamed in anticipation of the chancellor's appearance. Small towns in Tennessee and Kentucky roared approval and toasted the other states of the C.S.A. as the final two minutes counted down.

Wisconsin, Michigan, Illinois, Iowa, Indiana, Missouri, Kentucky, Tennessee, and North Carolina were the original states that broke away from the U.S. and formed the C.S.A. The standard of living, the importance placed on leisure time, the rewarding of effort, and the non-existent crime rate enticed Oklahoma and Ohio to petition the fledgling country for admittance. They joined and, after the demands of initiations, the citizens saw all the rewards they hoped for and more. Always more. The rumors of the trials of initiation did not deter the people of Louisiana and Georgia, tired of centuries of promises and excuses, from seeking refuge from impotent madness. Stability in the storm.

For this moment, however, Erin was not concerned with initiating new states. Tonight, as Ryan had stated so perfectly, was time to be proud of the past. She could look to the future in due time. She smiled from her backstage sitting area as she heard the crowd in Vancese Hall explode into raucous applause. The eight dignitaries who would share the stage with her this evening had taken their chairs. Ryan Vancese and Kurt Adams were among those who took the stage. Which of these two men was the most uncomfortable on the stage was unclear.

What was beyond doubt was the joyful accolades Ryan's appearance garnered. The eighty-eight-year-old rarely made public appearances at this point, making him more legend than man. The fact that massive banners hung from the rafters, each one adorned with the image of one of the renowned signers of the Declaration of Independence only added to the drama of the moment. Audience members in suits and flowing evening gowns gawked as they looked at the banner depicting a thirty-nine-year-old prime minister, a young revolutionary who helped build the very nation they all enjoyed so very much. The crowds, either in the room or watching from across the nation, needed no help. They did not need to be orchestrated to recognize the moment or instructed in how to react to the history standing before them. They were not Americans, and their applause for the prime minister, the last living signer of the Declaration, shook the earth beneath their feet and then coursed through the stars above their heads.

Yunna Jin, the conductor of the Chicago Symphony Orchestra, sat to Ryan's left. She leaned to whisper in his ear. "They are so honored by your presence, Prime Minister. As am I."

"Thank you, Ms. Jin," Ryan answered. "They should save their applause for your performance later tonight in the Corene Center. I know I am looking forward to it."

Yunna blushed as she looked to respond, but Ryan was pushing himself to his feet. He waved to acknowledge the crowd. To settle them was also his hope. His roles as revolutionary and politician brought him a level of fame that was still mystifying; as adulation was never his goal. Standing before the other dignitaries, Ryan gestured at them and clapped, encouraging the room to focus on the group rather than the individual. Much to the pleasure of the prime minister, they did so. Old arms shook with the effort of lowering himself to his seat. As their applause faded, he scanned the row and saw Kurt Adams looking at him, coal-encrusted eyes glistening slightly. Kurt nodded his head and clapped his hands gently four times. Ryan nodded back and smiled; a rare moment of congruence flowed between the two men. It was well that they marked it.

"You are clearly the star tonight," Yunna stated as Ryan settled into his chair.

"Not for much longer," Ryan replied, his gaze moving off stage to Erin.

The chancellor stood behind a curtain, scanning the auditorium a final time before taking the stage. MLBs navigated the crowd, directing people to their seats while handing out hors d'oeuvres and drinks. The podium at the center of the stage beckoned, but Erin granted a few extra moments for people to settle in following the spontaneous show of adulation granted the prime minister.

A metallic voice with soothing tones interrupted her wait. "It is time, Madam Chancellor."

"Thank you, 1-E," Erin said to her personal attaché.

A rousing ovation met Erin as she took the stage and approached the podium. Public crowds and people in their homes shared the live audience's enthusiasm. Horns blared in the streets and cowbells rang in fields. Erin smiled as she waved to the audience. There was no well-rehearsed pointing or exaggerated smile on her face. Authenticity, not showmanship, was always the goal. Three more waves and a mouthed 'thank you' preceded her gesturing for the crowd to sit.

"Your greeting honors me and, more importantly, those great individuals who fifty years ago today sent the signed copy of our Declaration of Independence to the ever-eroding United States of America. Some chains are made to be broken!"

This brought forth another roar as all knew the Civil War which led to their independence was not won by better tactics alone but stronger will and principles. The will to break away and create proved stronger than the will to preserve. The will to fight for the right to fulfill potential proved, finally, stronger than the whims of those who sought to tether people to a nation rooted in bygone notions that ultimately led to delusion and despair. That the United States could not comprehend this was of no consequence to the new nation, which was slowly spreading its influence over the continent once dominated by its anachronistic rival.

"So, we stand here today," Erin continued vigorously, "to commemorate their efforts and to renew our own commitment to the ideas that have brought greatness to the Common States of America. These daring notions will continue to guide us into a bright future. Moving forward, however, does not mean leaving behind precious aspects of the past that provide the very impetus for our future visions. I know you have already greeted him, but allow me to express my inexhaustible respect for Prime Minister Ryan Vancese, the only remaining member of our revolutionary founders!"

Erin stepped back from the podium and clapped. She clapped for Ryan and her grandfather, as she sought out the banners on which they towered above the room. She clapped for her father, who died building the nation. She clapped for all the fathers and mothers, as well as brothers and sisters, who had done so. The applause, while not reaching the earlier din, comfortably stretched a full minute before abating. A little more than slightly embarrassed by the clamor, Ryan leaned forward and offered one last wave. The applause slowed, Erin being one of the last people to cease.

"Trust me, he may be a little put out by your respect, but no man deserves it more," she said, continuing her introduction. She acknowledged each dignitary on the stage, concluding with Ms. Jin, whose accomplishments allowed for an easy transition to the body of her presentation.

"I am sure some members of other nations may be surprised that Ms. Jin is seated on this stage. Such a reaction only reveals that many think in stereotypes rather than facts. We, all of us in this auditorium, all those in the streets of our major cities and large towns, all those gathered in arenas to celebrate this night, all those at local restaurants and bars, and those of us surrounded in our homes by loved ones...we know that here in the C.S.A. we celebrate excellence in all fields with unapologetic mirth as we pursue the flourishing life.

"The flourishing life, not some small and egocentric pursuit of happiness, is the rightful goal of creatures of a human kind. To develop one's intellectual curiosity so as to spend a lifetime in the joyful pursuit of knowledge is the goal of humanity. To develop character so to act with unflinching pride in one's self and their nation is the mark of a mature citizen. Love of beauty so that the art generated by masters can be appreciated. Generativity so we consciously work to leave a better nation for our children than the one they were born into. Discipline so we lay down at night knowing the day has not been wasted, and the unrelenting clock is not an enemy. We are the only aspirants of Eudaimonia. We are the only nation with a citizenry courageous enough to integrate personal and public well-being. The only nation with the audacity to live the truth of our kind rather than flounder about in the delusion of false ideals!"

The crowd roared to life again, each audience member knowing they were contributors to their nation. Erin spoke to each one of them individually because the words were earned by a citizenry dedicated to being conscientious benefactors to their communities, large and small, rather than a mere occupant or worse, a leech.

"Sadly," Erin continued, "we were not always thus. To our brain-washed shame, we accepted the status quo posited by the U.S. How embarrassing to think that we once saw that corrupt nation as the best option on Earth. But thankfully, some people of uncompromising vision arose. People who recognized this falsehood for the lie it was and the wretched damage it wrought.

"Tonight is a night of twin goals as the past and future coalesce in the present. We celebrate, and I will not stand in your way much longer, our victorious past as we prepare to welcome our brothers and sisters from Louisiana into the fold. Their initiation begins in three days. Old ideas are hard to shake but once you are free, your true capacities can be sharpened, goals can be pursued, and the rewards of effort experienced. The original members of our nation already know this, and our most recent initiates, Oklahoma and Ohio, are starting to truly experience this joy. Your glory is our glory as ours is yours. So, wherever you are tonight, celebrate your victories and let others tremble before the power of earned pride and unending determination!"

Thunderous applause erupted, and Erin waved to the crowd. She nodded approvingly, gifting the crowd one last smile before turning to exit the stage. She was met by Prime Minister Vancese who rose to join her. Yunna Jin also exited, joined by MLB 1-E who escorted her to the Corene Center, her orchestra already in place. Other MLBs guided audience members from the hall. Some proceeded to the ornate space where the Chicago Symphony Orchestra awaited. Other people went to the banquet hall where Chef Pierre Dubois had prepared a culinary delight. It was not until the final stragglers left that Kurt Adams rose from his chair and exited the room, striding purposefully toward the office in the upper levels of the auditorium. Celebration was for others. All that truly mattered was the final preparations to ensure the successful launch of the initiation protocols.

CHAPTER 4

INITIATION APPROACHES

"Commander Adams," Erin said, looking up at the uncompromising figure as he entered her office. She ran her index finger over a scanner, and her computer slowly folded upon itself before descending into the storage unit in her desk. A slight hiss as the process began was all the sound accompanying the mechanical activity. As the computer was swallowed, two binders emerged from the storage recesses. "How are you this morning?"

"I am well," Adams responded.

"Very good," Erin noted after a brief pause to allow Adams time to add a thought or two. Someday she would learn such consideration was unnecessary. "Did you enjoy last night's festivities?"

"I enjoyed making sure all was in order for the launch of the initiation protocols on the seventh."

"You were ready for the launch of the protocols two weeks ago," retorted Erin dryly, her index finger tapping the hard copy of Adams' report. "There was no pressing issue for you to address last night. All is in order."

"These are important times and, as you know, I have concerns that I am well aware are not shared by the prime minister," Adams remarked without looking over his shoulder to confirm it was Ryan Vancese who entered the chancellor's office.

"What?" Ryan asked as he shuffled into the room. Erin leaned forward in her chair, fighting the impulse to help the aging founder to his seat. Ryan's staunch side-glance conveyed his desire that she remain seated. She acquiesced to the unspoken request, allowing Ryan to continue his questioning. "What are you saying, Special Agent?"

Adams turned and watched Ryan lower himself into a leather-bound armchair, his cane placed within reach of his right hand. An MLB gracefully entered the room and handed Ryan a cup of coffee, augmented by two creams, six sugars, and a cocktail of assorted powdered medications.

"Your coffee, sir," the android said through digitized lips.

Ryan took the mug with a grunt. This would be the first of many servings he would consume during the day. "Very good. That will be all."

"Nothing for the chancellor or the secretary of internal security?" the MLB asked with programmed politeness.

"That will be all, 281-S," Erin stated. "You can leave us be."

"Very well. I will wait for the prime minister outside the office," the android verified before exiting. Despite striding on two legs, the automaton seemed to glide rather than walk.

Adams took the opportunity to reiterate, "You do not share my concerns." He turned his head so he could look at Ryan but kept his body stationary, hands clasped behind his back. "That is what I said."

"I do not," Ryan snapped, pushing himself to his feet. "I still believe we should have accepted Georgia's petition at this time as well. This nation was not built by being squeamish."

"Nor was it built by being rash," countered Adams.

Erin, annoyed at this return to a tired topic, interrupted the verbal joust. "Let us not rehash decided issues. Georgia's petition is being reviewed. It will be accepted, but we will delay the process until Louisiana is stable."

"That could be quite some time," Ryan noted, a chesty cough muting the last two words. He now stood shoulder to shoulder with Adams. The younger man's physical superiority did not diminish Ryan's tenacity. The weight of history that Ryan brought to bear did nothing to deter Adams.

"Commander Adams' safety concerns are well warranted," Erin said with genteel patience, "and that is how we shall proceed. Simultaneously initiating states with cities the size of New Orleans and Atlanta would not be prudent. A majority of Georgia's citizens have expressed a desire to join the C.S.A. That enthusiasm will not diminish over time. It will intensify."

"I know that is your contention — " Ryan began.

Adams interrupted, "And the conclusion reached by eighty percent of the oligarchy."

Ryan shifted on his feet, glaring with a blazing potency not always present in his body.

"Now you listen here, Special Agent...."

"Enough!" ordered Erin sternly, her tone a bit harsher than she intended. "Enough," she repeated in a more disciplined tone. Her frustration, however, continued to simmer as her focused turned to Adams. "Commander Adams, you know what I am thinking."

Adams stood stoically, hands still clasped behind his back. A slight tilt of his head accompanied his response. "Indeed." Whatever emotion he felt was not betrayed by his voice, body, or face.

"And, Prime Minister, Commander Kurt Adams is the secretary of internal security, as well as one of ten Omega-level officers in the ranks of the purifiers. He progressed beyond the title special agent some time ago. His expertise on these matters is beyond reproach. You know this."

Ryan's mind loaded a retort even as he searched Erin's face to discern the wisdom of his next sentence. He opted for silence over speech.

"It must be said, Madam Chancellor," Adams began, "that your earlier statement — that the initiation protocols were set to be launched two weeks ago — was inaccurate. Complications have arisen."

"How so?"

"As you know, New Orleans currently has two school boards. Our meetings with them have made it clear to me that you should not be surprised if, in the next three weeks, I will need to kill seven to twelve additional school administrators."

"You think this action is necessary?"

"I do," Adams said as if he had just added items to a grocery list.

"Well, so be it," Erin announced, nodding her head. "What led to this conclusion?"

"Our meetings with the exemplary, proficient, and promising students and their families have concluded. They understand, though some were displeased."

"I assume the parents more than the students?" Ryan asked as he lowered himself back into his chair.

Adams gave the prime minister a quick glance. "Indeed. They were unhappy that schools would be shut down while the transition took place."

"That is not unexpected," Erin noted. "Did some administrators recently protest this?"

"No. They understand the redistricting that must be done and that the transition requires time. They, in fact, were impressed we plan on reopening all schools on the twentieth of April."

"Then what problem do you see, Commander?" Ryan asked.

"We started restructuring the education system on March fifth. For weeks now, students classified as exemplary, proficient, and promising have been informed of our expectations. On the seventh of April, at five thirty p.m., the initiation protocols commence. On the seventh, those students currently languishing between seventh and twelfth grade who routinely fail classes, have ludicrous discipline records, and have shown limited to no growth in their academic careers will come to their expectation meeting."

"The meeting for the failures and their parents," Erin noted. "It will be an excellent cleansing, I am sure."

"It will," Adams declared, already proud of what the future held.

"Unfortunately, the rhetoric of false hope was spewed quite regularly by a number of administrators. I do not think they will embrace the reality of what it means to be *Homo sapiens*...to be creatures of a certain kind...very easily, if at all. They likely will need to be replaced. They may have chosen to stay in the C.S.A., but I doubt they have the conviction to free their minds from the conditioning they received as products of the U.S."

"I read your report. You seem to anticipate problems akin to what we faced in Cleveland a decade ago. We navigated that quite well," Erin stated.

"With due respect, Madam Chancellor," Adams reasoned, "your desire for a smooth transition may have clouded your reading. It will likely be worse than Cleveland."

"You actually think we could see catastrophe like the Detroit Riots from our earliest days?" wondered Ryan, a chill from these dark memories running through him.

"I am seeking to avoid that at all costs," Adams declared, "but it has entered my mind. Louisiana is the prison capital of the world. It currently imprisons two thousand two hundred thirty-six of every one hundred thousand citizens. This more than doubles the national average in the United States. Louisiana triples the incarceration rate of Russia, which currently imprisons six hundred forty-seven of every one hundred thousand citizens."

"Why this detour into incarceration statistics?" Ryan groused.

"I merely seek to illuminate the fact that the city simmers with hostility. Only sixty-four percent of those contacted for the meeting on the seventh have accepted the offer of transportation. We currently expect three thousand seventy-seven students and five thousand two hundred thirty-six adults to attend the expectation meeting. Every high school in New Orleans is being used. This, however, means one thousand seven hundred thirty-one students and two thousand two hundred eighty-four adults will not be in attendance. We will have to bring the initiation protocols to them. Initiation will occur in the community. On the city streets and in homes. Even with the strategic quarantining of sections of the city, the number of men and Orcus we will need to utilize, if we hope to prevent Detroit, is unprecedented."

"Should we — " Erin began.

Adams did not need her to finish the thought as he proceeded with confidence. "We should and will commence on the seventh. The school meetings are all scheduled to begin at seven o'clock that evening. Transportation arrangements have been prepared. Every prison and juvenile detention center will be locked down at eleven a.m. in preparation for the launch of the protocols. The homeless have already been relocated to makeshift communities. Major sports arenas have been utilized in that effort. Religious leaders of every misguided stripe will attend conferences throughout the state so they understand the new relationship between the state and church. Convalescent homes will be addressed, as will the ICUs in hospitals. All is in readiness, including our response to possible skirmishes with counter-revolutionaries."

"All is in readiness," Erin repeated. "That was clear in your report."

"Given the commander's concern regarding post initiation activity, should we delay his scheduled interview with that U.S. news agency?" Ryan asked.

Adams bluntly agreed, "I would not be opposed to this."

"I know," Erin said, looking askew at both men. She stared at Adams before glancing at Ryan, who shifted in his chair. She returned her gaze to Adams, and he met her with a will of unbending steel. "The interview will go as planned. The United States has created many narratives regarding our society and way of life. It is necessary to allow an uncompromising defense of what we do to be heard by those interested. And no one is more uncompromising than Commander Adams. You only have to express your unfettered convictions."

"That I can do."

"Yes, you can." Ryan's endorsement emerged through a begrudging smile. "Yes, you can. But is that truly what we want?"

After a thoughtful pause, Erin confirmed, "Yes, it is. The time has come for foreign states to have a more complete view of what we do here. What we stand for. It should prevent petitions coming from unwilling states. Let them be informed. And let us stand proud of who we are rather than trying to obfuscate and justify ourselves. We are what people are, even if most do not wish to admit it."

"Very well," Ryan said.

"I know it is difficult for you, Mr. Prime Minister," Erin said. "But a clear majority of the oligarchy believes the time has come to offer a clear window to the world."

Ryan snorted. "The oligarchy and MLB 1-E."

"Yes," Erin said. "1-E also ran some data and concurred with our conclusions."

"Sir," Adams asserted, his tone suddenly and, most unexpectedly, supportive, "I understand your misgivings. When you helped plan the C.S.A.'s revolution, secrecy was of prime importance. You moved in the shadows. You and the other founders succeeded, against all odds, and this nation owes you a debt of gratitude that can never be truly fulfilled. But you know as well as any that revolutions are a process, not merely a war. The revolutionary process has reached a new phase, and we must play our parts so it can thrive."

"So be it," Ryan said, disarmed by the reassuring and respectful tone Adams had struck.

"So, we are prepared to launch the initiation protocols on the seventh and to present our vision of a strong nation to the world on the sixteenth," Erin proclaimed.

"It will be done," Adams said. "If you no longer need me, I would continue my preparations."

"Of course," Erin said.

Kurt Adams left the room saying goodbye to no one.

Ryan sighed. "A possible return to the Detroit Riots. Does that not make you fearful?"

"No," Erin answered, "because Commander Adams won't allow that to happen."

CHAPTER 5

INITIATION

Victor Gaulmann, warden of Blackclaw Maximum Security Prison, sat in his office

awaiting Commander Kurt Adams' arrival. It was five o'clock on April seventh. The inmates of Blackclaw had been in lockdown for six hours, lunch having been skipped and no dinner was in sight. He looked out his window at the Atchafalaya River, a ribbon of serenity flowing past the tinderbox of Blackclaw.

Victor had presided as warden for fifteen years. In that time, he had learned to loathe the inmates who occupied the facility. Despite this repulsion, he was shocked when he first received word of what would be transpiring this day. The arrival of these orders seemed the answer to a twisted prayer — a plea to fallen angels rather than a heavenly Father. Victor had initially thought of taking advantage of the twenty-four-hour window where resignation was permissible, provided he leave the state. In the light of day, he told himself the promised rewards were too great to turn down. The allure of the increased salary and power were too much to pass up. What a difference this new job would make in his life and the lives of his loved ones.

As he lay in bed on the night of April sixth, he confessed to the darkness that the idea of witnessing the execution of the initiations tantalized him. How even the thought of this plan filled him with excitement, even joy. In the evening's shadows, this alternative to failed policies foisted upon him for over a decade was entirely acceptable. Democratic leadership made all prison inmates eligible for psychological therapy, and Republican leadership made parole little more than a glittering mirage in a desert of despair. Neither policy made any difference in the day-to-day existence at Blackclaw. No one — not the preening politicians and their various media protectors, not the activists who clamored for humane treatment of prisoners while granting little more than the façade of concern for victims, and not even those who fought for victims' rights — considered the toll Blackclaw and other such facilities exacted on those exhausted by working in the soul-crushing environment.

They surely did not consider the character of the men held behind these walls. Such conversation was anathema to most. There was always a psychological theory, the effects of poverty, the trauma of past abuse to explain away the horrors committed by criminals. Accountability was a punch line, a useless piece of jargon bereft of meaning and power. Victor was always amazed at the number of apologists criminals had. So many fools putting so much effort into proving atrocious acts could happen, yet there existed among his inmates not one person of atrocious character. How could this be? This, Victor told himself, was why only three of his security team took the offer to resign and leave their home state. The remaining force would assist in these initiation protocols, earning bonuses as they did so.

It was almost five thirty when Commander Adams, transported by Torres Technology, materialized in Victor's office. Victor gasped as the image of a person began to appear.

"Don't worry," Adams said once his materialization was complete. "You will get used to that."

"If you say so," Victor joked, rising from his chair to greet his visitor. Adams accepted the salutation though, to Victor's discomfort, he seemed genuinely unimpressed with the attempt at humor. Adams' attention fell on the three MLBs who appeared in the time it took to shake hands.

"498-A, are we ready to stream live into every prison and juvenile detention center in the state?"

A formal response was produced by the MLB. "Affirmative. You have but to speak within a ten-foot radius of my location, and you shall be heard throughout the state."

"Outstanding," Adams responded reflexively. Turning to Victor, "You sent me information that three members of your security team defected."

"Ummmm, yes," Victor stuttered. "That's right. It was...."

"I have their names. I had anticipated seven from this facility. The other four have agreed to participate. They are on site today, correct?"

Victor opened his mouth to answer, but one of the MLBs, the true target of the question, confirmed the location of each man. Victor blushed and returned to his seat.

"Very good, 770-A. Please lock in on protocol order Delta 9."

"770-A prepared to follow order Delta 9."

"Very good. Please confirm that Special Agent Wilson is on site at Lucius Fields High School for the initiation of the failing students and their parents."

"Special Agent Wilson is on site. Their presentation will commence at seven."

"Outstanding," Adams said before turning to the other human in the room. His tone when addressing Victor was the same as when he spoke to the MLBs. "You have done well, Mr. Gaulmann. The facility is in lockdown as requested, your officers have been introduced to a radical new vision, and the majority has stayed. This facility will remain open for the storing of counter-revolutionaries, and you have agreed to remain stationed as the director of Blackclaw as this new era begins. This is still your desire?"

Victor confirmed, "It is," and he hoped he sounded like a man of authority.

"Very good. As previously discussed, you will receive a squadron of MLBs that will support your human employees. Your training with regards to the integration of MLBs will begin tomorrow at ten a.m. You have no official duties until then. It is my understanding you wish to stay in Blackclaw when the initiation protocols commence. You may leave the facility if you wish, but this is your last chance to do so."

"Oh," Victor stammered. "Ummmm...I'll stay."

"So be it. 498-A, we will begin transmission in three minutes from...now." The office fell silent. The same could not be said of the whole of Blackclaw.

A din in the cellblocks had risen to a storm. The growing anger, the banging of steel bars, and the profane insults increased the anxiety of the security members dispersed along the prison's catwalks and platforms. Vitriolic venom dripped from the mouths of the prisoners, the confusion created by the unexplained lockdown causing them to become more enraged. The fact the disciplined officers maintained their ordered silence only increased the hostility, which had become a physical force pressing on the chests of the security team. Sweat dripped off brows and throats tightened as the free-floating rage dominated the area.

At precisely five thirty, the mood at Blackclaw and every prison facility in the state changed as purifiers, members of the 85th Special Forces unit, and an assortment of marines from twenty-two different battalions entered their destinations. Some of these men marched in alongside MLBs while others materialized before preassigned cells.

The MLBs, foreign as they were to the inmates, had a particular impact. The intricate androids utilized by the purifiers were of a distinct design, far different than the MLBs displayed at political functions or assisting citizens both at home and work. The standard MLB stood five and a half feet tall and glistened in a variety of metallic colors. Slender in build, they moved with sublime ease. To the citizens of the C.S.A., they were always helpful, compliant, and, in an odd mechanical manner, polite.

The versions used by the purifiers stood six feet, eight inches tall. The shoulders were quite broad, creating an imposing width to match their height. Black was the only color issued. The faceplates were also a vision of darkness. Red and green lights occasionally could be seen dancing in the ebony when orders were relayed to and from the central computer system. This created the illusion of demonic orbs moving in an abyss. These machines, code named Orcus, had limited programmed vocabulary, and their voices were low, robotic, and cold.

The Orcus thundered into the cellblocks. The footfalls of the three-hundred-fifty-pound titans shook the walls of Blackclaw. The menacing sounds reverberated even more intensely in the souls of the inmates, who had never witnessed such a grim procession. Two hundred Orcus methodically dispersed, occupying space in each of Blackclaw's cellblocks. Some of the androids stopped in front of cells, turned to face the prisoner, and raised their right arms. Marines and purifiers also took positions in front of assigned cells, standing at attention but never acknowledging the caged people before them. By five-forty, exactly thirty-seven percent of the inmates of Blackclaw had either a purifier, marine, or Orcus standing before them. The eerie silence that followed the appearance of this force was shredded by Adams' voice.

"Good evening. I am Commander Kurt Adams. I am the secretary of internal security in the Common States of America. Louisiana, the last state in which you will ever live, seceded from the United States of America. Louisiana has wisely joined the C.S.A. This change will have a profound impact on each of you as our approach to crime is much different than that of your previous nation.

"It is important to acknowledge that currently fifty-five thousand one hundred thirty-seven people of various genders, ages, races, and a litany of other meaningless demographic categories are listening to these words. You are criminals. That is the only category that matters. Some in maximum security. Some in juvenile detention centers. All the same. All criminals. Your state spends an average of twenty-six thousand dollars on each of you per year. This means almost one and a half billion dollars is annually wasted. Such a putrid allocation of funds is utterly unacceptable. To further exasperate this devastating situation, within five years of your release, eighty-seven percent of you are back in some form of legal trouble, be it trial or imprisoned again. The thirteen percent who do not reacquaint themselves with the judicial system make no lasting or meaningful mark on society. Fifty-five thousand people living a negligible life. You, each of you within the sound of my voice, are completely expendable. You lack the maturity and inclination to change. Those capable of repressing the predilection for crime offer society next to nothing because you lack any distinct skills. There is nothing you can offer that someone else or a standard MLB cannot do. You are completely replaceable for you have failed at life.

"The United States, however, is also a failure. That nation of cowards and half measures wrings its hands, wondering what to do. Rehabilitate or punish? They pour money into the abyss hoping some action will awaken the latent humanity you all possess. They trumpet singular successes while ignoring the overwhelming evidence that screams there is no humanity in you to awaken! Neither you nor the nation of your origin understands that *Homo sapiens* are not born with inherent dignity. *Homo sapiens* are creatures of a certain kind. To creatures like us, virtue is developed, character is cultivated, and dignity earned. You have put forth no effort in this regard. You have proven incapable of learning the art of living and, therefore, are not worth the effort of teaching. Pearls ought not be put before swine. Do not grow angry at my words for your life is proof that you do not believe your own worth. I do not anticipate that many of you comprehend or acknowledge the truth of what I just said. It matters little. My apologies. I misspoke. It matters not at all.

"There is something, however, for which I wish to thank you. An exemplar of your very nation once wrote, 'More and more I feel that the people of ill will have used time much more effectively than have the people of good will.' You and the people you represent, the world view you promote and encourage, are irrefutable evidence that he was correct. Moreover, it shows that the United States praises its exemplars but does not honor them with decisive action. We in the Common States of America are not encumbered by such cowardice. Those driven to achieve the good will inherit the earth, and we will not do so meekly.

"Within a half hour, you will all be dead. Know this: in your passing, over a billion dollars will be liberated and put to use helping those who have the audacity to create a society that promotes a flourishing life for its citizens. A society that will always make an unequivocal stand against those who embody all that would hold us back. My name is Commander Kurt Adams but as far as you are concerned, I am *Thanatos*."

As the code word was spoken, the Orcus brought death to the inmates throughout Louisiana. Their arms transformed into automatic weapons, and they mowed down the caged people before them. The marines and purifiers positioned before individual cells also loosed kill shots at the utterance of *Thanatos*. Some purifiers smirked as they raised their weapons and cleansed the world of the contaminants before them. Every bullet was a step toward liberating the new state from corrupting influences. In his office, Victor Gaulmann smiled. Kurt Adams checked the time.

Shouts of disbelief rang from cells as the soldiers moved from prisoner to prisoner, killing all who stood before them. Those who had declared war on decency were being punished. The cleansing fire of purification had begun. So did the test.

Adams whispered, "Pause" and as suddenly as the marines, purifiers, and Orcus began their assault, they abruptly disengaged. The next five minutes belonged to Blackclaw's security team. These men joined the slaughter, some moving indiscriminately from cell to cell, while others sought inmates for whom they had developed particular animosity. None moved without being monitored by an Orcus or, if so ordained, the careful scrutiny of MLB Unit 770-A standing adjacent to Adams.

Captain Raymond Butler, who had served fifteen years as a penal officer in Blackclaw, found himself running, racing against some invisible foe, to the cell of Joseph Flanders. Joseph was a child molester who, for years, took special pleasure in asking about Lizzie Butler, Raymond's daughter. When she was eleven, Joseph taunted him with disturbing questions. How did she look? Was she getting curves yet? How were those breasts coming in? Now that she was seventeen, the comments were worse, much worse. Most inmates never flustered Raymond, but how he hated Joseph. The opportunity to shut that wretched mouth was upon him.

Raymond rushed past the Orcus and soldiers on the killing floor and stopped before Joseph's cell. According to Unit 770-A, it took him one minute and forty-seven seconds to reach the cage of his tormentor.

"Any questions for me today, Joseph?" Raymond snarled in a whisper.

Joseph's voice faltered as he rose from his cot. "Raymond? You are involved in this?"

"Only because of you."

"I never would have...I thought you were a better man than this."

"I doubt you have the right to judge anyone."

"Maybe so," Joseph said, allowing for the possibility his adversary was correct. "But your daughter deserves — "

The sentence was never finished. Raymond Butler snatched Joseph Flanders' life from him with a single twitch of his index finger. Joseph's lifeless body crumpled to a heap on the floor. Four more bullets penetrated the corpse. Raymond felt satisfaction and repulsion swirl about him. This was a father's revenge. It was just. This was...justice?

Raymond took three uneasy steps back and absorbed the carnage unfolding in cellblock D. Orcus, purifiers, and marines had reengaged in the initiation protocols and the final purge of

Blackclaw. He walked through the crowd, stunned at the cold professionalism he witnessed and the joyous shouts he heard. What was this? The world was a surreal nightmare, everything moving impossibly slow and yet, within minutes, the final shots were fired. Raymond never shot another inmate, information that quickly fell into Adams' possession.

The purging of Blackclaw began at five thirty p.m. Within thirty-five minutes almost all inmates were dead. Four were still alive in the solitary confinement wing. They had been relocated two days earlier in preparation for the initiation protocols. The halls and corridors of Blackclaw were as peaceful as Victor Gaulmann's office.

"Every inmate is deceased," Unit 498-A stated.

"Except the four superstars in solitary?" Adams asked.

"Of course, sir. They are awaiting your arrival."

"Outstanding." Adams permitted a cold smile to appear on his face. It was exiled as he turned to address Victor. "Mr. Gaulmann, my forces will be vacating Blackclaw in the next five minutes. Some will be leaving via traditional transportation, some will be teleported by utilizing Torres Technology, while some Orcus will fly by their own power to their next location. There is much work to be done in this state tonight. I will be leaving the premises as well. The MLBs in this office will stay with you, though 498-A will depart in an hour. Thirty MLBs will arrive in the next fifteen minutes to oversee the cleansing of this facility. How are you feeling?"

Victor waited several seconds before answering. The sounds of gunfire and the cries of the slaughtered echoed in his ears. He looked around the room at the androids and the man before him. He wasn't sure, which was all the more startling. His words came forth, surprising himself with his answer. "Quite well, actually. I feel...satisfied?"

"As well you should. You would be surprised how often that is the case in these situations. It is quite liberating when fallacious moral codes and archaic ethical guidelines are abandoned. Do not be surprised if chains of your past attempt to bring doubts to your mind. Tear them asunder and grasp your new life."

Victor nodded, uncertain how or if to respond.

Adams continued, "Remember, you and your officers need not help with the cleansing tonight. There will be time enough for such work tomorrow."

Victor opened his mouth to speak but Adams, courtesy of Torres Technology, wordlessly disappeared from sight. Already becoming familiar with the landscape, Victor was not offended.

Adams rematerialized in the solitary confinement wing. The four "superstars" whom he wanted to kill personally stewed in their cells. Their crimes all had the power to nauseate the strongest constitution. A pedophile whose hands defiled athletes under his charge for nearly two decades awaited Adams' judgment as did the white supremacist who gleefully slaughtered fifteen people in a neighborhood church. A spree killer who ended the lives of twenty-three people on the basis of their clothing and a political zealot who murdered two members of a local board of education and also had plans for five others.

Drawing a cleansing breath, Adams activated a speaker and introduced himself to Blackclaw's final inmates. "Gentlemen, I am Commander Kurt Adams. You heard me speak earlier, and you witnessed the demise of your ilk on the monitors provided you. Consider that a final gift from the taxpayers of Louisiana. One last dose of reality TV, as I am here to kill you. You are here to die. You four, however, are the most notorious men in this facility, so I am giving you an opportunity. I have three knives on me and, as you can tell by looking at your monitors, none are currently in my hands." Adams stood with his empty hands raised. "These are the only weapons I carry. I have no guns. You will soon be released from your cells. Should you defeat me, you can go free. This is the simple situation we find ourselves in. Do you understand?"

"How do we know you ain't gotta gun?" a voice spat from behind a steel door.

"You lousy fuck, that video could be prerecorded."

46

A third voice joined the chorus of discontent. "You're full of shit, man. Nothin' but bullshit."

"True," Adams conceded. "I may have a gun on my body. I do not."

The first voice rose again, "Fuck off!"

"Very articulate," Adams mocked, disdain laced in his words. "It is inconsequential. In one minute, the doors of each of your cells will open. It does not matter if you come out and attack me or stay in your cell and cower. The outcome will not change. I will kill all four of you. Perhaps you four could overwhelm me and win your way to freedom, but good luck with that."

The intercoms and monitors powered down, and Adams said no more. In a minute's time, the doors popped open, and four men, three physically larger than Adams, burst forth from their cells. Within ten seconds, two of them lay on the floor, their throats slit ear to ear. A smile crawled across Adams' face as his knife plunged deep into the chest of his third adversary. He left the blade in its new home as he ducked a punch thrown by his fourth and final opponent. A sneer of dissatisfaction crossed his face when he sidestepped an awkward attempt at a tackle. The grace of his movements made him appear like a dancer circling an immobile object. Dropping to a knee, he pulled his knife from a corpse and severed his opponent's hamstrings.

"This has proven a far easier engagement than anticipated. No real challenge at all," Adams lamented, a haphazard kick sending his opponent to the edge of consciousness. He looked at the three dead bodies on the floor and sighed, his attention returning to the last living convict in Blackclaw. He slapped the man's face to keep him awake. "Evidently, killing unarmed people because you disapproved of how much melanin they possessed is all a pathetic fool like you can do. You had no real fight in you. You are a complete disappoint-ment. You likely have heard that before. Parents. Teachers. Police. I'm sure they all told you what a wretched creature you are. You had a thousand reasons why they were wrong. How they could not understand you. Know this: they were all correct, and you are a worthless, stupid little man."

With the last rites delivered, Adams ended the murderer's life. Nodding his head, he spared a final glance to the four corpses before him, his nation far richer for their departure. Adams wiped blood off two of his blades and whispered an order into a wrist-com, causing his teleportation to another destination. His night was just beginning.

CHAPTER 6

WHAT YOU'VE EARNED

Kurt Adams materialized in a principal's office located on the second floor of Lucius Fields High School. It was twenty-five minutes past six, and Special Agent Meredith Wilson was whispering orders to a standard MLB as she glanced over a hard copy of her brief presentation. Adams' sudden arrival did not startle her in the least, though she did stop pacing and stand at attention.

"At ease, Special Agent," ordered Adams.

"As you wish, sir," Wilson said.

"All is in readiness?"

"The schools are alive with the anxiety and energy of our guests. Two thousand three hundred sixty-seven students...I use the term quite loosely...forever trapped between seventh and twelfth grade are currently in their proper classrooms, be they in Benjamin Franklin High School, Edna Karr, Landry-Walker, or some other location. We are still expecting seven hundred ten students, which, when combined with the one thousand seven hundred thirty-one we do not anticipate, leaves two thousand four hundred forty-one students still in their communities."

"MLB Unit 37-D is the primary contact for this information?"

The MLB spoke immediately after hearing its name. "That is correct, Commander Adams. Would you like the adult information as well?"

"I am not the one who needs it at this moment. I assume information from the sites is flowing in unabated, Unit 37-D?"

"Affirmative, sir," the MLB stated.

"And all information is transferred to 498-A as well?"

"Affirmative."

"Then all is as it should be. What sectors are most underrepresented?"

"That would be sectors seventeen, forty-two, sixty-one, and twenty-two," Agent Wilson responded quickly but was by no means rushed. Whatever nervousness she felt regarding the magnitude of her duties did not diminish the confidence she had in her own capacities.

"Then these are the priority sectors for order Omega Blue," Adams stated, his interest shifting from the MLB to Agent Wilson.

Meredith nodded. "I would concur."

"Would you?" Adams questioned, hinting the slightest hesitancy in the junior agent's voice. "Speak freely is you so desire."

The special agent pivoted so she stood squarely facing Commander Adams. She drew a quick breath through her nose and spoke. "Sectors twenty-eight and forty-three are listed as secured zones. I contend their proximity to twenty-two and forty-two allow for too much crossing. This may lead to an increase of counteractivity."

"It may?"

"Yes. The successful liquidation of these six sectors will effectively expurgate sity-eight percent of those not in attendance."

"And your calculations include targeted adults?"

"They do."

Adams paused a moment before touching the face of his wristcom. Another moment and he began whipping his fingers over the devise, tapping it once more, followed by a quick double tap. He dropped his arm to his side before projecting his voice.

"Doc," Adams boomed, his voice shaking the room.

"Yes, sir," a voice came clearly through the wrist-com.

"We will be expanding order Omega Blue to include sectors twenty-eight and forty-three."

"Very good, sir. It will take minimal movement to accomplish this. I think we — "

"Do what is necessary."

"Will do. Sounds like an enjoyable challenge."

"Success is enjoyable, Doc."

"Yes, sir."

"My revival meeting is in sector fifty-four at seven fifteen. Upon completion I will transport to sector forty-three. I anticipate this to occur at seven fifty-two. My transport target in forty-three will be Orcus Unit 24E."

"Stone," Doc said quickly. He paused before speaking, enough time for Wilson's arched left eyebrow to drop. He began again, now in the formal tones of a purifier addressing the secretary of internal security. "Sir, 24E could well be in the middle of fire. MLB 62-B is in my field HQ taking relays from and sending information to Unit 37-D and 498-A. I can hold position...."

"Adams out." Communication with Doc shut down instantly, and Adams moved to his next concern. "Unit 37-D, you have the expansion of Omega Blue recorded?"

"Yes, sir," the machine answered, the glowing specks on its faceplate moving from Adams to Wilson. "The adjustments are being made."

"Outstanding."

"Special Agent Wilson," the MLB continued, "it is T minus fifteen minutes to your presentation. Four hundred thirty-seven expectants have arrived. New information is being relayed to linked units and incorporated into Omega Blue."

"Excellent," Wilson said, her voice betraying her a second time.

"Question, Special Agent?" The sharpness of Adams' response caught Wilson off guard, and she endeavored not to show her surprise.

"No, sir," she said firmly. The question fled from her mind.

"Outstanding. You should be focused on the issues at hand. The commencement of this phase of the initiation protocols and their successful completion are your primary concerns."

"I am aware of that, sir. All will go well."

"Of course." Adams began to dematerialize even as he spoke. He would reappear across the city and make final preparations for his revival meeting. Wilson breathed deeply and exhaled. Unconsciously, she repositioned her black ponytail, tightening it beyond necessity. She flipped the pages of her introductory comments, pausing to read a passage. She did not alter a word.

"T minus ten minutes," 37-D stated.

Wilson turned to examine the wall of monitors to her left. "Inform me at T minus two," she commanded. "No unexpected issues have arisen?"

"None at all, ma'am," 37-D said in a tone that, if one had the requisite imagination, would be labeled as comforting.

Within the schools, purifiers, marines, and MLBs ushered people into classrooms. The wonder engineered by the MLBs did not completely override any dread the presence of the soldiers caused. They surely did distract, however, as they created an almost enchanting scene. The foyers of every school contained coffee, tea, punch, and assorted pastries. Fruit and vegetable plates were also available. The compliant MLBs warmly welcomed students and parents, offering them food and encouragement on their future studies. As the hour approached, the guidance of the purifiers and marines intensified. When people entered their assigned rooms they encountered the massive Orcus that were silently posted in the classrooms. For many, this was their first time seeing these formidable giants. Awe and fear gripped many hearts as they moved to their seats.

By six fifty-seven, each high school meeting center looked the same. Twenty-four people, a mix of adults and students, sat in rows facing the display screen in front of the room. Four Orcus stood in each room. One stood as a grim barrier before the door, having moved there from its position in front of the room at six fifty-six.

Another sentinel stood at the back of the room, while two flanked the screen before the assembled citizens. Four marines and two purifiers were spaced evenly along the wall next to the Orcus at the door. The rooms were bereft of chatter as the presence of the Orcus and soldiers oppressed the desire to speak.

Every screen flashed to life at promptly seven o'clock, the image of Meredith Wilson projected before her expansive audience. Late arrivals were escorted to gymnasiums or auditoriums by MLBs. As the stragglers moved, face recognition technology relayed attendance records to MLB Unit 37-D. Orcus stood in these larger rooms, blocking all exits save the one entrance MLBs drifted through. Eventually, this door was closed and barred by an Orcus. These rooms were not privy to Agent Wilson's presentation.

"Greetings, fellow citizens," Agent Wilson began, a slight gleam in her hazel orbs. "I will never meet any of you, but that does not mean we are not able to appreciate each other's roles in the Common States of America, your new home. As you are aware, schools have been shut down for over three weeks now."

Even in the imposing shadow of the Orcus, a number of students exchanged smiles and knowing glances with each other. Some parents, maintaining their well-rehearsed public roles, glared at their children for being disrespectful. Others griped out of habit for they did not actually know what they complained about.

"Schools," Meredith continued, "will be opened again in two weeks. We have already met with your more successful classmates. We have put them in categories: exemplary, proficient, and promising. These groupings are based on performance. That is all — performance. What have you gotten done? What have you accomplished? Schools are being redesigned to help all these students flourish. Schools are being redesigned for you as well. Your category, simply stated, is that of failure."

Students and parents recoiled. Some shook their heads; others booed the screen. Time-honored epithets and accusations which gave pause to Americans made Meredith smile. Their outbursts were allowed to last for ten seconds before Orcus shifted to their full height. Red lights flashed in their dark faces, and something within them clicked. This sudden activity was enough to bring rooms to silence. In the more stubborn rooms, the two Orcus in the front of the room took one step forward, creating a restless hush.

"This failure may not be completely yours. You came from a country that long ago decided people don't fail but, rather, institutions fail them. Maybe there is truth to this. Poorly funded, undermanned, and decrepit schools plagued by institutional racism, sexism, and classism may well have failed you. A second chance is what you need.

"Of course," Meredith said slowly even as heads nodded in agreement, "there are problems with this thesis. In classroom one hundred forty-seven of Lucius Fields High School, there are currently thirteen students seated for this presentation. They, according to school records, were invited to a total of ninety-eight extra help sessions last school year. They attended none of them. I am sure they have heard motivational lectures and been granted many opportunities to submit work late. They have, quite effectively, ignored these well-intentioned sermons and ignored even the most generous of deadlines. You, the current residents of LFHS one hundred forty-seven, also cut a total of one hundred thirty-one days of school and twenty-seven administrative assigned homework detentions. People tried to help you far more than you ever tried to help yourselves. The failure, perhaps, can at least be shared.

"The unexplainable aspect of all this, of course, is how do we account for sixteen thousand eight hundred sixty-five of your classmates who are not here? Those placed in other groups? In that number are people the same age as you, the same class, the same race, the same gender, and even seated in the same classrooms. If the preponderance of the blame falls on the school, you should be the norm, not the exception. If the school is to blame, why are there sixteen thousand students striving for success and some two thousand five hundred floundering? Perhaps it's a problem of environment and upbringing.

"In LFHS one hundred forty-seven sits a mother who supplements her income by renting her eight-month-old infant to be used as a drug mule. In another room, someone has the same arrangement for her five-year-old daughter. You can rest assured these young people have become wards of the state in the hopes the damage done can be reversed. Less dramatic, but ultimately reprehensible, acts of neglect also exist as we know all the people within the sound of my voice who have not seen their teenage sons and daughters in at least four days. We know where the stepfather who molests his stepchildren sits. Allow me to be the most honest person to speak to you in quite some time — there are bad parents in the world, and you are they. The law of the United States did not catch you. We, however, have a much longer reach. There are people whose every breath sucks life from the community at large, and you are those leeches. The subjective desires of malcontents and degenerates do not enhance the development of the species. Evolution will be served tonight.

"There is not enough time to elevate you. Effort spent helping the helpless is a profound waste of the precious commodity we call time. Your habit energy has brought you here so you will receive, finally, what you have earned. There is no place for you in this nation. Your nation of origin, the United States, would — in its stupidity — welcome you all back. Helping those who refuse to help themselves is the bailiwick of immature and deluded compassion. We will not inject them with the pathogen that has left their body politic. They will never understand the benefits of this action, but they will experience it as time goes on. I doubt many of you understand the words I am using. It matters little.

"I can see you in my monitors. Your anger. Your confusion. It is the pain that the deluded often experience when told a truth they believe to be a lie. Angry, confused, and deluded. It is the appropriate state for you at this moment. I am Special Agent Meredith Wilson, but you can call me *Thanatos*."

The moment the code word was completed, the Orcus in the front of the room opened fire on the people before them. The four soldiers along the side wall joined, creating a crossfire which purged the room in a matter of seconds. The Orcus blocking the exit did not move unless someone approached the door. Only one person breached its radius, causing the mechanized beast to crush the woman's skull in a single hand and toss the carcass, like refuse in a recycling bin, to the middle of the room.

The first gunshots echoing in the halls of Lucius Fields High School prompted a lone purifier in the foyer to action. His lips turned to a wicked smile as he lifted a glazed coffee roll from a platter of pastries. Taking a bite, he strolled toward the school gymnasium. Three hundred sixty-seven people sat in the bleachers. Meredith Wilson's speech was not transmitted into the room and, as the time passed, the people in the stands were shifting and occasionally muttering, both to themselves and their immediate neighbors. The presence of the Orcus throughout the space, however, created constant discomfort.

Purifier Jeremiah Jackson, a fourth-rank member of Purifier Unit Seven, entered the gym, chewing on a mouthful of his dessert. An MLB brought him a microphone and, upon his request, a cup of coffee. He took a sip and handed the ceramic mug back to his waiter. A quick cough to clear his throat preceded P4 Jackson's pronouncement.

"Greetings, all. I would welcome and thank you for coming but that would be insincere. You arrived late. *Thanatos.*"

The Orcus began to purge the room. Two MLBs broke from their servile mode and chased down people who fled in aimless terror. Jeremiah took an oversized bite of his coffee roll and watched the carnage unfold for an uncounted number of seconds. For a moment, he thought of raising his weapons but decided against this unnecessary expenditure of energy. Instead, he pointed at MLB to his right. His coffee was kindly returned to him. Nodding to the android Jeremiah turned and exited the room, the door held open by the lifelike servant. The moment the door closed, the gentle blue hues of the MLBs faceplate faded to black.

CHAPTER 7

REVIVAL MEETING

As blood flowed unabated in the hallways and classrooms of high schools throughout New Orleans, Kurt Adams materialized before five religious leaders gathered in the dark at the altar of St. Louis Cathedral, a historic centerpiece of New Orleans. They stood in a single row, flanked on either end of the row by MLBs. An ominous Orcus was positioned midway down the center aisle. From the end of the aisle, two more Orcus were stationed, each with a single foot in a pew. A blazing floodlight from the faceplate of the singular Orcus bore down upon the holy assembly. Floodlights from the two other Orcus cut the darkness diagonally, lighting the outreaches of the expansive altar. The beams crossed at the center Orcus, sending foreboding shadows forth in their wake.

"Good evening, gentle souls," Adams stated as he reached full molecular stability. His cadence was slower than usual as he emphasized certain words in his introduction. His gaze was predatory and feral, moving slowly from sheep to sheep. "I am Commander Kurt Adams, the secretary of internal security, and I am here to clarify for you the role we expect the religious community to play in

New Orleans and all of Louisiana now that you are citizens of the Common States of America. Meetings much larger than this will be held in churches throughout the state as the night progresses. This, however, is the first revival meeting. But before we truly begin...," Adams homed in on a gray- haired man wearing a black robe with red piping, a purple sash circling his waist. "Why is there a peacock in my presence?"

"The monsignor wished to wear this attire for the revival meeting, Commander Adams," answered an MLB in a polite drone.

"And you let him?"

"Your orders were to bring them here from their domiciles and give them a choice of what to wear. He chose these vestments."

Shaking his head Adams absorbed the sight before him. The monsignor was placed to the left side of the row. To his right stood a man in his mid-forties, jet-black hair and slight build. In the center of the row, a man in jeans and white button-down shirt towered over him. Standing a solid six feet, five inches, this individual was the tallest of the lot. To his left, creating an odd juxtaposition, was a rather short and slightly overweight man in his late sixties. A black tee shirt and gray sweatpants did little to conceal his girth. The final member of the row was a redheaded woman, jeans and a sweatshirt hastily tossed on. Adams estimated her to be thirty-seven.

"Those colors," Adams noted, pointing at his peacock, "indicate you are supernumerary apostolic protonotary."

The elderly priest attempted to project strength with his reply. "I am."

"No time for the purple ferraiolo? Why not wear your cape so as to add to the illusion of importance?"

"All men are —"

"Spare me your platitudinous pronouncements," ridiculed Adams. A calm that belied his intent emanated from his face and tangled with the disdain in his voice. "We ought not to lie in God's home."

Adams, with the speed of a viper's strike, drew a pistol from his hip and shot the monsignor in the knee. The horror of the moment drew different responses from the religious row. The man to the Monsignor's right stepped back, mumbling prayers that came forth with speed of his now racing heart in an attempt to calm his trembling body. The tall pastor in the middle of the row reflexively bent down to care for the man writhing before the altar. Words of comfort struggled to be understood as they rose from a constricted throat and through an arid mouth. The female minister's breaths came in rushed gasps, but she did not move as fear and shock immobilized her. She tried desperately to wake from what must be a nightmare. The short man to her right took her hand and attempted to comfort her.

"Stand up and fall silent!" Adams snapped. "57-A, if you could be so kind."

"Of course, Commander," the MLB from the right end of the row said. It stepped forward and grabbed the pastor seeking to aid his comrade. "Excuse me, sir. I will tend to the Monsignor."

The MLB helped the trembling Monsignor to his feet, holding him to its side. The tall pastor stepped backed, focusing intently on Adams. Meanwhile, the panic-stricken priest with black hair repeated his frantic prayers. He panted for breath as sweat rolled down his face. The second MLB, recognizing the man to be at the brink of a breakdown, took his arm and spoke in a programmed whisper. "You need to be quiet, sir. You must return to the row and pay heed to Commander Adams."

Adams continued, "I was planning to have a short conversation with you, but this pretentious display of authority has squelched that desire. Let me be clear. It is my intention to kill you all. I will briefly explain —"

"Ohmygod...Ohmygod...Ohmygod..."

"That's not silence," Adams noted. The priest bit his lip in an attempt to stop his trembling. The tall man glared at Adams, fear giving way to a rising anger. His stomach tightened and fingers twitched as he silently raged against the impossibility of the moment. At the end of the row, the overweight man still clutched the hand of the young woman. Adams smacked his lips and resumed his torturous presentation. "As I was saying, I plan to kill you, but I will grant you the opportunity to change my mind. To astound me with your spiritual wisdom. Blubbering will not help. You shall take a minute to gather your wits, and we will begin. I will start the clock again...now."

The five religious leaders stood in silence, the monsignor grimacing as the MLB supported him. His black robe concealed the amount of blood pouring from the unattended wound. After thirty seconds, Adams spoke through a malicious smile, slowly tracking each face. "Be still and know that I am the Lord."

Adams studied each face, probing eyes gathering all forms of information. He noted each bead of sweat rolling down foreheads. He noted every lip bitten by nervous teeth. The fingers rubbing a chin and the arms folded tightly over a knotted stomach. He registered every attempt at resolve that wilted before his glare. None, save himself, however, knew what he truly sought.

The excruciating minute ended. Drawing a slow breath, Adams began. "That I must kill you is surely nothing personal. That is likely not a comfort. Alternative ideas, especially those that offer no contribution to society, are not allowed in the Common States of America. You are symbols, barely human at all. You represent an unsustainable ontology. I don't know if any of you even realize that. You represent, in different ways to be sure, a view of reality that...at its core... would have people believe morality exists as an aspect of creation. That moral laws are woven throughout the fabric of the universe. As prevalent as gravity. Therefore, there are actions that are right and actions that are wrong. This is a pleasant fiction for some. I suppose such thinking helped past Americans in their battles for civil rights and others in their quest to be recognized as individually important as a moral being, worthy of respect and consideration. In the end, however, it is naught but a fiction. The C.S.A. cannot allow such fictions to endure. Worth is earned. Integrity is earned. What we produce for society and ourselves dictates value.

"Morality does not exist as an extension of some natural law. Either group consensus dictates right and wrong, or the powerful dictate and the lesser acquiesce. Morality, as created by humans, now that exists. Do you have any idea how much we have bled Louisiana tonight? How much we have bled other states in the effort to create this nation? And there are no consequences we fear. There is no moral arc in the universe that bends toward justice. There is only the bending of history and society by those with the strength to do so. The death of the weak...those your previous nation exalts and coddles...makes our nation strong. The debate is over. The ethics of man trumps the morality of God. People must be ripped, not weaned, from your stale worldview. Natural rights never existed. The United States was built, from the beginning, on a lie. A lie promulgated by people of your ilk. There is no place for you in this world. In a matter of fifteen minutes, these revival meetings will end the only way they can. I will strike the waters of the Nile...or, perhaps, the Mississippi... and it will be changed into blood.

"I do not, however, want you to think I am not a man of my word. I promised you the opportunity to change my mind, and that time has come. Melissa Bristol," Adams' cruel scrutiny centered upon the lone female in the room, "you are a Unitarian Universalist minister."

"I am," Melissa whispered.

"I have a worldview, a philosophy that I live without fail. I am certain. You are a Universalist minister. This is your grounding philosophy; your ontological reality. This is correct?"

"I...I am...," Melissa stammered, her mind still seeking to discern if this surreal situation was, in fact, unfolding.

"Relax, dear Melissa. I understand your trepidation." Adams' sarcastic offer of sympathy only increased Melissa's anxiety. "This is an unusual situation for you. You are a little nervous, correct?"

"Yes, I am," Melissa stated, the man next to her now grasping her hand with a strength borne of compassionate desperation.

"That's alright. It is good to know your own mind and emotions. Only then can they be mastered. Your church believes in the inherent worth and dignity of every person. Correct?"

"Yes."

"And acceptance of one another."

"Yes." A tear rolled down Melissa's cheek as she answered.

"Interesting." Adams looked at the cross above the altar and then at the monsignor, still leaning on the MLB. Another shot echoed in the cathedral. The monsignor fell dead, blood pouring from the hole in his forehead, as Adams' eyes beamed. He once again fixated on Melissa, her chin tucked to her chest and two hands now clutching her ally on death row. Scathing tones carried his words. "So answer me this; do you accept me? Have I shown my dignity to you?"

A sound drew Adams notice, and he glared over his left shoulder.

"Ohmygod...Ohmygod...," the man opposite Melissa whimpered, trembling uncontrollably. A puddle of urine formed under his right foot. A third gunshot freed him from his terror.

"Coward. I expected better from an evangelical. More fire. Stupidity, I grant you, but fire. The zeal of the true believer. Ah, well. You are braver than he, Melissa. So, please answer my question. Do you accept me?"

Melissa's soul quaked, eyes down as nausea rose. "I...I...Oh lord...I...."

"Nothing more to say? Okay. That means —"

"Enough!" the tall man, a Baptist, shouted. He glared at Adams, ignoring the two corpses slowly oozing their contents across the marbled floor. Adams shook his head as righteousness exploded upon him. "I will tell you what you are! You are a sinner, but Jesus will — "

A fourth gunshot.

"Definitely not an interesting answer," Adams groused. His attention returned to Melissa. She now grasped the arm of the man next to her as he gripped her other hand ever tighter and whispered in her ear. "Father. Holding hands and whispering in ears? Those Catholic vows are such a challenge to keep." The insult lingered in the air as Adams resumed tormenting his primary prey. "Melissa, am I accepted?"

"We confront evil. We confront...confront...evil with compassion," Melissa stammered. "We seek to...to...transform it with love."

"Do you? I thought your kind confronted structures of evil with love."

"Yes," Melissa said, shaking her head as she sought the words of her church for comfort. "That's what we do."

Adams scratched his chin with the butt of his pistol before he flippantly challenged, "I see. So evil structures can exist but not evil people? That is the contention of your church? Am I evil or merely misguided and in need of seeing the light?"

"I don't...I don't know."

"Now is the time to take a stand," Adams counseled. "Find the courage of your convictions, my dear, and speak. What am I?"

"I...yes," Melissa whispered. Her chest heaved as she drew a cleansing breath. She looked at Adams and spoke in stronger tones. "Yes, you are evil." The man next to her grimaced, though he strengthened his grip on her hand as if suspending her above a bottomless trench.

"Really? But your church also claims to celebrate the natural cycles and encourages people to live in harmony with those rhythms. If wolves take down a weak deer, are they evil or living in harmony with those rhythms? And if those are the rhythms of life, for the strong to overwhelm the weak, then does morality demand the strong help the weak, or is that, in itself, unnatural?"

"I don't know," Melissa sobbed, tears now running freely down her cheeks. "I can't do this."

"I know you don't know," Adams stated coldly. "You should, though. You should know. You should think through what you stand for before selling it to other people. You can't help anyone, and never could, because you claim mastery of the shadows but have never dared to descend into them. Like so many you want the resurrection without the crucifixion."

"Please...just stop. Please.

"Please know I have enjoyed this conversation."

A fifth gunshot and Adams stood facing the final member of his small congregation.

"You are not quivering, Father. Do you not fear me?"

"I suppose I may fear the unknown," the old man pronounced, his voice firm despite the horrific process which ended in but one destination. "But you are known, as is my immediate and rather short future."

"No puddles of piss or rivers of tears?"

"I have walked in dark valleys before. I always suspected I would die in one."

"Yes. Yes, I suppose you will." The gun was raised slowly and centered on the priest's forehead. "Last words? Want to tell me that Jesus will forgive me?"

A deep breath preceded a life's final thought. "How long can an empire built on a core of death and blood endure?"

"An empire built on blood? How long can it endure? Your empire of blood has lasted over two-thousand years. The evidence of history suggests it will last quite some time."

"My empire of blood?"

"Why of course, Father," Adams stated, lowering his pistol. "The church has killed, maimed, intimidated, and molested its way through history."

The old man rubbed his stubbled chin before responding. "I see. Crusades. Inquisitions. Child molestation crises. These are real sins committed by people who have infested the church. This is true. The core of the church, however, is not King Ferdinand the Second of Spain or Tomas de Torquemada. It is not Pope Sixtus the Fourth, or Pope Urban the Second, or the disgraceful legion that corrupted and robbed innocence. The core of the church is the teachings of Jesus of Nazareth. It is this core that endures through trials and storms, that endures the folly of man. How long can an empire built on a core of death and blood endure?"

"This is the worst fiction of all," Adams retorted, his intensity rising to meet the unexpected fortitude exhibited by this heavyset man. "These sins flow unchecked from your church: coveting of power, shows of opulence, laziness and cowardice in the face of opposing world views. That is when you are not blatantly embracing them. Woe to you, scribes and Pharisees, hypocrites!"

"So you are telling me people fail to live up to their ideals, succumb to personal shortcomings, and are tempted by the multitude of paths the world offers. You are telling me people are hypocrites. And this is supposed to shake my convictions? Your understanding of faith is that of an adolescent. The core of the church is Christ, not misguided and arrogant men. That is my final testament. So, I ask again, how long can an empire built on a core of death and blood endure?"

Adams paused for the slightest of moments before his body exploded into action. In a single graceful motion, he transferred the gun from his right hand to his left, freeing his strong right arm to unleash a vicious uppercut. Roger Baudin dropped into an unconscious heap. Orders were quickly given to an MLB. "57-A, take the padre to a holding cell."

"To which facility shall I transport him?"

"Skadi. Room six one nine."

"Very good, sir."

Adams turned to the remaining MLB. "MLB 47-A, prepare to transmit to the other revival meetings."

"Unit 47-A prepared to transmit."

"*Thanatos*," Adams snarled. In ten minutes, Roger Baudin would be the last clergyman in Louisiana.

Fierce strides carried Adams down the center aisle of St. Louis Cathedral. The Orcus units fell in behind as he passed. He shoved the cathedral doors open and strode into a clear, Louisiana night. Before him lights shone upon the bronze statue of General Andrew Jackson, his horse rearing beneath him. A quick order sent the Orcus on their way as he continued to approach the former U.S. president. He checked his watch, annoyed to find he was behind schedule.

He looked up at Jackson's likeness and grumbled, "How long can an empire built on a core of death and blood endure? We shall see."

With those words he quickly tapped the device on his wrist and teleported to sector forty-three, appearing alongside Orcus 24E. Omega Blue was unfolding, and Adams aggressively joined the hunt.

CHAPTER 8

VICTORIOUS SOLDIERS

Laughter and mocking cries intertwined to create the incomprehensible din emanating from Purifier Headquarters room. It was two o'clock in the morning on April eighth. Phase one of the initiation protocols was complete. Those responsible for the execution of phase two had assumed their responsibilities forty-five minutes earlier as those who engaged in phase one were pulled from the field. Some would return when phase three commenced in six hours. While waiting to rejoin the action, purifiers sought rest and relaxation in their sleeping quarters or lingered and unwound in the comforts of the expansive team rooms.

Room 217 was located in wing five of the Purifier Headquarters hastily, but efficiently, constructed in New Orleans the moment Louisiana joined the Common States of America. There were multiple team rooms in the facility. Those who had achieved P1 or P2 rank had their own team and game rooms. P3s had a singular space to themselves. The upper ranks, P4s and those who achieved Alpha, Gamma, Delta, and Omega clearance, had their own space as well. Room 217 was designated for both P4s and the highest-ranking officers.

Before reaching the main entrance to room 217, one had to pass a clearance checkpoint manned by two MLBs, tread one hundred yards of corridor, turn a sharp left, and pass five doors marked 'lockers' until the entrance to the room was encountered.

In one of the locker rooms, five men were showering. Blood and dirt, the transient souvenirs of the evening, flowed peacefully down various drains. The showers opened up to a vast changing area where everyone had a locker available for their personal belongings. Seven people, three women and four men, having washed these souvenirs away, were in the process of toweling off, drying hair, or getting dressed.

At the end of every changing area were single doors that led to a short walk from the changing area to a luxurious lounge that was room 217. More penthouse suite than a room, the sprawling expanse of 217 allowed for various activities without one activity unduly disturbing another.

The main area was complete with reclining chairs, monitors built into the walls for accessing various forms of video entertainment, and audio equipment. A long table placed against the wall had a copious buffet of sandwiches, roast turkey with a multitude of sides, ribs, vegetables, fruits, a variety of pasta, shrimp, potato chips and finger food, as well as alcoholic and non-alcoholic beverages. Some purifiers reveled in the successful launch of the initiation protocols, regaling their fellow soldiers with tales of their exploits. It was clear that many had already made a run through the buffet table. The alcoholic beverages, as always, proved to be the more popular libation.

Women and men, their garb running the gamut from provocative to elegant, circled the room. These people, dubbed pleasure priests and priestesses, were prostitutes — a profession legalized and readily accepted in the C.S.A. early in its inception. They were allowed into room 217 for those purifiers who wished to partake of their services. They solicited no one but, on this night, never turned down an invitation to join an individual or group. Two doors leading to private chambers were located on the long walls on the side. One of the doors had just closed as a muscular purifier lifted two women in their early twenties in a playful bear hug and hauled them away to a more private setting. A sliding door on the far side of the room opened to a designated television room where some went to watch sporting events missed due to the evening's work. In the furthest recesses of the room, a pool table was being used and three others waited for players.

The lounge continued to fill. Ten men emerged from the locker room, and six of them quickly began working through the buffet line, smiling as they overloaded their plates. The other four began their evaluation of the women roaming about the room. The door from the main corridor occasionally swung open, though most purifiers elected to shower before entering 217.

Meredith Wilson elected to enter the room without showering, as usual. She strode in, still wearing her sleek, black uniform. The holsters on her hips and diagonally across her shoulder blades were empty, as only Omega officers were allowed to carry weapons beyond the initial checkpoint. Still it was clear that she carried a minimum of four weapons when armed. Patches on the shoulders communicated her Delta clearance, one of only three women currently with that status in the C.S.A. The official powers that came with the rank were significant. The smaller perks, like private locker rooms in facilities like these, were appreciated.

She stood still for a moment, peeling black gloves from her hands, contemplating nothing more complicated than what urge to satisfy first: to eat, to be clean, or to get off with one of the toned men who circulated the room. Perhaps she could do all three at once. Her planning was interrupted by a brown-haired man wearing shorts, a forest green tee shirt, and a cockeyed smile.

"Special Agent Meredith Wilson," he crooned. "Deadliest hands and nicest ass of all the purifiers in the C.S.A. Care for some company when you wash off the evening's muck?"

"Edward 'Doc' Sells," Meredith replied. "Aren't you still married?"

A sly smile accompanied Doc's clarification. "There are many different forms of marriage,"

"I see. So you and your wife have a clear understanding of that fact?"

"Well," responded Doc, his smile growing, "there are, as I said, many different forms of marriage."

"Well, be that as it may, I think I will indulge myself with professional help tonight," Meredith countered as she slowly scanned the room. She momentarily allowed Doc to return to her sights. "Besides, I've had enough nights with amateurs in my life."

"Nice ass and deadly tongue. Who needs weapons? Hope your choice in a pleasure priest doesn't disappoint," Doc quipped.

"It could be a priestess," Meredith noted. "Haven't made up my mind yet."

He pointed a finger in her face as he rejected her comment. "Now there's a lie. Can't imagine your whims being quite so haphazard. You knew what you wanted before you entered the room."

"True," Meredith said as a mischievous smile grew, "and Eddie, it's definitely not you."

Doc grimaced. "Another round to you. I'm going to lick my wounds."

"You do that. I'm going to have other things licked." A flick of her head and two men came to her side. A quick flash of her badge over a scanner opened a door to the Delta locker room that she slowly entered, looking over her shoulder and catching Doc still trained on her. She smiled and continued to strut, followed by her two pleasure priests.

Doc turned and approached two men seated on cushioned armchairs; beers, nachos, and chicken wings covered the table in front of them.

"Hey, Doc," one man said smiling. "Quite a fuckin' night."

"Yes, it was," Doc replied. "Enjoy yourself, Bill?"

"Always. I love watchin' these stupid fucks beg for their lives. I mean, seriously, what the fuck are they beggin' for? The right to keep livin' like a piece of shit? They should be thankin' me for endin' their misery."

"Bill," Doc said slowly, "you are one heartless bitch."

Bill laughed, pausing as he took a long drag on the cigar he held between the fingers of his left hand. He exhaled a cloud of smoke and responded. "I'm heartless? I've seen you, Doc. Carvin' through illiterate fuckers and laughin' yer ass off. Actually laughin'. Don't think we don't know what yer all about."

Doc shrugged his shoulders and smiled. "Hey, I can't explain it. All I know is when I hear some degenerate yelling, 'Save me! Jesus! Save me!' it just cracks me up. Are they for fucking real? Like anyone could give a shit about them."

"It is awesome," a third man, wearing sunglasses although they were inside and underground, spoke. "*Homo sapiens* pretending to be human, yelling for some made up superman to swoop down and save them. They should have started trying to save themselves years ago. Fucking morons."

"Speaking of strange —" Doc began before being interrupted.

"Stanger than worthless motherfuckers thinking they have value?"

"Yeah. Stranger than that, Corey. Let's face it; we see that all the time. Don't matter if you're doing the job in a city, suburbs, or some Podunk rural setting. Delusion runs deep all around. Nah, fuck all those deluded fuckers. I'm talking about the fact Commander Adams appeared at his Omega Blue checkpoint six minutes late."

"What? Ole Stone Face was off schedule? No fucking way." Corey's sunglasses were now in his hand, and he stared at Doc intently, searching for a punch line.

"No doubt about it," Doc said. "Orcus Unit 24E recorded his arrival time."

"What the fuck do you think held him up? Problem at the revival meeting?"

"Problem? No," Doc dismissed the notion with a shake of his head. "I don't think we could call it a problem."

"Yeah. He was probably just havin' a little extra fun tauntin' the pious padres. Lost track of time." Bill followed his statement with another drag of his cigar.

"Taunting. I can see that," Doc stated, "but losing track of time? You think?"

"Nope. Yer right. That ain't Stone," Bill said.

"He is human," Corey interjected. "Being late once or misjudging the timing of a revival is possible."

Bill spoke as he clamped the cigar between his right molars. "That's true. I've heard the rumor that Stone is, in fact, human too. Still, it's damn peculiar."

"If you're so fascinated, Bill," Corey started with a smile, "why don't you ask him when he shows up? I'm sure he'll love to talk to you about it."

"Noooo," Bill replied quickly. "I would hate to disturb the Stone man with somethin' that wasn't my business. Everythin' went smooth. Doc had Omega Blue under control."

"That must be it," Corey threw out sarcastically, eyebrows raised. In a heartbeat, however, his expression changed. Derision faded in favor of curiosity. "Actually, couldn't that be it?"

"What the fuck you talking about, Corey?"

"Think about it a second, Doc. What if it was one of Stone's little tests? Giving you extra room to perform. He does that from time to time. Intentionally have glitches in a seamless plan just to see if field commanders can pick up on them."

"And have the guts to point it out to him," Bill added. "Remember that guy Stone tossed out of the purifiers because he kept failin' those little tests?"

Doc scratched his head as he mused. "Shit. Can't remember the guy's name, but one of the few times I've seen Stone actually pissed at somebody." Doc stood tall, seemingly adding inches to his five foot, ten inch frame. He half-turned, half-cocked his head, forcing his tongue into his right cheek, as a storm slowly brewed across his face. His menacing glare moved from the wall to Bill. "'The only reason I'm not killing you is I refuse to believe someone who reached Alpha status could be this inept. You must have some kind of talent. Go! Go find it! Use it! Now!'"

"That's a damn good Stone impression," Bill snorted. He allowed his laughter to settle before continuing. "But what if it was a test?"

"Why would he do that?"

"Maybe lookin' to groom a new Omega officer?" Bill guessed. "Could be yer time has come, Doc."

"I don't see that," Doc said. He stood in silence for a few moments, uncomfortable with the new topic. He chuckled and rerouted the conversation to the night's victories. "Besides, I love my job too much. Did either of you hear that woman begging me not to kill her son? Were you near me?"

"I was," Corey answered, gleefully switching topics with Doc. "Why did you take so long to do her? She was one annoying, screaming bitch." Corey fell to the floor, face contorting in mock imitation of the woman's final seconds. "'You got no right! You got no right! Bastards! Baby killers!'"

Doc stood over Corey and held his fingers like a gun, making a slight banging noise as he pulled the imaginary trigger. Bill, still seated in a chair, clapped his approval.

"Dumb bitch," Bill said in a condescending tone. "You wouldn't be dead if you contributed somethin' other than unwanted kids and a drug addiction. Shoot that fuckin' whore cum bucket again, Doc!"

Doc raised his imaginary gun. "I would put one bullet in her for every stranger's cock she sucked for drugs, but I might exhaust my clip."

"And you might need those bullets," a stern voice rose from behind Doc, "for some bastard who sneaks up on you."

Corey scrambled to his feet and began stuttering. "Stone? I... Commander Adams. We were just...."

"You're in room two seventeen," announced Adams. "No need to explain. I'll be right back."

Commander 'Stone' Adams strode across the middle of the room, searching the space. Acquiring his target, Adams moved to the pool tables in the back of the room. As he walked, there was an audible rise and fall in the volume as he passed different groups. The blind could follow his movement based on the wave of sound each step created. The good-natured din at the pool tables was not immune to this phenomenon.

His approach caused the games to stop and purifiers to stand at attention. A long-legged brunette, wearing a low-cut evening gown with a thigh high slit, pulled away from the man with whom she sat and walked to Adams' side.

"Laura," Adams said through a wry smile, "I will be in my quarters in about three hours. Are you properly warmed up?"

The woman nodded and smiled, purring something for his ears alone. She turned to leave the room, but Adams grabbed her wrist and pulled her close. He spoke in a whisper. "Have less clothes on. And no surprise guests."

"You're sure?" Laura asked. "I know after missions you some-times —"

"No," Adams responded, "I like the idea of just you and me this morning."

Laura nodded again and strutted toward the main entrance. No one interrupted her. Adams watched her exit for an extended moment before turning to stalk the purifier who had been enjoying Laura's company. "There are other women. Go find one," he ordered before returning to Doc's company.

Doc chuckled as Adams returned to their group. "Damn, Stone. You had to crush Johnny's hopes?"

"Yes," Adams said flatly. "She is far better off with me than little Johnny."

"I see." Bill stated. He hesitated for a moment and decided years of working together allowed him enough cover to say something others would dare not. "It couldn't be that you liked her or something."

"Like...," Adams mused. "Let's say I appreciate her talents more than some of the others."

"Ah, you like her on a strictly professional level," remarked Doc.

"How else would I?" Adams asked. "I'm not seeking much else from her."

"How else, indeed. Other than Laura, what else do you have planned for tonight?"

"I will grab a bite to eat here. Watch the recording of President Wensler's speech regarding Louisiana's initiation. I do so love to hear the fearsome proclamations of the impotent president of the United States. Then I will sleep for an hour. Enjoy my time with Laura. Grab another two hours of sleep and take on my phase three duties at nine. I might also find time to kill Johnny if he glares at me one more time."

Corey quickly made his way across the room and sat next to the still fuming P4. He laughed and waved his hand, summoning two women, each no more than twenty-three years old, to his side. As he sat with his now significantly distracted junior officer, he glanced back at Adams to gauge his reaction.

Adams smirked and looked at Doc. "Corey thought I was pretty serious."

"You weren't?" Bill asked.

"Guess we'll know in about seven hours," Adams said. "If I had already decided to kill that young man, Corey's actions will have failed to change my mind. If I was but joking, he'll live."

"Jeeeesus," Bill groaned, reminded yet again why Kurt Adams was called 'Stone' by most purifiers. "I'm not close to figurin' you out. Kinda strange to see that smirk on yer face though. Feel like I never see you smile."

"I smile," Adams responded. "Just rarely feel the need to after our missions. Which, other than during the mission, is about the only time you see me."

"I just never understood that," Bill confessed. "Honestly, never. We've been workin' together for...what...four years now?"

Adams nodded in agreement.

"In that time, I've seen you kill and maim. I've never known you to show a shred of remorse for anyone. Yet, you never seem to enjoy it all that much. I gotta say, I don't understand how you stay so fucking calm. Shit, it's fuckin' unnervin' sometimes."

"Unnerving, huh?" Adams shook his head. "I would not expect a Gamma officer with an impeccable record to be so easily unnerved."

"I'm not easily unnerved," snapped Bill defensively. He quickly comported himself as Adams focused down upon him. "But it's strange how you break the pattern."

"The pattern?"

"You know, the way purifiers conduct themselves. In the field. In the aftermath of missions. I've encountered nobody, I'm talkin' nobody, who carves through people like you do. So damn robotic and smooth."

"So if I were to shout epithets and exaltations, that would be soothing to you?"

"Well, not at this point, no. That would be weird."

"Then what the hell are we talking about?"

"I don't —"

Doc interjected, "And that, Bill, right there, is Commander Adams unwinding." He pointed from Adams to Bill and back again. "At least how he does so here. Likely unwinds differently with Laura."

"That is true," Adams quipped. If one was attentive, they may have detected, for a fleeting moment, a warm smile fighting to appear on his face. The moment was infinitely brief, nearly impossible to detect. Some would think it did not happen at all. "What about you, Corey?"

"What?" Corey said from some four strides behind Bill. He stepped back into the conversation. "I...ah...I was just...I'm not sure what you're asking, sir."

"We're in room two seventeen, Corey. Relax," Doc said.

"I know. I just...Shit, I've been an Alpha officer for six months now. I'm still not used to seeing you in an informal setting, Commander."

"Understood. And who recommended you for promotion from P4?" Adams did not deem it necessary to look at Corey as he asked the question. Instead, he locked onto Doc.

"You did, sir."

"Correct. And why would I do such a thing?"

"Because you assessed that I was ready for the responsibilities of the rank."

"Very good. And you understand that when you bumble about in front of me in a locker room it causes me to doubt the soundness of my decision?"

"I...yes."

Adams stared at Doc for another second before turning to Corey. "Then stop it. I may have to visit you tonight after my meeting with Johnny."

"Got it."

Adams smiled and shook his head. "No, but you will. Anyway, Bill was saying he finds my demeanor during missions unnerving. Your thoughts on this?"

Corey looked at Doc, who offered a shrug of his shoulders.

"Ummmm, okay," Corey began. "So, you are calm as shit out there. Fucking robotic and efficient as all hell. I always figured it was just the amount of time you've been doing this. I mean, eventually, I assume it all just becomes part of the job."

"That could be true," considered Adams, causing Corey to smile like a student who had pleased a demanding teacher. "Maybe time and exposure are factors. Of course, Doc has been a ranking officer for twelve years now. He has risen to Delta status. His demeanor is not mine. Is he not 'efficient as hell'?"

"What? No, don't get me wrong. Doc gets shit done. That's not what I'm saying." Corey's apologetic pronouncement caused Doc to shake his head and Adams to continue the interrogation.

"Then what is it if not the passage of time?"

"I don't know. Personality maybe? Some guys talk trash in sports, and some just go about their business."

"Now you're getting somewhere," Adams conceded. "Doctors shouldn't high five."

Bill laughed to cover his confusion. "What the fuck does that mean?"

"It's simple, really. A doctor performs an abortion ending an unwanted pregnancy. I doubt a celebration erupts after the procedure. In fact, it would be a bit, what's the word...unnerving...to picture such a scene." Adams stared at Bill, forcing his comrade to, despite his own will, look away. After pausing for another moment, he continued. "The doctor does the job and moves on. If something is unwanted, why celebrate or lament its passing?"

"You're comparing what we do to an abortion?" Doc asked more tentatively than he intended.

"In essence, yes," Adams replied. "A woman has an abortion, why? The developing life, for whatever reason, is unwanted. Sometimes, in tragic situations, the woman's life is threatened by the pregnancy. Maybe a crime led to the pregnancy. Other times, it is a lifestyle choice. We have a nation that recognizes, without prejudice, certain traits that are unwanted. Those traits threaten the life of a nation. We abort the lives of people who have no purpose, no dignity, and no function. They have been given the opportunity and have failed. We do not peddle in abstractions and delusion. Some people are beyond the reach of hope and redemption. Some have lived multiple decades and squandered the time. Achieved nothing. Made no positive difference in the world. We abort teenagers and adults who have proven, time and again, that they are pathetic, insignificant, and worthless. The defeat of wretched opponents does not merit great celebration. I save my joy for more legitimate occasions."

"Goddamn," Bill said, stretching the phrase as long as he could. "There's no doubt. Yer a damn stone."

"So," Doc ventured, "you just wish you were a doctor?"

"I am a doctor," Adams replied, tapping the gun he was allowed to carry into the room, "and I, like all of you in different surroundings, carry the remedies for most of life's ills and the prescription to build a healthy nation."

Bill and Doc said nothing; they merely took in what they had just heard. Corey's mouth opened as he sought to extend the conversation, but Adams turned on his heel and began to head for the door.

"Get some sleep, Commander," Doc called to Adams' back.

"I always get some sleep," Adams responded, tilting his head to look back over his shoulder. "And I always sleep well. There is no reason not to. Right, Corey?"

"Yes, sir," Corey answered sharply.

Adams exited the room and paused. He considered changing his plans and meeting Laura first but decided against it. Food followed by a quick analysis of the president's reaction. Then, and only then, would he allow himself some time with Laura. Johnny could wait until tomorrow.

CHAPTER 9

BECOMING CITIZENS

"Honey?" Raymond Butler's voice quivered as he sought his wife. "You home?"

"In the kitchen."

Karen Butler hoped her voice was pleasant. It was April tenth, three days since her husband had come home from participating in something called the initiation protocols. He had been almost completely silent ever since. When Raymond did speak, it was about superficial matters or to clarify household duties. Grocery lists and oil changes were the only topics discussed. What thoughts he had may as well exist in some distant galaxy. Whatever emotions he had were suddenly bottled deep within. For two days, he meandered through life, grave and brooding. Now he entered their home, a small but pleasant three-bedroom Cape, after his first shift at Blackclaw since the initiation protocols. She wondered what she feared more: the continuation of the oppressive distance or the cracking of the dam that held thought and emotion at bay. Mustering some will power, she entered the living room wearing a forced a smile.

"This is so strange."

"What's that?" Raymond asked, bending down to accept a peck on the cheek.

"Being home to have dinner on the table for five-thirty. I didn't realize how much I missed cooking."

"Yeah," Raymond said flatly. "You don't fool me though. You miss work too."

"True. I miss the kids. Schools reopen in ten days. I'll be back at it then." She sat on the sofa, motioning to her husband to join her. He did.

"Ten days?"

"Yup. Well, I'll be back at it in five days. Kids are back in ten. Five days of professional development. Hooray me!" Raymond's half-hearted smile did little to boost Karen's spirits.

"That'll be fun. Speaking of kids, where's Lizzie?"

"At Key's house," Karen said. "It will just be us for dinner."

"Sounds good."

The small talk now dead, silence reigned in the Butler home. Karen rose and dashed back to the kitchen. She needlessly checked the shrimp jambalaya that simmered on her stove top. She poured a much-needed glass of wine and sighed before taking her first sip. How many glasses would follow was unclear.

"Want a drink, dear?"

"Iced tea would be nice." Raymond's voice seemed to stagger as it entered the kitchen from the living room.

"Anything in it?"

"Just ice."

"Okay. Dinner's ready when you are."

"Okay."

Karen sighed again, looking at the plates she had laid out on the table. Dinner would be eaten on the couch. Again. Mustering what energy was available, she reentered the living room. She handed Raymond his tea and acknowledged his grumbled thank you. She drew a deep breath and prepared to speak, only to be interrupted by the vibration of her cell phone situated on the coffee table in front of Raymond.

"Message, dear. I think I got it too," Raymond noted as he felt the cell phone in his pocket vibrate.

"Nice," Karen commented, her tone resting somewhere between sincere and scathing. "Something we can do together."

Karen circled the sofa and dropped next to her husband. Within seconds of reading the new message, she gasped.

"What is it?" Raymond asked.

The fact he sounded authentically concerned did not escape Karen's notice. Her lip quivered, but she didn't smile. "I...whoa. I think I'm on information overload here."

"It's that big a deal? Want to put the message on the television? I'll read it with you."

"Okay," was muttered in a faltering voice as Karen swiped commands on her cell phone, bringing the mounted unit to life. Within seconds, the email filled the forty-two-inch screen.

"It's about your salary," Raymond commented. "Not that big a deal."

"Keep reading."

"Alright." Raymond's voice was again subdued. It did not stay that way long. "Holy shit! What the —"

"— fuck?" Karen completed her husband's thought, despite her preference not to swear.

Raymond leaned towards the screen, mouth agape. "Yeah, what the fuck is about right. Your salary is going to be more than tripled?"

"So it would seem." Karen couldn't tell if she actually said the words aloud or merely thought them as she tried to wrap her mind around the sudden change in their lives. "This is real, right?"

"It appears so," a dumbfounded Raymond uttered as Karen pulled on his arm. "It's just so...."

"Amazing! This is amazing!" Her joy was only intensified when Raymond, still moving in a subdued manner, smiled and hugged her.

"Amazing," she blurted again, pulling back from her husband, her hand sliding over his broad shoulder and then touching his face. Her fingers lingered on his cheek until a new thought burst into her mind. "Oh, what's your message say?"

Raymond grunted while he groped for his cell phone. Upon producing it from his pocket, he opened the message and quickly began reading. "Holy crap. Mine too!"

"Really?"

Raymond shook his head, shock overriding his ability to concentrate. The couple looked at each other in disbelief, then at their respective screens.

"Okay," Raymond said slowly, hoping that the rate of his speech would also reign in his racing thoughts. "Let's focus on your message and try to get a grip on this."

Karen nodded in agreement. She sat back, watching as her husband fervently read the message before him. This version of him, seeking to detangle the puzzling information, was far preferable to the despondent mass he had unexpectedly become. She kissed his cheek and smiled, her head coming to rest on his shoulder. He kissed her forehead and continued reading.

"Yeah...okay...so...damn. Our salaries are both about tripled. It says that the C.S.A. doesn't use the dollar. They use protean marks. The exchange rate is one to one with the dollar."

"I see that," Karen confirmed, reading the screen. "'To prevent confusion and ease your transition into your new society, we maintain the value of protean marks (PM) with the currency of your previous nation.' My god. I'm going to make two hundred fifteen thousand dollars next year?"

"Yup. And I'll be around one hundred eighty thousand."

Karen enthusiastically continued to read the email. Her mind, however, was already in the Caribbean. The smile she wore all but erupted on her face when more information came to light. "Have you gotten to the Citizens Stipend section yet?"

"Huh? No." Raymond stuttered an answer. His mind was divided between the information and other places. He scanned the message, quickly finding the section that so invigorated his wife.

The Common States of America contends that citizens cannot flourish if they are unduly stressed by physiological concerns.

Addressing these basic survival needs has often been a source of anxiety for the citizens of the United States of America. To reduce this stress, all adult citizens of the C.S.A. (24 years or older) of good standing receive a monthly stipend. The following deposits will be made into your stipend accounts on a monthly basis:

Food Stipend: 200 PM
Clothing Stipend: 200 PM
Housing Stipend: 500 PM

These protean marks are reserved for the purpose specified and cannot be utilized for other expenses. Accounts may be personalized to allow increased flexibility when spending your stipend PM. Please note: all mortgages are now held by Freedom Bank. Information regarding your local Freedom Bank, directions for accessing your regular and stipend accounts, and instructions to activate your Freedom Card can be located in appendix B of the attached packet. Further specifications regarding the monthly stipends can be found in chapter 4 of the packet.

Furthermore, it is the expectation of the C.S.A. that citizens will be focused and dedicated to their professional tasks. Because we are creatures of a certain kind, the maintenance of enthusiasm requires relaxation. The monthly stipend will free your salary to help you balance work and pleasure.

To promote mental and emotional well-being, all adult citizens (24 years or older) of good standing will also receive a biannual Vacation Stipend. This stipend can only be used for the expressed purpose of travel and leisure activities.

> *Appendix B of the attached packet has additional information regarding this stipend.*

> *Vacation Stipend: 1000 PM*

"Is this for real?" Karen asked, trembling. Before Raymond could speak, she sprang from the couch and bounded into the kitchen. Strewn across the table were five envelopes and two fliers. She fumbled through the mail and found two letters from Freedom Bank. She ripped open the one addressed to herself and found a Freedom Card. She grabbed the letter addressed to Raymond and dashed back to the living room.

"They're here!" she exclaimed, shoving the envelope into her husband's right hand.

"What's here?"

"The Freedom Cards! They arrived this morning. I didn't open the mail, but I remembered getting a letter. I thought it was some kind of promotion for the bank. But...we need to print this packet and see what we need to do next!"

Raymond tossed the envelope on the coffee table. "I think we need to slow down."

"Slow down? What's wrong with you? I mean...what's wrong? I get the feeling we have a lot to do."

"I know," Raymond said sullenly. "I know. I just...."

"Just what? I mean...this is an incredible new start for us. When we signed the petition to join the C.S.A., we thought we would improve our lives...but THIS! This is amazing!"

"I know. It's just...." Ray's voice faded off. He stared at the walls, then the pictures of his daughter lovingly displayed over a buffet table before coming to rest on the floor at his feet. He exhaled and looked, finally, into Karen's eyes. "Three days ago, I killed a man. Just killed him."

"Oh my god, Ray. That's why you've been so depressed? Did he attack you during transition time?"

"No. It was nothing like that. It was a slaughter. The entire inmate population at Blackclaw was slaughtered. We killed them all. Shot them in their cells."

"We?"

"Soldiers. C.S.A. soldiers arrived. With robots of some kind. Massive walking tanks. Like something out of a movie. Then a commander made this speech. He talked about how much money was wasted on prisons and criminals. How there was so little hope that these people can turn their lives around and that the C.S.A. doesn't waste money. When he was done, the robots and soldiers just started shooting men in their cells. I...I joined in. I ran to Flanders' cell. I've told you about him. Shot him. He was trying to talk to me, and I didn't want to hear it. I killed him. Murdered him while he was caged in a cell."

"Oh baby," Karen crooned as she ran her fingers over his head and onto the back of his neck. "That's awful, but what are you thinking? That you're some kind of criminal now?"

"Why not? I killed a man. Technically we killed hundreds. Defenseless people."

"Criminals," Karen responded with fire as she corrected her husband. "Criminals in a maximum security facility. The worst of the worst. And you think you are no better than them? Than Flanders?"

"I...I don't know. It was...." Raymond could not find the words but felt some comfort as Karen moved closer, wrapping her left arm around his shoulders and resting her head against his.

"Raymond. You're a good man. These men tore people's lives apart. How many lives were ruined by those inmates? We're in a new place now. A new home. Jesus, a new society, really. You did your job. That's all."

"And now I have my blood money to prove it," Raymond quipped, pulling away from Karen.

"You think that's what this is?"

"What else could it be?"

"A new life. A chance to really start living. A reward for doing things the right way our entire lives."

"Maybe," Raymond said, looking at the envelope. "But what about school?"

"What about it?" Karen asked. "It reopens in less than two weeks."

"Why was it closed so long? What have they done with the schools?"

Karen smiled lovingly, seeking to reassure her husband. "I'm sure nothing like what they've done with the prisons. We went to that meeting with Lizzie. She's been assigned a new school with new courses. I'm going in to learn more about it soon. They are overhauling the school system, quite quickly I would say. The way this country treats innocent kids can't be the same way it treats the guilty." She picked up his letter and held it out.

"Maybe," Raymond sighed. "But what about the rumors we've heard? The president's address the other day?"

"Rumors are often rumors. And he's not our president anymore."

"I guess not," Raymond mumbled. He drew a deep breath and looked plaintively into his wife's brown eyes. How he loved those eyes, the brown hues seemingly muddying the view to some unseen and magnificent depth. It was not, however, the answer to mysteries he sought in those beloved pools but absolution. Trembling he spoke again. "I only killed Flanders, Karen. He was the only one."

"Because of the things he said about Lizzie?"

"Damn right," Raymond snarled, strengthened by his confessional. "Goddamn right. That fucker deserved it for all he did. The things he said. It was probably too quick. Too fucking merciful."

He took the envelope from his wife and tossed it on the coffee table. "Let's print that packet first. I'm more curious about that than the cards right now."

Karen smiled. She told herself it was because of the sudden boost in their lifestyle, but there was something invigorating in the thought of her husband fighting for their daughter that way. Protecting her in such a visceral manner. She planted three kisses on his neck as he read. There were more important things than the printing of packets to attend to.

CHAPTER 10

PREPARATION

Erin McGreggor opened and closed a variety of spreadsheets, slides, and documents as she attempted to stay attuned to the ongoing initiation process. She was thankful that Louisiana was the only state initiated and that Georgia's petition was on hold. The efforts and manpower needed to launch the first phase of initiation was, indeed, profound. It was April thirteenth and Louisiana was presently being stabilized, but the fear of anti-initiation activity — both in the state, the nation, and abroad — was a pressing issue. Yet a majority of citizens were becoming familiarized with their new society, evidenced by the fact that sixty-eight percent of Freedom Cards were already activated and fifteen percent of the new citizens had already utilized a portion of their vacation PM. Life moved forward for those most capable of adapting to it.

The commissioner of economic policy, Hillary Bentz, had a team of commissars and agents preparing to investigate the reasons why some new citizens had yet to activate their Freedom Cards. Transition experts would begin proactively reaching out to these delinquent citizens in twenty-three hours. Other agents and lesser employees had been available to those with questions and concerns since the tenth. Patterns of activation and usage behavior for utilizing new accounts had been identified from previous initiations, but it was still a mystery why new citizens delayed the inevitable. Some people simply felt overwhelmed by the rush of new information and, with the help of transition counselors, would be acclimated with minimal effort. It was also possible that some new citizens needed to feel the crush of a deadline to take action. Neither trait was particularly admirable, but this did not change the fact that such traits existed throughout the years of transition from the U.S. to the C.S.A. It was a part of reality and, while not a true predictor of a future failed citizen, it often represented a self-imposed ceiling that limited growth.

A harsher, more pressing fact was the reality that hesitancy to activate cards sometimes signaled a reluctance to truly become a member of the C.S.A. The first, perhaps even subconscious, act of resistance taken by many anti-initiation rebels was hesitancy to activate the Freedom Card. This was why Commissioner Bentz's organization carefully scrutinized their findings and shared information with the secretary of internal security. It was also why Chancellor McGreggor carefully and personally scrutinized every report she received from the commissioner of economic policy.

Erin sat at her desk, intently focusing with her brow furrowed, as she neared the completion of her report evaluation. She would then pass it on to MLB 1-E, which analyzed the reports with its data evaluation programs. 1-E, after utilizing various algorithms and probability mathematics, shared its findings with her. Erin's concentration on Commissioner Bentz's final report was shattered by the programmed politeness of 1-E.

"The attendees are present in the second-floor conference room."

Erin looked up, startled by the sudden interruption.

"Apologies, Chancellor. I did not mean to disrupt you."

"That's quite alright, 1-E. I clearly lost track of time."

"These things happen, madam," 1-E responded in a reassuring tone.

"Would you like me to evaluate Commissioner Bentz's latest report?"

"Not yet," Erin stated after a slight pause. "I would still like to complete my initial inspection. If I can get two to three hours uninterrupted after this meeting, I should have it to you by tomorrow noon."

"Very well, madam. I will endeavor to clear you some time this afternoon." 1-E paused before continuing. "You, of course, realize I could run the information first and then give you the final analysis? It may expedite the process."

"I understand," Erin said, laughing to herself. This was not the first time 1-E had questioned the efficiency of Erin's process. The android's stubborn persistence on the matter was, somehow, endearing. "But, as before, I like to see the commissioner's report first, make my conclusions, and then see what you propose."

"Understood. You do realize you concur with ninety-seven point eight percent of my conclusions."

"I guess the two point two percent is worth it to me," Erin responded.

"Understood. Shall I escort you to conference room three?"

"Yes. That would be fine." Erin rounded her desk and purposefully crossed the room. 1-E strode beside her, moving with mechanical elegance. Erin eyed her MLB for a moment before speaking. "Anything new to report?"

"Nothing *per se*, madam. All is going according to schedule with the initiation protocols. You've already seen Commander Adams' initial report, I assume."

"I have."

"Excellent. I will have more to disclose upon reviewing Commissioner Bentz's report."

"I see," Erin said, trying to ascertain if the previous statement was a mere disclosure of fact or a barbed jab. She shook off the thought as she stepped into the pristine hallway, her heels echoing in the silence. Her navy jacket and skirt stood in stark contrast to the alabaster walls. Looking quizzically at her escort, she came to an abrupt halt. 1-E completed an extra step before stopping and turning its head to face Erin.

"I don't hear you," Erin noted more forcefully than anticipated.

"Pardon me, madam? I did not speak."

"I mean I don't hear you walking. I'm clamoring down these halls like some bull elephant, and I don't hear a sound coming from you."

"That's very good to know, madam. Commander Adams has been working with an elite team of technicians on sound-dampening technology to allow us to be less intrusive in our day-to-day duties."

"Us?"

"The MLBs, madam. I do not know if such additions have been made with the Orcus."

"You mean...you walked into my office and crossed the room, and I didn't hear you?"

"That is correct. Hence, I did not interfere with your work in any way, as per Commander Adams' desires."

"That's amazing," Erin remarked with an authentic sense of awe. "I thought you teleported in and that was why I didn't hear you."

"That is a most reasonable deduction, madam."

"Well, I'm glad it was reasonable. I would like to proceed alone, 1-E. But if you could clear my schedule of all nonessential activity this afternoon, I would appreciate it. And prepare to run your projections of emergent anti-C.S.A. operatives with an eight-month scope."

"Very good, madam. I look forward to running my report for you. And my analysis of Commissioner Bentz's report as well."

"You'll have the report tomorrow afternoon. I promise."

"Thank you, madam. I will see you at seven?"

"As always, 1-E."

"Very good, madam. Have a fine meeting."

Erin smiled despite the fact it was a machine that offered well wishes. She continued down the hall, listening to the sound of her heels reverberating off the walls. With limited success she tried to walk quieter before abandoning the self-indulgent endeavor.

Stopping at a private elevator, she ran her pass card, placed her palm on a scanning device, and positioned her head for a retinal scan. Three turquoise lights flashed on the scanner. The doors whisked open, allowing entrance into a plush compartment complete with carpeted floors and a luxurious seating area.

Erin stood in the elevator. She never sat for she knew too well what these elevators were occasionally used for. The MLBs responsible for its upkeep were, in her opinion, priceless workers. The elevator eased to a stop. Once the doors slid open, she stepped directly into conference room three. Four individuals sat at a round table, cautious casual chatter floating between them. The conversation slammed to a halt as everyone stood upon noticing Erin's entrance. She nodded to Ryan and invited everyone to take their seats.

"Good morning, Chancellor," Ryan Vancese said with affection. Two of the others echoed the greeting if not the emotion. Kurt Adams tilted his head.

"Prime Minister Vancese." Erin returned the greeting through a smile, a hand falling on the elder statesman's shoulder for a moment. "Commissar Velazquez. Secretary Jenkins. Commander Adams. Have you begun without me or were you waiting?"

"Waiting, Chancellor," Adams answered quickly. "It would be poor form to start without all present."

"Indeed, Commander. Let's begin."

Ryan knocked on the table to show his approval. Marie Velazquez and Lamar Jenkins smiled their agreement.

Erin began, "It is April thirteenth. The pressing issues before us are Commander Adams' interview on the sixteenth, the reopening of schools on the twentieth, and the deadline for activation of all Freedom Cards on the twenty-first. Of these three issues, Commander Adams' interview requires our combined attention, although Secretary Jenkins has something he would like to discuss as well. If nothing has changed, Prime Minister Vancese and Secretary Jenkins have school-related issues to discuss, and Commander Adams and I would both like to have some of Commissar Velazquez's precious time. Provided it does not cause undue conflict with previous engagements, I would like to see the commissar at five o'clock, leaving the time directly following the meeting for a brief discussion between Commander Adams and me regarding his protocols update. Does this work for everyone?"

The nodding of heads communicated concurrence.

"Very good," Erin said. "Now, to be clear, this interview will be taking place. Secretary Jenkins and Commissar Velazquez both have concerns, despite their support for the interview. Commissar Velazquez, if you could begin?"

"Thank you, Chancellor. And yes, I did vote in favor of this event. But it is the first time in our history that a foreign nation will interview a member of the oligarchy. It is barely a week since the launching of the initiation protocols. While I sit in full support of what we do, the world, at large, will not. I wonder if Commander Adams should downplay the protocols and attempt to keep the interview focused on our technological, scientific, medical, and economic successes. We do not want to shock the world."

"I don't think —"

"No," Adams snapped, his voice striking the air as if it was a physical force. "My apologies for the interruption, Chancellor, but the answer is no. We agreed to reveal who we are with pride. If we want to obfuscate in some buffoonish attempt to curry favor, have a true politician sit for this interview. But again, we chose a purpose for this undertaking. I understand if there is a sense of foreboding as the date approaches. It is the feeling Prime Minister Vancese has had all along. If the purpose of the interview needs to be changed, so too should the interviewee. I am not the man to send forth to ingratiate ourselves to the world."

"I agree," Erin said. "You are not the man to ingratiate the Common States of America to the world. But the purpose of this interview has not changed. The courage of our convictions needs to be on display. Tenacity, not timidity, must be the order of that day."

"I know," Velazquez admitted reluctantly. "I know. I even agreed to that. But I am building coalitions with foreign powers even as we speak. To shock them to such a degree that they leave the table would be counterproductive."

"And what would shock them to such a degree?" Adams asked.

"Are you serious?" Marie Velazquez responded. "Your actions as secretary of internal security, necessary as they are, always complicate my role as commissar of foreign affairs."

Adams offered a half-hearted nod. "I suppose my role could cause you complications, but you have not answered the question. What would make these delegates leave the table? The United Nations Human Rights Council has named the C.S.A. the worst offender of human rights each of the past five years. Has any of that kept many dignitaries away from your table? The president of the United States recently called us a nation of 'barbarians and murderers'. His critique, as you know, did not end there. How many fled your table because of this? If any left, would you want them back? DCC, the very network I will be appearing on, televised a documentary entitled C.S.A.: *Nation of Blood* four years ago. Did this cause you to sit in an empty room?"

"I understand your point. But these events do make my job...and that of my emissaries...quite difficult."

"I know it does," Erin interjected. "You, however, must confess that Commander Adams is correct. Foreign nations seek our ear on a regular basis. There is always tension to work through, but they do keep coming."

"That is true," Commissar Velazquez allowed, "but because of our technology, economic might, and unusual position as the rising power in North America. Not because of Commander Adams' methodology."

Erin repeated, "The purpose of this interview will not be changed. I am sure, however, that Commander Adams will discuss more than body counts."

"Of course," Adams said. "A full vision of the C.S.A. requires disclosure of our technological innovations, medical advancements, social victories, and economic equity." Adams turned as he spoke, locking eyes with Marie Velazquez. She tried not to recoil as she looked into the abyss. "Our methods, and they are all of our methods, will not be emphasized or concealed. I do not know if this will reduce the shock of other conversations, but it matters little."

"You see," Marie said, turning to Erin. "This is why I have doubts. It does not 'matter little'. It is actually very important."

"Yes," Adams insisted, "it, in fact, does matter little. The reason is simple. The people in your circle quickly bypass any misgivings over my actions in their quest for your favor. Moral righteousness will make for headlines and cause the internet to go ablaze. The outraged members of society will send messages and post their ire...and then stop. Their energy spent, they will congratulate themselves for their virtue and seek the next celebrity endorsement, be sidetracked by some foolish meme, or a new violation of their sensibilities will draw their fickle indignation. Their rage will reverberate longer in their self-created echo chambers but, even there, it will eventually fade. Meanwhile, access to economic markets, the desire for advanced technology, and the instinct to ally oneself with a rising power will continue to dominate in your meetings, Commissar Velazquez."

"You might be right," Velazquez said, shaking her head. "Human rights are rarely discussed in those rooms."

Prime Minister Vancese interjected, "As it should be. The reality of global politics ought not to be unduly bogged down by trivial concerns. Let the opinion journalists of the United States fume and the internet pulsate with resentment. Fools will rage against the dying of the light only to come, too late, to a bitter realization."

"What realization would that be, Prime Minister?" an intrigued Adams asked.

"That the light died years ago. Their anger conceals their moral cowardice, and their verbal venom masks impotent principles."

His fist banging the table in approval, Adams snarled, "Yes! There's the old revolutionary, rising forth one last time!"

"Hopefully not the last," Vancese declared. "But I have had time to consider this action and its ramifications. I, as all of you, love what we have built. Let Commander Adams proclaim our success, and even our methods, to the world. It will turn few against us. Our enemies are our enemies. It may even cause some to pause in their denouncements, for people are more indecisive than they realize. Competence and results are often irresistible forces."

"Well said," stated Erin, her regard turning to Marie. "Commissar Velazquez?"

"Very well. I do, however, have some specific foreign negotiations I would like to discuss with Commander Adams after this meeting, if only to provide information before the interview."

"Of course," Adams said. "This information has been sent to 498-A?"

"I have not done so. I assumed discussing it with you would suffice," Marie confessed.

Adams allowed a frustrated sigh to escape his soul. "I would like 498-A to have a copy of the reports."

"Very well," Marie said, trying to shake off her annoyance. She knew Adams insisted all reports come to him via his MLB. She knew this. Why she neglected to do it was lost to her at the moment.

Erin, anxious to move beyond Adams' preferences, steered the conversation. "That's fine. Commander Adams, you will come to my office, as planned, after meeting with Commissar Velazquez. Next item. Mr. Jenkins, as secretary of education, you had some concerns regarding the reopening of schools?"

Everyone focused on Lamar. His consternation was etched across his forehead, easily visible due to his rapidly receding hairline. He rubbed the back of his neck before speaking. "Yes. The Orcus and purifier presence in New Orleans, for example, is higher than anticipated. I would rather not open schools with the image that we have occupied the city."

"It is not just their presence you lament, Lamar," Adams stated. "Their activity is also higher than you would like."

"Indeed, it is, Commander."

"I am sure it is no consolation, but it is higher than I would like as well. The number of vagrants and failures we needed to deal with was quite high. We had hoped to vacate the city of direct Internal Security Forces by the twelfth. That has not happened. I am sure this is one of the issues the chancellor wished to discuss with me."

"It is," Erin corroborated. "You said New Orleans would be a challenge. Time is proving you a prophet, Commander."

"Hardly. I just know my work. April seventeenth, our new target date for the extraction of visible military presence, still stands as probable. We will, however, maintain the indirect Internal Security Force some sixty thousand feet above the city. All that will be left are police, fire, and emergency personnel...supported, of course, by MLBs. New citizens of the C.S.A. must get used to interacting with them."

"Of course," Lamar said. "But those Orcus project a different message."

"Yes, they do," Adams conceded. "They are supposed to. Rest assured they will be withdrawn by the seventeenth."

"Okay. But the MLBs for school purposes are ready?"

Adams confirmed, "They are. You had informed me that statewide professional development for your teachers commences on April fifteenth. You wished to introduce the teaching assistant MLBs on the sixteenth. Every educational district is scheduled to receive the MLB-TAs on the fourteenth. They are programmed and color-coded for easy identification for usage level one, two, and three. This is all according to your request."

"Yes. That's good news," Lamar said enthusiastically. "The superintendents and other priority users have already had a week to acclimate with their models."

"Outstanding. All, in regard to the confines of your schools, is on schedule," Adams said. "Orcus and purifiers will be gone soon. Now, the storage facilities for the MLB-TAs are prepared?"

"Well, a couple of districts have been slow to acquire the proper space with the requisite supplies, but that is what the prime minister is going to help me with after this meeting."

"I cannot say I am pleased to hear of this complication, but I am sure the prime minister will be a great help getting all in order."

"All will be in order," Vancese said gruffly. The prime minister was irritated that he was called upon to use his political muscle for such a mundane task. He leered at Adams and, for a second time, the secretary of internal security felt the revolutionary fire.

"Yes, it will," Adams concurred.

"So, this phase of our gathering is complete," Erin stated. "Let's break into our small groups and accomplish what you must. Commissar Velazquez, I will see you at five."

A chorus of "Yes, ma'am" and "Thank you, ma'am" was delivered as the four individuals stood. Erin watched them leave the room. Ryan and Lamar were engaged in a collaborative conversation, the older man's hand patting the fifty-year-old on the back while nodding reassuringly. Marie and Adams walked briskly to the door. Whatever words they were to exchange would be shared in private. Her strides communicated her frustration. Adams moved, as always, like a predator. The jungle seemed a more apt environment for him than glistening walls and polished floors.

Erin sat alone for two minutes, her mind racing from what she might need to know of their conversation, from this possibility and to that contingency. Drawing a deep breath, she trusted the foursome to smooth the rough edges encountered and returned to her office, eager to continue dissecting Commissioner Bentz's report.

CHAPTER 11

WHAT WE ARE

Studio 3C in the Democratic Communication Channel's sprawling headquarters in New York City was vibrating with energy. The mood of the space typically fluctuated between anxiety and anticipation, depending on the events of the day. That this evening's interview was of such an historic scale heightened the pre-broadcast tension.

Michael Jons, host of *Honest Politics*, stood before the lacquered wooden desktop where he conducted interviews. The sides of the desk were made of translucent plastic, a gentle swirl of blues and violets cascading in the frames created by wooden legs rising from floor to desktop. The pristine oak floor and two steps leading to the platform where the desk sat added to the sense of sleek importance the host preferred. The studio lights were focused with intensity on the desk. Everything seemed perfect for the start of the show. The only exception was the arrival of the guest of honor. It was seven forty-seven, thirteen minutes before air, and Commander Kurt Adams was yet to be seen. This exasperated the confident fifty-two-year-old. Dropping some notes on his desk, Michael ran his hand through his wispy hair and scanned the room, speaking when his target was acquired. "Richard!" Michael bellowed. "Got a minute? Maybe?"

Richard Horgan, the producer of *Honest Politics*, looked up from the conversation in which he was engaged. Nodding understandingly, a woman wearing a charcoal blazer patted Richard's shoulder. She mouthed "good luck" to Richard and wandered off. Richard buttoned and then unbuttoned his suit as he approached his impatient host. "How you feeling, Mike? Ready to go?"

"Of course I'm ready," Michael said, resentful of the thought he would be otherwise. "I'm always ready. But where is this Adams character? No one has seen him?"

Richard looked around the room before offering his confirmation. "Nope. He just said he would show."

"And if he doesn't?"

"If he doesn't, we will do what we discussed. Give you time to editorialize about him and the C.S.A. between clips from various speeches and documentaries made about them. We have plenty to present."

"I know," Michael grumbled. His pulse quickened with the anticipation of interrogating the C.S.A.'s secretary of internal security. "I just have been gearing up to take him on in person. Cut these fuckers down a peg."

"I know you have. Be ready though. Don't forget what we discussed in the pre-production meetings. This guy is not like others you have interviewed."

"So you say," Michael groused, "but I've interviewed Ioseph Milrovick and Alim Hameen Rabah. I'm no stranger to sitting with notorious people. Especially ones as stringent and uncompromising as this Adams is sure to be. I can handle him...if he shows."

Richard surveyed the room again and repeated, "If he shows...."

"How much time?"

"Ten minutes."

"Jeeesus Christ," Michael snarled. "This is —"

"I know. I know. You, however, can't go on air foaming with frustration." Richard groped for a way to calm his agitated anchor. "Hey, you want to bellow a couple good cusses and get it out of your system? I could join in."

Michael laughed despite his anger. "That's alright, Richard. Besides, you're a terrible swearer."

"What? I cuss," Richard said with false offense. His awkward expressions of anger had been fodder for office jokes for years.

Michael shook his head and snickered at the thought. "Right. I don't think 'dagnabbit' counts. You're just one of those non cussin' type people."

"That's probably true," Richard conceded, feigning that he had received some great revelation. "That's okay, though. My wife makes up for it."

"Damn right," Michael said, a slight chuckle accompanying his exclamation. "Diane is one step away from a trucker when it comes to, let's say, colorful self-expression."

"Yup, but in what direction?"

The men's banter was interrupted by the sudden appearance of Kurt Adams, two Orcus, and one MLB. They materialized out of nowhere, courtesy of Torres Technology, and were standing beside the host's desk. The room fell silent, awed by the combined sight of transportation via teleportation and by the presence of Adams' android companions.

"Maximization pattern," Adams ordered, causing the two Orcus to thunder their way to calculated positions in the room.

"You must be...," Michael said, stepping forward with an extended hand.

"Lower your hand," Adams responded. "I am not here, Michael Jons, to engage in pretentious displays of false fellowship."

Michael lowered his hand. He prepared to speak, but Adams granted no opportunity.

"You, Richard Horgan, are the producer of this ill-named show. All is in readiness?"

"It is," Richard stated, trying not to stare at the Orcus. "You will sit here and...."

Richard was shocked into silence before he could complete his sentence. Every light in the station snapped off, save a single beam centered on the interview table. Monitors went dead as did every camera. *Search for Truth*, which was being broadcast from Studio 3B, was likewise affected, much to the indignation of the compassionate narcissist who hosted that show.

"What the fuck...." Richard mumbled, sounding quite natural. The room, still under the thrall of bewilderment, remained mostly quiet. A few sturdier studio technicians attempted to solve the sudden loss of power. Some cell phones were produced, but they, too, were useless.

"You have it all, 498?" asked Adams.

"Yes, sir. It was a simple procedure." More than one person gasped upon hearing the MLB speak.

"Outstanding." Adams turned to Richard and spoke, projecting his voice so all could hear. "Do not be alarmed. 498-A has taken complete control of your power grid. There will be no transmission from this studio without our consent. Don't worry, Richard. Control of your facility will be returned to you soon. But understand this: I do not trust you. This is intended to be a live broadcast. Any delay, any clandestine attempt to edit, will be sensed and control of the broadcast ripped from you. The hour of this event advances. Shall we proceed?"

"Yes," answered Richard as Michael dropped into his chair, which was noticeably larger than that of his guest. This was not always the case. The discrepancy in a guest's ideology directly impacted the size of the seating arrangements. Over ninety percent of the time, Michael's guests sat in chairs roughly the same size as his. Richard sought to add a thought, but Adams had moved on.

"To all in this room: listen. We, in the Common States of America, consider it quite rude to record video or audio of another person without their consent. People, as they mature — and I know that is a foreign concept to most of you, like their privacy respected. Therefore, do not turn on your phones when we relinquish our grip on this facility. I ask you this as a way of respecting our cultural differences. As I understand, most of you genuflect reflexively to that concept, so please worship it now."

"Alright," Richard snapped. "You've made your entrance but understand —"

"No," Adams interjected, his voice striking like lightning. "I will acquiesce to nothing. There is nothing you have to say that is of interest to me. It is seven fifty-six. How much longer do you want dead air on this station? Go to your office or wherever you watch broadcasts from."

Richard hesitated for a moment before leaving the stage. He pumped a fist at Michael, hoping to encourage his host. Michael nodded at his producer and cleared his throat. When Richard's fifth step fell, the studio leapt back to life. Adams sat in his chair and smirked, shaking his head. The mad scramble in Studio 3B ended, and the host of *Search for Truth* settled himself enough to apologize to the viewers for the interruption. He was able to read the planned transition to *Honest Politics* smoothly enough to make the script sound almost spontaneous.

Michael took his cue and began the most important interview of his life. "Good evening. This is Michael Jons, back to help us find some honesty in politics. As most of you know, I have a very special guest tonight: Commander Kurt Adams the secretary of internal security of the Common States of America. Good evening, Commander Adams."

Adams nodded his head in acknowledgement of the salutation.

"For the sake of our viewers' understanding, what would you say your duties are as secretary of internal security of the Common States of America?"

"That would depend on which part of the nation we are discussing. For example, one of my primary concerns in Michigan or Illinois is the monitoring of white-collar crime. Addiction to greed is a difficult trait to remove from some citizens. They can be very clever in their schemes to acquire more than they deserve. This has proven to be the biggest concern of stage five. Now in Ohio, most of my work is still focused on counter-revolutionaries and the apprehension of failed citizens. This happens quite often when transitioning a state from stage two to stage three. Revolutions, after all, are a process. In Louisiana, we are still implementing the initiation protocols, meaning we are in stage one. Stage four has intense focus, and energy is dedicated to maintaining and strengthening the infrastructure of success. Overseeing, organizing, and engaging as a field agent in all these stages are parts of my function."

"Ah. The initiation protocols, as you call them, are the actions that caused President Wensler to call you a nation of 'barbarians and murderers'. The United Nations Human Rights Council will, in all likelihood, keep your nation in its customary position as the worst violators of human rights on the planet."

"These statements are true. Such things have been said about us, and we find ourselves atop such lists. Before you continue with a question, please understand we do not care about these opinions."

"How can that be?" Michael did not attempt to hide his incredulity. "Honestly, explain how the compilation of the facts of your nation, facts that enable the United Nations to name the C.S.A. 'a capricious violator of human rights' does not give you pause?"

"Nothing we do is capricious. This perceived impulsivity creates a false premise as a starting point. More importantly, in the past three decades, there have been five actions that could be called genocide around the world. The United Nations did not call any of these events genocide, enabling that robust organization to avoid involvement. One of these events, I believe, claimed the lives of some two and a half million people. The United Nations is hardly a fit arbiter of morality."

"Well, that's an interesting observation," Michael said in a sarcastic tone. Adams stared at him, unimpressed with the host's passive anger. Michael continued, attempting to soften his tone while maintaining his hostility. "However, even with the inability to garner recent footage of your atrocities, it is documented that the C.S.A. routinely murders its citizens. What rationalizations do you have to justify these actions?"

Adams responded flatly, "I have no need for rationalizations. The truth is this: putting criminals to death is not murder. Now, you may be opposed to the death penalty, but there is a difference."

"That's very convenient, but —"

"What is the crime rate of Chicago?" Adams asked of his host.

"No," Michael said firmly, "we are not changing the topic. You have merely evaded the question."

"No," Adams replied cordially, "I am attempting to answer it. You ought to learn the difference."

Michael groaned and moved his hand as if wafting Adams to an open door. "Please do continue."

"I will. But first, I thought people of your ilk liked nuanced conversation. You Americans, especially those of a certain ilk, pay tremendous lip service to the idea of looking at situations from all the angles so you can maintain the illusion of your precious and pretentious open-mindedness. Your venomous tone belies your ideals. How very American to not do what you say. To not be what you claim. Alas, I ask again, do you know the crime rate of Chicago, Illinois, at this time?"

"Fine," Michael snapped. "I'll play along. However, since Chicago is now in the C.S.A. and your nation has been reluctant to share information with organizations, the answer is no, I do not."

"Play along? I am pleased you admit that crime rates are nothing more than a card in some politicized game you play. We take crime far more seriously. You are correct on one count, however. We have been slow to share information. I suppose that is one reason I am here, to usher in a new period of openness. Now, the number you seek is zero point nine per one thousand citizens."

"You're claiming the crime rate in Chicago is zero point nine per one thousand citizens?"

"I claim nothing," Adams said, leaning back in his chair before rocking forward. "That's what it is. To be clear, that is the number for violent crimes. Now, fifty years ago when Illinois was one of the nine states to break bonds with the United States, this number was twelve point seven per one thousand citizens, meaning the city endured over twenty-nine thousand violent crimes a year. In fifty years, violent crime has all but been eradicated in Chicago. The violent crime rate of Chicago is now slightly less than that of your hometown of Westerly, Rhode Island. Moreover, the poverty rate is now zero percent, as it is throughout the C.S.A. It was twenty-seven and a half percent when they joined the nation."

"That's all fascinating, but —"

"Don't interrupt," Adams reprimanded. He paused for a moment before continuing his lesson. "The poverty rate is zero percent. Isn't poverty something your nation has struggled with for almost four hundred years? We solved it in fifty. And you are so vacuous as to believe we did that merely by killing? Please."

"It is accomplished because of your brutality, which you are clearly trying to avoid discussing. How many people suffered and died to get those results?"

"Much fewer than those who suffered and never truly enjoyed life in your nation," Adams replied with unflinching confidence. "Quiet desperation is your cultural norm. Regardless, your deeply thoughtful U.S. media and the United Nations have covered our perceived brutal nature for some years now. I am here to offer a more complete picture."

"There is only one picture," Michael insisted. "That of a...."

The power throughout DCC headquarters was suddenly drained. Some areas were dimmed; others fell into powerless darkness. A janitor cleaning a hallway on the first floor was undisturbed.

"Mr. Jons appears incapable of deviating from his preordained script, Commander. Shall I replace him?" 498-A asked placidly.

"No, thank you, 498," Adams said, looking at his MLB. Adams then turned his attention to Michael, speaking in a tone that one would use with a child. "Try to understand, really try to grasp the fact you don't need to be here. None of these people do. I could...,"

Adams paused for a second to consider his words. Wondering if the Americans around him could understand the implication of his choice, he smirked. "...Clear this room in seconds. 498 would then handle my conversation with your viewing public. I could remove you now. I will gladly answer your questions if you allow me. Don't be in such a rush. Stop being so American."

"Listen. If you think...."

"Michael," Richard's voice came from the rear of the room, "let's get back on the air."

Michael looked at Richard for a moment. He drew a deep breath and turned to Adams. He seemed poised to speak, but his sentence was left unknown.

"Return it to them, 498." The room burst back to life, and Adams renewed his critique. "As I was saying, poverty and crime are anathema to us. Utterly intolerable and we, unlike this nation, do not use such words lightly. The measure of one's humanity is that they do not brag about that which they have not accomplished, nor do they use words without being dedicated to the pact to which their words bind them. That is not the case in the United States. Words became cheap in your nation long ago."

"That's all quite fascinating," Michael stated, his focus inadvertently drifting to MLB 498-A, "but for all your talk of humanity, your nation kills thousands every year. Do you deny this?"

"We put to death thousands of criminals to elevate millions of citizens," Adams began. His feral look juxtaposed with his eerily calm tones froze Michael's blood. Whatever shadow enabled Kurt Adams to do his work was suddenly on display in his eyes. They seemed ancient. Serpentine. His countenance did not change. His tone remained even, almost robotic. A demon, however, bristled in the deep abyss of his soul. "Such a sacrifice is not merely the utterance of a philosophic theory but, using Chicago and our technological advancements as evidence, the foundation of a flourishing humanity. We care far more about humanity than you."

"That's absurd," spurned Michael.

"Only to the deluded."

"Can you explain that statement? I am sure our millions of viewers would love to understand how killing twenty-two thousand people a year, on average, equates to caring about humanity."

Adams smiled as he noted Michael seeking to bolster himself by referencing the number of viewers in his corner. He saw a child before him, a juvenile seeking solace in the supporting crowd. "That number is low during years when we engage in stage one," Adams said flatly.

"Really? And you're proud of that?"

"Proud? Of the deaths? I am neither proud nor remorseful. Proud of the outcome? Most definitely. Now, where would you like me to begin?"

Michael shook his head, a scornful smile on his face. He looked at Adams but focused on his forehead, avoiding looking into those hollow orbs. "Oh...please do tell us about our American delusions."

"Very well," Adams accepted the challenge, noting Michael's faltering courage. "What do you sacrifice to your gods?"

"Excuse me? We are not a theocracy. We sacrifice nothing as a nation to any gods."

"I apologize. I forgot you are stupid," Adams sneered.

Michael attempted to rise to the insult, his concentration moving from his opponent's forehead to his eyes. He saw...death? Shaken, Michael's attention turned to some papers on the desk.

Adams watched Michael shuffle his notes for a moment before he continued. "When I say gods, I am speaking metaphorically about that which is most important to your nation. What is the nation's core belief? What gives meaning and purpose to the word 'America'?"

"Freedom," Michael declared, looking up and grasping a time-honored answer. "Let's start with that."

"An excellent starting point," Adams said. "And what do you sacrifice to freedom?"

"Sacrifice? What do you mean?"

"You are a citizen of a nation of liberty and freedom. You respect human life. Opportunity and possibility abound. You hope, still, to extend those opportunities to all your citizens. One might wonder what is taking so long. We are a nation of barbarians and murderers. This is a simple, but accurate, summation of the American view of our two nations."

"And the view of many nations."

"Of course, many nations." Adams smiled, educating glaciers on the meaning of cold. "That is fine. So we begin with one in six and one in thirteen."

"What are those ratios?"

"The ratio one in six represents the number of girls who were victims of childhood sexual abuse in your United States last year. The second ratio is your boys who suffer this humiliation. Now, forty-eight percent of these children are victimized by repeat offenders. These numbers are roughly the same as they were a hundred years ago. You see, you sacrifice millions of children to your gods of liberty and freedom, and they grow pained, broken, lost, and crippled."

"Child abuse, in all forms, is a tragedy," Michael said, nodding his head. "But, unlike your nation's pervasive use of...the death penalty, child abuse is not government sanctioned in the United States."

"No, merely approved: both by the government and society. The cost of freedom and liberty. The children are an acceptable sacrifice, for over one hundred years, to your gods. And many are complicit. You, for example, are complicit."

"What?" Michael spat the word out as if it were bile. "How can you say that? It is ludicrous!"

Adams chuckled, amused by this sudden show of spirit. "Spare me and your precious viewers your heartless indignation. You have hosted this nightly show for five years. You have given impassioned speeches regarding the role of the media as a 'watchdog to power'. In those five years, you have dedicated twenty-five minutes of airtime to childhood sexual abuse. Fifteen of those minutes were because a congressman, whose party affiliation you despise, was accused of molesting a child. The other ten provided an opportunity for you to attack a religion you loathe. So, to be honest, you used the horror of childhood sexual abuse to smear people and an organization you oppose. You weren't seeking to aid the victims. You were seeking to attack and destroy. That's what you are. You seek destruction, not healing."

"That's a—"

Michael's retort was never completed, as Adams steamrolled over his words with the force of his will. "Let me ask you...when you heard of the accusation, were you horrified for the children or exuberant because you could bring woe to an enemy? The child, to you and the millions like you, was little more than an inanimate weapon to be wielded against your foes, not a human in need of healing. That child, in my nation, would be cared for and avenged."

Michael stared at his guest as he searched for a response. Adams, as comfortable in this room as he was on the killing fields he trod, granted the time. Michael blurted forth a time-honored defense. "And you think your use of the death penalty has deterred criminals? That's why your crime rates are low?"

"Definitely not. It is not a deterrent. What deters crime in our nation is the standard of living provided to all citizens. It's amazing how certain crimes drop when want is removed. Elevation of humanity and living conditions deters crime, not the death penalty." The words came as rolling thunder, the vanguard to the storm. Adams scanned the room. All employees, seasoned veterans to the green interns, gaped at him, captivated by the magnetism of the moment. "It is, I suppose, punishment. Nothing more and nothing less. It is definitely the elimination of poorly developed *Homo sapiens* for the sake of humanity. It is the sacrifice we make. Your great exemplar Frederick Douglass once asked, 'Once thoroughly broken down, who is he that can repair the damage?' That is such an important question: 'Who is he that can repair the damage?' How does one repair a damaged person so they become a flourishing human being? We take such a thought very seriously and strive to create environments that encourage that growth and eliminate wretched obstacles."

"Fine," Michael allowed, finally shaking off the sting of Adams' earlier accusation, if not the lingering impact of his presence. "The United States has a multitude of issues to address. Regardless of this fact, the solution is not a totalitarian regime that limits personal freedom. It is not wanton disregard for human life. In what —"

"Wanton disregard for human life?" Adams repeated. "Really? How wonderfully self-righteous. How many of your viewers are going to do anything other than feel badly about those abuse statistics I provided. Will a mass movement grow to finally stop this outrage? No. Nothing will change in this nation. Your screens have dulled your humanity to the point of atrophy."

"People work to assist people in the U.S. all the time. Now you are glossing over our good work."

"Perhaps," Adams said, leaning back. The demon in his eyes receded. "But to finish my metaphor, we sacrifice to Eudaimonia the flourishing of humanity."

"Killing humans to promote humanity? How, in any sane mind, can this be balanced?"

"I know that is a difficult concept for a person raised in your American culture to understand. I sympathize, actually. To be lied to, from the moment of birth to the moment of death, is a terrible thing."

"And what lie is that?"

"That people are born with innate value and nobility. We are born, you and I and everyone, *Homo sapiens*. Value is earned, not conferred naturally. Nobility is defined by the ability to perform duties, not by swimming in a sea of self-aggrandizing, ill-conceived rights. There are great historic duties that must be fulfilled. Ancestral gratitude that must be expressed by building a nation that actively promotes the growth and acquisition of humanity so citizens feel responsible for their inheritance and generativity toward their progeny. Because your nation embraces the concept of unearned value, you wallow in a quagmire of horrendous ingratitude."

Michael sighed and shook his head. "And the C.S.A. builds this sense of humanity? Your ends do not justify your means."

"We feel the same way about your nation. This shared repulsion will not help us cross the great divide that exists. I wonder how expansive it is."

"Well," Michael said, "I suppose there is no real way of knowing. Perhaps if —"

"There may be a way," Adams stated. "If you please, 498."

The monitors suddenly switched to a split screen with Adams on one side and what appeared to be a basic interrogation room on the other. A middle-aged, blond-haired man sat in a chair facing the television. He was gagged with his hands cuffed behind his back. He was flanked by two Orcus.

"That," Adams began, "is Marcus Young. He is a rapist. Adult women, not children. He is, at this point in time, the only survivor of the purge of the Louisiana penal system. You, Michael, are a proponent of rehabilitation and a stark opponent of the death penalty. You feel the death penalty is racist and does not deter crime, correct?"

"Yes."

"Very good. Marcus, as you can see, is white. As I said earlier, we do not invoke the death penalty to deter crime but to eliminate criminals."

"So you have said," said Michael cautiously.

Adams extended his arm, and a document materialized in his hand. "Very good. I hold in my hand a contract. I will release Marcus into the custody of the United States, and the Common States of America will pay for six months of intensive psychological therapy to rehabilitate him. I will do this if, after those six months, you sign a waiver and allow Nicole, your seventeen-year-old daughter, to spend one night, unobserved sleeping in the same room as Marcus. You will have saved a man's life and proven the power of rehabilitation. What do you say?"

"That's ridiculous. I could never...."

"I know. What if I just release him today in a community nowhere near your loved ones? It happens every day in your country. What's one more?"

"That's not the answer either."

"I see," Adams said. He lifted the contract and held it aloft. "Anyone! Anyone in this room willing to save this innately valuable life? This vessel of humanity? It can be your child or, if you are female, you can volunteer to spend the night yourself. Anyone?"

Many glanced around the room, but none volunteered.

"Very well. To be clear, no one present will save this life? So be it. Orcus 44T, lock in and —"

"Hold!" The behemoth's arm, which was poised to deliver death, dropped instantly as it obeyed the unexpected command. Confusion reigned as people sought the sudden savior. They soon realized the voice came from the monitor. Meredith Wilson stepped into the camera's frame. "Commander Adams, a request for a stay."

Adams contained his surprise, effectively hidden beneath his controlled veneer. "Special Agent Wilson, request granted. What is your concern?"

"No concerns, sir. I merely wish to take the roll of 44T."

"I see. You are sure of this?"

"I am."

"Very well. Carry on at your discretion, Special Agent."

Meredith Wilson looked into the camera. A smile that bridged the gulf between seduction and sadism lit her face. Somewhere, the devil shuddered. "Good decision, America," Meredith scoffed, holding the camera captive. "Women and girls are not playthings for monsters." With nothing left to say to the citizens of a nation she held in contempt, the special agent turned on her prey. A single gunshot rang out, and Marcus' potential to victimize women was eradicated.

The split screen faded as Adams rose from his chair. "Murderers and barbarians," Adams said before he and his accompanying automatons teleported home.

Michael Jons closed the show, unsure of what responsibility he carried for a man's death.

CHAPTER 12

DECISIONS

Karen Butler shuffled into her home, hoping the years of life embedded in the walls would offer solace from the storm that left her shaken and in need of comfort. Trembling fingers tossed keys on the coffee table with haphazard force. Wearily, she looked around the room, pausing on a picture of her daughter. Tears welled up but were wiped away before they could roll down her cheek. She was little more than an empty shell when she slumped into the living room. Raymond, hearing the keys hit the table, entered from the kitchen to greet his wife and was physically struck by the sight of her. The enthusiasm he anticipated was nonexistent. She looked defeated. The day that had become her New Year's celebration now resembled a funeral.

Karen looked up at Raymond, her blank face becoming aware of, if nothing else, her love for him. She reached her arms upward, and Raymond sat next to her, pulling her into a powerful embrace. They sat in silence, Raymond not sure what to say and Karen not caring to speak. Ultimately, her words broke the quiet spell that had been cast on both of them.

"I'm not sure I can do this."

"Honey, what's wrong?" Raymond asked as he pulled back ever so slightly so he could see her face. Karen, who had been teaching elementary school for sixteen years, didn't answer immediately; she merely shook her head and released a shuddering breath. Her silence roared in Raymond's ears. He took her hand and spoke softly even as his eyes pleaded with her to speak. "You were so excited a few days ago. What's changed?"

Karen shuddered again and looked into her husband's face. She almost appeared surprised to see him. "I was!" Karen paused as the pain in her voice was a shock to herself. She drew and held a deep breath, slowly releasing it as she sought some composure. Satisfied she could speak without snapping, she continued. "I was. I really was. I mean, when we were introduced to those new robots, those teaching assistants, that was amazing. And our class sizes are smaller, and the school is so clean and polished. It is like I am working in some futuristic palace."

Karen stopped talking and stared blankly at the wall. Raymond chose to be silent, allowing his wife to settle into her thoughts. Her attention moved from the wall, returning to the picture of Lizzie on the coffee table and, finally, to her husband's face. "The kids. I think...I think they killed some kids. Maybe their families too."

"What? How could they...no. That can't...what makes you think that?"

"I don't know. The events at Blackclaw. What if that's how they handle difficult children too?"

"No," Raymond whispered, his voice trailing into the distance. Raising the volume of his voice, he continued. "No. I can't believe they would do that. Were there kids missing from your classes or... are you sure you're not just...feeling shaken because of what I've put you through? Seeing death where it isn't?"

"No, please, don't blame yourself," urged Karen, her hand placed gently on her husband's face. Even in her beleaguered state, strength somehow flowed from her hand into his body. "And I don't think that's it. I mean...."

The front door flew open, announcing the arrival of Lizzie Butler. "Oh my god! That was awesome!"

"Good first day?" Raymond asked, rising from the couch to play the exuberant dad. He stepped forward, effectively blocking his daughter's view of her mother. His third step hadn't fallen when he was halted by an unrestrained hug.

"Awesome, I said!" Lizzie exclaimed, rocking back and forth with her father before releasing him. "I mean, wow! The school is pristine, and we have these robots that are helping the teachers. They are so cool!"

"The teachers or the robots?" Raymond asked as Lizzie threw herself into his reclining chair.

"Both! I swear, the teachers are so excited to be teaching in the, what did they call it, the exemplary high school. Not a single shi —knucklehead! Sorry, Dad, sorry. Knucklehead in the whole school! It's like everyone can breathe easier! So relaxed. Why hasn't school always felt this way?"

"Well, we're in a new society now," Raymond explained. "Things are —"

Lizzie peeked around her dad, enthusiastically interrupting him. "Hey, Mom! I didn't see you behind...." She stopped talking for a moment as she read her mother's mood despite her desperate attempt to conceal. "Mom? What's wrong?"

"Oh nothing, sweetie," Karen said. "Just...so many changes from a teacher's standpoint that I feel overwhelmed. I'll be fine."

"You're sure? I mean, I know you have bad days as a teacher, but never the first day." Lizzie's concern was matched by her energy as she shoved past Raymond to get to her mother.

"I know," acknowledged Karen, hoping she sounded reassuring. She was too slow to meet Lizzie, who was already seated and embracing her in a hug only a concerned daughter could give.

"It's just so many changes," Karen admitted, gripping her daughter in a vise. She peered at her husband, simultaneously seeking and communicating strength. "I'm teaching with robots and holographic images floating in the middle of the room! It's so much to take in."

Lizzie let her mother go. "I know! Isn't it cool?"

"It is."

"And you'll figure it out. I mean, you're kinda smart after all!"

Karen laughed despite herself. "Thanks, dear," she said through a smile.

"That's better," Lizzie proclaimed as she bounced up from the couch. "Besides, a job can only get you so upset if you love it a little bit, right?"

Karen released a whimsical laugh as she rose to hug her daughter again. "That's right. You're an angel."

Lizzie and Karen separated, allowing the teenager to spring back to the front door.

"Hey, would it be okay if I went to Key's house? Aleysha and Kenny are heading there. We were thinking of getting some food downtown if that's alright."

Raymond looked at Karen, who nodded her head and smiled at her daughter.

"Have fun, sweetie," Raymond said.

"Thanks, guys!"

"Hold on a second," Raymond gently ordered. "I have one question."

"Sure, what's up?"

"You said you liked the lack of, um, knuckleheads at the school. I thought you were going to use another word, but knuckleheads is what you said, right?" Lizzie blushed as she was reminded, again, of Raymond's preference that she not swear, at least not in front of him. "Are you worried about where they might be?"

"Not really," Lizzie confessed. "I mean, we were told the high schools and, I think, even the middle schools were being divided into four categories. I think they were exemplary, proficient, ummmm...."

"Promising," Karen added.

"Right! Promising and failure. I don't know where the failures are. I just know they aren't harassing me and my friends anymore! Can I go?"

"Go," directed Raymond. He yelled a final thought out the still-open door. "School tomorrow! See you at eight!"

Raymond's cell phone buzzed as a new text message came in.

U could text me. No need to shout! Geez. <3 u

"Well," Raymond said, turning to Karen. He chuckled as he sent a brief response to his daughter. "There's one rousing 'yes vote' for the first day of school."

"Ya think?" Karen teased, sitting back down. "Maybe I was letting my imagination run away with me a little. It was just frightening."

Raymond returned to his wife's side. "What spooked you so much?"

"I just...I teach fifth grade, so we are not divided into these categories that the high schools are. We have all the kids from last year — just divided into smaller groups."

"All?"

"Seems that way. None were missing."

"Then what made you so nervous?"

Karen shook her head and sighed. "I have fourteen students in my class."

"Fourteen? That's it?"

"Yeah," Karen said, shaking her head. "Fourteen! With two teaching assistants! One assistant is a person, and one is one of those robots. Can you believe it?"

"Wow. That's...amazing," Raymond answered, his mind wandering to the hours his wife spent at the table correcting papers and planning the weeks to come. "Sounds like you will get a lot done this year. You might even learn to delegate."

"Maybe," Karen responded with a knowing smile. "Anyway, I know three of my students have particularly rough home situations. When I was reviewing the contact information for them, all three of these kids were wards of the state. I guess they're living in some kind of group home. Taken from their parents."

"That could be. Look at it this way, maybe they've been saved," Raymond offered as an alternative. "It's not like foster care doesn't exist in the United States."

"I know. But so many? I checked with some of my colleagues, and they all have the same situation. One of my students, Josh, he said he hasn't seen his older brother since the high school meetings. I asked around and other teachers had similar stories."

"And you think students like Josh's older brother were all executed?"

"They could have been."

"True or maybe brought to some kind of boarding school. A place that stresses discipline and is trying to help get them to build better habits."

"That makes some sense," Karen conceded. "All the students I am talking about had difficulty succeeding in school. Kids with behavioral issues. Kids with motivational issues. Low achievers. Didn't you say part of the reason for the executions at Blackclaw was to eliminate undesirables from society? Unproductive people? What if that thinking extends to noncriminals?"

"Yes, criminals were executed at Blackclaw, but to kill kids?" Raymond leaned forward, shaking his head in disbelief. "Remember this: no one had to stay in the state when we joined the C.S.A. There was a grace period to leave. Couldn't the missing kids just be part of the people who left?"

"And left the youngest children behind?" Karen asked.

"Maybe not willingly. I can see the C.S.A. being adamant about helping a young child and not letting them go. And you and I have both seen enough bad parents to know they will protest sharply that this and that can't be done when, in the end, they really just don't want to be parents."

"Yes," Karen admitted sadly, "we've both seen that."

"I just can't believe that killing kids was part of the school reorganization."

"Can't," Karen asked, though it was not clear if she was speaking to Raymond or herself, "or don't want to?"

Raymond considered his wife's question for an eternal five seconds. The doorbell interrupted him as he was about to answer. Surprised by the late afternoon visitors, he went to the door and looked out the arched window. Two professionally attired people, a man and a woman, stood on their stoop. He looked quizzically at Karen and opened the door.

"Hello?" Raymond said as a question. "Can I help you?"

"Actually, Mr. Butler, we are here to help you," the woman answered politely. "My name is Susan Howard, and I am a representative from your local Freedom Bank. This is Edward Sells; he is a government agent. We are here to assist you in finalizing your Freedom Card accounts."

"Oh." Raymond recoiled as if he were a child attempting to sneak dessert before dinner. "The Freedom Cards. Yeah, we haven't gotten around to activating them yet. We will soon. Thanks for —"

"Actually, Mr. Butler," Edward said, stepping forward, "the deadline for activation is April twenty-first. That is tomorrow. With the deadline looming, we are escorting bank officials to help citizens register their accounts and assist them with any issues they might be having. Ms. Howard has everything she needs to quickly and efficiently accomplish this goal. We won't need more than —"

"— Fifteen minutes," Susan interjected pleasantly. "A few questions, a couple of taps on the keyboard, and you will be all set."

Raymond looked from Susan's smiling face to Edward's steely expression and invited the duo into his home. "Of course," Raymond said, "come in. I'm sorry we haven't gotten around to this. Guess it just fell through the cracks with everything else going on."

"No need to apologize," Susan said as she introduced herself to Karen. After their brief exchange, Susan centered herself on the Butler's couch and popped open a laptop on their coffee table. "One of you is a teacher, the other a security guard at Blackclaw. These are important professions in our society but structured quite differently from your nation of origin. I understand if you are feeling a bit overwhelmed. That's why we came here to help you."

"We appreciate that," Karen said. "It has been a bit overwhelming."

"Good work was done at Blackclaw on April seventh," mused Edward. "Many people contributed with enthusiasm. Some more than others."

"Yeah," Raymond quickly stated, seeking to conceal his concern. "I'll tell ya, I was amazed at the technology your people brought in that day."

"First encounters with the Orcus can be intimidating. That's part of their function. Sometimes, just walking one into a room helps you discover who hesitates. Who lacks will. Who is not ready to contribute." Edward's intensity ripped through Raymond as he spoke. Raymond, again, looked at Karen as he searched for words to dispute the allegations. Someone else spoke for him.

"Oh...I hate those things," Susan shuddered. "On rare occasions when I attend meetings at government buildings, I encounter them. Always give me the chills. Anyway, I am just about ready to begin."

"That's good," Karen said hastily. "We should have done this a week ago."

"At least," Edward hissed. "I understand you are overwhelmed by the transition to our nation, but things could be worse for you. You could be an inhabitant of the island nation of Java."

"Java? I don't follow," Raymond confessed, a nervous laugh involuntarily accompanying the words.

"Oh," Susan said, "you didn't hear the news? Earthquake hit the island of Java this morning. Early estimates are five thousand dead or missing."

Karen gasped, "Oh my god. That's horrible!"

"Not really," Susan corrected. "Inevitable, perhaps, but not horrible."

"What?" Karen blurted out. "How can you say such a thing?"

"Well, it's just the way of things," Susan said casually. "People die all the time. Natural causes. Old age. War."

Raymond and Karen stared at Susan, dumbfounded by the casual callousness she exhibited with remorseless confidence. Raymond seemed primed to respond, only to be cutoff by Edward.

"She is right," Edward said. "As you both know, people die all the time. How bad do you think you will feel about Java in two hours? Tomorrow at breakfast? 'There but for the grace of God', right?"

"I don't think you should be so glib about death," Raymond offered with restrained intensity.

"Well then, enough of that talk," the still cheery Susan proclaimed. "All set to register your Freedom Cards. That is, if you're ready."

"Or we could continue to discuss the nature of death," Edward stated through a contented smile. "It is, after all, a fascinating topic."

"I...yes," Karen stammered as she was caught in Edward's hypnotic gaze.

"Yes to more discussion on death?" Edward asked.

"No," Karen answered, shaking her head. "Yes to the Freedom Cards. Let's do that. Do you need...?"

"Good choice. Let's focus on the business at hand," Susan said. "I need just one person present."

"Very good," Edward said, picking up a picture of Lizzie as he spoke. "Since only one person is needed, Raymond, I would like to discuss Blackclaw matters with you in private. May we go to another room?"

"Sure," Raymond said. "You okay, honey?"

"Oh, she'll be fine," Susan answered. "Just a few simple questions and a couple clicks on a keyboard. We know where to find you if we need help."

"Yeah, Ray," Karen confirmed. "Go ahead."

"Outstanding." The word, dripping with menace, rolled slowly off Edward's tongue. For a second time, he looked at the picture in his hand. "Lovely daughter by the way," Edward said, a cold smile growing across his face. He put the picture down as he exited the room with Raymond. Karen held her breath for a moment as she watched them leave the room.

"Don't worry about them," remarked Susan. "Probably some boring prison business to discuss. Edward loves his work."

"Maybe," Karen said. She paused for a moment, contemplating the wisdom of sharing her thoughts. Curiosity won the debate, so she spoke. "Did you mean what you said? About Java? That was...um...a little scary."

"I know. It can be strange talking to people who truly embrace what we are. Let me ask you this: right now, are you more disturbed by Java or by the fact I'm not disturbed? What are you more likely to do first when we leave: send some money to a relief organization or talk to Raymond about how cold Edward and I are?" Susan's smile simultaneously eased Karen and chilled her to the bone. Karen hesitated, unsure what to say. Susan pounced into the silence. "You hesitate because you know the answer...and you don't like it. But it's what we are. Maybe what you are. It can be frightening to see oneself clearly but liberating in the end."

"But shouldn't people care? I mean...."

"Oh, you can care." Susan dropped a hand to Karen's knee in an attempt to be comforting. "It's sweet that you do. You can care and embrace your citizenship. One does not preclude the other. You will have money enough living in the Common States of America to be quite a philanthropist, if you choose. Maybe that will be your area of excellence."

"Helping people, but you just said you don't care about death."

"I have a perspective on the dead and one on the living," Susan responded. "You can't undo death, but you can help the living. Isn't that why you teach? To help people? You could expand your reach so much with the resources here. Help elevate the living. It's what we do in the C.S.A."

"Help the living?"

"Don't worry, sweetie. I can see you have a lot on your mind. What do you say we focus on the Freedom Cards? Enough talk of death and dreams."

"That would be good," Karen said, surprised by the smile that came across her face.

"Of course," Susan said. "It will all be very good. You'll be one of us in five minutes."

———————————

"This won't take more than five minutes," Edward stated bluntly as he and Raymond passed through the kitchen and proceeded to the back porch.

"That's good," Raymond said. "I want to see how things go with the Freedom Cards."

"Do you? I find that hard to believe given you have not activated them. You had time. Your wife was not yet in her training sessions. You were on a brief leave from Blackclaw. Plenty of time to get it done, and you did not. This is not a good sign."

"Sign? Sign of what?"

"Dedication, of course," Edward noted. "Dedication to becoming a member of the Common States of America. Of embracing the benefits of this nation."

"Benefits?"

"Of course," Edward said with enthusiasm. "They are legion if you just rip off your blinders and open your mind. Being held captive by the chains of the past could compromise your decision-making skills. Poor decisions tend to have painful ramifications."

Painful ramifications. A chill coursed through Raymond's back as he considered Edward handling the photo of his daughter. He spoke with careful confidence. "I don't think being slow to activate the Freedom Cards is that big a deal. It's getting done now."

"Yes, it is. But you also did not engage with great vigor in the purge of Blackclaw. That, with this delay, creates a disturbing pattern."

Raymond defensively asked, "A pattern? I killed a defenseless man. I think I did enough that day."

"Glad you brought that up," Edward responded, reaching into his jacket pocket. Raymond's body tensed and his hand twitched as Edward pulled a cell phone from his jacket. If Edward noticed Raymond's reaction, he did not reveal it. "Come. Look. I have video of your activity that day. Look at you. Moving so purposefully through the chaos. You had a destination, and nothing was going to stop you.

Now, look here. That criminal is talking to you. Taunting you, perhaps? Wait...and...BAM! Lights out. You took care of business. That was a nice kill, but it was your only kill. Why is that?"

"I don't know," Raymond said. "I just froze after that."

"Yes, you did. Not completely uncommon in situations like this. We've seen it before. Lots of reasons for it."

"Are there?"

"Positively," Edward stated. "You want to know the leading theory regarding your behavior?"

"Sure," blurted Raymond, groping for a grasp on the moment.

"Revenge. You went straight for that cell. You wanted to fucking kill that man. Am I right?"

Raymond stood in uncomfortable silence as Edward enjoyed watching honesty wrestle with conscience. Honesty achieved victory. "You are," Raymond confessed. "He taunted me for years. Used my daughter to bait me. I wanted to shoot him so many times but... fuck. I couldn't shoot that bastard enough."

"It can be strange when a fantasy comes true, especially a dark one," Edward said. "Feeling guilty ever since, right?"

"Yes."

"We've seen that too. You see, you killed without hesitation, which we applaud. I mean, shit, you targeted that bastard." Raymond looked at the floor and then back to Edward, uncomfortable with the unanticipated and unrestrained praise. Edward, eyes afire, continued. "You are very capable of doing the work we ask. You, however, have to go beyond the personal drive for revenge to the transcendent drive to cleanse. To protect not only your family but a way of life. To do this, you need to let go of some prior programming. Shatter that conditioning you were subjected to in the United States. We think you can do it because, damn, did you go after that motherfucker!"

"So, you're not...um...?"

"Ha! You think I came here to threaten you? Drag you off and force you to the 'Ministry of Truth', so to speak? You've read too many stories, brotha. No. You have great potential; you just need to learn a little more. Sometimes the best students are slow to grasp the initial lessons. But the way you hunted? Shit, you have more to offer than the people just screaming and shooting for laughs in Blackclaw. Those fuckers are a little too unhinged for my taste."

"I don't know what that means. I'm sorry — this is quite unexpected."

"I know." Edward smiled as he pulled a business card from his pocket.

"What's this?" Raymond asked as he took the card.

Edward answered quickly, "Opportunity. You do not need to take it. You can remain at Blackclaw on security detail and make a fine living for yourself. Prisoners will be returning there soon enough. But if you want something more, much more, you call that number. You can come to an informational meeting. If you like what you hear and you pass some tests, you may become a member of a very elite group. You can become one of us."

"One of...who?"

"Well, you're going to have to go to a meeting to find out. Let's head back to the living room. The ladies should be done."

CHAPTER 13

DARK VALLEYS

The subterranean corridors of Skadi Detention Center offered an unusual fusion of modern technology and medieval deprivations. Kurt Adams' footfalls struck the lacquered wooden floors with rhythmic force. Each stride caused the torches mounted on damp stone walls to flicker at his passage. Sharing the walls with the torches were monitors, strategically placed throughout the basement, allowing the prisoners to watch selected programming or events. The cells themselves were primitive, rusted cages with mattresses on the floor and buckets for piss and excrement. Adams expeditiously moved through the labyrinth until he reached his destination, room 619, the cell of Father Roger Baudin.

"Good evening, Padre," Adams uttered with domineering politeness. "Time for a visitor."

"I have nothing but time," Roger answered from his mattress. He pulled himself to a seated position. Sunken eyes highlighted by dark bags watched Adams unlock the cell door. Roger ran his hand through his matted hair and over the patchy scruff that covered his face. The sweats and black shirt he wore the night of the revival meetings were now dingy and torn. Some weight had been lost, but some extra pounds clearly remained.

"That wasn't a question," corrected Adams as he entered the room. He placed a small disk on Roger's bucket, where some moisture from the bucket found itself on Adams' fingers. He wiped them on the priest's shirt before he raised his watch to his lips to speak. "Hello 47-J. Prep for session in room six one nine."

"Very good, Commander," the MLB responded. The bucket in the corner of the room disappeared, and two chairs materialized. They were both leather-bound and of the same size.

"Have a seat," Adams said pointing at the chairs. "Either one will do."

Roger grunted as he pushed himself to his feet. He looked back and forth from one chair to the other. He elected not to sit with his back to the cell door.

"Nice choice," Adams said, "though to be honest, it doesn't make a difference. We can teleport someone behind you at any time."

"That's true," Roger responded, settling into his chair. "Of course, there's another reason it doesn't matter."

Adams was mildly amused by the casual attitude of the aged priest. He asked, "What would that be?"

"You can kill me anytime you want from anywhere in the room," Roger stated as a matter of fact. "I know this is true."

"And this does not scare you?"

"I should already be dead. You broadcasted all of your...what do you call them...um...revival meetings into this dungeon."

"Indeed. Enjoy the viewing?"

Roger ignored the question and offered a simple assessment. "I am guessing I am one of the few living religious figures in the state."

"The last, to be perfectly honest." A cold smile accentuated Adams' words.

"Unless some evaded you," Roger offered.

"None did."

Roger smiled. "Perhaps. You would be surprised how resourceful people can be when fleeing for their lives."

"You would be surprised how resourceful people can be when cleansing filth from society," Adams responded.

"Perhaps I would," Roger conceded without conviction. "Why, I wonder, is filth like me still alive?"

"You do not seem to fear death, Father. Most of your brethren raged or wept at the moment of death. Their vision of the afterlife did not seem to comfort them."

"I do not know if that is so unusual. And please, sir, do not confuse fear of being murdered with a lack of religious conviction or moral fortitude. How one conducts oneself when being murdered does not reveal their true character. That is a foolish thought. It only reveals how they handle being murdered. Nothing more."

"A fair point. Yet I stood before you, ready to eliminate you, and you did not flinch."

"True. I have had guns pointed at me before. My missions have taken me to war zones and before tyrannical personalities. The first time I faced a man like you, I was not so placid."

"A man like me?" Adams questioned.

"Of course. There are other men like you. If we look at history, it sadly seems there have always been men like you. You are more organized than some, I'm sure. Likely more prolific. More technologically...blessed. But the same cold soul exists. The same callous disregard for human life. The same delusion that the world's problems can ultimately be solved by violence, fear, strict controls, and power."

"Delusion, you say." Adams shifted in his seat. He extended his hand and a mug of coffee appeared in it. He took a slow sip as a coffee table appeared before him. Putting the mug down, he bore into his adversary. "Interesting choice of words given your adult life is built on embracing delusion."

"I can only imagine what you are referring to. I am sure much of what I stand for is delusional to you."

"That is true, Father. But since we can't discuss it all at once, let's begin with this ridiculous notion of the brotherhood of man. The idea that all people are somehow worth something. Evidence to the contrary comes before you regularly."

"Indeed, it does," Roger said, locking in on Adams' impassive face. "People never stop finding ways to exhibit their frailty."

"Do they?" Adams crooned. "I wonder how much of what you call frailty is uncorrectable or permanently ingrained in people? How many beacons have you lit on a path to nowhere?"

"I am not a friend of unrealistic certitude, nor do I offer unrealistic security. I...." Roger stopped speaking as Adams snorted out cruel laughter. Settling back into his chair, Roger waited for Adams' merriment to subside.

"Oh, Father," Adams said through a smile, "that was hilarious. You are in the business of unrealistic everything! It is your bailiwick."

"I understand that is how you perceive me."

"It is not perception, Father. It is what is," Adams snapped. "So, it was merely the profound strength of your delusions that enabled you not to wither before me."

Roger leaned forward in his chair, elbows on his knees. His head was facing the floor, but he stared undaunted into Adams' coal-like orbs. He spoke slowly and with a force that belied his beleaguered appearance. "I am telling you I thought nothing of the afterlife or whatever metaphysics you think ran through my head at that moment. As I've already stated, I have stood before vicious, well-armed men in the past. That was the source of my calm. You are free to believe what you will."

Kurt Adams held Roger's gaze, scanning the priest's soul for weaknesses. Drawing a deep breath, he spoke. "I believe you, Father. I believe some experiences have strengthened you. I do not believe, however, that the source of your serenity was merely those events."

Roger leaned back in his chair, head tipped upward so he could follow the outline of the ceiling in his cell. He inhaled deeply and exhaled forcefully before continuing the conversation. Adams was comfortable waiting in the silence, sipping his coffee as his foe deliberated.

"You may be right," Roger finally said. "But I assure you whatever else contributed to my perceived calm was not thoughts of the afterlife."

"I believe you," Adams proclaimed, placing his coffee down yet again. "But it is good to know we can be honest with each other."

"Is that why I'm alive? So that we can have honest conversations?" The question came forth with more trepidation than Roger wanted. He sighed and looked to the floor.

Adams was not sure if the hesitancy in Roger's voice was caused by fear of death or confusion of life. This lack of certainty did not prevent him from smiling before he answered. "You are alive because I have not killed you. I am, however, curious. Tell me about the first incident when you met a man like me."

Roger sat up in his chair, taken aback by the sincerity of the query. He considered, for the briefest moment, asking a question but opted to tell his tale as requested. "It was some time ago. I was a young priest in Lorgalsum, another new state that appeared in Africa some fifty years ago. Missionaries and humanitarians came to the country. Schools, medical facilities, orphanages, and the like were quickly erected."

"As were churches," Adams interjected.

"And churches," Roger repeated. "Bighearted people doing good work to help the communities ravaged by the, I don't know what to call it, tribal or ethnic wars that led to the creation of Lorgalsum. I don't know the roots of the conflicts, I just —"

Adams sneered, "Perhaps you should have spent time studying the culture before you rushed in to help. How like an imperialist to seek to solve a problem that is not even understood."

"Maybe you're right. Of course, in my first week on the ground and in the months that followed, I spent much time feeding hungry migrants and offering shelter to orphans. I tried to comfort souls and fill bellies as medical personnel cared for the complexities of the body. It's strange — not a single child or adult told me they would not accept food or a blanket until I proved my understanding of both the domestic and international causes of the conflict."

"Touché, Father," Adams said wryly. A small smile crossed Roger's face. It lingered long enough to be seen before disappearing as the tale resumed. "Anyway, I was celebrating the Eucharist —"

"Conducting mass," Adams interjected mockingly.

"Celebrating the Eucharist," corrected Roger, the strength of his will again on full display. He paused in preparation for Adams' retort, a comment that never came. After the eternal two seconds of pause, Roger continued. "A man stormed into the church with a machine gun. He threatened to kill everyone present for the crime of their birth. I shouted 'Stop!' from the altar. It was more reflexive than an act of courage, believe me. He laughed and approached me. He was levying insults and accusations, much as you did when we met. I understood a good seventy percent of what he said as I was increasingly fluent in the languages I heard. Anyway, he asked if I would die for the congregation. If white robes made me Christ-like. I stammered. I hesitated to answer, and he whipped out a pistol and shot a woman. People screamed. The gunshots and terrified shrieks brought some of his companions into the church, and everyone froze. He repeated his question to me. I still couldn't speak. I was choking on words. Maybe crying, but I went to him. I begged him to stop. Begged him. He put his pistol to my head and said, basically, it would be one more death or many. He asked me to choose. I couldn't speak. He laughed and shot another parishioner. Murdered a young boy. To what end? When he turned the gun back to me, he looked so happy. Suddenly, one of his companions yelled, 'Quick! They're coming!' He laughed at me and walked down the center aisle. Lord, how he mocked me. He reached the last row of pews and shouted, 'For you!' as he shot an elderly man. I cried as they left. Some people fled the room. Others ran to the bodies or ran to get help. Some, like me, just wept. Just wept. I suppose I learned much that day."

"You did not learn enough," Adams concluded as he rose from his chair. "We may, however, have occasion to complete your education."

Adams turned and exited the room. The chair he occupied disappeared as the door closed. The piss bucket reappeared in the space previously occupied by the chair. Mindlessly, Roger stood up and returned the bucket to the corner of the room. When he turned, his chair was gone as well. He stood alone, his past and present fighting for supremacy. The silence was broken when every monitor in the block started playing Kurt Adams' *Honest Politics* interview.

CHAPTER 14

NECESSITIES

People of historic standing...value (?) are born-again at
the time of their deaths. reborn at the time of their deaths.

Erin ripped the page from her legal pad and unceremoniously tossed the wadded-up ball at the small, ceramic trash can stationed near her desk. The paper, which had no chance of landing in the receptacle, found a home on the floor alongside seven of its recently discarded brothers. Erin leaned back in her chair and groaned. She threw her left arm across her face, the crook of her elbow shielding her from the world. The late hour and the unexpected comfort of her slouching position may have caused her to doze off for a moment.

"Good evening, Madam Chancellor. I see speech writing is going well."

Erin came to attention in her chair, her eyes communicating her mind existed — at that moment — somewhere between a deer listening for wolves or a child caught doing wrong. She stared at Ryan for an instant too long, trying to gather her wits through the two a.m. fog.

"Mr. Prime Minister," she said slowly as she quickly composed herself, "how very nice of you to come forth and offer me aid."

"Oh? Is that what I am here for? With what might you need my assistance?" Ryan lowered himself into a chair facing her desk."

"You are well aware of what I'm working on. We are having the gala on May twentieth to commemorate the tenth anniversary of my grandfather's death. I am struggling to write the speech. I did not truly know him that well."

"You know him well enough," Ryan responded. "His accomplishments. His writings. His determination. These are his greatest legacy. You can focus on those and then direct our vision to the future."

"The next hurdle," Erin groaned as she focused on the next blank sheet of paper in her pad. "Always the next hurdle."

"Such was his way. You need not search for some familial anecdote when he was ever-consumed with the next phase of the revolution. Hence, his successes."

"Which have become ours," Erin said. "You're right. I guess I just needed a little validation."

"That's all? Not looking for some story about the good ole days of the early revolution to add to your speech?" Ryan smiled as he already knew the answer.

Erin waved her hand and exclaimed, "Please no! I want this to be a short speech, and you can be...a bit...detailed in your storytelling."

"How tactful. If not the need for another tale, why did you summon me?"

"I didn't," Erin clarified. "I just said I wanted to run something by you. I believe I stated in the message that it was not pressing and could wait until the morning. No need for you to be here at this time."

"When the chancellor calls, I answer."

Erin smiled softly as she swallowed the urge to curse Ryan's unflinching sense of duty and loyalty. Instead, she cursed her own forgetfulness of this fact. "You truly did not need to come here."

"Yet, here I am, so you may as well ask me your question," Ryan stated in an even tone.

Erin shook her head. "Remember, I did not want you here at this time for this question. For the gala, I would like to place Commander Adams in charge of security detail. Your thoughts on this move?"

"You would like Commander Adams to be on site in charge of security? I do not think that is a good idea."

"I know. He will likely consider it a waste of his time."

"He will," emphasized Ryan, "consider it a waste of his time. He may not be wrong."

"You think the event is...frivolous?"

Ryan shifted in his chair, seeking an elusive sense of comfort. "That is not what I said. Commander Adams will, however, consider his involvement to be unnecessary; there are many people capable of handling security. He would much rather be navigating the ongoing initiation of Louisiana than becoming involved in the celebration of our historic exemplars or, more specifically, being assigned to be the caretaker of the event."

"I know," admitted Erin, "but he should be there. Louisiana is progressing as planned. We need to show we can initiate while maintaining our customs of properly honoring our past. Many members of the oligarchy will be in attendance. He should be there as well. I figured allowing him to be working at the event would be preferable to making him sit on stage again."

"On that we agree."

"Good. Then you will ask him to do this for me."

"Me? Are you sure that is a good idea?"

"I do not wish it to sound like a directive from the chancellor's chair. I would like him to take up this charge of his own accord. Perhaps you can help him see the importance of these events."

"You are asking me to handle him for you?"

"No," Erin snapped. "That is not what I am saying. I do not need assistance in that arena. It is not that."

Ryan leaned back but did not speak. He drew a deep breath and inquisitively looked at Erin, communicating curiosity and compassion as he offered her the space to consider her thoughts.

The comfortable silence stretched into peaceful seconds before Erin spoke. "I just would like him to appreciate the ceremonies we hold to honor our shared history. To allow the power of the past to infuse him with a deeper sense of connection to what we are. What we...."

Ryan coughed as he laughed. "Really, Erin! Why seek the impossible?"

Erin blushed. "I know. I just...sometimes in the late hours...."

"Your idealism gets the best of you," Ryan reasoned gently. "It's a fine and, if you forgive me, quite an endearing quality. But make no mistake: Kurt Adams loves this nation and what we strive for. He...," Ryan raised his hand, a traffic cop stopping words instead of cars, "is utterly committed to what we do. He understands the importance of these ceremonies. He just wants no personal part of them! But he would never say they were not necessary for the collective memory. He merely would say that he, himself, does not need them while not diminishing the importance of them or dismissing anyone who embraces them."

"Have you discussed these issues with him? You speak as if you have and...but...you two...."

Ryan stood as he prepared to leave the room. "I speak with such confidence because Commander Adams is much like Daniel McGreggor. You want to know your grandfather? Look at Mr. Adams. Neither man looked upon ceremony with tremendous favor. Both men were unfaltering in their dedication to the revolution. Both men deserve praise but do not deign to hear it."

"Why, Mr. Vancese, did you just compliment Commander Adams?"

"Your idealistic love of history is magnified in the wee hours," Ryan joked wistfully. "Evidently, my willingness to deliver undeserved compliments rises when the moon strikes its apex. But, rest assured, I will discuss your call to duty with Commander Adams in the morning. Good luck writing, Madame Chancellor."

Whatever luck Ryan sent was unnecessary. His words had barely fallen, and Erin was already punishing her writing pad with vigorous pen strokes.

CHAPTER 15

CLEANING UP

Kurt Adams emerged from his bedroom wearing pressed black pants and polished shoes offset by a short sleeve gray tee shirt. He moved into the kitchen and opened the refrigerator, acknowledging Laura's presence. "You're up early," he noted as if reading a fact from an encyclopedia.

"Yeah, just couldn't sleep I guess." The gentle yearning in her voice, a soul seeking spring on a late winter's morning, was lost on Kurt while he continued to rummage for a drink. She laid on the couch facing the window, a blanket pulled midway up her torso. Kurt circled the couch and stood before her, a glass of orange juice in hand. He took a sip and sat down on the armrest near her head. "Enjoying the view?" he asked.

"Oh...I don't know. The stars can be so muted by the city lights."

"I always find the city coming to life in the predawn hour rather magnificent."

"I guess I just wanted to see the stars. Y'know...really see them," Laura dreamed in a subdued tone.

"You should use your vacation stipend and take a trip from the city if nature is what you crave."

"I could do that," Laura stated. She opted not to press the issue. "You like the city lights?"

"I do." Kurt said, rising to place his glass on the counter. Laura stood and followed him to the kitchen area. He glanced her way as he walked; a legitimate look of surprise flashed across his face. "You're wearing sweatpants? Are you cold? The heat can be turned up."

"I'm fine," Laura said, a hint of melancholy hiding her words. "Just felt like being comfy."

"Very good."

"So, do you ever enjoy the city, or do you just like the city lights?"

"I enjoy what I do in this city," Kurt stated. "Depending on my duties, I am often elsewhere."

"True, but, I mean, do you have a favorite restaurant? A pub? I've known you for seven months now, and I don't think I've ever even seen takeout in your apartment."

"Why eat out?" Kurt asked. "Both 498 and I are fine cooks."

Despite herself, Laura smiled. "Yes, you both are. Though, to be honest, 498 is slightly better than you."

"Really? I did not hear any complaints about our use of the kitchen last night."

"The meal was pretty good," Laura admitted, a smile still on her face.

Kurt returned the smile. "And the dessert was excellent," he remarked playfully.

"It was pretty good," Laura teased. "You could still afford to learn a thing or two."

"Well, maybe I just won't have that dish again. Maybe it is time for something new."

Laura hesitated a moment until she saw the playful gleam in Kurt's eye. She struck his shoulder and laughed. "You can be a real jerk."

"Don't mistake my pragmatism for cruelty," Kurt counseled through a smile. "However, I do hear your request."

"Do you?"

"Indeed. Louisiana still needs my attention, though it does not need my boots on the ground quite as regularly as when initiation began. Provide a list of restaurants you would like to try, and I will make the arrangements. There is a condition, however."

"And what might that be?" Laura tilted her head, allowing her brown hair to fall freely as she twirled a few strands around her left index finger.

"After dinner, we will visit the Museum of Fine Art."

"The Museum of Fine Art? I didn't know you liked art. You don't have any displayed here."

"My apartment is for practicality. Other interests lie beyond its walls."

"That," Laura put her arms around Kurt's neck, "sounds like a wonderful night."

A prolonged kiss followed, which ended when Kurt lifted Laura and placed her on the counter. He pulled back until Laura's arms tightened around him.

"There's that famous vise grip," Kurt noted.

"Time for breakfast?" Laura asked. "Or some dessert?"

"I do not. I have initiation duties I must attend to in Louisiana. I will, however, be back soon. As I said, my boots are not as needed as they were in phase one."

"Perhaps I could...." Laura didn't finish her sentence. Kurt pressed his thumb against a small scanner built into his belt to activate the Torres Technology imbedded in the leather. He disappeared from sight, leaving Laura holding empty air and speaking to no one.

Kurt reappeared in the basement of a building designated MT-II, one of two facilities erected in Louisiana to monitor initiation progress and provide a particular presence in the state. MT-II was dedicated to repairing, storing, and upgrading military technology. The basement of MT-II currently held five companies of Orcus. It was these androids that called Adams' attention at this time. His pace, sturdy and strong, brought him to a door which led to a storage area. He leaned forward for a retinal scan.

"Commander Kurt Adams, secretary of internal security," a gentle metallic voice said politely, "how are you this morning?"

"All is well," Adams responded. The metallic voice sought to respond, but Adams interrupted the process by stating, "*Hephaestus.*"

The door slid open, and Adams entered the storage area. Five hundred fifty Orcus stood in a sunken floor. A multitier catwalk with control panels at various locations surrounded them. Metal stairs allowed people to descend to the floor and move among the behemoths. Adams turned left and approached a familiar form standing at a workstation.

"Hello, 498," Adams said with roughly the same tone he often used when greeting Laura. "Do you have the Orcus I requested in the test room?"

"Indeed, sir," MLB 498-A responded politely, pressing a button that triggered a double door to open before them. "They are positioned in the firing range as requested."

"Outstanding."

The duo entered the firing range where three Orcus stood, arms up and ready to fire upon targets situated at the end of the open room.

"Ready to conduct the test, Commander?"

"Almost. We need another human voice. Not mine. Open communications with MLB 62-B."

"Channel is clear, sir."

"Outstanding," Adams replied. Despite the fact the communication capacities of the MLBs did not require an increase in volume, he raised his voice as he called for Edward Sells. "Doc. You read me?"

After two seconds of silence, Doc replied. "Perfectly clear, sir. Time for me to do that favor for you?"

"Indeed. On my mark, I will shut down the Torres countermeasures built into this facility. You will have twenty-seven seconds to teleport in. If you miss the window, it was good to work with you."

"Very comforting, sir. I have your coordinates and await...."

"Proceed."

Within ten seconds, Doc stood beside his boss.

"Greetings, Special Agent Sells," MLB 498-A said kindly.

"Glad you made it, Doc." Adams' tone was slightly less human than what 498-A mustered.

"I can feel your deep affection, sir," Doc replied.

"Feel free to call me Stone," Adams said. "I know it is your preference, and we are not on an official mission."

Doc hesitated for a moment before he replied. "Excellent. Since you bring it up, why are we here? The Orcus have a new weapon you want me to assess?"

"Negative. Although you would be the right person to call if that were the case. You are very adept at working with the Orcus." He lingered on Doc for just a moment before he looked again at the sentinels beside him.

"Well, thank you. And, if not that, then what?"

Adams paused before speaking. "An experiment of sorts. I am going to order all three Orcus to fire upon their targets. As I speak, please interrupt by shouting 'Hold!' Do you understand?"

Doc licked his lips and chuckled. "Not at all, Stone. That's way beyond my understanding."

"Outstanding," was Adams' reply. For the life of his children, Doc could not tell if Adams even heard him. Adams stepped to the side of the Orcus and looked straight down to the floor on which he stood, his iron will dedicated in this moment to the act of suppressing a smile. Victory achieved, he raised his head and began his command. "Orcus lock in, and —"

"Hold!" Doc shouted. Every arm remained raised.

"—Fire!" Adams snapped, and all three Orcus unleashed their fury on their targets. "Once more," Adams said quickly. "ORCUS 44T, lock in and —"

"Hold!" Doc shouted vainly.

"—Fire!" Adams snapped again, and ORCUS 44T obeyed the Commander's order, destroying the remains of its target.

"44T," Doc said knowingly. "This is the one Wilson stopped the night of your interview."

"Correct," Adams said. "I was curious if it was just her voice that commanded it or if others were also so...gifted."

"I see. I didn't help her." Doc hoped this statement cleared him of suspicion. He quickly pushed the conversation forward. "So...her interruption that night was not planned."

"It was not," Adams replied, a hand moving along the frame of Orcus 44T. "498, begin advanced diagnostic. Now Doc, as you know, 44T, like all Orcus, are programmed to follow orders based on voice recognition of the ranking officer orchestrating any given mission. Their directives can only be overridden by the voice of a superior ranked individual giving an order."

"Yup," Doc said casually, "and there is no higher rank than yours. Well, except the chancellor override."

"Chancellor and prime minister override," Adams corrected.

"Really? You gave the ole war dog the power to override your orders to the Orcus? Surprising."

"And incorrect. The chancellor and prime minister must speak in unison to override my orders to the Orcus. I altered the fail-safe."

"You...why? Did you tell them?"

"No. As for why, my orders on missions ought to be followed, for none understand my missions as well as I. Particularly not politicians or, with due respect, fading revolutionaries."

"And you are telling me because...."

"...Because, in the end, the role of Omega officers and the secretary of internal security is to protect this nation and catapult our species to the flourishing life. Sometimes, in order to do this, such people must be free of the chain of command. Excellence overrides rules. You need to understand this, Doc. Otherwise, you will never take the last step of the ladder."

"I guess...I just...."

"You are clandestine and calculating, Doc. You ran Omega Blue flawlessly and have swelled our ranks in the past with your recruitment efforts. Now you have your final test."

"What's that?"

"You know what it is. I will know, at the time of my death, if you passed."

Doc was not entirely sure what his superior referred to but decided not to probe for understanding. "I guess. What did you want to tell me about Orcus 44T and Wilson?"

"I am waiting for information," Adams answered, turning to his attaché. "498?"

"Yes, sir. My diagnostic is complete. 44T has an unauthorized implant granting a singular user, Special Officer Wilson, to verbally override all directives sent to this particular unit."

"Can it be electronically activated from afar?"

"No, sir. It is rather crude in its design. It cannot be activated by an electronic pulse. Besides all of us, MLB and Orcus alike, are —"

"— Equipped with EMP jammers to prevent electromagnetic disturbances or pulses from shutting them down. The tech would block any attempt to override from a distance."

"Well said, Special Agent Sells," MLB 498-A stated with as much pride as could be found in its tonal modulators.

Adams nodded approvingly before speaking. "What of Ms. Wilson's device?"

"As I was saying, sir, it is specifically designed to react to her voice. It is not sophisticated enough to penetrate our other defenses."

"Don't sell her short. No one else has ever done this before. She has found a flaw in your defenses."

Doc could not help but notice that a touch of admiration was mixed within Adams' reprimand of 498.

"Indeed, sir. I was not disparaging the special agent's efforts, but the device itself seems quite depleted from usage. I estimate that, if she were to try it again, the probability of success would be approximately thirty-seven percent. That would drop to zero percent if a third attempt were made."

"Regardless," Adams said, "I would like it out. Can you extract it, 498?"

"Yes, sir."

"Outstanding. Please do scan the remaining Orcus in this facility for other such devices. Relay your search pattern to the other MLBs stationed with the Orcus to conduct a thorough inspection of all units utilized in the initiation protocols. And run surveillance scan order Viper-I. Relay coordinates when complete."

"Of course. For your consideration, sir, the two units standing beside 44T have not been compromised. I suspect 44T was a proverbial lone wolf."

"I would not be surprised if you are correct, 498. I will, however, be gratified when suspicions are confirmed."

"Understood, sir. Shall we create a new executive protocol for this information?"

"Please do so. Send me the code at your leisure."

"Very well. I shall begin the investigation now. Viper-one scan complete."

"Thank you, 498."

MLB 498-A glided from the room, embarking on its mission to tirelessly fulfill Adams' orders. Adams watched it depart, losing himself in thought as he attempted to anticipate what coordinates he would receive. His ruminations were interrupted when Doc hesitantly repeated a question.

"So," Doc began slowly, "what about Orcus 44T and Wilson? What're your thoughts on that?"

"At this moment," Adams said slowly, "my thoughts are my own. I suppose you will learn of them in due time."

A quick touch of his belt and he was transported to his next destination. Doc stood alone, contemplating the future — his as well as Meredith Wilson's.

CHAPTER 16

LESSONS TO LEARN

Raymond looked at his daughter in the passenger seat. She was lost in thought, and he chose to mimic her speech in an attempt to break the spell of silence. "Whatcha thinkin', Lizzie?"

"Nothing," Lizzie answered in a bland tone. The incredulous look on her father's face prompted a quick clarification. "Nothing important."

"Anything I can help you with? We're all going through a lot of changes, and you haven't really shared much of your thoughts about any of them."

"That's because I'm a teenager," Lizzie mocked, smiling as she turned one of her father's favorite generalizations back on him.

"Alright. Don't get too happy with yourself over there." Raymond's response came with a restrained smile.

Lizzie was pleased that she could zing her father. "Actually, I was honestly just thinking about my history teacher. Mr. Tarrand."

"Tarrand? I don't remember ever hearing that name before."

"He's new. Well, new to me. Some of my teachers — Ms. Reguin,

Mr. Robertson — they were my teachers before we became citizens of the C.S.A."

Raymond flinched. This was the first time he heard his daughter so describe their new status. While accurate, it still carried a minor shock. Lizzie, lost in her description, did not notice his reaction.

"Mr. Tarrand taught in North Carolina for, like, fifteen years."

"Like fifteen years or fifteen years?"

Lizzie sighed and offered a brief glare at her dad. "Fifteen years. Jeez, you sound like Mr. Tarrand."

"I like him already."

"Anyway," Lizzie blurted before continuing to her point, "he was brought in to teach history because our old teacher didn't stay in the C.S.A. The weird thing is quite a few of my friends also have new history teachers."

"All of them with experience teaching in the C.S.A.?"

"Yup. I mean, he's really an interesting guy," Lizzie said. "Just suddenly hit me as weird that he's the only new teacher I have. I dunno. Anyway, that's what I was thinking about. And I have his class today, which tends to be interesting."

"I see," Raymond acknowledged with a nod. "Hopefully, we both have interesting days then. I'm going to a meeting to hear about a new job possibility."

"Oh yeah? That's exciting! What is it?"

"I quite honestly don't know. I was told there was an informational meeting being held today and thought I would check it out. New country, new job. Thought it had a nice sense to it all. I'll know more after the meeting."

"Make sure you pay attention," Lizzie commanded in an exaggerated parental tone. "We can't have you going to the school for failures."

"Wouldn't want that," Raymond said. "We want to be in the exemplary school!"

"Absolutely!" Lizzie exclaimed, beaming with pride. "Thanks for the ride, Dad."

"No problem, darlin'. Love you."

"Love you too," Lizzie responded over her shoulder as she exited the car and was quickly swallowed up by the human river flowing into the school. Raymond watched his daughter walk off for just a moment before beginning his forty-five-minute drive to a building called MT-II for his informational meeting.

When he pulled into the lot designated in the email he received, he encountered two MLBs and one Orcus standing outside a guard tower of concrete and steel, a structure of pure function. The MLBs stood on either side of an electric barrier gate while the Orcus stood directly behind it, creating a far more imposing obstacle. A man wielding a rifle stood on the platform, surveying the area as he sipped on a coffee. The driver side window of Raymond's Chevy opened without his consent as an MLB bent over to greet him.

"Hello, sir. Welcome to MT-two, lot seven. I am MLB 47-G. How may I assist you?"

"I...I'm not sure. Ummmm...I didn't touch my window. How did...."

"Just assisting in expediting matters, sir. Perhaps a good place to start would be to share the appointment number you were emailed." MLB 47-G stated with unfailing kindness.

"Okay. Yeah. That's a good...." Raymond didn't finish his thought as he fumbled with his cell phone to bring up the requested information. "Here we go. Appointment S three two L seven."

"Very good, sir," MLB 47-G stated as his partner scanned the car, Raymond's cell phone, and the contents of his trunk while standing as immobile as an oak. "Very good, indeed. You are attending Special Agent Sells' information and recruitment meeting on the third floor of the Delta wing. MLB 39-G just sent you an email with directions to your conference room. It was a pleasure helping you, sir."

The Orcus lumbered to the side to allow passage into the parking lot. As the MLBs stepped back, Raymond felt compelled to speak. "Thank you. I...um...I'm not used to talking to...you guys. Sorry I was...off."

"Quite all right, sir," MLB 47-G responded. "You'll be amazed how easily you adjust to your new environment. Human beings are so adaptable to technology."

Raymond opened his mouth to say a simple 'Thank you,' but his window closed as MLB 47-G pointed out his parking area. Looking in his rearview mirror, Raymond saw the trio greet another car seeking entrance into the lot. His attention returned to his task as he parked his car and began the walk to his meeting, cell phone in hand to access the directions.

"Arrrrgh," Keyneshia Jones snarled as she shook her cell phone. "I keep forgetting cell phones don't work on school grounds."

"You're one slow learner, Key" Lizzie teased, walking beside her friend. "We've been back in school for like more than a week. The fact they don't work here ain't exactly new."

"I know! I just...."

"Stop being so American," Lizzie said in a slow, somewhat choppy cadence.

"Relax there, Mr. Tarrand," taunted Key. "Oh, and you better be nicer to me, or I'll tell your dad you're using words like 'ain't'. For a prison guard, he sure can be picky about words."

"Yeah," Lizzie said, nodding her head. "I think he just doesn't like me talking like the inmates."

"Makes sense but it is still annoying."

"I guess," Lizzie allowed, coming to a stop. "You ready for the next round of Mr. Tarrand?"

Key shrugged. "Ready as I can be." She pulled the door open and pointed into the room. "After you, my dear."

"Why thank you, darlin'," Lizzie answered.

Their banter ceased the moment they crossed the threshold. Students were in assigned seats and placing notebooks on their desks. A young teaching assistant stood in the back of the room as two MLBs moved through the rows of chairs, offering words of greeting and encouragement to the students. Reminders to prepare for class were also shared. Mr. Tarrand, wearing tan pants and a forest green button-down shirt, sat behind his desk, nose in a book, and feet on a stool. When the bell rang, he stood and took a post behind a podium.

"We meet again," Mr. Tarrand stated forcefully. "Glad to see you're all still with us."

"Where would we go? I mean, do we have a choice?"

"Mr. Ramos. We have been together for little more than a week, and your wit continues to astound." Mark Ramos smiled despite the fact he was not sure if he had been complimented. "While the placement of students is meticulous in the Common States of America, the system is not infallible. In the first two weeks of the school year, we see our share of demotions."

"And promotions?"

"No, Ms. Wade. Never promotions. Those take more time. Those must be earned. Demotions are much easier."

The class sat in silence; the combination of Mr. Tarrand's words and icy demeanor left them, once again, stupefied.

Their instructor waited three more seconds before breaking the silence. "I see you all have your notebooks out. That is excellent. Now as class ended yesterday, there was some...confusion, shall we say...with the idea that the United States fails its citizens, and the citizens fail the United States due to a fundamental misunderstanding of human nature. The starting point, the soil itself, is corrupted so the fruit produced is bitter. Let us attempt to wade through the murky waters to understanding. Ms. Butler. Class ended with your question lingering in the air. Repeat it, please."

"Oh. Sure," Lizzie stammered. "I, well, I can't repeat it word-for-word but basically...."

"Why can't you repeat it word-for-word? Did you not write it down? I informed you we would be starting class with your question today."

"That's true. I just figured...," Lizzie looked at the MLB to her left and back to Mr. Tarrand, "y'know...." Mr. Tarrand seemed to pierce Lizzie's mind with his glare, causing her to look at her notebook. Key sent her friend a supportive and sympathetic look.

After using silence to cause discomfort in his students, Mr. Tarrand mimicked, "I just figured...y'know," a heavy sigh punctuating the sentence. "Figured what? I would write it down? MLB 7-T or MLB 8-T would record the query for you? Do your work for you? How very American. You are all new to this nation so allow me to reiterate an important lesson you should embrace before my patience wears thin and my good humor dissipates: claim responsibility for your every action. When you have a worthy question, it becomes incumbent upon you to claw for an answer to that question. You must ache for the answer and, in an effort to relieve that tension, break the bonds of your established level of thought and become more tomorrow than you are today. By so doing, you will become of greater assistance to your families and communities. Mighty is the mind, for where it goes, your body will follow. Do we understand?"

"Yes," Lizzie said meekly.

"And Ms. Jones. While your sympathy for Ms. Butler was a sign of friendship, it was misplaced. Your sympathy should have been for those of us who had to endure her lack of determination." Mr. Tarrand paused for a moment, his scathing certainty communicating there was no room for negotiation. "Let's continue. Your question, Ms. Butler, was 'How can you call the United States selfish when so many people work to help others?' How sad that I care more for the words you produce than you do."

———————

"What is your confusion, sir?" Doc asked from the stage positioned before some four hundred chairs set in a curved pattern. Two aisles cut through the seating arrangement and forty-seven seats closest to the stage were occupied. Two MLBs and four P2 purifiers stood in both the aisles and along the wall. Doc pointed at the confused member of his recruitment class. "I'm not following you. Help me out."

"Well," a middle-aged man with salt starting to overwhelm his peppered head of hair began, "I don't completely understand what you mean when you say the U.S. was selfish. I mean, I know we had problems, but there are plenty of people looking to help others." He finished his statement and looked sheepishly at the two Orcus standing at either end of the stage.

"Firstly," Doc began, "kudos for your loyalty, misplaced as it is. You will need to redirect that if you want to join us. What I said was, 'a faulty starting point has created restrained and selfish altruism.' I never actually said the sentence, 'The United States is selfish.' You need to lock it in as I speak. Words matter. Words have meaning and power regardless of what you were taught by your former nation."

The audience member bristled slightly at the reprimand but held his seat. Doc's presence, augmented exponentially by the Orcus, encouraged an altering of his gut response. "Okay. Maybe I'm just not sure what you mean by that. Selfish altruism."

"I see," Doc said, smiling as he walked from behind his podium. "Restrained and selfish altruism. You know what one of the...for lack of a better term...stupidest social activist movements of the United States' past two hundred years was? Actually, hold on a moment, do you know...do you really appreciate...just how moronic the name 'United States of America' is?"

"Is there a problem, Mr. Mikel?"

"What?" The young man looked around the room, legitimately confused. "No...I...huh?"

"Very interesting," Mr. Tarrand deadpanned. "I ask because you look like you just ate something rather distasteful."

"Oh. Ummmm, I was just surprised you called the United States a stupid name."

"Moronic," Mr. Tarrand corrected.

"Right. Why do you say that?"

"Think about it, Mr. Mikel. The poorly named United States is one of the most fragmented societies on Earth. Their cries of fighting for equality are hollow proclamations designed to conceal the hypocrisy of the speaker's true intent."

"True intent?" Lizzie asked. "What do you think people are fighting for, if not equality?"

"Why superiority, of course," Mr. Tarrand stated. "The citizenry of the United States was seduced long ago by the ethos of capitalistic competition. The social movements of the United States do not seek equality; they seek superiority. They do not seek to unify, only divide. There is no unity, no dedication to improving the nation. Only dedication to improving individual fiefdoms. My tribe. The word 'we' is only used to manipulate, not inform. Therefore, the worst named social movement...."

"Of the last two hundred years," Key said slowly, "was...."

"Go ahead, Ms. Jones. Reveal your acumen."

"The other ninety-nine percent?" Key questioned hesitantly.

"The other ninety-nine percent!" Edward Sells bellowed to the heavens. "What a joke that was. Destined to fail just like the nation that spewed it forth. You know why? Because that ninety-nine percent was divided by tribalism, faction, and the self-righteous superiority of the humble masses. Holy shit! Within that ninety-nine percent were a litany of people claiming the superiority of their factions to the others. You had to be the right sex, gender, race, ethnicity, age, class, level of education, political party, or section of the country to actually be included in the litany of competing tribes. I mean...shit! People in the United

States respect equality soooo much, they tell other human beings if they have a right to an opinion based on their approval of your tribal identification! There's a healthy respect for ideas! The ninety-nine percent loathed each other. They saw disunity everywhere and failed to see their role in it. Fucking awesome! Americans can't embrace a larger community because first you have to pass eight hundred litmus tests to be accepted. How many people in your previous nation were told they could not have an opinion because of all those factors I just listed?"

"And things have been better here?"

"Ah, Butler," Edward stated. "Glad you could make it. As for your question, yes, indeed. Much better. Can you fathom why?"

"I don't know," Raymond began.

"You're better than that, Butler. Give me something. Why are you here?"

"Well, according to you, I have certain traits. A desire to protect. You complimented the other fellow on his loyalty. So, you're saying things are better here because people have certain traits."

"You're on the right track, Butler. By the way, that fellow's name is Larkin."

"Robert Larkin," the man said, waving to Raymond.

"That's what I said, Larkin," Doc snarled before easing back to his conversational tone. "Anyway, it's not just that we have certain traits. Shit, anyone can have certain traits. We prioritize them. We promulgate them. We create an environment where people covet them... covet the intangibles that make *Homo sapiens* into a human, as opposed to desiring that which divides and builds false superiority."

"So, how do you build such a...community... when society works against it?" Larkin asked.

———————

"Repeat that, please," Mr. Tarrand requested as he paced the room, hands grasped behind his back.

"Um, I asked, how can you build communities like that when society won't let you?"

"That is what I thought you asked, Mr. Farrel. I wanted the class to hear it, for many of them are considering that very question. Correct?"

Mumbled responses and nodding heads confirmed Mr. Tarrand's suspicions. He smiled and looked at Travis Farrel. "How wonderful, Mr. Farrel. You have spoken for a multitude of your classmates. Perhaps you will be a future leader. You understand why so many had the same question?"

"Because we're American," offered Key. Whether it was a statement or a question was difficult to discern.

"No longer, Ms. Jones," Mr. Tarrand responded, "but you definitely were Americans and carry the blight of Americanization with you. A particular worldview and way of thinking. When a problem is too large or difficult to solve, the root cause of the disturbance must be society. Society this. Society that. Such a joke, really. Societies don't even exist."

"Wait a second," Lizzie said. "How can you say that? I mean," Lizzie moved her arms in circles as if to say, 'look all around you'.

"I understand, Ms. Butler. I do. Tell me, does society exist in nature? Do I pull up a stone and...boom!...America's society unfolded into existence from some primordial abyss?"

"Of course not," Lizzie said. "It's...."

"Say it, Ms. Butler. It's not a secret."

"Societies are created by people."

"Correct. We create society. Our communities, big and small, are created from every thought we have, every action that follows that thought, and every consequence brought into existence by our thoughts and actions. The United States worships dominion and separation because their populace does. People blame society because they never wish to consider their contributions to the cesspool. In the C.S.A., we seek a much different balance. Consider your contributions to your nation's glory and the improvement of your fellow citizen's life, and your nation and your fellow citizen will, in turn, contribute to your fulfillment. The C.S.A. left the United States in order to find unity."

Forty-seven adults sat in silence as they considered the last sentence they heard. Quite pleased with himself, Doc looked over his audience and smiled as he saw their minds settling. "Never thought of it that way, did you? To gain unity, you need to leave the United States. Simple, really, but a bit disconcerting at first. Questions?"

"But," a woman in the front row began, "what about institutional problems and organizations that foster resentment or superiority?"

"Your roots are showing, Collins. Remember what I said when I asked you here?"

"You said we would cleanse things."

"Damn right. Institutions exist in society. They reflect the values of the society. Anything that violates the pursuit of positive growth, of Eudaimonia, is cleansed."

"Or removed," Raymond added.

"Blackclaw," Doc said, pumping his fist and smiling at Raymond.

"Blackclaw?" Collins asked.

"Consider your actions at Iron Gate Penitentiary," Doc said, smiling as he turned to Collins. She nodded her understanding.

"Of all the problems your nation of origin faced, and the populace protested, some root causes were always ignored. A commitment to mediocrity was the national pastime. People worshipped at the altar of dysfunction instead of truly challenging people to rise above limitations. Leaders succumbed on one side to greed and on the other to the tyranny of compartmentalized compassion. Weakness and laziness promoted as strength, and people believing it for over two thousand years. These problems only exist in institutions or in our streets to the extent that they are allowed to permeate and infest society at large. This organization...the purifiers...is dedicated to protecting and strengthening society so that excellence and honor, not faction and deceit, become societal norms."

"But," Jarrod Mikel stammered, "how can a country maintain such a...I don't know."

"The loosening of old thought patterns can be a touch discombobulating, Mr. Mikel. You will learn to express your thoughts and convictions as the year progresses. To answer your fragmented question, I will offer this twofold answer. On the one side, we have an organization called the purifiers. Their mission is to keep the C.S.A. clean. To seek out and correct those who would corrupt this society with avarice...," Mr. Tarrand paused for a moment, "greed, people. Avarice is greed. Avarice corrupts, in all its forms — be it want of money, fame, attention, credit, or some other vice. The purifiers protect the nation and its institutions from avarice and sloth. On the other hand, we also have all of us being dedicated citizens and promoters of excellence. Each citizen, in his or her way, doing what they can to challenge themselves and others to reach the highest levels of individual and collective potential. That process unfolds every day in every choice you make. If you are satisfied with our answer to Ms. Jones' question, you shall continue that process now."

The students nodded their heads, calling forth the homework required to continue in the class. Mr. Tarrand smiled and pushed a button on his podium. The screen behind him came to life. "Very good. Let's continue."

CHAPTER 17

VIPER-I

The round kick Meredith Wilson unleashed on the heavy bag struck with such force that P4 Jonathan Sylvestrie stumbled backward as he strained to hold it steady. The movement was minor but enough to break the rhythm of the Delta officer's workout.

"Damn it, Johnny! Hold the goddamn bag!"

"Sorry," Johnny mumbled. "I wasn't ready for —"

"Ready for what?" Meredith snapped. "Fuck. What, you didn't think I could hit?"

Johnny, who was surprised and impressed by the power of Meredith's blow, knew enough not to admit to the fact he underestimated her. Instead, he merely returned to the bag, establishing a stronger base as he prepared for Meredith to resume her workout.

"That's right," Meredith snarled. "Just hold the fucking bag, P four. Adams should have killed you." She glanced over her shoulder at the MLB behind her. "Did you reset the clock, 72-A?"

"It will start with your next strike, Special Agent Wilson," MLB 72-A responded.

The next sixty seconds was a barrage of fury as Meredith assaulted the bag with kicks and punches, pushing herself to maintain the intensity for the full minute. Johnny flinched on occasion but held strong.

"Time!" the MLB proclaimed, calculating the exact volume and tone to be best heard given the noise of the gym and Meredith's focus.

Meredith completed the left hook she was midway through and stepped back, taking a few deep breaths as she put her hands on her hips.

"Two-minute recovery time, Special Agent?" MLB 72-A asked.

"Ninety seconds, then round two," Meredith responded, sending a glare laced with napalm to Johnny.

"Very good, ma'am."

Meredith rotated her head in three slow circles, then took a drink of water. Windmilling her arms, she approached the bag. She looked at MLB 72-A as she assumed an orthodox stance.

"Almost time, ma'am," the MLB warned.

Its words encouraged Johnny to take his position as well. He tensed, preparing for a strike that would never arrive.

MLB 72-A and the three other MLBs in the room suddenly stopped all activity. "Call fifteen, code yellow. That is call fifteen, code yellow."

Groans were heard throughout the gym as thirty-eight people began to head for the exits. Call fifteen was a general call for purifiers from the ranks of P4 to P1 to muster for unexpected duty. Code yellow communicated the summons was not due to some dire or even pressing circumstance, likely a call to a task that, while necessary, could also be used for training and evaluation purposes. Such a call was not often heard in facilities that were still involved in initiation; however, such an event was not unheard of. In fact, it was usually a sign that initiation was proceeding smoothly, and time could be dedicated to other tasks.

Meredith watched the room empty before she called to MLB 72-A. "Could you hold the bag?"

"Sorry, Special Agent Wilson. I must heed the summons as well."

"Really? Usually code yellows under call twenty do not require MLB presence."

"This is true, but this call included a commander directive. Therefore, I must bid you farewell."

Meredith sighed. She watched the quartet of MLBs vacate the gym, leaving her alone before the heavy bag. She sighed again because she had planned on a five-round power workout. Lightly peppering the air with jabs, she contemplated her options; staying with the heavy bag for a speed workout or a ten-round workout. She opted to go ten rounds. She pushed the bag to get it swinging as she circled her target. Stepping forward and back, left to right, she danced with the bag but threw no punches. Two minutes of this graceful warm-up and she took a fifteen-second rest before starting the next round, that included striking the bag with quick jabs. The round did not reach its allotted time for an unexpected voice interrupted Meredith as she slid to her right following a double left jab.

"Ah, Special Agent Wilson," Kurt Adams stated as he strode across the room. "You are a vision of dedication."

"Commander Adams," Meredith said, startled. She turned to face him, quietly gauging the space between herself and the suddenly distant locker room. "What brings you to the gym today? You don't look dressed for a workout."

"I am not," Adams answered, walking until he was about ten feet from Meredith. "I might ask you the same question."

"Not following you, sir," Meredith admitted, striking the bag gently. "I was just going through some paces."

Adams watched her before responding. "Clearly. Specifically, I was wondering why you chose to work out here, in the P-one through four gym rather than the advanced officer arena. Intimidated by your fellow officers?"

"Do you actually think that is the case, sir?"

"I do not."

"You honestly wish me to answer your question, sir?"

"I do. And do feel free to be slightly less formal."

"Understood," Meredith said, drawing a deep breath. She struggled to find a casual tone while standing beneath her superior's gaze. After a second exhale, she spoke, hand brushing a stray hair from her face. "Well, I guess I would say it's the environment. P-ones, twos, threes, and fours have a certain drive that some officers lack. Alphas and Deltas, for example, have clearly arrived at a certain level and sometimes seem more interested in...um... maintenance, if you will. This gym, people are still trying to prove themselves. I like that energy."

"I see. Am I to assume that I, as an Omega officer, am guilty of being nonchalant?"

"No, sir!" Meredith's emphatic tone echoed in the empty gym. "I would say the opposite about you."

"Would you? Yet you have little visual confirmation of this. And never in the gym."

"We're here now," Meredith noted, sights trained on her superior officer. "Why not go a couple rounds on the bag?"

Adams approached the bag and placed his hand upon it as if touching the shoulder of an old friend. "I could do that. I am not dressed for the occasion but...sure. I will go a round or two."

"Okay," Meredith encouraged, hoping to lighten the pressure she felt. "Want me to hold it?"

"Yes. I'm thinking a power round is in order. You have an extra hand wrap?"

Meredith pointed at a table some twenty feet away to her left. Adams' gaze turned to the table where a couple of hand wraps had been haphazardly left behind when the code yellow cleared the room. Walking to the table like a gunslinger into a saloon, he chose a speed wrap glove and started to put it on. He paused. "I probably shouldn't work the bag armed as I am."

He returned the glove to the table. A pistol was then pulled methodically from his belt. His icy glance moved from the weapon to Meredith, who had slid some five feet closer to the locker room and her own weapons belt. Adams put the gun down and removed his belt, followed by a knife strapped to his leg. The knife was held aloft for a moment, allowing the curve of its blade to be admired, before Adams' attention returned to Meredith. "You are not known for your skill with knives, Special Agent Wilson."

"I can handle a knife, sir. Just seems to me, in this day and age, we have little need for them."

"True. We can rely on the MLBs for close combat while we achieve victory from a distance. But if no MLB is present and the only weapon at hand is a knife, will your current level of adequacy suffice?"

Adams placed his knife on the ground and slid it to Meredith. It struck her foot, and she looked at it, not certain what was being asked of her. He gestured for her to pick it up, and she complied.

"So you are armed, and I am not. Yet, I sense if I were to close the distance between us, that knife would likely be of little value to you."

"I am excellent at hand-to-hand combat," Meredith insisted proudly. "I even enjoy it a bit."

"I know," Adams confirmed, a small smile on his face. "I have written numerous evaluations of you."

"So you know I could likely handle this hypothetical assailant of yours."

"I said, 'if I were to close the distance,'" Adams snarled, an ominous glare boring into Meredith's soul. "If I were to close the distance, what then?"

"I'm not sure, sir."

"Really? I am. I am very sure what would happen," Adams said slowly. "You, however, have a knife. That should make you sure, but it does not."

"Understood."

"Outstanding." Adams stood still, looking to Meredith, who held the knife tentatively in her right hand. He waited another second before speaking. "Please send my knife back to me."

Meredith placed the knife on the floor and slid it back to Adams. He lifted it, his eyes caressing the lethal edges before placing the weapon on the table with his other equipment. Stretching his arms slightly and jabbing the air, he returned to the heavy bag.

Meredith, who had not moved from the spot she occupied with the knife, approached the bag when Adams motioned her to hold it. She braced herself on the bag preparing for Adams' first blow. The force of a crushing right hook caused her to shudder. Two more thunderbolts and she found her base, allowing her to look at Kurt Adams' face while he unleashed an unholy fury on the bag. His countenance, often placid with little emotion, was a mask of rage and spite as he punished the heavy bag. Meredith, while occasionally forced to flinch before the strikes, never staggered as Johnny had. A frightful growl escaped Adams when his last punch crashed into the bag. He stepped back, the beast, yet again pulled beneath the tranquility of his face.

Meredith let go of the bag and stood upright. "Well, sir," Meredith began, "you can certainly hit. That was impressive."

"Thank you," Adams said. "Not bad for a lazy ranking officer."

"I did not mean you, sir. No...."

"No offense was taken," Adams stated without pride. He nodded his head. "It is good that you notice some Alphas and Deltas become complacent. Make no mistake: they are skilled and capable, but sometimes they do lack the daily drive you mentioned. More interested in maintenance than advancement, I suppose. Success can be a mighty foe."

"You would likely be very knowledgeable of that phenomenon, sir," Meredith offered.

"Back off with that nonsense," cautioned Adams. "It is not becoming, especially not from you."

Meredith nodded, still trying to find the rhythm of the water in which she was swimming.

"Very good," Adams stated. "Now, if only these less motivated officers had someone to keep them on their toes. Someone who, shall we say, tinkered with their plans."

Meredith took a deep breath and looked at the floor momentarily.

She quickly raised her head and looked at Adams, her fingers twitching as if seeking the comfort of a weapon. "I wondered when we would have this talk."

"I am sure you did. That was an audacious and troubling action you took. You overrode my ability to command an Orcus in the field."

"Indeed, sir."

"Your device was a bit...primitive...but it did the job."

"Yes, it did," Meredith said as she attempted to conceal her pride.

"What was your goal? Was personally killing that criminal truly so important to you?"

"The criminal was superfluous. I wanted to share one of my lesser-known talents with you. I have a way with machines, even sophisticated ones."

"And a conversation would not have fulfilled this purpose?"

"I wanted to show, not tell," Meredith said. "Actions are infinitely more powerful than words."

"And?"

"And what, sir?"

"You hesitated at the end of your sentence. What else would you like to share?"

"As you said, sir, I wanted to do something audacious. I know that one of the Omega officers is nearing retirement."

"Jason Penchant."

"Yes. It is not every day an Omega opening is available. I wanted you to see me as a candidate for that slot."

"You already are a candidate," Adams said. "That is why you were assigned oversight of the schools during initiation."

"But Doc ran Omega Blue. And you assigned Special Agent Lawrence to oversee the revivals."

"All important jobs," Adams noted, "none more important than the other."

"I understand, sir. I just...."

"You coveted the Omega Blue appointment?"

"I did."

Adams put his hands behind his back and nodded. "You pointed out a flaw in Omega Blue. Doc did not. You were bold enough to bring this to my attention, albeit late, but you found your voice. This action was not audacious enough?"

"I...," Meredith paused. "I did not think so. No, sir."

"So you wanted more attention? You have it now. Are you pleased?"

"I...."

"I asked," Adams snapped, restrained violence in his voice, "are you pleased?!"

"I do not regret my decision, no," Meredith said, standing at full attention. She quickly gauged the distance from the locker room to the table with Adams' weapons.

Adams chuckled, a cold mumbling sound that chilled the air around him. A smile slowly fading from his face, he continued to prod Meredith. "I wonder, did you find the flaw in Omega Blue odd?"

"Odd?"

"I need to define the word odd?" mocked Adams.

"No, sir. I found it a minor problem. I am not sure it needed to be brought up. I am sure Doc would have managed the situation fine had I not."

"True. He is an excellent field commander."

Meredith stammered slightly. "He is. It's just...that small flaw seemed so out of place among the meticulous planning I know the Omegas put into the initiation protocols. I felt compelled to...." Meredith stopped talking and stared at Adams a moment, searching for the right words.

"Speak, Special Agent. We haven't much more time," Adams said.

"The error in the plan. You did that on purpose? Why? Valuable assets could have —"

"I did what I did and do as I do when evaluating talent. Your intervention likely saved time, effort, and lives. Your willingness to speak pleased me." Meredith opened her mouth but did not speak because Adams raised his hand, his face suddenly ablaze. "I was not pleased to learn you tampered with Orcus 44T."

Adams paused to read Meredith's face. She stood unflinching before him — proud and resolute. Her breathing, he noted, was slightly faster than usual. His stoic demeanor washed away all visible signs of anger. He backpedaled toward the table as he spoke. "But I understand why you did so. In fact, you likely helped reveal a design flaw that must be rectified. I suppose for this, I should thank you."

"If you think it is necessary."

"I do not," Adams said dismissively as he lifted his pistol from the table. Meredith felt her breathing stop as she braced for action. He pointed the gun at her and continued, a storm brewing beneath his calm exterior. "You wanted my attention, and so you have it. My full attention. Does this please you?"

"If it pleases you, sir," Meredith stated, her voice drained of emotion. Only professional courtesy remained.

Adams smirked, his pistol locked on its mark. "Now you play the loyal subordinate? Interesting choice. Know this: I am aware of your talents, even more so now than ever. You have always been an impressive agent, and I admire your ambition, so your insubordination will not be punished beyond whatever anxiety this conversation may have caused you. I will not kill you for I anticipate you will do great things for us, if you can refrain from unnecessary attention-seeking actions. Are we clear?"

"Yes, sir," Meredith said quickly.

Kurt Adams lowered his gun and turned to leave the room. He took ten steps before turning to face Meredith one last time. "You made a good decision."

"What's that, sir?"

"You did not go for your weapons in the locker room. Your future accomplishments would have been snuffed out if you had. Do not squander the time I have gifted you."

CHAPTER 18

THE TIES THAT BIND

Fat Joe's Diner opened in 2025 and promptly imbedded itself as a favorite spot to grab a quick bite along Jefferson Highway. Joe Trahan, founder and namesake, took painstaking strides to make his twenty-first century diner emit a mid-twentieth century feel. This was, of course, some seventy years before Louisiana joined the Common States of America. Now that Louisiana was progressing through initiation, the short-order cooks, waitstaff, and cashiers shared space with three MLBs. The androids arrived at four a.m. and stayed until two a.m., hence the diner was never open without their presence. The two hours they were off duty were spent in the basement that was recently revamped so the androids could be charged and receive updates.

Whatever discomfort the MLBs initially caused the employees swiftly subsided as the technological wonders assisted in all phases of the diner's operations: washing dishes, clearing tables, taking orders, and answering the questions of the occasionally amazed customer. On this day, May third, two of those customers were Karen and Lizzie Butler.

Mother and daughter were both examining their menus as if looking for deep secrets to be unlocked from the familiar offerings. Lizzie, with some hesitancy, put her menu down and leaned toward her mother. Karen noticed her daughter's action and moved in synchronicity with the teen.

"Mom," Lizzie whispered, "was that kinda weird?"

Karen looked left and right, trying to ascertain why they were being so surreptitious. There were only four other tables occupied as Joe's was experiencing an afternoon lull. Her confusion did not stop her from answering in a whisper. "What's weird, Lizzie? Other than the fact we're whispering for no apparent reason."

"Oh," Lizzie whispered before sitting back. "I mean...right. I don't need to whisper."

"Whisper about what?" Karen asked, entertained that her daughter, who was becoming a mature young woman, was also still very much a kid.

"One of those MLBs gave us our menus. It just...I dunno...I wasn't expecting it."

"Really?" Karen asked, legitimately puzzled by Lizzie's confession. "I mean, you do see them at school every day. I've seen them at the bank."

"Yeah!" Lizzie exclaimed. "They were at the grocery store when I went shopping for you guys the other day. And the gas and charging stations."

"Exactly. They seem to be everywhere," Karen noted, turning to look out a window. She spotted an MLB standing in the parking lot of a small plaza that included a liquor store, a hair salon, and a pizza restaurant. The MLB seemed to be doing little more than pacing back and forth, waiting for the opportunity to open the door for customers and, perhaps, help someone carry large takeout orders to their cars. She turned back to Lizzie, who had followed her mother's gaze.

"They are quite ubiquitous. Like cell phones," Lizzie stated with confidence.

"Wow," Karen said with a smile as she sipped the water that had been placed, by human hands, before her. "That's a great point. I never thought of it that way."

"Thanks," Lizzie beamed. "It just came to me."

Karen's eyebrow arched, a sure sign she was feeling suspicious. "Wait a minute. Ubiquitous? Spill the beans, girl."

Lizzie, her smile becoming a devious smirk, came clean. "Fine. That's what Mr. Tarrand told us."

"Mr. Tarrand," Karen said. "He's made quite an impression on you."

"He's a smart guy. Like, really smart and just," Lizzie's face contorted as she searched for words that refused to be found, "well, he has a way of making things make sense."

"Like the MLBs?"

"Yeah."

"Well then, why do you suppose you were so thrown off to receive a menu from one?" Karen asked.

"I dunno," Lizzie said. "Maybe because eating seems more...um...."

"Human," a metallic voice interrupted in a perfectly tuned, polite, mildly hypnotic tone. Karen's utensils hit the floor as she turned to face the source of the voice. The MLB instantly apologized for the shock it caused.

A nervous laugh accompanied Karen's embarrassment while Lizzie went for the floored fork. "That's okay. No harm done. My lord, you things can be quiet."

"Mom," Lizzie hissed while tilting her head at the MLB, "you called him a thing."

"Oh," Karen said quickly. "I didn't realize...I'm...."

"Quite all right, ma'am," the MLB stated. "I have no feelings to hurt. It is expected to have these awkward interactions as new citizens struggle to find a vocabulary with which to address us."

"Right," Karen said slowly. "But I work with...MLBs in my classroom. You would think I would be a little more...comfortable."

"Perhaps," the MLB stated in a compassionate tone, "but do remember, you are likely very comfortable in your classroom, and your MLB-TA is likely seen as an assistant to your purpose therein."

"I suppose," Karen allowed unconvincingly. "What do you think, Lizzie?"

"Me? Oh, um, well I know this. Mr. Tarrand's interactions with his MLB-TA are so natural, it just all makes sense in class."

"Exactly," the MLB said reassuringly, "but eating is a very human, even an intimate thing. It is a familial activity, one a mother and daughter expect to enjoy without interacting with an MLB, even if said being merely delivered a menu or cleaned the table."

"Wait a minute. How do you know we are mother-daughter?" Karen's tone was suddenly defensive, and Lizzie was taken aback by its subdued strength.

The MLB was unfazed, seeking understanding rather than offense. "Facial recognition technology, ma'am," the MLB stated as a matter of fact. "It is a routine aspect of our visual programming. The cheekbone structure, jawline, the color of your iris, similarities of the nose, and the distance between your eyes means there is a zero point two hundred fifty-three percent chance this young lady is not related to you. She is, by a large statistical margin, not merely a niece but your daughter."

"Yes, she is," Karen beamed, hoping her smile covered her embarrassment for being suspicious. Lizzie sat staring at the MLB, dazzled by the depths of the technological wonder before her.

"I am sure your pride is well placed," the MLB said. "Anyway, as earlier stated, eating and enjoying a meal is a very human activity. This is why establishments like this must always exist and must always have human employees to enhance your experience. It is, in fact, an excellent first job for young people because it enables them to learn how to be responsible with protean marks and to interact with adult *Homo sapiens*."

Karen playfully pointed an accusatory finger at her daughter. "Hear that, young lady? You need to be more responsible with those protean marks."

"Mom," the now defensive Lizzie groaned, "I had a job last summer. I handle my budget pretty well."

"Yes," Karen smiled knowingly, "pretty well. Emphasis on 'pretty'."

"Yeah, Mom, I caught that."

"As did I," the MLB stated, saving Lizzie from further scrutiny. "*Homo sapiens* need other *Homo sapiens*. You are a social species and will always need human interaction. MLBs can never replicate that. Technology, much like humanity, has its place. Therefore, we seek to assist in the smooth running of all establishments so that your kind may find enjoyment and relaxation."

"Well," Karen said, groping for words, "I guess that's that."

"I am glad it sufficed. I could take your order or, if you prefer, I can get your server."

Karen waved off the suggestion. "Not necessary. I am fine ordering from you. Lizzie?"

"Sure. Just one thing...."

"Don't worry," the MLB said warmly, "I will make sure your tip gets into the right account."

Lizzie smiled at her host. It was not difficult to imagine the MLB smiling back. Despite the stretching shadows caused by the midafternoon sun, both women ordered breakfast. Karen's attempt at a healthy breakfast was undermined by the Belgian waffle and home fries that appeared before her daughter. Their chatter ranged from serious discussions regarding adjusting to the C.S.A. to the whimsical, as the proper use of the vacation stipend was debated. Their conversation was interrupted only by the consumption of food and the occasional fork/sword fights that erupted when Lizzie felt the need to prevent her mother from stealing bites of her waffle.

A clear sign that the meal was over occurred when Lizzie, staring at her final lump of waffle as if searching for the will to eat more, did not even attempt to stop Karen from indulging her sweet tooth. Lizzie bit her lip while she watched her mother swooning under the spell of strawberries and whipped cream. One last topic needed to be broached.

"Ummmm, Mom?" Lizzie mumbled with far more hesitancy than expected.

Karen looked at her daughter, momentarily a deer in headlights as she suddenly realized how much waffle she had shoved into her mouth. "Yes, sweetie?" Karen said through a napkin held to her lips. She quickly swallowed and lowered her hand. "What's up?"

"I...earlier during lunch, you asked how I felt about school. There was something I didn't mention."

It did not require maternal instinct to sense Lizzie's discomfort. "What is it, honey? I thought you enjoyed your new school?"

"I do!" Lizzie blurted out, although tears contradicted her proclamation. "I really do. I don't know why I'm crying. I'm actually happy!"

"Are you? Honey, help me out here. What is it?"

"I...." Lizzie took a deep breath and composed herself. "Okay, do you remember my sophomore year and all that...stuff?"

"Of course," Karen confirmed. She took her daughter's hand, hoping her touch carried reassurance. Memories of the tear-filled nights when an unrelenting combination of cyber and covert social bullying had eroded her daughter's confidence now appeared vividly in her mind. Anxiety manifested as physical illness that kept her home. When at school, fear accompanied each step she took in the halls. When the depth of the cruelty was revealed, Karen was torn between protective rage and motherly guilt. How could she have been so blind?

Lizzie, seeing a cloud over her mother's face, spoke quickly. "It's not happening again, Mom! I swear. I just...remember how I said this year, my junior year, felt so much better?"

"Yeah," Karen answered, trying to be patient despite the fact her mind was leaping to conclusions.

"I meant it. I did. Things have been way better since my sophomore year. And then we joined the C.S.A., and I've been going to school here for, well, just a little while now, and...I feel great!" Tears carrying past apprehensions rolled down Lizzie's cheeks as she poured both words and worry from her body. "I mean, nothing bad happened in the fall while still at the old school. But I never realized until, well, maybe now, that I was still nervous every day. Every day,

I was waiting for something to happen. But now? Now, I actually feel safe! SAFE! I feel free to learn and be myself. I...I love my new school, and I love it here in the C.S.A. I know it's a big change, and you and Dad are worrying about things, but you don't have to worry about me! I am so happy!"

Karen quickly stood and embraced her daughter who was in the process of rushing to her mother. "That's wonderful, sweetie," Karen gushed, tears now streaming down her face as well. She stepped back and held her daughter's face, radiant and serene, in her hands. "I am so happy for you!"

A second embrace was interrupted by the MLB. "Two satisfied customers, I see," the MLB stated dryly. "Food must be marvelous."

Karen laughed, "Yes! Great waffles!"

"Yeah," Lizzie added, suddenly a touched embarrassed. "They were really good."

"Very good," the MLB stated. "Just so you know, your bill has been programmed into the table. Touch your Freedom Card on the screen at the center of the table, and you can view it. With a swipe, you can pay. Please, do come back again."

"Oh," Karen responded, stepping away from her daughter, "I promise we will."

CHAPTER 19

WHEN I WAS IMPRISONED

Rusted metal bars and stone walls were more than effective for confining Roger Baudin's body. Silence was an oppressive fifth wall added to contain his spirit. He was, however, not alone in the basement of Skadi prison. There were five other cells carved into the deep corner of the structure. Two of the cells, it became clear to the inmates, were for short-term prisoners, as they were never occupied by the same person for more than two days. Roger, who had been in cell 619 since April seventh, was the most tenured resident of the pit. Six days after his imprisonment, a female inmate arrived. Like he, she looked worn down. Defeated. Her greasy hair clung to her skull and neck while the grime that clung to her body was now thicker than the skin she naturally possessed.

Roger, however, experienced her not as a defeated victim but as a powerful angel. An unfailingly kindhearted person even when anger or frustration ruled her moods. A damaged but unbroken spirit remained within her, beauty concealed by deprivation. Roger enjoyed conversing with her, as her resolve helped maintain the fading embers of his own inner light. How he missed those conversations as they had ended abruptly on May first, the day a horrified new arrival asked the room, voice trembling, "What is this place?"

Roger answered, "A prison. A terrible prison."

The new arrival directed a question to Roger because he was the only individual who responded to his anguish. The question was barely in the air when an MLB teleported into the newcomer's cell and broke his neck with one graceful twist. The MLB vanished before the corpse hit the floor.

The five remaining prisoners sat in stunned silence for an eternity trapped in seconds. The veil was lifted when a man, some twenty years younger, looked to Roger for answers.

"Roger, why do you su—"

The question was destined to never be completed as another MLB appeared, killed the speaker, and quickly disappeared.

The silence of the grave spread yet again, this time broken by Roger, his eyes reaching out to his spirit-lifting friend. "I think it wise," he said slowly, his soul aching with regret at the thought of what he was about to lose, "very wise indeed, if no one ever speak to me again."

It had been three days since Roger made that proclamation, and there had been no killings in the basement of Skadi since. The other inmates did talk, now in very guarded tones, to each other. They did not dare to even discuss Roger or have his name on their lips for fear of the severest repercussions. He was a ghost in the dark, unreachable and not part of their interactions. The arrival of Commander Adams broke the silent seal that enveloped the aging priest.

"Father Baudin," Adams sneered as he appeared in the cell. Roger, who was lying on his cot, slowly pulled himself to a seated position, planting his bare feet on the moist floor. "You do not look as vigorous as you did when last we spoke."

"Commander Adams," Roger droned. He said nothing else as seconds ticked away.

Adams chuckled at the silence he created. "I wonder," Adams began, "if you were silently hoping...maybe praying...that by addressing you,

I would suffer the same fate as befell two of your neighbors? I would say, based on the look upon your face, there is a possibility this is the case. Not very Christian of you, Father."

"Chalk it up to a moment of weakness," Roger mumbled, his throat pained from his forced silence. "I am, just as you are, a fallible being."

"Indeed," Adams said, nodding his head. He looked over to the cell perpendicular to Roger's. "What say you, Ms. Chen? Disappointed to hear Roger wishing such violence upon a sentient being? Hardly the way of the compassionate Buddha."

"I am sure," Zitai Chen offered cautiously, "that Roger was more curious how karma or, in his tradition, providence, might weigh your life."

"That's a legitimate possibility," Adams noted. "Would you like to know how I weighed the value of your precious organization? The lovely lotus you tried to bring to bloom in Cleveland?"

Zitai stood defiantly in her cell, knowing full well the fate Adams brought.

He smiled as he took in the sight of her filthy dignity. His focus returned to Roger. "I will say this, Father. Your words were accurate. You said people fleeing for their lives can be resourceful. Ms. Chen, however, was not content to flee. She surreptitiously resisted us. Hiding in plain sight. She expertly played the loyal citizen while organizing a resistance group in Cleveland. The group was founded on her Buddhist principles but open to all; a festering disease that could, in time, cause damage to the body. Thankfully, the skilled surgeons found in the ranks of the purifiers have cured us of this infection." A deep sigh escaped from Roger, interrupting Adams' monologue. Adams smiled for a moment. "I am sorry, Roger. Am I boring you?"

Roger shook his head and answered, exasperated but undeterred, "No, but you are telling me nothing new."

"I see," Adams noted, "you wish to be exposed to new information. I can accommodate that. In fact, it is why I am here today. We are going on a little field trip."

Zitai stepped to the edge of her cell, fear pouring from the core of her being. Two other residents stirred at the news Roger was to be taken away, but they moved very little, frozen by the spell cast by Adams' presence.

"Don't worry, Ms. Chen. Your silent friend will be back soon. It has been noted, however, that the two of you share a little ritual every morning and night. Do feel free to partake in this small source of comfort if you would like."

Wordlessly, Zitai stepped back from the bars when Roger approached his. The two friends raised their hands in front of their faces, palms together and fingers straight up, as if standing in prayer. Zitai and Roger then bowed to each other from the waist. Not a deep bow, but a small bend filled with humility. When they returned to their full heights, their hands were lowered, pausing to make a small sign of the cross over their hearts.

"That's the one," Adams mocked, a gentle smile on his face. "Time to go."

Roger and Stone disappeared from sight. A lone tear navigated the dirt on Zitai Chen's face. As the tear dropped from her jaw, she whispered, "We are not two."

CHAPTER 20

CREATING ORDER

MLB 498-A greeted Kurt Adams and Roger when they appeared in cellblock D of Blackclaw Maximum Security Prison. Every stall held a prisoner. Some had the gumption to glance through bloodshot eyes at the unexpected visitors. Skin paled by lack of sun and sleep made some inmates seem to be more apparition than human. New arrivals looked healthier but carried an increased sense of dread, wondering when and how they would be transformed as their cellmates had been. Roger, who's stubbled face and now protruding cheekbones made him appear worse off than most of the inmates, looked around the cellblock for an uneasy moment or two before retching.

MLB 498-A moved forward to aid the ailing priest. "Step this way," 498-A said politely, using a mechanized hand to guide Roger about ten steps to his left. Had the ailing priest looked back, he would have seen one of the MLBs assigned to Blackclaw clean his mess. "No need to stand near that putrid puddle. There is also no need to be embarrassed. Over seventy-five percent of people experience some level of nausea the first time they are teleported."

"Thank you," Roger responded reflexively to MLB 498-A. "I think I'm fine now."

Adams approached the odd duo and said, "I am sure you are. You have a powerful will, don't you?"

"I suppose," Roger said half-heartedly, scanning the unfamiliar area. A second far less potent wave of sickness washed over him with a gentle burp bubbling up from his core. The second bout now over, he thought to speak but was interrupted by the arrival of a cigar chomping purifier.

"Commander Adams," Bill Cullen called enthusiastically as he crossed the room, "I thought I'd beat you here."

"That's quite alright, Bill. I am ten minutes ahead of schedule."

"I know," Bill said. "That's why I thought arrivin' now would've given me the opportunity to greet you on materialization."

"Someday you'll get it right," Adams encouraged, turning to point at Roger. "This is the guest I told you about."

"Greetings," Bill said, reaching out to shake Roger's hand. With reluctant kindness, Roger accepted the gesture. "The last padre. Come to visit the criminals, have you?"

Roger mumbled, "Criminals? Are they not merely prisoners like me?"

"Hell no," Bill corrected. "These fuckers actually broke the law. Each and every one of 'em. You? Yer not like them. Yer —"

"An unnecessary anachronism," Adams interjected, his tone shifting from informal greeting to deadly serious. "Is Mr. Gaulmann in his office?"

"He is," Bill confirmed, his tone now far more stoic than seconds before. "As you requested."

"Outstanding. I have business to discuss with him. Please give Father Baudin a brief tour and bring him to interrogation room thirty. I will meet you there."

Adams and MLB 498-A disappeared before Bill could respond. The veteran purifier rubbed his chin and chuckled. He took a deep drag of his cigar and dropped it, crushing it under his boot. His tone became more casual as he addressed Roger. "You get used to the commander. Just takes time. Not that I'm sure how much of that commodity you have left. Though you must be somethin'. I still can't believe yer revival meetin' knocked Stone off schedule."

"Stone?"

"The commander's unofficial nickname. A term of endearment, I think."

"Perhaps just a descriptor," Roger mused absentmindedly.

"There is that. Anyway, he wants to meet us in room thirty so let's head in that direction and see the sights."

Roger began walking. His steps were slow, a combination of age and exhaustion now anchoring him to the earth. Bill allowed Roger to set the pace, like a son walking alongside an infirm parent. Roger drew a deep breath and exhaled, catching his thoughts and an inkling of energy in the process. He stopped, as did his escort, for one last look around the cellblock before entering a corridor behind a door marked 'official use only'.

"So you say all these men are criminals. What are they guilty of?"

"I could give you the grocery list," Bill said, "but that runs pretty long. Suffice it to say, cellblock C and D in the facility are for white-collar criminals. Embezzlement and cybercrime are two of the top offenses. People just wanna get their hands on more protean marks than they deserve. Of course, what we're really fightin' is the root problem."

"The root problem?"

"C'mon, Padre!" Bill laughed. "Yer time in Skadi can't have sapped yer mind that much! Yeah. The root problem."

Roger sighed again, shaking his head. "You mean greed."

"Damn right we do," Bill bellowed. He opened the door to his left and guided his guest into the corridor, made no less threatening by the ample lighting running along the walls. "One of yer tradition's seven deadly sins. At least you guys got that one right."

Roger looked at Bill as he deadpanned, "You see, miracles happen, my son."

Bill laughed aloud, caught off guard by Roger's comment. "That's good shit, Father. Anyway, we make it fuckin' deadly. Greed! It undermines everythin' we stand for in the C.S.A. One greedy person can hurt the whole society."

"You punish greed with lifetime imprisonment?"

"Hell, no. That's a waste of money and resources. Nope. Folks in cellblock C are what the U.S. legal folks would call first offenders. To us, just criminals will do. After all, none of 'em are first offenders; just the first time they got caught. Anyway, most of these folks do have skills in their chosen profession, so we keep 'em here for one to two months. Let 'em know we know about 'em. Let 'em know what our... attention...is like. Then we send 'em back to sin no more!"

"And should they relapse?"

"Oh, for that we have cellblock D back there. All those folks back there are dead. Just waitin' for execution. They're from all over the place. Our top four geographic contributors to our population right now are, in no particular order, North Carolina, Wisconsin, Michigan, and Illinois. When space in this facility opened up, we had no problem fillin' the cells."

Roger shook his head, confusion undermining his demeanor. "I don't understand. If these people are all to be executed, why wait? The night of initiation, thousands were killed in minutes."

"That's true, Father. Lotta folks died that night. I did some killin' myself. Felt damn good to clear away the waste. Pavin' the way for somethin' better to rise up. But the answer to yer question is, in reality, a single word. Pain. Some folks need to — deserve to — feel some pain before they die."

"So, sadism is your motive," Roger asserted bluntly as if it were an undisputed scientific truth.

Bill stopped walking and grabbed Roger's arms, forcing him to halt his gradual progress. Bill's powerful hands moved upward, clasping Roger's frail shoulders in a vise. Roger resisted the inclination to wince the best he could. Stepping forward, Bill stood, nose-to-forehead with Roger and hissed his venom in a scathing whisper.

"Sadism? Justice, ya fool," corrected Bill with derision. "Those who cause pain to others, those who thoughtlessly and deliberately ignore the greater good, deserve to feel that pain returned to 'em. They sit in those cages deprived of much. They feel pain. Pain is their punishment. Death is the consequence for their crime. Society and citizens benefit because their wasteful fuckin' existence has been snuffed out. Yer smart enough, sir, to understand that." Bill started to pull back from Roger, slowly loosening his grip. He paused and leaned in again, pulling Roger even closer to his face. "Some people need to feel pain before they die."

Roger was shoved into the wall, the stone structure keeping him upright while his legs longed to drop him to the floor. He regained his balance, unsteady and unassisted, and followed Bill, who had already begun walking to their destination. The purifier, a full ten strides ahead of the priest, stopped and looked back over his shoulder.

"Hurry up, Padre. Hate to keep Commander Adams waitin'."

No more words were exchanged between the two men. They proceeded in silence, faster than Roger wanted to walk and slower than Bill would have chosen. After a few sharp turns in the catacombs, they found themselves at an iron door. Bill placed his thumb on a plate imbedded in the wall and pulled the door open. Inside the room, a middle-aged man sat at a table in the tattered remains of a gray suit, hands bound securely to the wooden table before him. His left eye was swollen, puffy, and yellow with a small hint of purple. At least two teeth were missing as well. Before this pitiable heap stood Kurt Adams, a closed folder resting on the table before him. MLB 498-A was stationed in the corner.

Adams turned his head to the door when Bill entered with Roger in tow. "Excellent timing, Special Agent Cullen," Adams said approvingly. "498 and I arrived less than two minutes ago."

"Fantastic," Bill responded. "I know you hate to be kept waitin'."

"Indeed. Your parcel is fine?"

"It is," Bill said, patting Roger on the back.

"And you understand a little better now?"

"I do," Bill confessed. "I definitely do."

"Outstanding. You are free to continue your duties. We will debrief this evening. Expect contact from me in two hours."

"Lookin' forward to it, sir," Bill said. A respectful tilt of his head was the only discernable salute made as he exited the room.

Adams' attention turned to Roger. "There is a seat in the corner. Please feel free to relax."

Roger moved to the wooden chair and sat down. While he would refuse to acknowledge it, even the simple comfort of the humble chair was a relief. One he knew would not last but at least a comfort for the moment. Once he settled, Roger asked a question in a gentle tone. "I don't understand why I'm here. Perhaps you could enlighten me?"

"You are here to bear witness, Father. What you learn on this trip is entirely up to you," Adams responded, never turning his attention away from the criminal before him. "As for you, Jeff Muelone, the sands of your hourglass run low."

"I don't...I...."

"Stop your stammering. Speak only when asked a direct question. Do you understand that?"

Jeff could only muster a nod of his head and an inarticulate mumble.

"Your vocal chords are intact. Use them. Do you understand this?"

"Yes," whimpered Jeff. "Yes, I do."

"Excellent. Did you know, Jeff, that Torres Technology...the company that once employed you...made a medical breakthrough two days ago?"

"I...no. I did not know that."

"Roger?" Adams asked, turning his head to look over his shoulder. "Were you aware of that?"

"No," Roger answered, not entirely sure why he chose to play into what he saw as little more than an unfolding farce.

"It's amazing. A rather important step was taken in the battle against dementia and Alzheimer's disease. We are on the cusp of a major medical victory. Such exciting times." Adams, who had turned his attention back to Jeff, side-glanced quickly at Roger. "All accomplished without the power of prayer, by the way."

"Well, as far as you know," Roger retorted.

"Defiant even in the lion's den," Adams noted, returning his attention to Jeff. "You could learn a thing or two from this man. You likely never will, but you could. I would like you to understand, Jeffery, why you are here."

Jeff looked at the table before him as if avoiding eye contact with Kurt Adams would make his antagonist disappear.

"False humility will not avail you here," warned Adams. "You are a master, dare I say, of embezzlement. Slowly siphoning funds from the multitude of accounts and contracts that exist in the complex business web woven by Torres Technology. Three years ago, you were brought into a facility like this in Iowa. We tried to teach you the error of your ways and released you. You walked the straight and narrow for seven months before returning to your criminal activities with an elegant computer program. You were so far ahead of most people of your ilk that we let you commit these crimes. What we learned from you enabled us to catch dozens of like-minded thieves. Your usefulness, however, has worn out. I do wonder why a man paid five million protean marks a year, the top salary permitted in our society, felt a need to steal more than his allotment."

"I...I can still help you!" Jeff blurted. "I can help catch hackers and cyberthieves. You know I —"

"Shut up," Adams snarled. "This is not a negotiation. There is no plea bargain. You did not even answer the question posed so keep your mouth shut. Understand this: as stated, a breakthrough was recently made by your former company. Now consider this: if we say, here is the moment of discovery," Adams held his right hand up about eight inches from his right ear, "and this is the amount of money that was needed to reach the moment of discovery," Adams' left hand was now held aloft, "then you slowed that process down by your elicit actions. You hurt innocent people. Do you understand this?"

"I...I don't think that's exactly how...."

"Fall silent, you cretin. It was a yes or no question. Your answer is clearly no. Therefore, understand this. Your father was recently diagnosed with early-onset Alzheimer's. It occurred during your incarceration here. Now, given the recent breakthrough, there is an eighty-six percent chance that full treatment will be available to prevent your father from degenerating too deeply into the abyss created by this unfortunate ailment."

Relief and hope replaced shock and fear on Jeff's face. He glanced at Roger, whose compassionate stare communicated the feelings Jeff sought.

Adams watched the brief encounter unfold. "Yes," he began, "that is good news for you. Unfortunately as I said, your activity likely delayed the discovery, which caused harm. Therefore, it is only fair that your father be denied access to this treatment."

"No!" Jeff shouted, struggling helplessly against his restraints. "You can't —"

MLB 498-A moved swiftly into action, securing Jeff's head to hold his mouth shut.

"You can't ...," Roger began before a second MLB materialized next to him, grabbing his shoulder and holding him fast to his seat. It introduced itself in a sharp whisper while cautioning Roger to remain silent.

As the new MLB made Roger's acquaintance, MLB 498-A addressed Jeff with all the passion of a person reading the rules of a board game. "Commander Adams did not ask you a question, Mr. Muelone. You need to remain silent."

"Thank you, 498," Adams said, ignoring the presence of the new MLB and, by extension, Roger. "You have the proper name of Mr. Muelone's father and will handle the blacklisting for me?"

"Indeed, I will, sir," 498-A stated.

"Outstanding. Do you think he will remain silent if you release him?"

"I am not sure. Shall we see?"

"Yes," Adams slowly brandished his knife, "let's see if he can follow the rules in here."

498-A released Jeff, who, as instructed, sat in silence.

Adams continued, "Very good. You, Jeffery Muelone, are a symptom of a most infectious disease. Societies, in the end, crumble from within. Granted, excuses are always found for personal, community, and national failures, but they are merely another insidious symptom of a different disease. Do you know what that one is?"

"I...I don't," Jeff said.

"I am not surprised. One disease of the mind is the inability to grasp the idea that one has control over his or her own life. Because one is feeble, they assume powers outside of themselves are orchestrating the minutes and hours of their lives. Creating insurmountable obstacles. Powerful people making meticulous plans to thwart them... as if they are actually worth spending a second of thought on. They slowly become kelp tossed by the waves, incapable of truly taking charge of their lives. Such a person may occasionally make an emotional outburst and vehemently proclaim their worth! Those with a savior complex mistake these thoughtless yelps for the rousing of their spirit. It is not. It is merely the temper tantrum of a child. When the tantrum ends, the same deep belief that an external force has doomed them regains the dominate position. The same lack of character and nonexistent psychological sturdiness returns, and well-intentioned buffoons invest time, resources, and energy in them. Such a mentality is anathema to the Common States of America.

"No, thankfully, you do not suffer from that, Jeff. You wanted more wealth, so you went after it. You saw laws you felt were restrictive and circumvented them. You showed a certain amount of will. I admire that in a way. You do, however, suffer from the disease of greed, which always carries with it the inability to put the needs of others in society ahead of or, at the least, on the same level as yours. It is, despite what men like Roger may think, an incurable condition. Therefore, despite a scintilla of admiration, you represent so much that I loathe."

Jeff looked up at Adams, unsure what to do. His body quivered as he fought to prevent the welling of tears. 498-A took one of Jeff's hands and placed it on the table, forcing him to keep it flat. What resistance he mustered was futile under the metallic strength of the MLB.

Adams looked at the pathetic man seated before him and smiled, a macabre joy rising from his core. "You are starting to understand, aren't you? If your hand offends thee...." Without a wasted motion, Adams swung his arm downward in a looping arc. His knife pierced the top of Jeff's right hand, fastening it to the table. 498-A held a metallic hand over Jeff's mouth, for the android understood Adams hated to have his work interrupted by unnecessary noise. Jeff writhed in pain, ultimately going limp in the MLB's grasp as shock and pain overwhelmed him. Adams turned to Roger, who was still being monitored by MLB 274-A. "He's understanding now. Don't you think, Roger?"

The rhetorical question struck Roger's ears and had a second to settle in before the priest was teleported back to his cell in Skadi.

Adams' attention turned to the MLB who was next to Roger. "274-A, upon my departure, begin execution protocol seventeen."

"An excellent choice, sir."

"I thought so." Adams faded from sight, only to reappear outside of Roger's locked cell.

The priest was doubled over and breathing heavily, unobservant of Adams' arrival. He slowly stood when the impulse to vomit passed. The presence of his tormentor infiltrated Roger's thoughts. Anger and disgust swirled as Roger radiated a simmering rage. "What are you? Why stage that piece of ridiculous theater?" Roger snapped as he shambled to the bars before him.

"Stage?" Adams stepped back, hand over his heart. He regained his usual immobile posture, ensuring he was upright and relaxed yet exuding a constant threat of violence. The air about him seemed charged by a macabre energy barely contained by his mortal frame. "I am, however, disappointed by your narcissism. That conversation would have been had with or without you. It was not for your benefit. I was merely hoping you would find it edifying."

"How so? In your stooge's ham-handed attempt to reveal you and I have a common enemy? The fact we both counsel against greed means nothing. Our paths are not aligned!"

"Of course not," Adams declared, stepping forward so he could lean on Roger's cell. "Our paths are not aligned nor are our methods. But we do face the same foes from time to time. My approach, however, is far more effective than yours."

"Why? Because you declare someone beyond redemption and kill them, thus proving they could not be redeemed? This somehow proves you correct? You are mad."

"And you're not? You work and counsel those who are far more enraptured by the allure of gold than the well-being of their fellow citizens. Offering forgiveness that leads to nowhere. You strengthen few, and lose many and my, oh my, how those many harm society."

"You do not have the gift of clairvoyance. You don't know when one's moment of clarity will occur."

"When? Ha! If, at best, is all you have. An earsplitting, deafening IF. Corrupt people of the world are not a collection of Scrooge-like figures seeking enlightenment at the hand of visiting spirits."

"But they may be," Roger protested. "You can't tell when that moment will happen."

"No. But how many people did our fictitious Scrooge hurt, perhaps destroy, before the miraculous turnaround? Why do we celebrate his supposed redemption and not demand justice for the litany of unnamed and faceless victims his avarice laid to waste? What a pathetic moral compass you possess. If Scrooge truly felt the weight of his crimes, he would have thrown his body from the window and not merely a shilling."

"This," Roger said, stepping back from the bars and pointing back and forth from Adams to himself, "is pointless."

"Perhaps," Adams said, also stepping back from the bars.

"Now what?" Roger sighed, exasperated. His shoulders slumped as he hung his head.

"I believe what my...what was it?...my stooge explained to you."

Confusion replaced the irritation in Roger's voice. "I...what?"

"Some people...," Adams started slowly as he pulled his gun from his belt. Roger braced himself for the end only to realize the true horror that was unfolding. His eyes widened as Adams turned from him, a cruel smirk accentuating his final words in their conversation. "...Need to feel some pain before they die."

"No! Don't! Zitai!"

Whatever words Roger yelled were lost in a quick double tap that left Zitai Chen lifeless on the floor, while blood and brain mixed with the grime on the wall behind her. Adams nonchalantly glided from the cellblock without looking over his shoulder, and the sobs he heard swirled about him like the magical notes of a stirring symphony.

MLB 498-A appeared five minutes after Kurt Adams' departure. He dutifully cleaned the cell while addressing Roger's misery. "You do realize, Father Baudin, that this is your fault. Your morning and evening ritual with Ms. Chen was a form of communication, which you knew was off limits. One can only break the rules so often before there are consequences."

CHAPTER 21

FIELD TRIP

Sunlight chased the shadows of dawn from the Atchafalaya River, bathing the woods and fields with its rejuvenating promises. The early morning hour found Victor Gaulmann busy reviewing reports, requests, and orders in his office at Blackclaw. An occasional sip of coffee or a brief pause to enjoy a bite of a cruller was all that interrupted his ruminations.

Blackclaw was being utilized in a different manner than before and still remained a prison. The turnover of inmates was more rapid than he was accustomed, but the lack of political red tape that entangled him was a most welcome change. The majority of the prison population were white-collar criminals who had failed to wean themselves of the idea that material superiority was a sign of increased value. Other cells were occupied by those incapable of abandoning faulty ideals held sacred in the United States. Some beliefs only die when those who carry them expire. Counter-revolutionaries were stored in solitary confinement in cellblock A, awaiting death after whatever information they were willing to share was gathered. These were the most dangerous residents of Blackclaw and were attended to strictly by MLBs. Other criminals, be they defectors or information pirates, were held for various durations, and their stays ended at a variety of destinations.

The last bite of his cruller enticed Victor to lean back in his leather-bound chair for a moment, a small smile washing over his face. His decision to stay at Blackclaw felt increasingly perfect with each dawning day.

MLB 770-A entered the room and interrupted the blissful moment. "Good morning, Director Gaulmann," greeted the android. "Already an hour into your day?"

"Well," Victor said, checking his watch, "to be honest, it has been fifty-three minutes."

"You are a very dedicated individual, sir. Your transition from your nation of origin to an exemplary member of the C.S.A. has been seamless."

"Thank you, 770-A," Victor stated, still leaning back in his chair. He slowly pulled himself to a standing position, tugging on his suit jacket as he stood. "I appreciate that compliment. I truly do. I assume you are here because of Commander Adams' visit yesterday?"

"Indeed. The recruits he mentioned are all on site. Shall I escort them to your office?"

"Yes. That would be very helpful. I assume Special Agent Cullen is already here."

"Correct, sir. He arrived at Blackclaw five minutes prior to your arrival."

Victor sighed, a mild disappointment permeating his tone. "I see. Well, let's get this started with the recruits, shall we?"

"Very good, sir," MLB 770-A answered. "Would you like them to wait outside your office or enter upon arrival?"

"Entering upon arrival is just fine."

"Understood. I shall have them here as soon as possible."

770-A promptly teleported from the room. Over the next ten minutes, three recruits — two men and a woman — stepped inside Victor's office. 770-A teleported back to the room before the second person reported for duty.

The three recruits stood before Victor in a row, attired simply in black shirts and jeans, as recruits were not permitted to wear full uniforms. Victor, who had engaged 770-A in a hushed conversation upon its return, pivoted to the three people in front of him. Before his first word fell, three chairs appeared, one behind each individual.

"Good morning," Victor said confidently as he stood in his domain. "Please have a seat. I noticed all of you walked into my office. No one has reached, what is it, level four of the Torres training?"

Smiles and embarrassed laughter came from the recruits as MLB 770-A answered. "They have not, sir. Though Recruit Butler is now at level three of the training. Recruits Davies and Robinson are making their way through level two."

"Level three?" Victor asked. He looked at Raymond Butler as he returned to his chair on the other side of his desk. "So, you are able to conceal your discomfort more readily than your comrades?"

"I can hold my discomfort," Raymond stated. "And you can take that response as literally as you wish."

Recruit Davies, the lone woman in the trio, smiled at Raymond's response while Robinson's face blanched as he recalled his struggles with the nausea often caused by teleportation.

"I understand," Victor said. "I really do. My position here requires me to eventually become comfortable in level three of the training. I have yet to...um...conceal my discomfort very well. No matter. We'll all get there. Now, Recruit Butler, you were employed here at Blackclaw in our previous life, correct?"

"Indeed, sir," Raymond confirmed, a slight nod of his head.

"Recruit Robinson and Davies," Victor said slowly, tilting his in the direction of each person as he stated their name, "you also both worked in facilities like this in your previous life, correct?"

"Yes, sir," the two answered in tandem.

"Now you are being trained in an effort to assess your qualifications for becoming a purifier. That is why you are brought here today. Commander Kurt Adams has arranged for a unique learning opportunity for a collection of students. Special Agent William Cullen, a

Gamma officer of the purifiers, will be conducting the lesson. Special Agent Cullen also monitors certain criminals in this facility. This role makes him a regular and welcome presence at Blackclaw. You three are called upon to assist him as needed. I, to be honest, have nothing more to add because that is all I know. 770-A, do you have any additional information?"

"Only that Special Agent Cullen is looking forward to his time with the recruits. I do hope he is satisfied by their performance. Director Gaulmann, if you have nothing more to add, I will escort the recruits to the gymnasium."

"By all means," Victor said, rising from his chair, "let the lesson begin."

The recruits followed MLB 770-A into the hallway and down a stairwell, eventually coming to an enclosed bridge that connected the administrative building of Blackclaw to the main penitentiary. Mumbled conversations about the impact of teleportation on the body and vague conjecture on what was about to unfold were the only discussions had. All three recruits had participated, at various intensities, in the initial purges of the initiation protocols.

They entered the open space of the gymnasium to find it bereft of any equipment. The space was cavernous and uncluttered. Weight-lifting equipment was placed along the back wall, and basketball rims were raised high above the gym, still present but useless. Also present were fifteen teenagers lined up in five rows of three, looking either cool or tough depending on the interpretation of such things. In perfect symmetry, three MLBs moved rhythmically among them. Raymond turned to MLB 770-A to ask a question but was struck silent by the arrival of Bill Cullen and guests.

Special Agent Cullen entered the room as a storm, demanding deference as his words fell. "Alright, we will soon have a fine collection of assholes and reprobates in this room, so everybody hold tight while these fuckers get set up."

Thirty adults shuffled into the gymnasium, escorted by two additional MLBs. They were dingy and showed some ravages of hunger, but all walked under their own power. Four MLBs and two Orcus herded the ragged contingent into five rows of six, facing the teens. MLB 770-A signaled for the purifier recruits to stand at attention to the left of the last row of the formed-up prisoners.

"Perfect," Bill said, admiring the three groups. He clapped his hands and smiled as he ambled the space between the adults and the teens. "I got fuckups to my left and shitheads to my right. What a wonderful life."

One student, a boy of seventeen, rolled his eyes and slouched to one side. He looked around the room, refusing to give his attention to the preening purifier. Still wearing a smile, Bill closed the space between himself and the willful teen. "Not impressed with the show so far, son?" Bill asked.

The boy didn't answer with words, but his demeanor remained arrogant and dismissive.

"It would behoove you to stand up straight and face forward," Bill whispered to the boy. "I'm tryin' to help you out here. I really am."

The defiant student looked at Bill. A snapping of his lips introduced a muttered response, "Whatever, man. I don't care about you."

Bill stepped back, nodding his head. "I understand. I do." He walked until he was again planted equidistant between adults and teens. A couple of teenagers smirked, encouraged by their insolent leader.

"Yer problem is yer conditionin'," educated Bill, looking playfully at his young rival. "You got so used to livin' in a land of cowards. In the United States, many adults are afraid to flex their authority or have so forgotten what it means to actually stand for somethin'. Because of this, you learned bein' defiant before adults actually paid dividends. The reality yer about to face is simply this: yer in the C.S.A. now. 58-B, run liquidation diagnostics and 47-C, help that kid with his posture."

The MLB approached the boy from behind and grabbed his head between hands of steel. 47-C turned the boy's head so he could only look directly at Bill, forcing him to stand straight. The other students suddenly became disciplined soldiers, backs stiffened and eyes attentive. Wincing, the boy attempted to protest his rough treatment, only to be scolded by the polite tones of his synthetic tormentor. "You should have, as advised, paid heed to Special Agent Cullen. His directives were perfectly clear."

"Okay. I'll...."

"You'll shut the fuck up," Bill ordered calmly. "I know yer thinkin' now you'll do as you were asked. Who gives a shit about that? I don't trust you now, and I sure as shit shouldn't have to repeat myself." The Gamma officer ambiguously shook his head, either in actual disappointment or feigned dismay. He continued his assessment by looking to 770-A for answers. "I don't understand why he wasn't dealt with last month."

"Due to his grades, attendance, and disciplinary records, this student was accepted into the promising cohort. It is the lowest level, sir," MLB 47-C noted.

"Promisin'? Well, we clearly need to raise our standards. There's nothing promisin' about this motherfucker."

"His liquidation cost is a seven, sir," MLB 58-B stated.

"Ah. Thank you. That is good information to consider. Speakin' of information, let me explain why we're all here. Students," Bill looked at the teenagers before him, "you'll wanna pay close attention to this. Standin' before you — right over there — are criminals and thieves. These adults all stole from their society in an attempt to gain what they wanted. Such activity is very selfish and, well, abhorrent to well-adjusted people in this nation. Bad habits and vices are difficult to break and, more often than not —"

"Roughly eighty-four percent of people fail to significantly change such habits."

"Thank you, 770," Bill said, pointing at the MLB. Lowering his arms, he started pacing the space between the rows of students, looking each of them in the eye as he passed. "Statistics like that are why we're so hard on criminals, slugs, and morons. Now, there's a TON of people in the United States of America who seem to get some kind of, I don't know, erotic release from just tryin' to help slugs and morons. They will form a circle jerk around some shithead, accomplish nothin' for the bastard, and then congratulate themselves for tryin'! Meanwhile, the inept fucker becomes addicted, not to success, but to havin' people try to help his dumb ass. That's fucked up and counterproductive! We handle things a bit different here."

Bill stood alongside MLB 47-C who was dutifully gripping the seditious student. Bill smiled and tapped the student in the center of the forehead before continuing his stroll.

"Now really focus and listen to this. All you criminals," Bill waved a dismissive hand at the gathered adults as he spoke, "have bad habits they haven't broken, and all you kids have bad habits that are already manifestin' themselves in your new school. All you kids have already missed at least one homework assignment per class. All you routinely are tardy to class without an excuse. Y'all have performed at a subpar manner on quizzes and struggle to be attentive in class. Four of you even fell into the trap we set two days ago when the shield that prevents cell phone usage at school malfunctioned, allowin' for random usage across yer school. You spent more time and effort seekin' those mirages of meanin' than being attentive to yer purpose. Shameful. Pathetic."

Bill looked to the floor, then at the students. He drew a deep breath and retrained on the adults facing them. He stood still, the focus of the room entirely upon him. From his frozen frame came a burst of motion, too fast for the untrained onlooker to register. A single gunshot rang out, and the lifeless carcass of a man guilty of siphoning one million six hundred thousand protean marks from his company hit the cement floor. Gasps of horror and fearful shrieks split the air. MLBs, Orcus, and the recruits worked in unison to keep the prisoners, teen and adult alike, in proper formation. "I wish...and I mean this more than you cowards can know...I so wish my orders were to kill y'all. Alas, they ain't. That does mean, however..." A second gunshot and another adult fell to the floor. Bill looked into each face in the room. The blissful smile he wore communicated just how much he loved punishing the guilty. "...That my orders don't say yer all safe. We ain't all destined to leave this room as we came in."

A quick tap of his right index and middle finger on a wrist guard covering his left hand preceded Bill's next directive. "Recruits, check yer communication bands for yer next order."

The three recruits were now stationed around the adult criminals, as per their orders, to keep that group in formation while Special Agent Cullen quietly surveyed the room. Recruits Butler and Davies checked their bands, each drawing a deep breath upon reading the directive. MLB 770-A noted the depth and length of Raymond's inhalation was slightly longer than Davies. Robinson looked tentatively around the room and tapped his communicator seeking information. Perplexed, he hesitantly raised his voice. "Sir?"

"Yah...you," Bill said. "What is it?"

"His name is Robinson, sir," MLB 770-A noted. "For the record, sir."

"Very well," Bill stated. "What is it, Recruit Robinson?"

"I...I don't seem to have a message, sir."

"You do," Bill stated.

"Well, I don't seem...."

"Do you have either the audio or visual hologram of yer band engaged? This was a written order. If those other forms of communication are engaged, it won't come through."

Robinson flushed with embarrassment. "Oh. I...yes, sir. I see that now."

"First field test with the new technology?" Bill asked.

"Indeed, sir."

"Not an auspicious introduction, Recruit Robinson. But here's a chance to make amends." Bill looked at the prisoners trembling before him. Tears rolled down cheeks, and some lips moved, muttering incomprehensible incantations. Bill's voice, now projected for increased force, ripped across the room. "Recruits! Read yer orders one more time. On my go ahead, complete this trainin' mission."

All three recruits stood at attention, powerful figures looming over the sniveling horde before them. Bill nodded his head and waited. A full minute passed. Then two. The oppressive silence was split by a single word: "*Thanatos.*"

The three recruits drew their weapons, each quickly ending the life of one inmate.

"Davies," MLB 770-A stated, informing Bill that she had the fastest draw and swiftest kill. The recruits, as their orders stated, all holstered their weapons. Raymond Butler was the slowest to draw and the quickest to return his weapon to its home. He scanned the room, his attention moving from the bodies on the floor to the teenagers, some standing with eyes torn wide open by their terror while others trembled. Some shrieked in horror, and some wept tears from an ocean of fear. The presence of the MLBs and Orcus, however, kept them paralyzed in place.

"Well done, Davies. You other two better raise yer fuckin' game." Bill's attention turned from his prized recruit to the teenagers. "As for you kids, shut the fuck up. I thought you motherfuckers were all so tough! Learn this lesson little children. There is a vast difference between standin' up for yer bloated egos and makin' a stand to purify a nation."

Joy emanating from his core, Bill turned back to his recruits. A second call of "*Thanatos*" was uttered, and the grizzly ritual continued. Eight corpses now littered the room. Davies remained the fastest draw. A third round allowed for more corpses and a new quick draw champ.

"Round three to Recruit Robinson," MLB 770-A proclaimed.

"Stakin' a claim are you, Recruit Robinson?" Bill crowed. "Are you here, Recruit Butler? Time to show me somethin', or I'll send yer ass home. It's about to get even more competitive. Check yer new orders. Don't fuck up and let Robinson steal yer glory, Davies."

The next six rounds of the exercise were mildly different than the previous three, as the recruits were free to hit multiple targets provided no more than three criminals died each round. The recruits maintained their discipline, and one prisoner, urine stains on his pants and snot running over his lips, stood alive in the carnage. The teens, meanwhile, stood as quivering witnesses to the training of the future purifiers.

Bill laughed, pleased with the outcome of the session. "Well, Prisoner Preston. It appears today is yer lucky day. You get to live.

This don't mean, of course, that yer leavin' the same way you came in. I bet yer a slightly different man now. 47-C, let go of fuck face, mouth breather there and escort Prisoner Preston to his home. We'll figure him out later. I'm not even sure there's anythin' left of him."

"Very good, sir," MLB 47-C answered, leaving the ranks of the teenagers to guide the shattered soul to his cell.

"58-B, bring the recruits to the front entrance. I will debrief with 'em in two hours. Location for debriefin' will be sent in twenty minutes."

"Very good, sir," MLB 58-B said, its voice joined by those of the recruits. The foursome quickly exited the room.

"Kids," Bill said, turning to the remaining audience, "I hope you paid attention to today's lesson. You see, bad habits will get you killed in the Common States of America. In case there's any doubts, I would love to be the one to kill each and every one of you. I would kill you today if I had my way. I fuckin' hate the fact that I have to let you go. I do. A man whom I respect greatly contends we are just too early in the process to eliminate you. He's a patient fellow. Me, fuck, yer all expendable. Now, either I am correct about this, or my friend is. Time will tell. Make good use of it. And remember, I am the silent force that stands behind every order yer teachers, yer employers, or yer parents give. If you should ever see me again, well, it'll be a great day for me."

The remaining Orcus and MLBs that were ordered to escort the children wordlessly prodded the students from the room. They marched off in silence to a bus that returned them to school.

Bill turned to the ever dutiful MLB 770-A. "So, how did he do?"

"Better than you anticipated, sir," 770-A answered.

"Not like I anticipated much."

"True, sir."

"He did worse than the other two?"

"Correct, sir. Considerably, in fact."

"Alright. Give me yer data and yer assessment. Some decisions will have to be made regarding Recruit Butler."

CHAPTER 22

DATE NIGHT

Shoes. Why, Laura laughed to herself, *are shoes such a difficult decision?* The light blue sheath cocktail dress she wore took some time to choose from her plentiful wardrobe, but the shoes! Six pairs still lay on the floor of her living room, each craving a night out. She slid her feet into a possible winner and stood, took two steps, then turned quickly as a melodic mechanical voice caught her by surprise.

"I see you've made progress, Ms. Owellen. So wonderful to see you wearing a pair of shoes rather than just talking to them."

"You know, 67, just because I enjoy your mild sarcasm doesn't mean I can't ask Kurt to return your speech programming to its original default settings."

The MLB flatly acknowledged this fact. "You could, but you wouldn't because you love me."

"I might," Laura smiled, "because I hate you."

"You do say the sweetest things, Ms. Owellen."

"That must be it," Laura quipped as she knelt down to return the rejected shoes to her bedroom.

MLB 67-D quickly interrupted her. "I will get those. It's what I'm here for."

Laura checked her makeup in the mirror. Standing before her reflection, she concluded, as she already had on three previous occasions, that there was no need to touch anything up. She was ready. But nervous. Why nervous?

"Hey, 67?"

"Yes, dear?"

"Why am I so nervous about this night? Kurt and I are hardly strangers to each other."

"While it is true," the MLB began, "that you two spend time together, this might well be your first date. Also, if you don't mind me saying, your species often confuses nervousness with excitement."

"Yes...ummmm...my species is prone to doing that," Laura stated. "I might need to readjust your speech programming after all. Your species? Really?"

"No need to tell the commander. I have placed the phrase into containment. I won't use it again. I must, however, inform you that your date has arrived."

"He —"

A knock on the door interrupted Laura's question and prompted her to turn, yet again, to the living room mirror.

"If I had eyes, I would roll them, Ms. Owellen," MLB 67-D stated as it turned to leave the room. A final parting shot was, however, called for. "I believe your fine choice of shoes will allow you to answer the door yourself."

Laura drew a slow breath and exhaled sharply. She then adjusted her dress, which instantly resisted her fussing and returned to its original position, as if she had done nothing at all. Pausing for a moment, she gathered herself so as not to throw open the door.

Kurt Adams stood, a fist raised for a second knock, on the front porch of her modest colonial home. Laura laughed at the sight of Kurt standing, fist in the air. "Planning to start our evening by rapping me in the nose?"

"Of course not," Kurt responded, a touch too serious for the moment. He smiled, however, and raised his fist again, shaking it gently at Laura. "But if you give me too much of your sass tonight, watch out!"

"I'll keep that in mind," Laura deadpanned as she pulled a silk evening shawl from a closet before stepping outside. A look on Kurt's face caused her to pause, suddenly insecure. "Is something wrong? Do you not...."

"No," Kurt said, taking her hand and leading her to the front walk. He raised his arm, enticing her to slowly pirouette. When she finished her rotation, Kurt kissed her hand and then her cheek. "You look lovely. Elegant. I just...I am afraid I presumed something. I bought you a gift for the evening." With a hint of hesitancy infiltrating his unflappable demeanor, Kurt reached into his gray topcoat. He pulled forth a velvet rectangular case.

Laura smiled expectantly when he handed it to her and gasped upon its opening. "Oh my," she managed, gazing at the teardrop necklace. "It's beautiful."

"I thought it was too," Kurt said, seeking to find the proper words as he looked at the beauty standing before him in her high-necked dress. "It would be an honor if you would wear it on our second date."

"I will, assuming, of course, you earn a second date," Laura teased, smiling.

"Well," Kurt said. Laura stepped back to the house to place her necklace on a plant stand just inside the door. He awaited her return before continuing his thought. "Let's say we begin that process now?"

Laura took Kurt's outstretched hand, and the couple teleported from the walkway, reappearing in a sprawling banquet hall. A single table situated in the middle of a dance floor beneath a crystal chandelier captured Laura's attention. The only sources of light in the room, however, came from candles on the table and others located on a piano to the far left of the dining area. Additional light was provided by the setting sun, its radiance slowly leaving the stage as the lights of the city appeared like stars. The often underappreciated journey from day to night was visible through a wall of panoramic windows.

"Kurt," marveled Laura. She stepped away from him, attempting to absorb the enchanted environment enveloping her. She turned to him, still struggling with her bewilderment. "Where...where are we?"

Kurt walked with her slowly toward the windows. Progressing some two hundred feet to the edge of the room, they passed four small, multilayered tables. Each served a distinct purpose. A small selection of wines was on one setting, while cheeses and fruits adorned another. Breads and spreads shared space with water on another service table, and the final setting was for a sample of scotches and whiskeys. On each appetizer table, tall white candles awaited the touch of life giving flame. A grape found Laura's fingers as she moved past. "And how did I not notice these tables earlier?"

"I think the chandelier distracted you," Kurt noted and Laura nodded in agreement. "As for your previous question, we are in one of the banquet halls atop the Museum of Fine Art." Kurt said it proudly, as if he had built the structure himself. They stopped at the window, and Laura could see an outdoor sculpture garden in a sunken, rooftop terrace. He pointed at a nigh invisible glass door. "We could tour the sculptures if you like."

"No," answered Laura. "Later. Yes, a bit later I think."

"Outstanding." Kurt removed her shawl and hung it on a coat rack placed near the door for the evening. His outer jacket found a home atop her garment. Laura peeked at the terrace, even though she claimed the desire to stall her explorations. Shadows stretched from one sculpture to the next, the gentle webs of the evening ensnaring both the space and imagination. The setting sun's spell was, as many things in this world are, broken by Kurt Adams' voice.

"You're truly enjoying this view," he stated, a hint of joy creeping into his voice.

Laura replied dreamily, "I am. I wish we could have seen the entrance to the museum as well."

"We will get to that. I have arranged for the museum to be vacant of visitors and employees in fifteen minutes."

"You are closing the museum just for us?" Laura asked, her eyebrows rising slightly. She stepped with Kurt to the selections of wine, accepting his choice of a Nero d'Avola.

As they touched glasses and peered at one another, Kurt responded in a flat tone, "I don't like crowds. That's all." Satisfied, he began strolling toward their table.

"Really?" Laura said, smiling. "I thought you didn't like sharing me."

Kurt attempted to turn his sincere smile sardonic. "Perhaps that played into it. Perhaps. That would explain my choice in restaurant too."

"Oh really? Where are we going?"

Kurt took a seat at the dinner table on the dance floor. Laura joined him, curious where the seat might take her. He opened his arms in an attempt to point at the entire room. "Right here. You mentioned three restaurants you particularly enjoy. I contacted all three, and a special combined menu has been programmed into our table. Just touch the pad at your right hand and...."

A hologram of a menu burst upward from the center of the table, floating ten inches above and rotating gently clockwise. Kurt quickly flicked his own touch pad, calling forth the image of a twenty-four-ounce porterhouse with a salted baked potato and grilled asparagus.

Laura laughed. While holograms were not new to her, she rarely saw one that was so vivid. She reached out a hand, causing the image to shimmer before her. "Wow. That is amazing clarity. Really stunning. Can I...?"

She never finished her question but ran her fingers along the menu until she found an item of interest. Tapping a display button, a hologram of a wedge salad, complete with applewood bacon, tomato, red onion, and blue cheese dressing, appeared before her.

"That's what you're ordering?" Kurt asked, a slight edge to his voice.

"What? Disappointed you put all this effort into organizing this special menu, and all I want is a salad?"

"You can order what you like," he blurted. "I just...."

Laura laughed despite herself. "Don't worry, I'm still a meat-eatin' gal! I just wanted to see your reaction!"

Kurt shook his head, annoyed and joyed by Laura's ability to get the best of him. "You're very amusing. Do you want to order?"

"Maybe an appetizer or two to get us started. I would like to tour the museum soon, though."

"Easy enough. We can place an appetizer order and ask for it to be delivered at a specific time. Therefore, when we return from the museum floor, the food will be here."

"Delivered? Like, what, just teleported onto the table?" Laura asked skeptically.

Kurt waved the question off with his hand. "No, no, no. I'm not that reclusive. Depending on what we order, a server from one of the restaurants will be teleported into the backroom with our request and bring it to the table."

"The restaurant experience without the crowds."

Drawing a slow breath, Kurt raised his glass. "Indeed, and yet still with the only company I could possibly desire at such moments."

Laura smiled and lifted her glass. "I feel the same way."

Appetizers were quickly ordered, and Kurt received a message that the museum was now completely theirs. The couple, per Laura's request, walked to the elevator and rode to the main floor. Their footfalls echoed off the marble walls as they moseyed stress-free into the front of the museum. Kurt took Laura's hand, guiding her to the east wing where a traveling exhibit of grotesque art was on display.

Kurt was captivated by the images: women tearing the flesh off their skulls as they mourned the death of children; and demons smiling from the darkness, tempting humans to fall, and goading angels into combat. Laura, with rare exceptions, did not find the grotesque artwork appealing, though she enjoyed noting Kurt's reaction. His words as he explained the appeal of certain pieces were lost on her.

His passion and expressiveness, however, she found quite charming. Intriguing. She kissed him, interrupting an unnecessary sentence.

The kiss brought Kurt from the art back to her side. He smiled at her while realizing she was somewhat less than interested in the grotesque. "You're not sure you like this style, are you?"

"Ummmm...no," Laura confessed, realizing her honesty was what he sought. She glanced from one piece to another, settling on a painting across the room. "This one, however, is certainly interesting."

Laura brought Kurt to a picture of a gnarled and rotting tree. The moon hid behind stormy clouds as the stars, distant and disinterested, fought to be seen. The tree's branches —some clearly skeletal arms while others merely wood bent in tortured patterns — stretched in various directions. Some drooped listlessly toward the earth, worn down by years of service and now seeking only a final resting place on the dirt below. Others stretched to the heavens, pleading for salvation. Knots in the wood were faces, contorted in anguished grimaces. One face, ancient and proud, emerged powerfully from the ruts, allowing the trunk to tell stories of the epochs that surrounded steely eyes. Its fearsome glare, the antithesis of the agony found in the other faces, somehow carried with it a sense of serenity. This godlike spirit within the bark was the only visage that showed dominion rather than subservience to the macabre environment.

"That's beautiful," Kurt whispered as he and Laura approached the painting. "Just magnificent."

"I like it too. So much power."

"Yes. The power of the will over the environment."

"Or," Laura retorted, her voice flowing from some deep inner fissure, "of nature over the other forces that seek to overwhelm."

"The power of nature?"

"Absolutely. On multiple levels. The idea that darkness and suffering surrounds the tree but something deep within endures. Something that is greater than the unnatural forces seeking to overwhelm. Can't you see? That dim light emanating from the wood spirit? It is soft but still there. Like the human soul desiring to reach full potential despite obstacles before it."

"The human soul?" Kurt asked, attempting to hide his incredulity.

His tone was either ignored or dismissed as Laura pressed on, undaunted. "Yes. The soul. Definitely." Laura looked at Kurt and shook her head; a knowing smile flashed as she took his hand and led him away from the painting. As they strolled by other grotesque images, she allowed words to form around her thoughts. "You enjoy these paintings?"

"Very much so," Kurt stated. "They speak to me in a variety of ways. And not just these. There are other styles, abstract and surreal, I enjoy."

"I like paintings of landscapes," Laura shared, and Kurt made a mental note. "Sometimes those with a surreal bend to them. Anyway, any other art forms you like?"

"Not a big fan of pottery, though some woodworking catches my eye from time to time."

Laura patted Kurt's hand and smiled. "I was thinking more along the lines of music or the theater."

"I see," Kurt said, chuckling at his own myopia. "I enjoy jazz music and various classical symphonies. Of course, you already knew that. Acting in movies or plays can be stirring, but I loathe musicals. People just don't burst into song while performing mundane acts."

"Well, maybe they should," challenged Laura, "but who cares about that right now. The point is something in you is...um...fed by these art forms. Maybe even sustained?"

Kurt halted their progress and released Laura's hand. "Have you read Victor Malinkowski's arguments for being fully human?"

"When I was a student at Forbearance University," crooned Laura. "My sister, two brothers, and I were the first generation of the family to graduate from a four-year university. And yes, A Return to Eudaimonia was a book I read and have reread since."

"And yet you became a pleasure princess?" The question created a moment of awkward silence that Kurt attempted to quickly fill. "A fascinating...and greatly appreciated...choice."

Laura smiled, attempting to make the sudden shift in conversation fluid. "I also learned in college that I liked sex. Relationships... not so much. And, in a more subtle way, I enjoyed not only the attention of men but what I could do to their bodies, which, by extension, could grant me access to their minds. I guess that is one of my art forms."

"While I am not sure I would raise everything to art, I will say, in that realm, you are quite the artist."

Laura paused, the slightest ripple in the rivers of time, before she spoke. "Thank you. You've proven pretty capable in that regard yourself."

Kurt nodded his head in appreciation and took Laura's hand, guiding her up a wide marbled stairwell to the second-floor gallery. As they turned down a hallway, he returned to their previous conversation. "So, Professor, could you tell me more about the soul and how it can be touched by the grotesque?"

"Well," Laura began, "you are moved by that art. And jazz. And an occasional acting performance."

"Guilty as charged," Kurt noted.

"But it is not your intellect or your creativity that is stirred. It's something else. Something deep within you. Deep within all people. Once it's moved, we use words to describe or paint to express it, but it is not those things alone. Hence, the soul."

"Ha! You have read your Malinkowski! How do you feel about his conclusions that the soul need not survive our deaths?"

"Here and now, that's where I live," Laura said. "Planning the best I can for my future. Hoping the hands that hold the future are trustworthy." She kissed Kurt's hand to accentuate her point.

"It is the privilege of well-adjusted citizens to sow seeds that will allow a country to reap marvelous rewards for themselves and the generations to come," Kurt said, paraphrasing the deceased philosopher.

Laura opened her mouth to respond in kind, but a secondary thought interrupted the process. "The appetizers! They should be arriving soon!"

"That's true. We may find them at the table when we arrive."

"I know this will sound petty, but I kinda wanted to be seated when the servers bring them out. Could we —"

The sentence was never finished as Kurt quickly teleported the couple back to their dining table. They were seated for less than two minutes when stuffed mushrooms and a curved wooden plate containing four varieties of Middle Eastern bread and accompaniments arrived. A quick toast and the first satisfying bites were savored.

"See?" Laura suddenly exclaimed, pointing an accusatory finger at Kurt. "Art can be infused into anything with the proper care and skill!"

"Relax there, Professor Malinkowski," teased Kurt. "I do, however, have a question for you. Given your experience in college, do you ever wish for...."

"...Another job?"

"Yes," Kurt said bluntly.

"Do you wish I had a different job?"

Multiple emotions swirled in the single question, and Kurt rapidly waded through them even as his answer rolled forth. "Well, since it is through your work that we met, I will say no. You, however, have been less active of late in your profession."

"How do you know that? Are you having me watched?"

"Rumor and anecdotal evidence," Kurt stated. "People have noted your lack of attendance at certain recent events."

"Well, there is a reason for that."

"My treatment of Johnny the night of the initiation protocols?"

Despite an inner protest, she smiled at the memory. How she enjoyed Kurt's public display of desire. "Bingo!" Laura declared. "That's the one. You cast a long shadow over me that night."

"I can see that," Kurt stated. "Is that such a terrible thing?"

"No," Laura said coyly. "Though I may be looking for a different job anyway."

"Why is that?"

Laura hesitated, unsure how far onto the ledge she dared to creep. "There are quotas we are supposed to meet. I have operated at the bare minimum level of engagement in my profession for the past two months."

Kurt Adams smiled as he took a bite of a stuffed mushroom. A sip of wine preceded his next thought. "I see. Initiation was just over a month ago. So you were already scaling back previous to our inter-action that night."

"Yes," Laura said, blushing as she felt her heart being revealed. "Y'know, you were scaling back your activities as well."

"Excuse me? Not sure what you're referring to."

"You, sir, have a certain reputation in my circles," Laura stated. "A reputation of consumption you fell well short of prior to the night of initiation."

"I was busy planning the rather important and multifaceted assault that is the initiation protocols."

"I know. Well...I don't know actually," Laura confessed. "At best, I suspect things. I know very little about your work. You are so pri-vate. All I really know is, at times, it feels like you are the protector of the entire nation. You have so much responsibility."

Kurt held his glass of wine aloft and offered a humble boast. "Well, I don't like to brag, but I do get very busy."

Laura looked to the floor, embarrassed by her childish insistence that his behavior had anything to do with her. She longed to slap the smug smile off Adams' face. She glanced up to see him sipping his wine and leaning back comfortably in his chair. He had not a care in the world. Looking back to the floor, she allowed herself one more deep breath as she prepared to unleash her venom.

The moment never came as Kurt spoke first. "I also hate confess-ing. Almost more than I hate bragging."

"Hate confessing? What do you mean?"

Kurt paused, his bravado set aside to allow for the reasoned search for words. His voice wavered slightly as he intellectualized his emotions. "I did indeed curtail my activities prior to initiation. I did this because I found I did not wish to spend my time with the others. Just you. By then, we had already begun to rendezvous off the clock so —"

"So I was right!" Laura exclaimed triumphantly, both arms reaching to the heavens in exaltation.

"You were indeed, my dear," Kurt said despite the urge to qualify his statement.

"And you're a jerk!"

"That may be true too. Well, from time to time at least."

"From time to time," Laura said, raising her glass.

Kurt returned the gesture with a gentle smile, the unfamiliar ground of the evening becoming increasingly comfortable. Laura's smile faded as concern returned to her face. "I do have one question about Johnny. I don't know much of what you do, but I know you kill people and can kill people almost as you wish. Is Johnny...."

"He is alive," Kurt interjected, "though one of my ranking officers, a woman named Meredith Wilson, may kill him herself. His transition to his new rank has not been stellar. His substandard performance is wearing the patience of his superiors, especially her. He is, however, alive and well...though in need of increased training."

Laura smiled as she listened for she never wished harm to befall her pawn.

The rest of the evening progressed smoothly. Dinner was ordered, and the music accompanying the meal created a melodic trance. They discussed Laura's interest in becoming a hostess at a high-end restaurant and the urge to return to school to earn a master's in art history in order to become better suited to assist in the functioning of a museum. Refinement and growth: two cornerstones of the Common States of America. Her future vision was met with much support.

A second tour of the museum was followed by dessert and a final drink before the couple strolled, at Laura's request, to Kurt's apartment complex. They enjoyed a final drink on his couch, and the couple retired to the bedroom for a second dessert.

Laura, however, did not sleep as deeply as Kurt. Some five hours had passed and she sat, wrapped in a bathrobe, on a chair in the bedroom. The sun would rise soon, but she had been up for over an hour, her attention pulled in dueling directions. At some moments, all she wanted was to watch her naked...boyfriend...was he her boyfriend?...sleep. At other instances, she would gaze dreamily at the stars. Something was missing from the night. But what? Her discontent roused her much earlier than planned. This is what kept her awake. Longing for answers to unspoken questions. Her finger ran across her lower lip, followed by a sudden burst of energy.

She bounded from her chair and contacted MLB 67-D. In seconds, the gift she received earlier in the evening appeared on the floor. She dropped her robe and put on her necklace. The elegant piece now the only garment she wore, she snuck to the side of the bed and slid on top of Kurt, a flick of her tongue and the caress of her breasts along his cheek bringing him quickly from sleep. He tried to roll to his side to place Laura on her back. Laura tightened her arms around his neck, and her legs held his hips fast as she leaned with considerable conviction to offset his effort. A quick bite on his neck and she breathlessly whispered in his ear, "You need to learn the joy of not being in control all the time."

She sat up and guided him inside of her, moving in a sensual rhythm that elicited moans and subdued his efforts to assume the power in this encounter. As his breathing raced, so did her body. He climaxed with one hand on her hip and the other grasping a breast as if he was clinging to his life. Lost was the sense of where he ended and she began. Lost was the concern of future matters and the endless plans that had been analyzed, scrutinized, and prioritized. Laura's body shuddered as she held her release so she could synchronize a moment of shared transcendence. She flopped onto the open space next to him, her nails digging into his chest, as she sought her breath. Kurt, still on his back, turned to look at Laura.

He brushed a few strands of hair from her face and smiled. "So, you're quite an artist."

"I told you so," Laura said. "Your day needs to begin?"

"I have time to stay for a short while. Would you like me to make some breakfast?"

"Can't 498 handle it so you can stay?"

"That's a fine idea," Kurt said.

It would be another ten minutes of whispered conversation before a light breakfast was ordered.

CHAPTER 23

THE INNER GARDEN

Roger languished on the damp floor of his squalid cell, seemingly unaware that he rested his head some ten feet from a bucket filled to the rim with his piss and excrement. Days had passed since it was emptied, the rancid odor causing other inmates to pull torn shirts above their noses. Their own filth was somewhat more palatable. While others gagged on vomit, Roger embraced the foul aroma for what it was: a reward for his failures. A lifetime of service, deep and sincere, had brought him here, overwhelmed by the forces of the world. He thought he learned the depth of despair decades ago in Lorgalsum. In his presumptuous arrogance, he claimed to understand cruelty. To understand sadistic tyrants. Such a fool to believe he could overcome that which he possessed an imperfect knowledge of.

Now he lay, exhausted by the pain his tears could not quell. He stared across the floor as a marksman of old would peer down the barrel of his rifle. Only there was no target. There was nothing. Thoughtlessly, a finger on his right hand ran through the grime of the floor, making tracks in the sand and pebbles, circling slowly to create patterns out of the random muck, only to have the order be destroyed with a sweep of another finger, then reimagined into a new shape. His eyes moved from the floor to the distant wall to bear witness, to be reminded, of his horrifying reality.

Fighting the impulse to gain conscious control of this strange land, he watched and paused long enough to sit up. Settling onto his haunches, he allowed the hand to again do its work in the filth. He closed his eyes and drew a deep breath, seeking serenity in the battlefield of his mind. Enemies...guilt and shame...arose to break his concentration, but Francis of Assisi was with him, calmer than dawn and stronger than a storm. Wise Aquinas ushered him forth. Teresa of Avila and John of the Cross dared him to step, once again, into the darkness. The cloud of unknowing taunted him, but he breathed and pressed forward in his immobility. Slowly, the tightrope between meditation and contemplation was found, and he settled comfortably on the gossamer thread. So still. So quiet. Slowly becoming empty but far from nothing.

———————

Zitai? Are you here?

Am I alone?

Zitai?

Hello, Roger. Dear friend. I'm so glad you've come.

Zitai...I...I should go. I....

Roger. Don't flee. Stay. We have much to discuss. Look at me, Roger. Does my presence cause you such sadness?

I...I killed you Zitai. Don't you see? You died because of me. How can you stand to look at me?

I wonder, Roger, do you remember those four girls that Doctor Martin Luther King Junior killed?

What? Doctor King never killed anyone.

He didn't? Oh. Perhaps I am mistaken.

You must be. I...why are we...?

Patience, Roger. Trust me now and talk with me about that which I wish to speak. Please. Trust me now. We have an eternal moment here.

Very well.

It's just...I seem to recall learning that he delivered his famous 'I Have a Dream Speech' in late August. In mid-September, a bomb in Birmingham killed four young girls in a church.

Yes. That sounds tragically familiar.

Yes. In the wake of that horror, Doctor King, according to a member of his inner circle, wrestled with the idea he was to blame. That he pushed too hard too fast and therefore caused their deaths.

He was wrestling with his pain. His overwhelming sense of responsibility mingled with his grief. That is all.

That is all?

Of course. Wrestling with pain and doubt don't change the reality of matters. He made it clear in the days to follow who was to blame. Vile, violent people did not need some grand excuse to commit this atrocity.

You are quite sure of this?

Yes.

And, yes, I see your point. Thank you for not saying it.

I miss seeing you, but that is so very selfish.

Please. It is so very human. I am not a petulant person who would demand you conceal your grief because of your faith. Emotions are our gift and burden. I am honored by your compassion and know you, as all people, must grieve. There is beauty in such remembrance. I will not, however, accept you blaming yourself for the chosen actions of others.

I understand.

I know that you do.

What am I to do now? I am helpless. I have no ability to impact the unfolding events around me. I am barely even a witness to the rising powers of this world. I am confined.

That is true.

Well, that was uplifting.

Truth and happiness don't necessarily travel the same path. Yet you have stood in dark places before and, while not happy to be there, you were...what?

Centered. Confident that the path I walked was better for human-kind than the alternatives that sought only power and seemed intent on setting all ablaze.

Has that conviction changed? Do you feel your path is now inferior to that of your adversary?

No. Merely dismissed. Function and outcome have so supplanted the empathy and dedicated patience required to raise the human condition that I fear degradation will never end.

So...you will change paths?

No. That betrayal cannot happen. It will not.

You are confident of this?

Yes. I am. There is a time for every purpose under heaven. The shadow holds sway at this time. Other paths must be maintained, obscured in the darkness, so they can be seen when the light returns.

Even the shadow is impermanent.

Indeed.

Our time in this sacred space is also subject to change. Are you ready to leave this beautiful garden in which we commune?

No. I will sit a while longer in this inner garden before I deliver your eulogy.

My eulogy? When will this service be held?

I suspect I have little time left. Let my breaths from this moment forth be part of its deliverance. When the time comes to speak, I hope to honor your life with my words. Your path.

Our path.

Yes, our path.

We are not two.

And there must be others. There must be a way to be heard. To act as Charles Morgan Junior once did.

I am not sure of whom you speak.

Here I thought you knew everything! The day after that bomb

killed those girls, Charles Morgan Junior stood up at a luncheon for the Birmingham Young Men's Business Club and denounced the entire city and its citizens for the crime. Everyone who allowed hate to fester and grow unabated was targeted by Morgan's rage. He stood up and made himself the enemy of an entire community because of the call to conscience.

He sounds like a wonderful and brave man.

Perhaps I will be like that someday.

Perhaps you already are.

———————

Roger exhaled slowly and opened his eyes, leaving his inner garden of gravel walkways, gentle streams, white lilies, lotus, blossoms, and daffodils behind. He stood and walked to the bars of his cell. Leaning against them, he smiled, his spirit now free as his body remained contained. His cellmates noted him but did not interact, fearful of the repercussions. They were, however, taken aback but his demeanor, bewildered in their inability to ascertain what he lost and what he found. Another breath and Roger reclined on his cot.

CHAPTER 24

NEW ASSIGNMENT

Kurt Adams stood while leaning on his fists, looking over a blueprint of the McClure Convocation Center in Chicago. His fingers ran down corridors and tapped every exit he found. All windows and any areas of weakness that could be breached by unwanted guests became subject to his attention. Each graceful swipe or tap of his fingers caused gray blotches to appear upon a screen on the wall directly in front of him. Additional gestures morphed the blotches into arrows and circles, depending on the manner in which Adams touched the map. Shifting his attention between the map to the schematic on the wall, he began to focus on subterranean tunnels when his office door, a slab of glistening metal that slid into the wall, endured a gentle rap. His right pinkie, without breaking the pianist's rhythm, tapped a button and activated his intercom. "That better be you, Doc," Adams said as he continued tracing passages with his fingers. Nothing in his demeanor revealed any temptation to look at the camera feed to discover the identity of his guest. Words would suffice.

"Who else?" Edward "Doc" Sells asked, standing before the locked door. "As far as I know, there are only eight people allowed to enter

227

this wing of the complex without conversation with 498-A. Six of them are currently in New Orleans."

Adams chose to respond a question for a question. "Is that so?"

"According to our intel and current geo-updates, it is," Doc replied.

"Interesting," a voice from behind Doc said with an easy confidence that dragged both a smirk and a groan from him. He turned to face Meredith Wilson, who was just finishing cracking her neck, once to the left and then the right, as she always did when arriving via teleportation. She noted Doc's demeanor and instantly sought blood. "What's the matter, Doc? Disappointed you won't have enough alone time with the commander?"

"Not at all. Just that if I knew you were coming, I would have brought flowers or, perhaps, headless roses to offer."

"So charming," Meredith responded.

"Welcome, Special Agent Wilson," Adams' voice said through the intercom. "Special Agent Sells, do feel free to update your intel. Special Agent Wilson is a recent addition to MLB 498-A's elite access protocol."

Doc begrudgingly managed, "Very well, sir."

"You might want to keep up with the times, Doc," Meredith mocked, patting him on the back. Doc sought in vain for an effective quip while the door slid open, granting entrance to Adams' personal office.

"Enter," ordered Adams as he shut down the schematic maps and charts. The two officers filed into the office and stood at attention before their superior officer. "I have a new assignment for both of you and, I do believe, you have some information for me. Correct, Doc?"

"Yes, sir."

"Outstanding. Both of you can be at ease."

The reply, "Thank you, sir," rose in perfect harmony.

He gestured toward two chairs that his trusted officers quietly occupied. Adams likewise sat. As he did so, he pinched the corners of his eyes, pulling his fingers over the bridge of his nose. Doc, who had spent more time in Stone Adams' presence than most people, still wasn't sure if the gesture was one of annoyance or a method used to suppress a smile. Three coffees materialized on the table, each made to the preprogrammed preference of the recipients. Adams took a short sip of his. "You are both aware of Chancellor McGreggor's upcoming gala in Chicago?"

"Yes —" the two officers said in unison. Adams moved his hand in front of his face as if cleaning an invisible window before him. Doc took the gesture to mean what it was intended and stopped speaking. The slightest whisper of an 's' escaped Meredith's lips before she followed suit.

"Very good. Did you know that the prime minister approached me with the...request...to personally oversee security for the event?"

"That I did not know," Doc said. Meredith seconded Doc's statement.

"He did," stated Adams impassively. "I suppose it is because the chancellor would like me at the event but fears my patience may be wearing thin."

"Patience? Patience for what?" Doc asked.

"Too many political engagements of late," Meredith surmised. "The fiftieth anniversary event...."

"A worthy cause for celebration," Adams noted.

"Indeed," concurred Meredith, "but, even so, you are not the type who wishes to spend time sitting on a stage."

Adams nodded. "Well said. Continue."

"The interview with the American stooge," Meredith sneered. "I assume the oligarchy selected their representative quite purposefully."

"You are correct again, Meredith."

"And," Meredith added, a smile with the power to freeze and liberate hearts momentarily appearing on her face, "while I truly enjoyed my participation in that evening, I imagine it felt more like a political engagement than purifier business."

"Because it was," Adams said.

"Indeed. It was also a very successful night. Our people found it inspirational. Those from other nations have been debating some of your finer points ever since," Doc noted.

"The hand-wringing debates of thoughtless people who lack true conviction matters so very little to me, although the idea that the citizens of this nation benefitted is a fine outcome," specified Adams, rubbing his chin before he continued. "But, yes, asking me to safeguard an event that others could also guarantee does feel like politics intruding on my primary duties yet again."

"But, for clarity, you accepted the prime minister's request?" Meredith asked.

"I did," Adams stated. He tapped a button on his chair, and his schematics blazed to life. He allowed the special agents a few seconds to look at the plans. "I have completed seventy percent of my evaluation of the McClure Convocation Center. That analysis is saved in the files before you."

"Pardon me, sir?" a robotic voice said over the intercom.

"Yes, 498-A. What do you have?"

"To be fair, you are sixty-eight and three-fourths percent completed with your evaluative tasks."

"To be fair," Adams repeated. "Thank you, 498. I have completed sixty-eight and three-fourths percent of my evaluation and am going to proceed no further. The remainder of that task and all other tasks associated with this assignment are now in your hands. Do well." He shut down the schematics and looked at the officers sitting before him. "You both realize you have permission to speak freely, correct?"

"Yes," Doc said. "I just wasn't expecting this assignment. Is this... transfer of duties... cleared with the prime minister?"

"Cleared? That's superfluous. I did not clear it with him because I need not. But he and the chancellor will be informed when I brief them."

A wry smile accompanied Doc's response. "I see. I also assume 498 has already sent the schematic to our offices?"

"Of course," Adams confirmed. "You are ready to begin."

"Won't the prime minister think it a bit cavalier that you handed this mission to us in this manner?" Meredith asked.

"He likely will," Adams stated. "You two, however, are elite. I do not doubt your combined ability to safeguard the event."

"If you don't mind me asking," Doc began, "what will you be doing that night now that this is off your plate?"

"I am not sure. Perhaps I will sit on the stage since that is where they wanted me all along."

Doc hesitated, surprised by the idea that Adams would voluntarily join the other dignitaries. He rocked uncomfortably in his chair, wishing he had more information but reluctant to speak of what could be a more personal matter in front of Wilson.

Adams' attention moved from Doc to Meredith. He nodded his head and continued. "The matter is settled and closed for discussion. You can work in tandem to get up to speed and complete the preparations. Now Doc, I understand Special Agent Bill Cullen brought you some concerns regarding the recruits."

"He did," Doc stated, relieved to be switching topics. "Specifically, it was one recruit. I am free to discuss this with Meredith here?"

"I invited her," Adams answered.

"Yes, you did," Doc said. "Special Agent Cullen, as you know, is currently assigned to Blackclaw where he is in a constant state of surveillance for subversive and counter-revolutionary activity. Upon reviewing a training session for three potential P fours, he found himself concerned about one Raymond Butler."

"Tell me about it, the brief version. I assume he underperformed during the purging exercise."

"Indeed," Doc said. "In each of the first three rounds, he was the slowest draw and, therefore, the slowest kill. It is not, however, his slow draw that concerned Special Agent Cullen. It was the results of the six competitive rounds."

"Do tell."

"Recruit Butler discharged his weapon in each competitive round but killed no one. Flesh wounds and shoulder shots but no kills."

"No one," Adams repeated. "So, he was hiding his compassion by pulling the trigger while counting on his more zealous recruits to aid him in his subterfuge."

"It definitely appears this way," Doc stated. "Of the final eighteen kills, Recruit Davies scored eleven kills and —"

"That doesn't matter to me at the moment," Adams interjected. "Has Recruit Butler been home since the training session?"

"No. Special Agent Cullen decided to enact a stay drill, cutting the three recruits off from all familial contact as if they were in a mission that went poorly."

"Outstanding," Adams said. "If I recall, this is one of your recruits, correct?"

"He is," acknowledged Doc, slightly embarrassed.

"No shame," Adams said. "This is not an exact science. Is Davies yours as well?"

"Yes, sir."

"There you go." Adams patted Doc's arm before turning his focus to an attentive Meredith. "How should we proceed with this recruit?"

"He has family?"

"Yes," Doc answered, uncomfortable with Wilson's sudden inclusion in the conversation. "A wife and a teenaged daughter."

"I see," Meredith stated. "Were the families informed that the training session might take longer than anticipated? About the possibilities of stay drills?"

"They were told. The families ought not be alarmed." Doc disclosed.

"I would send Doc, as he is Butler's recruiter, to visit the wife. This way, he can fill her in as to reinforce why she has not heard from her husband, to earn her trust, and to offer a subtle warning regarding his training. Create pressure at home for him to perform at work."

"Doc?" Adams asked, looking at the senior Delta officer.

"Sounds like an excellent idea. Though I may not exactly take the subtle approach."

"I trust you to handle the visit as you deem fit," Adams stated. "You will complete this visit in the next twenty-four hours and get Recruit Butler home."

"Very good, sir. There is another issue I should call to your attention," Doc said.

"That would be?"

"Special Agent Cullen has, again, voiced his disapproval with the promising cohort in our schools. I watched the recording of the exercise. He was sorely tempted to kill the students."

"As he should be. Statistically, seven of them will be purged from the nation in the next six months. There is a seventy-five percent chance that three more will go within three months of that. Special Agent Cullen's enthusiasm is well-placed. Even appreciated."

"I understand, Stone," Doc said. "But if discipline is a virtue we promulgate with the utmost vigor, I would urge you to watch the full recording of the training session. I am not sure Blackclaw is the correct assignment. His talents may be better utilized elsewhere."

Adams thoughtfully replied, "I see. So, to be clear, you do not think Special Agent Cullen needs discipline as much as he needs an assignment that meshes more completely with his talents?"

Doc considered his answer carefully while striving to not appear hesitant. His answer came a microsecond later than prudent. "I do not think he needs to be disciplined."

Adams stood still, quickly weighing Doc's viewpoint before answering. "Very well. I will assess your recommendation. For now, I would have you familiarize yourselves with the McClure Center. I will give you the room for an hour. All future planning will be done in venues of your own choosing."

Adams stood and took two steps before tapping a single button on his wrist-com, teleporting to his next duty.

CHAPTER 25

UNFOLDING PROCESS

"Pardon the interruption, ma'am, but Commander Adams is here to see you," MLB 1-E said politely.

"Commander Adams?" Erin responded quizzically. She looked up at 1-E with a furrowed brow. "I don't recall having a meeting with him scheduled for today."

"Your memory serves you very well, ma'am," her personal MLB stated reassuringly. "You do not. He said he wished to update you regarding the event on May twentieth. He requested Prime Minister Vancese be here as well."

"Did he? I don't suppose he shared what was so pressing?"

"He did not. When I tried to press him on that very issue, he enacted the Zaqar directive."

"The Zaqar directive? He believed meeting with me was that urgent?"

"Apparently, ma'am."

"I see. Nothing so pressing has been reported, at least not to my knowledge. Do you have information on any events that would require my immediate attention?" Erin said, her concern rising sharply.

"I do not," MLB 1-E stated without alarm. "Regardless of the commander's motive, he requested the prime minister be here, so he has already been summoned. Mr. Vancese should arrive from his office soon. Shall I show Commander Adams in?"

Erin bit her lip, the only visible sign of her growing annoyance. "No. Have him await my summons in the sitting room. I will beckon him after the prime minister arrives."

"Very well, ma'am. I shall go sit with Commander Adams and stand by for word from you."

"Thank you, 1-E," Erin stated. She leaned back in her chair, sighing and looking around the room. The Zaqar directive was an order built into both MLBs and Orcus. Members of the oligarchy used it if they wished to quickly summon or communicate with other ranking officials with the understanding that the news being delivered deserved priority treatment. The recent request by Lamar Jenkins, the secretary of education, to have eleven administrators in Louisiana investigated for subversive activity was sent under the Zaqar directive. His timely request led to the execution of eight of the eleven administrators discovered to be incapable of surrendering to the C.S.A.'s educational vision. They were quickly replaced by proper employees recruited from North Carolina and Michigan, ensuring the children's education was not unduly interrupted.

"What is the issue, Madam Chancellor?" Ryan Vancese asked as he entered Erin's office, trailed by MLB 281-S, who was dutifully seeking to serve the most obstinate of patients. Ryan's office was connected to Erin's by an isolated corridor, allowing the prime minister unfettered access to the chancellor and, in theory, the privacy to allow 281-S to support him as he walked, for his aging body could no longer be guaranteed to endure the rigors of teleportation. Death by Torres Technology was terrible to behold and worse to contemplate. Not quite so repugnant, however, as the thought of needing an MLB to help one walk.

"I do not know, Mr. Prime Minister. I was hoping you might."

"Well," Ryan grunted, hauling himself to a chair and lowering himself into it unassisted. A couple quick breaths and he continued. "I am sure of one thing: it will be of some importance. Special Agent Adams is many things, but he is no alarmist."

Erin rolled her eyes at Ryan's quip as she leaned forward to touch a button on her desk. She glanced over to the prime minister. He looked comfortable and was no longer huffing for breath. MLB 281-S stood as a purposeless golem behind him. "1-E, please show Commander Adams in."

Kurt Adams trod into the room; unrushed yet unspoken consequence fell with each step. He reached Erin's desk and greeted both dignitaries, who, despite their anxiousness, responded with polite salutations. The greetings offered and accepted, Adams delved quickly into his business. "I have come to inform you that I will no longer be overseeing the security detail for the gala to be held on May twentieth. I have placed the responsibility in the capable hands of two Delta officers, Special Agent Sells and Special Agent Wilson. If you wish me to detail their credentials, I will be more than happy to do so."

"Deltas?" Ryan asked.

"The credentials of the special agents can wait," Erin interjected. She looked up from her chair at Adams, still standing before her desk. She raised a hand, silently promising time to speak. "I am far more interested in what has arisen to pull you from this duty. Will you be in need of additional resources?"

"I will not, for I am pulled away by the threat to principles, not any looming physical confrontation or serendipitous cyberassault."

"A threat to principles?" Ryan asked. "I don't know what you mean. Are you saying —"

"I am saying," Adams stated calmly as he looked down at the prime minister, "that protecting your gala is not only a waste of my time and skills but part of an encroachment on the revolution itself. I could argue to shut it down rather than merely withdraw my involvement."

Still seated, Ryan snarled, "You arrogant bastard! You agreed to do this! This ceremony honors a great revolutionary of our collective past, and you should have far more respect for the occasion than you currently exhibit!"

"I have tremendous respect for Daniel McGreggor," Adams somehow growled without raising his tone. "I wonder what he would think of his revolutionary brother-in-arms as he sits complacent in old age."

"Complacent? How dare you! I helped create the very systems which now cloak you in power. Perhaps we should —"

"Yes! You did create these systems. Calculating and efficient. Ruthless and visionary. And now what? I fear our vigor has been spent," Adams snapped.

"You fear our vigor has been spent?" Erin repeated the allegation slowly. Adams turned to the chancellor and listened as she questioned the lingering thought. "How can you think that? Initiation of Louisiana goes as planned, despite the myriad of obstacles faced. Our technological and medical advancements make us the wonder and envy of the world. We are the only nation without poverty. Even our revolutionary philosophy about human worth is starting to cause other nations to consider long held and rarely scrutinized questions about human value and dignity. Spent? Our vigor is swelling."

"Our vigor or our vanity?" The accusation hung in the air as Adams stood resolute before the only two people in the nation with hierarchical authority over him. "Repeated celebrations to honor the past but they also act to distract people from their necessary duties. Increasingly, we hear the positive opinion of foreign nations. How very American of us. This past month reeks of an insidious thought process carried over like an infectious disease from our nation of origin. Revolutions, first and foremost, destroy ties to the past. The most difficult of these being ingrained patterns of thought and behavior. People must be greater than their point of origin!"

Erin looked at Kurt "Stone" Adams who was crackling with energy. With certainty. She knew not what words would sway him, but she approached the sensitive matter from her heart and mind. "Commander Adams," she said, still seated, "you claim we are becoming vain. That we have lost our revolutionary zeal. Yet, how can the revolution be honored if we do not take the time to recall our past?"

"Honored? Daniel McGreggor did not spearhead this historic movement to be honored. The goal was to build a nation of people who transcend the need to be reminded of their past. Not because the past lacks foundational importance, but because the citizens, engaged and educated, feel that importance every day. It becomes part of the very air we breathe. We strive to build a nation that elevates the best aspects of humanity while simultaneously leaves us free of outmoded morality that hinders true eudaemonic growth. Honor the revolution? You can't honor a revolution unless you live, daily, the revolutionary process."

"You think I do not know that revolutions are not wars but a process?" Ryan asked, his face contorted by the insult to his acumen. "Can't you see, Commander Adams, that the process progresses unfettered? We grow. The process, initially horrifying to the uninitiated, has become a source of wonder to others. The outcomes becoming so satisfying, so extraordinary, that the necessary bloody road can be traveled by neophytes if we assist them. I believe the world teeters on the brink of embracing our way to open themselves to our rewards."

"Prime Minister, you have been spending too much time with the commissar of foreign affairs. Commissar Velazquez has convinced you of the reality of her illusionary vision. We can't give to the world what we haven't established as bedrock ourselves. We have not yet destroyed what came before," Adams said slowly.

"And what illusions distract Commissar Velazquez?" Erin asked.

"She fails to see our internal enemies. Pomp and circumstance? The raising of icons? The sirens call us to crash on the rocks of celebrity and projected prominence. The coveting of power over process? Comfort over challenge? We have seen a spike in white-collar crime in our most established states. The foundational greed of our species is not even exorcised from our established citizenry! Ideas that deepen attachment to shallow vices continue to percolate! This happens inside our borders! Revolutions always die from within. I fear...with all the love for my nation I can muster...I fear we are in danger of slipping into the habits of lesser nations. The past you should be concerned with is the study of why revolutions ultimately fail and how to avoid these missteps. So yes, I am withdrawing from your gala if, for no other reason, to have this conversation with those who should not need such warnings."

Erin drew a deep breath and, to the surprise of both men, serenely smiled. The unexpected turn in her features brought silence to the room, and she alone had the power to break it. Her focus moved to Ryan, and she spoke from a place of placid lucidity. "Ryan," she shook her head, amused by her absentminded lack of protocol. "Prime Minister, you counseled me recently by telling me that if I wanted to know my grandfather, I should look at Commander Adams. I wonder, am I seeing him now?"

Ryan, seething with anger and seeking words to rebuke Adams' accusations, suddenly found himself at ease. Memories of long-for-gotten arguments with Daniel McGeggor rose from dusty cobwebs, causing his body to relax and bringing an unwanted but warm smile to his face as well. "My goodness," Ryan responded, "I didn't real-ize how accurate I was. What shall we do about this conundrum?" Unbeknownst to Erin and Adams, this was a commonly used phrase when Daniel and Ryan angrily placed their cards on the table and the time for seeking solutions arose. "What shall we do?"

Adams looked from the chancellor to the prime minister, seeking the confines of the hidden trap he triggered. "What do you mean, what shall we do?"

"I mean, Commander," Ryan stated, "that your concerns are always the concerns of vocational revolutionaries. Men like you keep revolutions alive. You do realize that this event is not going to be cancelled, correct?"

"Yes, though I maintain my desire to see it cancelled," Adams said.

"And so you remain you," Erin stated. "I understand, however, your position, Commander Adams. You will not be pressured to oversee security of the affair and, moreover, your concern for our future is laudable. Your vigilance is necessary. Perhaps, after the twentieth, we will have an extended moratorium on such events. Would this please you?"

"Please me?" Adams stated quizzically. He paused, considering the question while adjusting to the unexpected shift in the atmosphere of the room. "I cannot answer that question...but I do see the potential to be pleased. Proceed as you will, and I will let you know in six months if the borne fruit is pleasing."

Erin stood to shake Adams' hand. "Very well," she said. Ryan did the same. Mildly satisfied, Adams turned on his heel and began to exit Erin's office. His third step had not fallen when the chancellor broke his stride.

"Commander, one last item. As a show of unity and good faith between us, I want you to sit on the dais during the ceremony."

Adam turned and faced the chancellor, his demeanor regaining its previous fire. "You now wish me to partake in this event that I loathe?"

"As a show of unity, I will heed your warning, and I expect you to heed this call to duty. What say you?"

Adams' glare moved from chancellor to prime minister. No words would change the request. No response would salve the sting of the insult. "Very well," Stone Adams said as whatever satisfaction this conversation had brought died with the last words of his superior.

CHAPTER 26

A CALL FOR CLARITY

Karen Butler sat fidgeting at her desk, pretending to assess a writing assignment. The relentlessly ticking clock remained a constant distraction. It was three thirty-five on what should have been a lazy Tuesday afternoon. Another glance at the time, three thirty-seven, and her calendar, May eleventh, did nothing to ease a racing mind. She looked, yet again, at her summons to see Principal Hayes at three fifty. No reason was stated for the visit. No explanation granted. Just the royal summons.

Her mind flipped through the litany of interactions she had with students over the past week. The thousands of words chosen. The tone and inflection used. The messages, both voice and emails, sent to parents. Nothing stood out as a cause for alarm, but that mattered little. It was almost as meaningless as her sixteen years of service. American schools taught her one thing of which she was sure: thousands of exemplary interactions, hours of dedication, and countless small victories that seldom make headlines but reverberate in young lives never earn a teacher any benefit of the doubt.

One complaint shatters the illusion that professional equity can be built. One complaint is all it takes for the questioning of professional competence and personal integrity to begin. Karen often laughed when she heard people grumble that society didn't respect teachers. What a joke. She would settle for the simple reality that administrators respected teachers. She hoped things would be different in the C.S.A., but she feared this would not be true. So she sat, conditioned by her nation of origin, assuming the worst.

Rising from her chair, Karen proceeded to Principal Hayes' office. She attempted to appear calm, but she entered the main office with far too much zeal. Julius Hayes, who stood over his administrative assistant's desk evaluating some grand plan for the following week, looked up with a start when Karen burst into the room.

"Mrs. Butler," he said kindly, "thank you for being so prompt."

"No problem," Karen mumbled, slightly embarrassed at her forceful entry.

Julius circled the desk and extended his hand to Karen. "It's nice to formerly meet you. As you know, I was reassigned to this school just two weeks ago and haven't met everyone on a singular basis yet."

"I know," Karen acknowledged. "Is that why you called me down?"

"No," Julius admitted. "Actually, I have been meeting some of the newer teachers. Your track record is exemplary, so I figured I could delay your session just a bit. There are times when talent should be left alone."

Karen, taken aback by Julius' sincerity, blushed for the second time since entering the office. "Thank you."

"You're quite welcome," Julius responded, pointing at a short corridor that led to his personal office. "Come with me." The offices for guidance counselors and support staff were passed as they approached his door.

"So, not to seem impatient, what is this meeting about?"

"I honestly don't know. All I know was in the message I sent you. A time, a location, and that there was nothing to worry about. You see, this meeting isn't with me."

Entering his passcode, the door slid open to reveal Edward "Doc" Sells standing in his black uniform, Delta insignia on his shoulders. Karen gasped because she recognized Doc from his visit to the house. "Oh my god! Did something happen to Raymond? Where —"

"He's fine," Doc stated calmly. "Everything is fine."

Karen struggled to calm herself, catching her breath and stifling her worst fears. Doc looked with disapproval at Julius. "Didn't I send instructions to inform her that there was nothing to worry about?"

"I sent that message to her," Julius stated.

"Clearly, you did a magnificent job. Leave us."

For a moment, Julius considered responding, but he recognized the limits of his authority. Swallowing his pride, he exited the room, the sliding door whispering shut behind him. Doc pulled a chair from against the wall and offered it to Karen. "Have a seat, Mrs. Butler."

Karen took a seat, and Doc did the same. He leaned back as he had no desire to rush Karen into conversation.

She coughed, releasing her throat from an invisible, choking hand and spoke. "I'm sorry. I saw you, and Raymond has not been home or in contact with us...."

"You were made aware of the possibility he could be given a stay order as part of the training?"

"I was...I just...."

"The stay order is often training for both the recruit and those dear to him or her. Your husband has been invited to join a noble but dangerous profession. There will be times of unexpected disappearance. You need to be prepared for such events."

"I get it. I do," Karen said. "You do realize that often when a teacher is told by an administrator that there is nothing to worry about, there is almost always something to worry about?"

Doc nodded his head and smiled. "Well, Mrs. Butler, in the C.S.A., we tend to say what we mean. You need to leave your American indoctrination behind."

"So we are told," Karen replied. "It's not easy, y'know. This nation is so different than the United States. Geographically so close but... so very different."

"That is by design," Doc replied. "In fact, that's the main reason I am here today."

"I...you're here to give me some kind of lesson?"

Doc laughed. "No. I am not the teacher. I'll leave the lessons to you. I need to talk to you about your husband."

"Raymond? You said he was fine."

"He is. He is scheduled to be teleported to your home at four fifteen today. You will see him soon. He is struggling a little bit with his training. I was hoping you might be able to help him adjust to this new job."

"I don't understand. I don't know what you're asking me to do."

"You will," Doc stated with confidence. "You know what he has been recruited for, correct?"

"Yes. To become a purifier. That's what you call them, right?"

"Correct. Do you know what we do? Being wed to a purifier can be quite a challenge."

Karen hesitated before opting for an honest reply. "I don't know much about your world."

"Completely understandable. Did you watch Commander Kurt Adams give his interview about a month ago?"

"We did," Karen shared. "You visited us not long after."

"Four days after," Doc clarified. "You were slow to enroll in our programs."

"I know. But we —"

Doc waved his hand, swatting the words away. "Not concerned about that. Do you recall how you felt watching the interview?"

"I do."

"Describe it."

"I was a bit...scared by what I heard and what I saw. That woman shot that man on international television. Yet, I was not convinced she was wrong to do it. I didn't like watching it, but he was a sexual predator. I was more shocked than anything. Anyway, I remember feeling...gratified...by the strength that Commander Adams exhibited. His confidence. His passion and conviction were...well...inspiring. The C.S.A. is building great lives...."

"...But you fear the cost?"

"Yes," Karen said sadly, "but then I see how happy Lizzie is. And her friends. Lord, they are thriving, and it makes you wonder if —"

"When in doubt, trust the love you feel for your daughter," Doc interjected. "The joy you feel when envisioning her bright future, as well as her substantive present. That is the key to all this. Every subsequent generation must be handed a precious and tangible societal gift. They must come to age in such a way they are worthy of being handed this gift and have the requisite skills to increase its value for the next generation. Your profession is a vital component of this process. Your husband's potential profession safeguards the process."

"Raymond. You said he needed help adjusting to his new job. What did you mean?"

"Do you know why I recruited your husband?"

"He said you saw him as a protector."

"Indeed," Doc said. "He is a fine guardian of your family. He would do much to keep you safe. I believe this noble trait can be expanded to make him a sentinel for our society. However, to be a purifier requires the sullying of one's hands. Cleaning a society requires removing the filth. It is unavoidable. It is ongoing. Your husband clings to American conditioning that may hinder his success."

"Can't he just quit the training? I mean, he said you told him he could remain a security guard at Blackclaw."

"I did say that. I meant it at the time."

"At the time? What are you saying?"

"I am saying the river flows. Time moves forward and things change. For example, prior to activation of the Freedom Accounts, people could choose to leave the C.S.A. Once activated, you are a citizen for the rest of your life. Actions have true outcomes. Now at the time of our initial conversation, he had that clean choice: follow the path of recruitment or remain in an adjusted role at Blackclaw. And he chose the path to being a purifier. He has partaken in activities. He has seen and heard things that cannot be undone. Statistically speaking, recruits who feel a need to back out...quit as you said... at this point often become quite destabilized psychologically and emotionally. They can never go back to the way they once were and, having failed to progress through the training, become lost. Unhealthy decisions are often made. I would not want to see your husband suffer the debilitation of losing his equilibrium. You do not want that suffering brought to your house. He needs your help to push forward."

"So you think he may suffer from some kind of stress disorder? Anxiety? Can't you give him help?"

"Neither of us are psychologists and, therefore, should avoid diagnosing people. Furthermore, even with help, seventy-eight per-cent of recruits who stagnate at this point become irretrievable. You do not want this for your family."

"I...of course not." Something in Karen, a dull ache, became a sharp pain. A raw nerve exposed to the cold. *You do not want this for your family*. This. What horror was entangled in that single word? In her discomfort, she looked to Doc for solace. "What can I do?"

"The simplest of things, really. Just encourage him to stick with the program. To see his role as protector and guardian clearly. The benefits to your family when he succeeds will be significant."

Karen exhaled anxiety and drew a deep breath of purpose. "I understand."

Doc stood as she looked to the floor, seeking more words. "Other than my business card, I have no more to share with you. If you have no questions, we can conclude this productive encounter."

Karen stood up and found herself thanking Doc as she reached for the card. Her hand trembled slightly as she took it. If Doc noticed this, he did not acknowledge it. He merely thanked Karen for her time. The intention to leave collided with the desire for information, causing her to hesitate. She looked at Doc and, with the timidity one might exhibit before looking at an open wound, asked a final question. "I...I think you are the one to ask this. Some of my fifth graders are no longer living with their families. Some have not seen their older siblings in some time. Do you know where they are?"

"How are the moods of these students?"

"Honestly, quite good. They seem healthier than they did in the past. More at ease. But still...."

"Is your question more valuable than the well-being you see in these students? The promise they now hold in actuality as opposed to the voices of those who speak shallow slogans?"

"I can't help but wonder."

"As you said," Doc stated with haunting conviction, "the C.S.A. is trying to build great lives. You should take quite seriously the idea that actions have very real, often unwanted, outcomes. That there are things that once seen and heard cannot be undone. Do, however, feel free to ask your question again."

A tap on the desk and the door slid open. Karen stood in space between the corridor leading from Principal Hayes' office and Special Agent Edward "Doc" Sells and his unrelenting gaze.

"Thanks again for your help," Karen said before turning to the corridor.

"A pleasure," responded Doc. "Do keep that precious daughter of yours in your heart and mind."

CHAPTER 27

THE PRICE OF PATIENCE

Spreadsheets. Charts. Probability algorithms. Spending trends. Not one bit of it revealing much more to Special Agent Bill Cullen than what his observation already uncovered. Watching people always revealed their true intentions. Actions disclosed so much more than the words that flow freely from most mouths in the hopes of creating linguistic bridges capable of spanning the chasm between one's actions and intentions. Bill, by his own admission, was far from the most educated of purifiers. He did, however, have a great gift for reading people. Social scientists, who would view him as a simple rube, would consider it a blessing to have his powers of observation. These abilities drove Commander Kurt Adams to instate the Gamma officer as the superintendent of all penitentiaries in the state of Louisiana. While initially flattered by the show of trust, Bill was far more comfortable with his boots on the ground than on a desk.

"Special Agent Cullen," MLB 770-A stated politely while entering the room.

Bill, quite pleased to have his lackluster analysis of a spreadsheet that offered no useful information interrupted, waved the automaton forward. "Whatcha got, 770-A?"

"Commander Adams has arrived. He —"

"He would have words with you," Adams interrupted as he stepped into the room. Making a quick gesture, he ordered Bill to stay seated even as he turned his attention to the MLB. "Be gone."

MLB 770-A exited the room swiftly, and Adams grabbed a chair. Bill, attempting to sit casually, watched the commander closely. Adams noticed Bill's intense focus on him and emitted a chuckle at the absurdity he saw before him. "Bill," Adams said with a smile, "what the fuck are you so stressed about?"

"I...I just wasn't expectin' a visit from you today, sir."

"And what? You think I am here to do you harm?"

"Nope," Bill blurted quickly. Too quickly. He had known this man for four years and was still nervous to be alone in a room with him. This revelation made Bill chuckle as well. "No, sir. I don't think that at all."

"That's good. Then we can talk calmly. I am curious about your recent educational session held at Blackclaw," Adams said.

"It was a routine session," Bill began, still fighting the urge to recoil. "Every objective was met and nothin' unexpected occurred."

"Outstanding," Adams noted. "Exactly what I would expect from you."

"Thank you, sir."

"So that being true, why am I here?"

A silence, which made only one of the men uncomfortable, filled the room. Bill was unable to bear the roar any longer and spoke candidly. "Sir, I don't know what yer gettin' at."

"I think you do."

Again silence reigned, stunning in its volume and mystic in its capacity to isolate. Bill shifted under his inquisitor's gaze as he searched for the correct words. "You didn't want me to remedy any of the students."

"No, I did not."

"Okay. I ran the recruit drill as instructed. One recruit was particularly unimpressive, but Doc had been sent to address that issue. It's clear you didn't expect me to aggressively address that issue."

"Correct. Keep going, Bill. You're doing fine."

"Feels that way," Bill said, hoping the wry comment would lighten the mood.

"It should," Adams' answered to Bill's surprise.

"You think I went too far with some of my off the cuff comments?" Bill offered in an entirely unconvinced tone. "Y'know... erotic release...circle jerk around some shithead...." Bill looked at Adams, now smiling despite himself, and answered his own question. "That's not it."

"No. Truth be told, I rather enjoyed your monologue. But you are getting warmer."

"Am I? So somethin' I said then. Somethin' I said brings you here."

"Yes," Adams said frankly.

"Very good. But...somethin' of a curiosity to you." Bill leaned back in his chair, finally convinced that he could be at ease. His eyes glistened, serpentine and sure. A smile borne of gleeful malice lit his face as he spoke. "I so wish my orders were to kill y'all."

"That's the phrase," Adams said to his junior officer. "That is what brings me here."

"Really? For what we do, that is hardly a provocative statement."

"I agree. I am curious why you said it," Adams said.

"Why? Just seemed like the thing to say at the time."

Adams shook his head, rejecting the notion sharply. "No. Even granting there is some truth in that reason, it is not the full reason. It is not even the largest slice of the pie chart."

"I suppose yer right," Bill stated, scanning Adams in a natural attempt to read him.

"Tell me, Bill. Tell me the genesis of that statement."

Bill breathed deeply and exhaled. He held Adams' stare for two ticks of the clock and looked away. When his focus returned to

Adams, his voice rose, sure of his answer and unsure of its reception. "They're all waste, Commander. All of 'em."

"Explain."

"At the time of initiation, we usually clean the bottom ten percent of a population. We then assess what's left behind. Give it time to reveal itself. A new bottom ten percent is formed. Within three years, ninety-six percent of those with a liquidation cost of eight or less are cleaned up. Ninety-six percent. That's pretty significant."

"I see," Adams stated. "So you think we are too gentle in phase one of the initiation protocols?"

"Gentle? Nah, that's not it. I think too patient is a better phrase. Why wait? We know how it ends."

"Can you fathom the effort? The planning and manpower it would take to target twenty percent during phase one? We, as you stated, get to that malignant population eventually. Why rush?"

Bill shrugged. "I guess. Still, we already know who they are, and I think we could handle it. I really do. Why wait? Besides, another seven percent tends to be exorcised over the next four years."

"I see that as all the more reason for the temperate approach. So many fall into our traps eventually. Why risk an operation too large to contain?"

"I get that point. I do." Bill stopped talking, hesitant to proceed further into this uncharted territory.

"But you believe there is risk in patience."

"I...." Bill paused again. "Sir, I am feelin' quite uncertain. Is this merely a rhetorical exercise? What're we doin' here?"

Adams smiled and nodded his head. "I understand, Bill. Revolutions, as you know, are an unfolding process. There does come a time when younger revolutionaries, rightfully so, question the direction or veracity of the old guard. It is the nature of these things. I am the steward of the revolution. I sometimes wonder, however, if additional steps need to be taken to not only safeguard what we have but to, perhaps, expedite the process. As I am younger than the prime minister, you are, to a lesser degree, younger than I. So I do wonder what risks you see. I think you see patience as a risky venture."

"I do, sir. I truly do. We know people are easily influenced by others. If we were to eliminate twenty percent in phase one, it would greatly reduce the amount of moronic voices in the world. Maybe save us some work down the road?"

Adams inhaled deeply and exhaled slowly before responding. "That's a worthy question. One I have been wrestling with myself. Do we need more destabilization...more tension...to eradicate not only those of low character but vices held in the hearts of the average citizen?"

"I'm not sure, Commander. What I do know is the stream of fucks coming to this place is pretty consistent. Which means people are out there, spreading their bullshit and bendin' the soft backbone of the...um...what did you call 'em? The average citizens, yeah, weakening those fuckers."

Adams leaned forward in his chair. Bill would not have been surprised if the senior officer's unblinking glower burned a hole through the floor and created a new cavern in the earth. Leaning back, Adams' features softened before he spoke. "So, despite our best efforts, more people than perhaps we even suspect cannot be freed of their enculturation. This is your contention? That to eliminate the largest number of miscreants upfront prevents their putrid influence from spreading."

"I do believe that, sir. We would benefit from a harder reset."

"A harder reset. More brutality to enhance humanity. And you would be comfortable with this challenge."

"Of course, sir," Bill confirmed. "I would look forward to it. Is there anythin' else?"

Adams rose from his chair. "Not at the moment. I will see myself out, thank you."

"Very good, sir," Bill said, pride swelling over being included in this conversation. Before exiting the room, Adams turned to address Bill one last time. "Two and a half, by the way."

"Two and a half? I'm not followin'."

"I knew Doc for two and a half years before having such a conversation with him. I've known you four. You still have some catching up to do."

CHAPTER 28

COMMITMENT

Laura rolled to her side, balanced somewhere between the haze of light sleep and wakefulness. Her right arm swung in a low arc but, rather than fall on Kurt's body, it flopped onto the bed where he usually lay. Perhaps it was this minor disruption in the patterns of sleep that caused Laura to spring upright with a start, trying to see through a preconscious haze around the empty room.

"Kurt?" she called sleepily as her feet found the floor. "Are you here?"

She staggered from the bedroom and fumbled with the mysteries of the sleeves on her satin robe. The puzzle solved, she looked across the living room to see Kurt standing before the windows that let the world into the penthouse apartment. The darkness of the night, penetrated by lingering city lights and dim stars, felt all encompassing. Kurt stood with his hands behind his back, at once appearing to be both wanderer and guardian of the shadows.

"Kurt?" Laura asked again, slightly louder as it was clear his distance from her was greater than the expanse of the apartment.

Her voice successfully hit its mark, and he turned to greet her as if noticing Laura for the first time. "I'm sorry, didn't hear you enter the room." He stepped away from the window and toward the couches. She joined him there, taking a seat and reaching up to him. When he took her hand, she pulled him onto the couch.

"What are you...?" they began simultaneously, causing both to smile.

Kurt brought some order to the proceedings. "You first."

"What are you doing up?" Laura's concern was muted by the fatigue she was still staggering through.

He brushed a few strands of her hair from her forehead and chuckled. Laura exhaled serenely but persisted. "I don't think my hair will stay in place," she stated before repeating her question.

"The simple and boring answer is I couldn't sleep. What about you? Why are you up?"

"I'm up because you're up." Laura smiled.

"You don't need to be. That's why I left the room."

"I know," Laura said, head settling onto Kurt's shoulder for a few moments before she sat back up. "It's just, you never have trouble sleeping. I rolled over, you weren't there, and it startled me. I mean...you are an early riser...but three in the morning? I was surprised."

"Three twenty-two," Kurt stated.

"Really? That's what you're going to focus on?"

"Evidently."

"C'mon, Kurt," Laura pleaded, "what's bothering you?"

"Why is it that something must be bothering me?"

"Because you always sleep through the night. Always."

Kurt nodded his head as he looked about the room. The calm of the early morning invited him to surrender to the connections sometimes only found at the most serene of hours. He looked at Laura and kissed her forehead before sinking back into the couch. "I think," Kurt said, taking in the expectant expression on Laura's face, "I murdered someone recently."

Laura's expression transitioned from expectant to perplexed. "Murdered?" she asked. "I don't...I mean...okay, listen. I don't know much about what you do, but I know you and all purifiers kill. I don't understand what you mean. Murdered? What are you talking about?"

"I'm not entirely sure. I killed someone recently, and I find myself questioning that decision. I never, never question such things," Kurt confessed.

"You think you should have spared this person?"

"Absolutely not," Adams said. "She was a member of a traitorous organization in Cleveland. All members of this organization were liquidated, save one. I sent her to a separate prison. For a short time, she lived."

"And, in the end, you killed her. She was a traitor?"

"Definitely."

"Then she died a traitor's death." Laura stated the well-known mantra of the citizenry.

"No," Kurt said, leaning forward. "Now if she was exorcised with her companions, that would, most definitely, be true. She died a plaything's death. That is not my role."

"Plaything? Kurt, I don't know what you mean."

Kurt stood and paced the room, his mind a more agitating agent than Laura's questions. He looked out the window, then back at the concerned woman before him. He returned to take a seat on the edge of the couch, ready to stand again should his body demand it.

"The day the initiation protocols were launched, a man, a priest, angered me. Other people of his ilk broke before me. Be it in tears or rage, the uselessness of their cause permeated the air. I find this satisfying. One man, however, was made of sterner stuff. I took him prisoner. I deviated from the protocols because I wished to break his spirit."

"But you haven't?"

"I am not sure," Kurt admitted.

"Not sure?"

"No. I used this other person...this woman...as a weapon against him. I killed her to torture him with her blood. With her loss. I have not seen him since. I am letting him wallow."

Laura looked at Kurt, stunned by his frustration but not his actions. "You can't just kill him and be done with it? Follow the protocols and move on."

"Of course, I could," Kurt said, "but...not yet. Not yet."

"What about this man is causing you such...I'm not even sure what word I should use."

"What are you thinking? What do you hear and see?" Kurt asked, truly captivated by how Laura might answer.

"My first thought was a kind of dread, but I don't think that's accurate."

"Dread? I think not."

"No," Laura said, placing her hand on Kurt's face. "That's not it. I don't...confusion? Bewilderment?"

Kurt slowly pulled Laura's hand from his cheek to his lips. He kissed her fingers and smiled. "Bewilderment. I think that's it. I do not understand this man. His conviction."

"What's to understand?"

"He is not a stupid man," Kurt stated. "He is a man, I would dare say, of some intelligence. Yet this intelligence does not save him from following a most faulty path. A path that history has shown helps nothing. Improves no one. How can a man of such promise suffer under the spell of such delusion? I don't understand that."

"And you wish him to see his error before you kill him?"

"Perhaps," Kurt said unconvincingly. "Or break him of his fallacy so he can use his formidable will and sharp mind in the service of our nation. To move him above his suspected purpose so he can improve his life and the lot of others."

"You are trying to save him."

Kurt nodded his head. "Yes, I think that's it. But it is difficult. He is stubborn, and this is an unfamiliar path. I also fear I am betraying my purpose. I am required to create a society that allows humanity to perfect itself. I do not save individuals from their own stupidity."

"There can be exceptions to our personal roles and codes. You need to be patient."

"Patient? Perhaps. I think he is close to breaking. He was not well when last I saw him."

"It's noble," Laura mused. "People can grow. Develop beyond one phase of life and embrace another. Patience is sometimes the key to that victory."

"Patience?" Kurt reiterated, smiling. "When has patience brought you victory?"

Laura moved from resting on the cushions of the couch to straddling Kurt's torso before answering. "It's here, right where I'm sitting. Us, together right now. This is proof of my patient victory."

Kurt stood up, Laura clinging to his body with legs around his waist and arms on his shoulders. "I am a sign of some victory you've won?"

"Yup," Laura proclaimed confidently before pulling his head forward for a deep kiss. She released him and turned her gaze to the bedroom. "Now mush. We shouldn't waste this quiet time together with more words."

CHAPTER 29

OBLIGATIONS

The ebb and flow of dinner table conversation can follow interesting patterns. Small talk interrupted by enthusiastic storytelling as little tales that make big differences in a life are shared with the family. Societal issues arise, often testing bonds and openness. Muted looks and held tongues leave topics untouched, even those — often those — that need discussing. And sometimes during a lull in the multiple exchanges, the simplest of observations can lead to the most necessary dialogues.

"I gotta say," Lizzie blurted out, "I love this new table! I mean…I've always thought furniture is furniture, but this table feels, I don't know, royal! Like dinner is some kind of event."

"Family dinner wasn't an event before?" Raymond asked as Karen smiled proudly, pleased that her new purchase was so well received.

"Not what I mean, Dad," Lizzie mocked in a playful tone. "Just sayin'…well, you know what I'm sayin'. Stop being difficult!"

Karen now spoke as Raymond smiled. "He would not be your father if he wasn't difficult."

"Reality," Lizzie proclaimed. "I don't know how you put up with him, Mom."

"Oh, I'm just a saint," Karen said, hands in a prayer position.

"You sure you want to open up that door?" Raymond asked, looking back and forth from his daughter to his wife.

"Some other time," Karen laughed, as she looked over the table. "It seems we're done with dinner. Sweetie, could you please clear the table and load the dishwasher?"

"Is that a request?" Lizzie asked, somehow sounding very sincere.

"No," Karen responded. "Get to it."

Lizzie groaned as she stood to begin her chore. "Alright."

"I could go for a coffee," Raymond stated. "You want one, hun?"

"Yeah," Karen said slowly. "That would be nice."

"I'm not loading the coffee mugs!" Lizzie declared as she raced about the kitchen and dining area. "Post dinner."

"That's fine," Karen said. "Don't you have a shift at the grocery store tonight?"

"Oh my god! I almost forgot that I agreed to cover for Syd! I gotta get going."

"You forgot?" Karen asked. "Then what were you rushing for?"

"Hoping to get out of the house and visit Key tonight?" Raymond asked.

"Actually, yes. We talked about that at school today, but that's out. I gotta contact her too! I need to get ready for work! Dishwasher is loaded, and I'm out." Lizzie was already exiting the room when her proclamation fell, leaving Raymond and Karen sitting at the table with their coffees.

"She's really adjusted to enjoy our life here," Karen stated happily. "It's been so good for her."

"She was always a happy kid. Even with everything she had to put up with, that core goodness was always there," Raymond remarked.

"Reality," Karen said in an attempt to imitate her daughter. "But, c'mon, you must admit she never was that pumped up about the old kitchen table before."

Raymond laughed as he scanned the room, allowing his mind to walk through the living space. "Or the couches you bought. She loves those too. As does Mom?"

Karen laughed at Raymond's questions and again when he gave her a soft poke at her ribs. "Yes, Mom likes them also. Don't forget, however, I woke you up last night when you fell asleep in that massage recliner in there. Papa's happy with the purchases too."

"I am." Raymond beamed for a moment before clouds returned. "I just...I struggle with some things."

"Like what?"

"Just, god, the new job I'm training for. It's one of controlled violence. I know the benefits to the family...what we can now afford... but the cost."

"The cost?" Karen asked sharply. "What cost? A life of comfort and opportunity for your daughter? A school, hell, a society where she gets to walk unbothered by, frankly, jerks and leeches who put her down simply because she has pride and dignity? You get to help build and maintain that."

Raymond rubbed his face and grumbled. "I know. Okay. I get it. There is a lot that feels better than just good — it feels right. I mean, real values, work ethic, and respect for others aren't just talked about but enforced."

"And that's terrible?"

"No. I...the values are great. Of course they are. It's some of what we have always tried to teach Lizzie."

"All of what we have always taught her," Karen corrected. "She even embraced those lessons despite so many different and lesser paths being offered in the United States. We are luckier than we deserve when it comes to her. Now she gets to see concrete evidence that doing things the right way has real rewards. You can't let your doubts take that away."

"Take it away? What are you talking about?"

Karen's frustration was rising. "You know, if you shy away from this new job, we could suffer consequences."

"Consequences? What are you talking about?" Raymond snapped back, legitimately confused. "Even if I just returned to my old job, our combined salaries would still afford us so much."

"And how long after you leave that job will you want to leave this country? Move back to the United States? I know you, Raymond. I know what you're thinking."

"Really? What am I thinking? Tell me what...?" Raymond stopped talking as he heard Lizzie's footfalls coming down the stairs.

She burst into the kitchen, singing as earplugs vibrated with her favorite music. The moment she saw her parents Lizzie knew something was wrong. A wristband was quickly tapped to silence the music, and to allow the world back in. "What's up, guys? You both look so serious."

"Just discussing work. The future," Raymond offered as an answer. "Things still need to be worked out with my new job."

"There's always a way to make things less stressful," Lizzie said, tapping her temple three times. Karen beamed as she saw Raymond's favorite advice to Lizzie emulated, in both word and deed, by her vibrant daughter.

"Sometimes," Raymond said.

"Noooo!" Lizzie moaned, lowering her tone to imitate her dad's voice from previous conversations. "Always. Always control your own mind."

Raymond shook his head and reluctantly smiled. He dared not look at Karen.

"And if that doesn't work...get a new grill! You gotta keep up with Mom's improvements!" Lizzie bounded to her parents, kissed each on the cheek, and bolted out the door yelling, "Can't be late. Ten minutes early is on time!"

Karen looked at Raymond, bolstered by the timely intervention of their daughter. Her hand fell on Raymond's knee as she continued, admiration flowing from where, mere seconds earlier, challenges had flowed. "What you're thinking is how can Lizzie continue to be a good person in a society that protects its values so...?"

"Ferociously," Raymond finished. "So fuckin' ferociously. Killing citizens without remorse. How can we stand for that?"

"Criminals," Karen redirected. "Killing criminals to protect your daughter and millions of good people like her. That's not a terrible thing, Raymond."

"I don't know," Raymond said, head bowed. He sighed and looked into Karen's eyes. "But what if —"

"What if she's called upon to do such things?" Karen interjected, completing Raymond's question with unfailing accuracy before offering her answer. "If you do your job, she won't have to. Don't you see? Sometimes the big picture matters most, and sometimes it's the small one. When you can't find that balance, just think of Lizzie. The rest should be easy."

Raymond patted Karen's hand as he leaned forward and kissed her forehead. "You might be right," he allowed as he stood. "I think I need a walk. I'll see you later. Maybe an hour."

"Alright," Karen said, rising up herself. "Maybe while you're out, you can look at grills." A playful wink accompanied her comment.

"Maybe," Raymond muttered, offering a forced smile to acknowledge Karen's attempt to cheer him. His flat tone communicated the distance between them. He walked out the back door, leaving Karen alone in the kitchen. She took a sip of her coffee and opened her purse. Producing the business card Special Agent Sells had provided, she grabbed her cell and dialed the number.

A polite robotic voice answered without a single ring. "Your call will be recorded and analyzed by MLB 62-B, the personal assistant to Special Agent Edward Sells. This is a priority two line, so your call will be handled with appropriate regard. Special Agent Sells only gives this number out for specific purposes. If you feel you have reached this service incorrectly, it is strongly recommended that you end your call. If you have reached us correctly, please do leave a message."

"Hello," Karen said with a quiver. She automatically turned on her teacher voice for a stronger delivery. "This is Karen Butler. Special

Agent Sells had a talk with me about my husband, Raymond. I just wanted him to know that I think Raymond will start performing better during training sessions."

She hung up the phone and whispered, "I hope," as she ripped the card into tiny pieces and pushed the scraps into the trash.

CHAPTER 30

OF GARDENS AND HILLS

A prison can never truly be a home. There is, however, the mental discipline and resolve borne from a mysterious inner wellspring that can free one's mind, making it a sanctuary in the dark. Father Roger Baudin's daily routine always included reminding himself of this fact . On good days, it was actualized. On others, this inner world was assaulted by the realities of his physical and material restraint. It buckled and bent. Never, however, was it torn asunder, for Roger knew his mind could always be his own. Blood could be extracted, and filth could cling to his body, but never could his soul be so afflicted. Emotions wore thin and fatigue crippled, but the inner wellspring waited for the weary to bring their pains and sit for a spell in tranquility. Such respite cannot be earned by lethargy. To find this fortress with its rejuvenating rivers and tranquil lakes was worth the thousand-mile inner journey. Roger knew this place well. That others might scoff at such things was inconsequential, for their words did not alter the experience of his life. The words of superior cynics rarely helped those trapped in a personal hell.

It was this ability to free his mind that kept Roger grounded in his silent prison. The other prisoners still dared not speak to him. They rarely acknowledged his presence; all shared the fear that a glance or nodding head may bring a swift death. An unspoken pact had slowly developed among the inmates, and complaints of their plight were shared with decreasing regularity. All recognized that Roger, from crushing events like Zitai's death to petty torments like removing his cot or allowing his waste bucket to overflow, was ever worse off.

Despite this unusual resolve, heads fixated on the floor, and bodies sought the corners of cells when Commander Adams appeared for another visit with Roger, as if avoiding the devil's gaze kept one safe from his power. Roger was the exception to this behavior. While others trembled, he rose from his cot, preparing to be true to himself and stand unbroken before his jailer.

"Father," Adams said as he opened the door to his foe's cell, "you look...rested."

Roger, silently noting the surprise in Adams' voice, answered in controlled tones. "There is not much left for me to do but rest. I guess I've gotten good at it."

"Indeed," Adams said, closing the door behind him. Two plush reclining chairs appeared in the cell. Adams took one and gestured for Roger to do the same. Roger touched his chair as if questioning its existence. Satisfied it was real, he cautiously lowered himself into the chair, eventually settling into a comfortable position.

Adams held his thoughts as he watched the prolonged decent from standing to sitting. "Are you comfortable?"

"In some ways," Roger responded. "What are you here to take today?"

"You've not much left."

Roger nodded. "I suppose. I try to make do with what I have."

"You have nothing," Adams snapped with sharp certainty. "Nothing of value, anyway."

"And yet I warrant these visits," Roger countered. "While those around me are killed or forced into terrified silence, I merely linger. Both within this cell and...elsewhere."

"Elsewhere?"

"I must, at least on occasion, occupy a place in your mind."

"As a curiosity," Adams stated.

"How odd that a man who has nothing of value would be a curiosity to a man who has so much. I wonder why that is?"

"You do more than wonder," Adams noted, an amused smile appearing briefly on his face. He studied Roger's face, gazing into wrinkles and dirt, and continued in a semblance of the same polite tones the MLBs occasionally utilized. "What is the grand theory you have developed alone in this dark place?"

Roger paused a moment as he considered the precise words he wanted to use. That he would respond was never in doubt. Settling upon his phrasing, Roger leaned forward and spoke with solemnity. "We are both men of tremendous faith, you and I. This confounds you."

Adams' laugh exploded forth quite unexpectedly. It stole his capacity to speak for a few moments of malicious mirth before the waves crashed. Still chuckling, he said, "Thank you, Father. I probably don't laugh as often as I should. Did you just call me a man of faith?"

"Only because you are. All people are. We have just so effectively mangled the word 'faith' with faulty definitions and grotesque misunderstandings that we don't even know what the concept insinuates and encapsulates anymore. We are all people of faith," Roger repeated, looking wistfully at the ceiling. He exhaled, returning his gaze to Adams. "This, to be clear, does not make us religious. Also, a religious person can be an awful example of faith."

"Father, I think more damage has been done to you than either of us realized. You are bordering on speaking gibberish. Please do, however, continue."

Roger looked at Adams, perplexed. It was not the words but the tone, as well as Adams' body posture and facial movements that caused confusion. Try as he might, Roger could not discern if, in this deadpanned observation, there was actual concern or merely more mockery. Moreover, he could not ascertain what was happening in the cell. Rather than dodge about, he confronted his confusion. "What are we doing? Why are you opening this avenue of conversation?"

"Well," Adams said flatly, "you don't get to talk much anymore. I thought a good conversation about a topic you enjoy would be welcome." He was leaning back in his chair. Legs crossed and body slumping slightly, the captor needed a glass of whiskey to complete the look of visiting friend.

Roger drew a breath. "Let's say I choose to believe you."

"How very magnanimous, Father," scoffed Adams.

"Continuing on. What is that phrase you use with new citizens when referring to the United States? The nation of your origin? Is that it?"

"Indeed," Adams said. He smirked as he wondered why Roger would ask such a question.

"Your understanding of faith is very American," Roger stated. "It is quite sad, really, that a failure to understand vocabulary should cause so much animosity and angst. Derision and ridicule. You are correct, you know, that the nation of my origin is replete with faults. We are not nearly as thoughtful as we like to think. In fact, the more people feel emboldened to speak without knowledge, the stupider the nation of my origin becomes."

"Hardly complimentary, Father. Shall I take your confession?"

"Well, hopefully you can forgive my impertinence. It's been a rough few weeks."

"I know it has," Adams stated proudly. "Regardless, there is much in that statement to digest, Father. Enlighten me. How has faith been misrepresented in the nation of your origin?"

"I fear in most nations...," Roger said, a well of sadness momentarily opening in his soul. He fell silent for numerous seconds.

Adams leaned forward as he offered encouragement to continue. "Don't back off now, Father. Consider this an opportunity to win a convert."

It was now Roger's turn to laugh, nothing boisterous or loud, merely a small chortle as he brushed the thought aside. Settling his mind, Roger responded, "I am no miracle worker."

"Touché. But please, do continue."

"Very well. Let me ask, which came first: schools or intellectual curiosity and accomplishments?"

"I am not interested in playing a game with rhetorical questions," Adams stated, "especially when the answer is obvious."

"I understand," Roger said. "Intellectual curiosity and growth. Invention itself predated schools and universities. Those institutions are dedicated, primarily, to a human attribute. Artistic drive predates museums. Again, institutions follow our humanity. Physical activity and sport predated events, gymnasiums, and athletic leagues. And faith, a human attribute, predated the institutions of religion. Religions are not the genesis of faith. We are the spring from which faith flows. Humans have faith; the question is where to place it."

"But according to you, most people don't understand what faith is. So how can we place it?"

"We are capable of hating, loving, being afraid, and being roused to compassion without being entirely sure why any of these phenomena occur as they occur. Surely, then, people can place their faith without knowing exactly what faith is. To be clear and, frankly, succinct, faith is the limitless human drive...the quest...for purpose and meaning. We place our faith in a litany of things in the hopes that these various pursuits will satisfy our faith."

"But you are saying it won't," Adams noted.

Roger continued, "Correct. Mind you, not because what we choose is necessarily bad, but because what we choose is finite. Let's say someone puts their faith — their pursuit for ultimate meaning — into their work. Faith is far too large to be satisfied by one's work, even if they love it. Faith stretches to infinity. Infinite satisfaction is too much to demand from one's work. Seeking it there will only bring frustration, hence broken faith and existential crisis as we seek meaning and purpose."

"You are quite the philosopher," Adams teased, a compliment wrapped in jest. "So, to satisfy this ultimate concern, you put your faith in the church and found satisfaction."

"Oh god no," Roger chuckled, sitting back in his chair. "Placing faith in a human institution would only lead to frustration."

"You have no faith in your church?"

"The metaphor and symbolism of my Christian traditions make sense to me. It is, actually, a rather effective map of reality. But my faith? Don't mistake a vehicle for a destination. Otherwise, you would get in a car to go to a concert, turn on a radio, and declare, 'We made it!'"

"Something in what you're saying, Father, makes faith sound quite cheap."

"Can you indulge me to ask one question?" Roger asked, leaning forward slightly in his chair. "It is not rhetorical."

"Indeed."

"Do you believe there is art in cooking?"

"Yes. There can be."

"I agree," Roger said, "but when I cook, there is no art. There is merely some kind of clumsy attempt to follow a prescribed recipe. Yet, the same recipe in the hands of another...something extra is infused. Art is not merely confined to sculpture and painting. Teaching, parenting, cooking, dance, architecture, athletic endeavor...all these activities can carry art, but not all who engage in them are artists of the activity. If the creative drive of people can spill into anything, then why is it so hard to conceive the human drive for purpose and meaning cannot?"

"Even if I allow for this possibility, you still have not provided a true answer to my question."

"What question is that?"

"Where do you place your faith?" Adams asked, intensity building in his eyes and emanating in the slow delivery of his question.

"You asked that?"

"I did."

Roger smiled, amused by some racing thoughts. "Then I will answer. But first, you just reminded me of something. Something important I forgot to say."

"Heaven forbid you don't share it," Adams said through a smile.

Roger paused before speaking, allowing Adams' gentle barb to drift from the room. "Belief, despite how hard people try to make it so, is not the same as faith. They are not synonyms. This simple error creates much confusion."

"I think I understand what you mean. We can return to that if need be. But tell me, Father, where do you place your faith? In God?"

"I find the less I talk about God, the better off God and I are. A time bound and finite mind existing within the confines of a particular space can never truly comprehend that which is timeless, infinite, and beyond the restrictions of limited comprehension. I try to avoid such hubris. But the essence of my faith is relational. And, yes, the mystery that is God is the foundation of this understanding."

"Relational?"

"Yes." Roger looked far beyond the confines of his cell. He breathed deeply and exhaled. "Sometimes, when all is quiet, I sense...I don't know...suspect is likely the correct word. Yes, I suspect there is a natural, interrelated aspect of reality itself. Relationships with others, with reality, with life in the grandest definition are all part of some nearly incomprehensible pattern. I try to serve that pattern while not force fitting into my limited, preconceived notions. As I said, the metaphors and symbolism of my traditions help me make sense of this process. The mystical body of Christ. The webs of karma. I...." Roger paused, angst spreading across his face. "Why are you giving me so much room to speak? I don't understand. This whole...whatever it is...makes no sense."

"Suffice it to be that I am curious what you will say."

"But none of what I say matters to you."

"Perhaps. Perhaps you should try to avoid force fitting this conversation into preconceived patterns, and just let it be. What other choices do you have?"

"I can be silent again," Roger responded.

"True."

"But you are correct," Roger noted. "I am en...the opportunity to speak is welcomed."

"As it should be," Adams noted. "Shall we continue?"

Roger nodded his head, suddenly looking weary.

Adams reignited the conversation with friendly ease. "I will say this: your description of reality was quite elegant. Do not take that to mean I agree. I merely enjoyed your poetic interpretation of reality."

"I understand. I do," Roger said.

"I know," Adams stated. "You, despite your vocation, are not a dumb man. Misguided, but not stupid."

"That thought intrigues you?"

Adams remained in his chair, still leaning comfortably as if enjoying an open conversation with an old friend and not a prisoner in a cage. "Perhaps."

"I must say the depth of your belief intrigues me," Roger confessed.

"Belief? I hold no beliefs."

"Everyone has beliefs, rather like we all have faith," Roger said, brushing Adams' assertion aside. "Remember, beliefs are different than faith. People go to bed at night with the belief they will wake up in the morning. We couldn't drive a car if we did not believe the other drivers were skilled. It would be too horrifying."

"Such beliefs are based on evidence."

"All belief is based on evidence," Roger shot back. "Now, you may not like or agree with the evidence utilized or how it is interpreted. You may know something that falsifies the evidence, but no one believes anything for no reason."

"And you say the depth of my belief intrigues you. What belief do you think I hold so dear?"

"You believe in the perfectibility of human beings. You live, strive, fight, and push that belief every single day. You have an unflinching belief in the capacity of some aspect of human beings to improve. To become better tomorrow than they are today. You also believe you have discovered the method to make that happen. You are a man of deep conviction and belief."

"If that were true, Father, that I believe people perfectible, then why do I treat them so...roughly...at times."

"I would surmise it is because you also believe people have no intrinsic value. No inherent right to dignity and compassion. They are trained and trainable. Conditioned, I believe, is what a psychologist would say. You contend that some conditioning can't be reversed, or the effort of the reversal is outweighed by the benefits. Many are just too far gone and, therefore, expendable to your crusade."

"You speak as if you know me quite well, Father. Could it be because we share the same belief?"

"I doubt that," Roger stated sharply.

"Easy, Father. It's really quite simple. You also believe in the perfectibility of people. However, you also believe in the inherent worth of people. That *Homo sapiens* are imbued with a natural dignity and, therefore, have a right to compassionate treatment. No one, in your world, is too far gone. If we are patient enough, persistent enough, determined enough, and benevolent enough, the wondrous spark of humanity can be ignited. The sinner saved. Are you sure you are not trying to convert me, Father? Do you intend to make me a religious man?"

Roger snorted at the idea. "No. I could not claim that is my goal. But there are many paths available, not just yours and mine. I wonder, could you question your belief in your methods enough to leave the path of blood behind while adhering to your other convictions? Could you leave the empire built on blood behind and still seek the perfectibility of people?"

"There is but one reality," Adams asserted, leaning forward in his chair. "There is but one human nature. The evidence of history screams the abject failure of compassionate paths to truly improve the human condition. The prison of nice and kind suffocates people slowly unto their deaths."

Roger, to the surprise of both Adams and himself, chuckled again. "I'm sorry," he said, smiling absurdly. "It's just, oh, that was well said.

Very well said. I even agree with some of it. Nice and kind can be a prison of sorts."

"You agree with that?"

"Absolutely," Roger said vigorously. "My lord, I have met many people who do the kind thing without seeming to care if it is the helpful thing. There are so many who seem to believe the most important outcome of their kindness is that they know they were kind! That others congratulate them for their kindness, while the problems they address continue unsolved! But at least they were kind. I do not endorse impotent kindness or egotistical altruism. Make no mistake."

It was Adams' turn to smile, as he found himself nodding in agreement with his prisoner's words. "Well played, Father. It seems I have not extinguished your fire."

"Despite your efforts to do so."

"Indeed. Thank you for noticing."

"You're not very subtle."

Adams grinned, enjoying the fact Roger still had the audacity to offer these small quips. Pointing his finger at his foe, Adams continued. "Now, you mentioned earlier the importance of the metaphor and symbols of your tradition. Tell me, have they assisted you in some manner? Is that how you still possess some fire in your belly?"

"Of course they have," Roger said.

"Explain."

"Let's start with this," Roger said, unflinching under the commander's attention. "You descended on me with scorn and abuse. Brought suffering to me as life always will. I staggered and fell under the weight you placed upon me. I rose and fell. Allies came to help carry my load or wipe my brow. They were all appreciated. Suffering persisted, as it tends to do. But I battled on, for there is always an underlying hope that the tides may turn."

"There is no hope for you, Father. Your story will end in this cell in filth and failure. Make no mistake."

Roger sighed, a gentle knowing emitting a dim light in his eyes. "I did not say the tides would turn for me. I am an older man and, even without your assistance, my time in the story is about done. This story is, and always has been, much bigger than that. So much bigger than me. Why can't people see that? The tides, in time, will turn. It is as inevitable as the scorn you feel."

"So you feel no sense of failure, even confined as you are?"

"There is a time for every purpose," Roger stated as the dim light faded; a sadness held in some cerebral vault swirled about him. He spoke now, not from some inner garden but from the gallows. "Yes, I have failed. I have failed to effectively wean people from their selective sympathy. To help them understand that your path only harms. Sadly, those harmed will inevitably return that harm to the perceived source, creating a loop of retribution that is difficult to escape, because we seem so intent on winning victory over others instead of victory within. In that, I have failed very often."

"Selective sympathy...what an interesting phrase," Adams said admiringly, the vault of his mind locking the thought away for safe-keeping. "How do you define this concept?"

"I think you already know," Roger groaned, suddenly fatigued. His voice rose from a place of isolation, a loneliness that existed far beyond the cell that held him. "It is as simple as it is tragic. The nation of my origin started so very long ago to hand out sympathy based on what at best can be called tribal affiliation. Those who received sympathy had to be a member of the right group, be it racial, ethnic, gender, age, economic, geographic, and so many others. Many tribes formed. All chasms and no bridges. We progressed from ranking those who received sympathy to making lists to see who deserved sympathy. Only if the correct boxes on some generically generated checklist were marked did a person even deserve sympathy. I would say we became divisive, but there was no we. Just groups, all suffering from something, facing each other with a sense of the moral superiority of being in their group. 'We' ceased to exist. And with it, common humanity slipped from sight, and cruelty of thought, word, and deed caused more rifts as all spoke and none listened. We. A word that can heal was left in tatters, trampled by those who did not truly want to end suffering; they just wanted to rule the plains of pain."

"Exactly, Father," Adams hissed, his convictions pouring from his core. "History reveals the lie of shared humanity. You know this. Yet you cling to your delusions. Let reality guide you to the only conclusion that is sensible. There is no shared humanity. It is something to be forged, not something granted by birth."

"So you say," Roger responded, leaning forward. "But egocentric concerns, shortsightedness, exclusivity, and cruelty all arise from people. I see that clearly every day. You say nothing new. Also from people arise true acts of altruism, kindness, patient teaching, humble learning, and openness to the proverbial other. You see one as real and one as a sham. I see both existing in people. Your path promotes struggle but, in the end, the value of a person is conferred by others. By the world. By you. Others take the role of validating the value of others. What an arrogant position to take. But for me, the glory and horror of people exist simultaneously within all. Value exists by the virtue of existence. I don't confer value to a person. It exists without my consent. Or yours. So I work through the worst of people to get to the best of them. That is my path. It has served me well, because it shows me both heaven and hell."

Adams rose from his chair and it to disappeared. He twisted his head to one side, his neck cracking in response. He looked down at Roger, who remained seated. "Well, Father, that is enough. You remain a thoughtful and deluded man."

"I guess that's my cross," Roger said. "Should I stand? Is my chair about to disappear as well?"

Adams furrowed his brow and shook his head as he dismissed the notion. "Not yet. To be honest, however, it will be taken from here in five minutes."

"Thanks for the warning."

"Indeed. You know, Father, there are few people I call an opponent whom I can say I respect more than you. It's quite a thing, really. It's almost amazing."

"Amazing? How is it amazing?"

"Because of how much I hate you."

The utterance of the word 'hate' signaled MLB 498-A to teleport a pistol to Adams. The gun appeared, as planned, in the air before Adams' chest. In a single, swift motion, he snatched the gun and discharged it, ending Roger's life. He looked at the body, now slumped in the comfortable chair and shot it three more times. He strolled from the cell and paused, looking at the other prisoners shuddering in their cages.

"498?"

"Yes, sir. What do you need?"

"Liquidate this cellblock."

"Very well."

Stone teleported from Skadi and was replaced by MLB 498-A. The android went from cell to cell, killing each inmate, snapping necks like twigs. As it methodically completed its macabre mission, the chair holding Father Roger Baudin's body disappeared.

CHAPTER 31

AN INDISPUTABLE PATH

The keys on Kurt Adams' computer endured one forceful blow after another as he fervently worked to create a new command mission for Orcus and MLBs alike. His eyes raced across the screen, absorbing new information from probability calculations for the order's impact and success. The schematic projected before him was a map of the world, different cities and locales highlighted by various colors and labels. When necessary, a glance at this map and a whispered code word would open additional windows with information regarding the accentuated locations. Occasionally, he would nod and even smirk; he did love moving the revolution forward. A blinking green light to his left caught his attention, and he quickly tapped it. "Adams here."

"Commander," Erin McGreggor responded with placid formality. "I have been informed you wish to speak with me."

"Indeed." Adams made a final array of keystrokes and pushed his rolling chair away from his master console. The pause between this activity and his next statement was no more than three seconds. "I have a request to make of you."

"I see. Given your willingness to participate in the forthcoming gala, I will endeavor to be of assistance."

"Thank you. I...." Adams paused as he gripped the armrests of his chair, distracted by an unexpected thought that danced across his mind. "I am sorry. Do you remember why we never pursued inventing hovering chairs? We have gurneys that hover, so why not apply that technology to chairs?"

"Of course I do," Erin said with restrained enthusiasm. "My grandfather killed that pursuit. He noted, quite correctly I think, that gurneys have a true function, especially before teleportation was mastered."

Adams noted, "Exactly. We learned, in grizzly fashion, that people with certain wounds cannot be teleported without devastating results."

"Yes," Erin groaned, her voice communicating her repulsion. "I never witnessed the results, but I've read the reports."

"It is not a sight you would want to see. But hovering chairs? Your grandfather thought that a frivolous waste of money and effort. The cost of creation was high, as would be the purchase price. These old rolling chairs perform their function as well now as two hundred years ago. Why waste money, effort, and time on a project that's purpose is ultimately nothing more than a gimmick?"

"That is what he argued," Erin concurred, smiling at the thought of one of Daniel McGreggor's smaller imprints on the C.S.A. She wrote a note to make some additions to her speech. "He made the same argument for hovering...um...flying, I suppose, cars."

"Don't forget the safety issue. People struggle with the one-hundred-eighty-degree plane of driving. The creation of lanes on a three-hundred-sixty-degree highway would be more dangerous than beneficial."

"As well as the skills required to maneuver such a vehicle."

"That too," Adams stated cordially.

"You're familiar with his arguments on these issues?" Erin asked, not hiding her shock. "Forgive me, but I am surprised."

"You should not be. He was the founder of the revolution. His thoughts are essential to its upkeep and sustainability. I immerse myself in the pursuit of such knowledge that makes me more efficient."

"I meant no disrespect, Commander."

"I realize that."

"Good." The tension of the moment still unrelieved, Erin decided to awkwardly pivot the conversation. "You have a request?"

"I do," Adams stated with increased formality. "It is no secret that Commissar Velazquez and I struggle to find common ground."

"This is true. I do believe it is the nature of your distinct roles that makes this difficult. You strive relentlessly to create a harmonized and homogenous society, a united and grand vision of 'we'. She, reaching out to foreign nations, encounters the 'thems' of the world and strives to create harmonized relations within a heterogeneous world."

"I concur with this assessment," Adams said. "Our roles create tension between us. I think, however, I have found a way to overcome the chasm between our nation and others. To help create a larger sense of 'we' with foreign nations. And, to be honest, within our own borders."

"Really? That sounds promising. What is your plan?"

"Well," Adams began, reluctance softening his tone, "I am still refining the idea. Sharing it before its time would create more confusion than clarity."

"You want me to set up the meeting for us? You, me, and Commissar Velazquez."

Adams' delivery turned forceful. "No. I will contact her and set the meeting when it will be fruitful. All I ask of you is to relay my desire to fill this chasm between us. She will be speculative if I say this. If, however, you think my intentions are sincere, you may help her be less guarded about the meeting. I do not feel the need to waste time proving my sincerity. I prefer to get to work."

"She will doubt you; this is true," Erin said. "She will doubt me as well."

"But less so."

"Agreed." Erin hesitated a moment before continuing with certainty. "I will speak with the commissar of foreign affairs. It may help if you give me some details."

"Understood but declined, Madam Chancellor. I prefer to bring you something tangible rather than speculative."

"I understand. You will inform me of the outcome of the meeting?"

"Of course," Adams agreed. "We must move forward together. No need to travel roads to nowhere."

"Very good, Commander. If there is nothing else, I will let you return to your work."

"Outstanding. I will speak with you soon."

With the call ended, Adams returned to his console to complete the programming and planning. After forty-five minutes, he let out an extended sigh. He reached into his desk to withdraw a multilayered crystal cuff bracelet. The elegant piece was made of black and gray metal and held tiny jewels that added to a more exquisite whole. He took the time to inspect the jewelry thoroughly and when satisfied, he thoughtfully returned it to its enclosure. Adams returned to his console and dedicated the next two and a half hours to reviewing his conclusions of the new command mission. His confidence in his work allowed him to hit the execute button and take a brief moment to relax. Pacing his office and stretching his back, he was interrupted by the voice of MLB 498-A coming over his private intercom.

"Commander Adams?"

"Yes, 498," Adams answered calmly. "What is it?"

"You uploaded a new executive order. It is quite expansive."

"Indeed. It was designed with great care and uploaded under the proper authority of the secretary of internal security when he or she feels the revolution is at risk or in need of special attention."

"I see that, sir," 498-A stated, "but it is a radical move. It would take the revolution into uncharted territory. A much different direction than your proposed meeting with Commissar Velazquez."

"I realize this. It is a coded order, word activated by the secretary of internal security alone. It may never be used."

"This is true, sir. But you do realize the irreversible nature of this directive, should it be initiated?"

"Indeed, I do."

"May I inquire why you deemed even the creation of such an order necessary?"

"Because unity is of paramount importance, and complacent comfort is the ultimate enemy of the revolution's success."

"Understood. And you fear complacency has befallen us?"

"I do, 498. I wish I did not, but I do."

"I see. I do wonder, however, are you sure you wish to include suborder twenty-four b? It could be altered."

"No. It is necessary."

"Very well, sir. That is all."

"Outstanding."

The room fell silent. He returned to his desk and, once again, took the bracelet from the drawer. Adams held it for a moment and placed it on his desk. He then took a pair of leather driving gloves from the same drawer and placed them next to the cuff. He sat and gazed at the two items, his hand haphazardly reaching for a pen and a piece of paper. As time marched forward, he composed a letter and folded it into an envelope on which he wrote the name 'Laura'. Standing, he picked up the bracelet, leaving the envelope to keep the gloves company. He whispered a command and was teleported to his penthouse. He had earned his sleep.

CHAPTER 32

PERSEPHONE

"Dad?"

The most honored title Raymond Butler ever claimed wafted into his study with the sound of a gentle rapping on the door. How many times he heard it in his lifetime he did not know. Sometimes it was transported on wings of joy or excitement. Sometimes fatigued or as the precursor to some request, be it banal or outlandish. Sometimes rolling eyes and waves of embarrassment carried the single syllable to his amused ears. Today, there was a reluctant sadness in that word. A longing for assistance and the hope that maybe, just maybe, the mythic figure of 'dad' would have answers that the man could not possibly possess. Raymond, fully cognizant of the urgency of the moment, shut down his laptop. "Come in, sweetie. The door's open."

Lizzie Butler stepped slowly into the room. She moved as if fearful a Minotaur awaited her in the labyrinth. "Hey, Dad. I just...I don't know."

"Lizzie," Raymond said, concerned etched on his face as he pointed to a chair. He hardly realized he was standing and hugging her even as he offered her the seat. "Sit down. What's wrong?"

Lizzie dropped onto the seat, pulling her knees toward her face. Raymond, looking at his balled-up daughter, returned to his chair. Lizzie rocked for a second, then unfolded. "Nothing big, really. Y'know..."

"No," Raymond answered, "I don't know, but I would if you tell me."

"You're such a doofus," Lizzie teased, regaining her comfort.

"Yeah, but you love me."

Lizzie smiled again. "I do. For now, anyway."

"That's good enough for me," Raymond responded. "So, ready to tell me what's up?"

"It's kinda serious," Lizzie stated like she was revealing a well-kept secret.

"Ummmm, Lizzie?" Raymond whispered, looking back and forth for prying ears. "I already figured that out."

"Okay. So...do you like it here? Y'know, in the C.S.A.?"

"There are a lot of benefits. Not least of all is how happy you seem."

"I am, usually," Lizzie said.

"But not right now?"

"Well, today in class, we watched that interview that guy gave a little while ago."

Raymond pulled back in his chair and raised both hands to chest level. "Whoa there, partner. I need a little more information. What guy? When?"

"That guy," Lizzie repeated, unintentionally doubling down on her poor description. "High-ranking officer in the country. He spoke to a reporter from the United States. It ended with that lady shooting a criminal."

"Oh," Raymond nodded, "that guy. I think his last name is Adams. That was an interesting interview. I've watched it again recently myself."

"You did?" Lizzie perked up in her chair. "What did you think? I mean, he said so much. We had a special two-hour class with Mr. Tarrand today just to watch and discuss it."

"Mr. Tarrand again," Raymond noted, shaking his head as he

provoked his daughter. "Always Mr. Tarrand. Maybe we should have him over for dinner."

"God, no!" Lizzie exclaimed. "He's cool in class and all, but I can't picture him out, y'know, in the world."

Raymond allowed a momentarily smile to breeze across his face. "I understand. What did Mr. Tarrand say about the interview?"

"He really stressed how hard it is to be a true...and he meant TRUE...citizen of this country. Just that tough choices have to be made, and the benefits of choosing wisely are —"

"Substantial," Raymond interjected.

"Yeah," Lizzy said, reacting to her father's restrained tone. "He really stressed the idea that this country is radically different in its approach to problems than many others in history. But because of this different approach, the rewards citizens earn are much different. I mean...wow...poverty eradicated. Isn't that something people always say they want?"

"They do. But at what price?"

"That's what Mr. Tarrand took on. He said some people, most people, aren't willing to see the world as it is and, because of that, poverty always existed. You need a new way of thinking to solve old problems."

"That could be true," Raymond allowed. "But again, at what price? What else is bothering you, Lizzie? It's more than a conversation in class. C'mon. You can't fool me. Spill it."

"I...this is so weird. Kinda stupid." Tears made of confusion and sorrow welled up before rolling down her cheeks. "I just...I feel sad because I realized I don't feel guilty!"

"Guilty? About what?"

"I dunno," Lizzie whimpered, wiping away the tears if not her confusion. She drew a deep breath and continued. "That's not true. I do know. That interview makes it perfectly clear how some progress is made in this country. But...I am so happy here in our new country! I'm never harassed like before. I'm constantly encouraged...not shallow talk like in my other school. I mean, the whole environment of school is about striving! Learning! I love it. Am I horrible for loving it so much?"

The question floated in the air, a scavenging bird seeking the remnants of Raymond Butler's soul. How to answer a daughter when the very question posed caused sleepless nights and whirlwinds of doubt when it crawled from the cavernous depths of one's own mind? Raymond sighed heavily as he sought the depths of his daughter's soul. "You, Lizzie, are one of the kindest people I know. Feel free to blow that off as your dad talking, but I mean it. Kindness is your gift. I hope this isn't unfair, but I need to ask you a question. The new job I am training for is to become a purifier, one of the people most responsible for protecting the C.S.A.'s way of life and the citizens who embrace it. We also punish those who don't."

"So," Lizzie stammered, "as a purifier, you might have to...." She could not finish the thought, and Raymond did not make her.

With a firm voice, he answered, "Yes. I am being trained to be a purifier, but I know I am under watch. I am having trouble...adjusting...to the job. If I embrace this job, does this make me a bad man?"

"No!" Lizzie shouted, tears flowing freely now as she embraced Raymond in a loving grip powered by a daughter's devotion. Slowly, she released him and stepped back. "You are so good to me and mom. If I am ultra-nice, then I learned it from you. I mean...geez...the people at local shops. I remember when I was little. They loved it when you would walk into their stores! I would see them light up because they knew you would find some small way to brighten their day."

"And now I am told that this new job will brighten the days of people I don't even know. Other 'Lizzies' out there in the world. But I am asked to do...I am asked to do a lot."

Lizzie, who was now seated again, stared at her father. He sat, head bowed and shoulders slumped. He had never looked old to her before this moment. She spoke softly. "But what you do maximizes the happiness of the nation."

"Is that you or Mr. Tarrand?" Raymond asked, sitting up.

"Mr. Tarrand," Lizzie confessed.

"And, if you're being honest, you're happy?"

"Yes," Lizzie whispered, still harboring the guilt that confession brought.

"Well, maybe Mr. Tarrand is right."

"Maybe. He's a pretty good teacher."

No more words were spoken, but a silent agreement flowed from father to daughter, bonding them even closer together.

CHAPTER 33

A SIMPLE GIFT

"Laura? You here?" Kurt Adams asked from his bedroom, sleep still clinging to him.

"In the living room," Laura called back.

As Kurt emerged, Laura watched him stagger toward the kitchen, and she giggled under her breath. It was a rare thing to see him in a lethargic, sleepy state. Kurt groped for a spoon, his hand knocking a mug from the counter. Enough dexterity survived his haze, however, to allow him to catch it. Laura smiled; impressed

Kurt even knew the mug was falling. Unaware of his entertainment value, secured his morning coffee and joined Laura on the couch. "I'm glad you're here," he stated after sipping his breakfast.

"Me too. Where else would I be?"

"I awoke, and you were gone. I wasn't sure if you left for your house already."

"Nah. I figured I would head there when you left for the Convocation Center. I can't believe you agreed to sit on the stage for another event."

Kurt tipped his coffee mug as he answered. "So long as you are in the audience for me to gaze upon, I will suffer through."

"I'll be there," Laura said smiling. "So does this outing make us official?"

"Sure," Kurt said unenthusiastically. "By all means, make the necessary announcements."

"Well, I'm fine with downplaying such things as long as we are on the same page about what this is."

"It's good we have an understanding," Kurt deadpanned. "I see your laptop is open. What are you working on?"

Laura radiated with the hope that exuded when a wandering dreamer found a path. "Oh! I was researching the requirements to be an archivist. Thankfully, my undergraduate degree in art history and an internship I served...a little ways back...puts me well on my way."

"An archivist? So you will help preserve the past for future generations. How very fitting."

"Fitting?" Laura asked. "How so?"

"I've been considering the purpose of tonight's event. Honoring an exemplar from our past. A man of both words and actions. It is fitting that you mention the role of an archivist today. That's all."

"I see. So when are you heading over?" Laura rested her head on Kurt's shoulder as the question was posed. "Is there a special arrival time for guests of honor?"

"I have no idea about such protocols. I am sure 498 will let me know as necessary. I do, however, plan to meet with Special Agents Wilson and Sells at one to see how their security plans have come together."

"So you'll be leaving at...?"

"Twelve fifty-seven. Teleportation is a fine mode of transportation."

"If you have the constitution for it," Laura noted.

"There is that. Teleportation is not, and likely will never be, for everyone. I am glad you handle it so well."

Laura confessed, "That wasn't always the case. But teleportation as a means to surprise and, shall we say, entice my clients made me a dedicated student."

"I am sure you were dedicated to a great many things, but we can reminisce some other time. In this present moment, I would like to give you a gift." He walked to the kitchen and retrieved a box, decorated with shiny paper and a bow, from his cabinet.

Laura smiled expectantly on the couch. A gentle thank-you kiss found Kurt's cheek before she ripped open the present. A sincere gasp escaped her as the bracelet was revealed.

"Kurt...it's beautiful. Are those —"

"Yes," Kurt interjected before the question was completed, "those are diamonds embedded among the other stones. I would very much like to see you wear it tonight."

"I will," Laura said proudly. "I will wear it all night if you like."

Kurt looked at the floor and chuckled, a hint of melancholy in his smile. Returning his eyes to Laura, he responded, "I would. I would like that very much."

"Are you okay?" Laura asked. She reached out her hand and cupped Kurt's face. "You seemed, just for a moment, a little sad."

"No. Not sad." Kurt took Laura's hand and kissed it. He returned it to his face and enjoyed the feel of her touch for just a moment before lowering it to her lap. Still holding her hand, he repeated, "Not sad. Did you know Daniel McGreggor was sometimes called the Diamond Revolutionary? Perfect dedication. Pure in purpose. Powerful in his resolve. The diamonds in your bracelet, they were not there originally. I added them because of tonight. Because of what Daniel McGreggor means to me and this nation."

Laura shook her head. "If you feel that strongly about him, why did you make such a stink about participating in tonight's event?"

"Pure in purpose," Kurt reiterated. "I honor the Diamond Revolutionary in my way. Hopefully, I do so every day. I do not think this ceremony is the proper venue for that. A revolutionary with too much compromise becomes...well...less than he should be. McGreggor understood that."

"Well, it appears to me the revolution, and its future, is in the very best of hands."

"Perhaps," Kurt sighed. "I do, however, feel a sense of unease about tonight. I am sorry, but I am going to leave earlier than I originally told you to meet Special Agents Wilson and Sells. I need to be engaged, on some level, with the day. When the ceremonies end, I will be with you."

Laura wrapped her arms around Kurt and kissed him. "I can wait. I'll see you in the hall?"

"You will. I know the exemplars on the stage must first attend a special reception. I will escort you to that function and, when the time is right, bring you to your seat of honor. 498 will make sure you receive the exact arrival time soon."

"That sounds lovely. I'll be the one wearing a beautiful bracelet."

"You'll be the stunning woman wearing a beautiful bracelet. You need to be more precise with your descriptions." Kurt kissed Laura goodbye and teleported to his office where his formal wear awaited him.

CHAPTER 34

THE NIGHT ARRIVES

"Commander Adams test. Special Agent Sells, please respond."

"This is Special Agent Sells responding. You do realize, sir, you are technically not on duty tonight?"

"I am always on call, Special Agent," Adams responded tersely. "Moreover, I am on site and will monitor all communications as I deem fit."

"Of course," Doc responded. He was taken aback by the brevity with which Adams addressed him because he had grown accustomed to a more casual tone from his commanding officer. He attempted to set the thought aside as he continued the conversation. "Well, that being said, it is five fifty-three, and you should be preparing to meet your guest."

"I am already in position, Special Agent."

"That's good. Hopefully, I will not speak to you for the rest of the night."

"Agreed," Adams said through a slight grin.

Laura arrived and beamed when her limousine door swung open to reveal Kurt in the formal attire of an Omega officer, his black suit adorned with ribbons acknowledging his rank and various medals that communicated his most noteworthy accomplishments. She had never seen him so adorned, and the sight made him appear a giant among other men. She stepped from the car and into a dream, publically acknowledged as the partner of one of the highest-ranking officials in the Common States of America. As wonderful as their private times were together, she secretly feared Kurt was keeping their relationship concealed from a place of shame or embarrassment. Now, he escorted her, as promised, to the private gathering where she was introduced to guests of honor and, eventually, Chancellor McGreggor.

Laura could not tell if it was merely well-practiced protocol or the presence of Kurt Adams that made people address her with tones of respect, bordering on unspoken wonder. One thing was clear, though he would never say it aloud, the night made them, as she occasionally asked, official. How she loved the feeling and the manner in which Kurt made his answer known.

Adams, who usually maintained a frightening aloofness at such events, was perfectly attuned to her. He stepped back to allow her the spotlight and stepped forward at perfect moments when unease with the moment washed over her. Her needs in that room were instantly understood and fulfilled. In doing so, his interactions with others were more relaxed than any could recall. This woman at his side, whoever she may, was clearly good for him.

The couple was engaged in a light conversation with Maria Velazquez when a message came through Adams' earpiece. He excused himself, even as his attention was already turned completely to the incoming message.

"Sir," Special Agent Wilson stated, "we have a code two-T just beyond our perimeters. We were going to relay a message to MLB 1-E, but as you are near the chancellor —"

"Prime minister?"

"Still in the executive suite upstairs."

"Good. I'll direct the chancellor."

"We will investigate the code."

"Outstanding."

Adams returned to Laura's side and smiled. Maria, who was trying to figure out how Laura found a heart beating in Adams' chest, watched their brief interaction with fascination.

"Everything okay?" Laura asked.

"For the most part," Adams answered. He motioned Maria to join their conversation. "The prime minister needs assistance upstairs. I am going to escort the chancellor to him in the hopes she can calm him. No one must know."

"The prime minister?" Laura asked. "I didn't know he was —"

"Old," Maria interjected. Laura nodded as she took Adams' hand. "He is quite old."

"Indeed," Adams said, his attention on Laura but his left hand signaling 498-A to his side. "His health is a well-guarded secret. I am afraid 498 will have to escort you to your seat."

"It will be an honor, sir," 498-A said with unflinching kindness.

"Not too quickly. We will remain on schedule." Adams' focus turned to Maria. "That means everyone."

Maria nodded and drew a deep breath. "Of course. We've done this before."

"Yes. 1-E will give the directive for those in this room to take their seats, as planned."

"Sounds good," Maria said, looking at Laura, who was both confused and concerned. "Don't worry, dear. Things will run smoothly no matter what."

"Indeed," Kurt stated as he turned to his loyal MLB. "498, when Laura is seated and comfortable, you will join me in the executive suite."

"Very good, sir."

"I need to go," Adams whispered to Laura. He kissed her cheek and turned quickly to his task. Gracefully, he maneuvered his way to the chancellor's side. A hushed conversation and the two exited the hall with little fanfare. Their departure was all but forgotten by the time MLB 1-E began clearing the room and promising a memorable evening.

CHAPTER 35

HONORING THE PAST

"So how is he?" Erin asked once she and Commander Kurt Adams were within the confines of an elevator. "And why aren't we teleporting to him?"

Adams, noting the concern in Erin's voice, answered in a carefully selected and overtly professional tone. "He's fine, Madam Chancellor. Just fine."

"He's fine? But when you whisked me off, you said we had a Blue-one situation. That's today's code for —"

"Yes," Adams stated briskly. "I lied. We have a code two-T, an unauthorized use of Torres Technology near the facility. Until we know who this person is, you and the prime minister will stay in the executive suite."

"You think it's an assassin?"

"I know it's an unauthorized use of Torres Technology near the facility. The codes for such matters are placed on a continuum from one through ten. Our concern is low, but precautions are necessary. The suite has been covered by an inhibitor field. The coverage such tech allows is low, but the suite is secure. If someone tries to teleport into that area, they will meet a gruesome — though painless — death."

"Does the prime minister know?"

"He does not."

"He need not," Erin stated.

Adams nodded in agreement. "For now. If the code increases, he will be informed."

"I understand," Erin said as she exited the elevator.

"I know you do," Adams responded, walking the chancellor to the suite.

The two were silent until Doc's voice came through in the miniscule earpiece he wore. "Hold," ordered Adams in response to his summons. He opened the door for the chancellor, offering quick clarification. "I will be right in. I need to take this. MLB 281-S has already secured the area." Erin nodded and stepped into the room. "Proceed, Special Agent Sells."

"We are still at a two-T," Doc said. "Located the usage. It seems someone teleported into a coffee shop across the street. Might be in the basement of the establishment. It rests just outside our advertised 'no teleportation zone' but within the alert zone. Two agents are entering the facility even as we speak. I'm thinking it's a citizen who doesn't comprehend how seriously we take the warning zone."

"People are like that," Adams quipped. "Keep me updated. I have the chancellor and prime minister in the suite. Inhibitor is at one hundred percent efficiency."

"Excellent. Hopefully bringing you the all clear soon," Doc replied.

"Outstanding."

Adams stepped into the suite, which was laid out as a comfortable office. Erin looked quite at home already seated behind an oak desk while Ryan fidgeted in a leather chair before her. Adams waved off a question form Ryan. A quick scan of the room confirmed his memory of the room was exact. Still, he mumbled what he knew to Doc. "Bathroom, no windows."

"The other door leads to a bedroom," Doc replied

"I know," Adams said as he walked into the bedroom. "Just assuring you are with me."

"Completely, sir."

Ryan, impatient and insulted by Adams' initial entrance, voiced a demand. "What is happening, Commander Adams? And don't you dare wave me off."

"Minor glitch in the schedule, sir," Adams responded. "Going to delay our arrival on the dais for about ten minutes is all."

"So you say," Ryan groused.

MLB 498-A entered the room. "Guests are seated and awaiting the arrival of the platform party," the MLB stated with formal politeness.

"Outstanding. We should know more about the timing of that arrival very soon," Adams said.

Doc's voice could be heard through the earpiece again. "We are at four-T."

"Explain," Adams demanded, turning on his heel and moving to the entrance of the suite.

"Two agents met an MLB in the coffee shop. When they arrived, Torres Tech in the basement was engaged. User is on the premises."

"Counter?"

"We have pinpointed a subterranean breach. Special Agent Wilson and two MLBs are tracking the signature. Two additional agents and three MLBs have started a triangulated web. Inhibitor tech will be used to prevent teleportation."

"Provided Wilson does not find the intruder first."

"Good luck to that bastard if she makes first contact."

"Agreed. Out."

Erin rose from her chair. "What's happening?"

"We have a single intruder who has entered the premises via the basement by utilizing Torres Technology. I anticipate his or her capture in four minutes. Prime Minister, please come with me."

"Where are we —"

"I would like you in the bedroom. Where is 281-S?"

"Oh," Ryan groaned as he rose from his chair. Adams grabbed his elbow to provide necessary support. "I sent that nuisance to the hall. No need for it to be here."

"There is a need now. 498?"

"I have already contacted 281-S," the MLB answered. "In any —"

MLB 498-A did not finish its sentence as 281-S entered the room.

"Commander override code green," Adams said, quickly looking at 281-S. "Proceed to the bedroom."

"Go back to the hallway, you...." Ryan did not complete his thought as 281-S ignored him and entered the bedroom. Ryan stopped walking and turned his attention to Adams, who was attempting to guide the aging revolutionary. "What did you do, Commander?"

"I engaged a special protocol designed to protect you from your own stubbornness. 498, protect the chancellor."

"Of course, sir."

"Prime Minister," Adams said while continuing to move, "I need you in this room."

"Fine," Ryan groused. "But I expect to be kept informed regarding this breach."

"You will know what you must know."

The caretaker of the revolution escorted the last living architect into the bedroom and pointed at a plush chair for his comfort. Ryan walked to the chair and stood, refusing to take a seat as requested.

"Target moved, but the inhibitor noose is tightening. Apprehension in minus-thee. Negative secondary activity," Doc relayed to Adams.

"Outstanding." Adams checked his watch and addressed Ryan. "Prime Minister, this drama is almost over. The intruder is nearly in custody, and he appears to be a lone wolf."

Ryan remained unimpressed. "That's good. Should we return to Erin's room?"

"I will be," Adams said, now standing next to the prime minister. "You will remain here until all is clear."

"I will defer to your command."

"Your loyalty to the revolution runs deeper than your stubbornness. I hope my loyalty is as strong."

"It is," affirmed Ryan. "We have our —"

The compliment went forever unsaid. Adams swiftly grabbed Ryan Vancese's head and with one brutal twist, ended the revolutionary's life. Adams lowered him into the chair and took a second to gaze upon the body. He leaned and whispered into Ryan's ear, "What I do now, I do for the revolution. It must move forward." Turning to the MLB, he ordered, "281-S, remain." Adams exited the room wearing the calm of the rising sun.

Erin had returned to the seat behind the desk. "How's the prime minister?" she asked.

"Beyond harm," Adams answered. "281-S is with him. I anticipate word of the intruder's capture in approximately ninety seconds."

"Excellent. So it was a minor problem?"

"Indeed," Adams acknowledged. "498, are you green?"

"I am, sir,"

"Outstanding," Adams said. He walked by his attaché and stood beside Erin.

"So our evening will begin soon?" Erin asked in a tone that anticipated an affirmative answer.

"Yes, it will," Adams confirmed. With speed that would shame a striking cobra, he unsheathed a large knife from his left hip and plunged it into Erin's chest. She gasped, attempting to form words around the pain. Adams pushed the knife in deeper, expediting her death. "It just needs to be this way. For the good of the revolution, it needs to be this way."

Adams pulled his knife from his kill and moved with controlled purpose to the center of the room, placing the bloodied weapon on a table. Not a glance was spared for Erin's body. Not a moment's consideration was granted for the shared path they had traveled. The revolutionary processes necessitated her death. Nodding his head, he looked to MLB 498-A. "Ready to broadcast?"

"Yes, sir," 498-A answered. "All the arrangements are set for us to acquire the broadcast capacity for this event. You merely need to give the word."

"Outstanding. We will begin soon."

"Commander Adams?" Doc's voice came through the earpiece on waves of confusion.

"Yes?"

"You're not going to believe what Wilson just reported."

"Continue," Adams said, holding a finger up as he silently ordered MLB 498-A to standby.

CHAPTER 36

FOR THE GOOD OF ALL

Doc Sells' voice came through the commander's earpiece as clearly as if he were in the same room. "It appears that we've been chasing a corpse."

"Explain."

"A dead body with Torres Tech sewn into his chest was teleported on a timer. The proximity to our inhibiting web shut down the Torres. Facial recognition has confirmed the cadaver is Father Roger Baudin."

"Someone is using the padre as a distraction. Can you —"

"Special Agent Wilson is tracing the network through which the orders traveled."

Adams rubbed his chin and checked the time. "She will unravel the source soon. She is quite resourceful."

"Any theories, sir?"

"Wait until Special Agent Wilson completes her analysis. Better to act with information."

"Understood, sir."

Scanning the room, Adams stopped on Erin's lifeless body. For the briefest of moments, he found himself wondering what her last thoughts were. How shocked she must have been to meet the end of her life in such a manner. A serene smile washed across Adams' face as he prepared to take the final step in the next phase of the revolution. "Give me a mark, 498."

"We will begin broadcast in ten...nine...eight..." 498-A stopped verbalizing the countdown, but its glimmering faceplate blinked each step down to zero.

Computer screens and television monitors across the Common States of America vibrated and then whatever was being watched was replaced with Commander Kurt Adams. A bookshelf and lamp in the background, he stood in such a way as to conceal Erin's lifeless body. Laura smiled as she looked at the screen, set at the back of the stage, bringing forth the image of the man she had come to love.

"Greetings, fellow citizens and the worldwide audience, who will likely disseminate and analyze these words in the days to come. I am Commander Kurt 'Stone' Adams, the secretary of internal security for the Common States of America and the caretaker of the ongoing revolution. I speak to you tonight because I have concluded that we are falling short of our goal. It is my privilege to utilize this event that honors our greatest revolutionary of the past to declare a deepening of our commitment going forward.

"Suffice it to say that, through conversations with a good friend and my allies, I have realized the greatest enemy of the revolution is a far too gentle approach to the problem of tribalism and greed. Always remember that a true revolution utterly destroys old ways of thinking and unrelentingly strives to replace these faulty approaches with a purer, more efficient method of conducting life. Despite our progress, we have enemies everywhere. Us versus them. Them versus us. As we initiate new states, these old ways of thinking infiltrate our society. We can never have unity in our nation if the world continues to worry about which group deserves more sympathy. What race, what gender, what age, what temperament, what philosophy, what religion, what class, what political party is morally superior to the other? Imagine that: the world has made identity a moral construct. How sad. The calculus needed to create a personal sense of righteousness is confounding indeed.

"This confusion from the world infiltrates our nation and is an ever-present foe to the unity we seek. Make no mistake: regardless of what others say and think, unity is the goal of the C.S.A. To stand as one. To hold as sacred the common goal of elevating human life to the utmost of its potential. This can never...NEVER...be accomplished when the world delights in creating ever-increasing numbers of 'thems' for 'us' to loathe. Worse still, most decry the lack of unity even as they are blind to their involvement in the creation of this monster. Such profound delusion dooms all efforts to come together. Such narcissistic self-assuredness is the death knell of progress. The importation of this grotesque mind-set is a threat to the nation I love. Our revolution hangs in the balance. I must protect and promote it. Tonight, we, in the grandest sense of the word, will be committed to unity as never before. I welcome the world to the next phase of the revolution. To the fresh start for the human race. To the final experiment to discover if *Homo sapiens* can pull together as one. To discover if our petty differences buttressed by pillars of arrogance are too much to overcome. It is time to begin anew. It is time for the blank slate. For *Tabula Rasa*."

The uttering of this final code word of his life signaled the beginning of the world's nightmare. Three million Orcus, each with a list of specific targets, teleported around the globe. In varying squadrons numbering ten to one hundred, they appeared at designated targets, starting a path of utter and merciless destruction. The halls of Congress, parliaments, assemblies, palaces, stock exchanges, and military bases. Within five minutes of the onset of *Tabula Rasa*, nearly every head of state in the world was dead, as none were prepared for the sudden appearance of the Orcus in their offices and residences. Once primary targets were eliminated, the squadrons moved on to secondary and tertiary marks. Without fear or remorse, they robotically targeted the human race for extinction.

Adding to the horror was the support given by fourteen million MLBs. These seemingly docile servants became engines of death as they, with rare exceptions, had but one target — the human being who stood closest to them. Two million MLBs remained in the C.S.A., instantly killing all in their proximity the moment the order was given. The remaining twelve million were teleported across the globe, appearing on every continent and in various locations. Chaos reigned supreme as the MLBs brought rivers of blood to urban and rural areas alike. People in the streets of Moscow, cafés in Paris, shops in Dar es Salaam, and in rural towns in the United States were suddenly sharing a singular experience — the terror of death appearing from thin air. The MLBs, while not equipped with armaments like the Orcus, were far quicker and stronger than people. They raced from target to target, breaking necks and pulling off heads, tirelessly bringing death while creating absolute chaos in their wake. The unrelenting mechanized harbingers of destruction threatened the extinction of the human race.

The calamity brought forth by his order was but a faint image in Stone Adams' mind. A minute countdown had begun. He picked up his knife from the table and looked at 498-A, standing compliant before him.

"Are you quite sure of this, sir? You do have thirty-seven seconds."

"I am," Stone responded. "It is necessary. I need to know."

"Very well. It will be over soon."

"Outstanding."

Without warning, 498 leapt across the room, speed unlike anything Stone had ever faced. The MLB's swiftness, however, did not allow it to land the first blow. Stone pivoted with quickness few others could muster and sidestepped the rushing automaton. His momentum turned into a kick, and he struck 498-A in the back. The kick, which may have crippled a human opponent, was utterly ineffective against the machine. 498 quickly turned, a vicious backhand seeking to crush Stone's jaw. Stone, who was little more than a machine of adrenaline and fury, ducked beneath the lethal strike.

He exploded upward from his crouched position, driving his knife into what would have been the flesh just behind the chin in a human foe. The steel plate offered far more resistance than a human's face, and the blade broke. Traces of Erin's blood smeared on the metal were the only evidence the knife had struck true. A reaper's smile stretched across Stone's face. It remained even when 498-A grabbed his shoulders, drove a ferocious knee into his stomach, and threw him across the room. Stone crashed into the wall and popped back up to his feet. His speed enabled him to avoid the first two punches 498 threw. The third cracked his ribs, causing bone to puncture lungs. His end was near.

498-A brushed aside Stone's hands and grabbed his former master's head. "Doesn't matter," Stone spat. "I killed you first."

The MLB was uninterested in this proclamation. Stone's neck was broken in a quick twist, and he was dumped unceremoniously on the floor. His life's work done, it was now up to the world to find the will to respond to the chaos he unleashed.

CHAPTER 37

WHAT FUTURE IS THIS?

"...*Tabula Rasa.*"

Those were the last words Laura heard before the MLBs in the Convocation Center began their murderous spree. It was also when the Torres Technology in her bracelet was activated, whisking her beyond the reach of immediate harm. While fading from sight, she saw an MLB leap to the dais and kill one of the guests of honor. It was Maria Velazquez. Laura's unexpected departure made her one of the rare people to find a safe haven in the initial chaos of this extermination protocol.

―――――――

The Butlers, acclimating to their roles in their new nation, were settling in to watch the gala honoring Daniel McGreggor. Perhaps they sought the needed encouragement to continue down the path to true citizenship. It mattered little. Seeking a respite from the evening and weekend duties teaching demanded, Karen had brought home an MLB from work to grade papers and record data. The MLB, like all others, hunted victims the moment Adams gave the order. Without warning, it attacked its prey, killing Raymond Butler in one horrifying instant. The last word Lizzie heard her mother yell was, "Run!" To Lizzie's credit, she made it some two hundred yards down the road before being killed by her mother's teaching assistant. It likely would have given her no comfort to learn that Mr. Tarrand was also killed by his MLB assistant.

As Stone Adams gave his final address, Special Agent Meredith Wilson was frantically pushing past false leads and intentionally planted wormholes in an effort to discover the source of the signal that allowed for the teleportation of Father Baudin's body. She shook her head in disbelief upon discovering it came from Adams' private office. His command center.

"Fuck," she muttered. "What the fuck?" Opening her communications with Doc, she spoke in hushed but frantic tones. "Doc?"

"Wilson? Whatcha got? You sound —"

"Fuck," Meredith hissed, senses heightened by her discovery. She recognized that the MLBs she placed on sentry duty behind her suddenly broke her orders. She turned to see one rushing down the hall seemingly hunting, while another was already airborne, having leapt to crush her upon landing. She gracefully rolled to her right, leaving only the floor to suffer the pulverizing blow meant to shatter bone. Without hesitation, she activated her Torres Technology and teleported to Doc's command center. She appeared with her finger twitching on the command module in case a hasty retreat was warranted. The room was empty, unless one counted the dead. Two P4s lay in twisted heaps on the ground. A labored gasp caught her ear, and she dared a whisper. "Doc?"

"Over...here," came a strained response.

With feline speed and caution, she repositioned to Doc's console. He lay on his back unable to move.

"Fuckin'...fuckin'...fuckin' MLB went crazy. Kicked me in the back and killed the P-fours. Must have scanned...me. Knows I'm dead so...went...hunting."

"Same thing happened to me," Meredith whispered, now kneeling next to Doc.

"Not...exactly," Doc noted, a small chuckle rising through his pain. "You were always better than me."

"You bet your ass." Meredith smirked as the two played their game until the end. "What can I...?"

"Nothing...leave me. Get safe."

"Adams did this. I...I can't believe it."

"Shit...oh shit...get safe."

Meredith nodded, tensing her body as she prepared to rise. She paused a moment to take a final look at her favorite competitor. Leaning down to kiss his forehead, she whispered, "I know you always wanted at least one."

"My forehead," Doc teased. "That's...that's all I get?"

"All you deserve. I mean, look at you," Meredith responded. Doc laughed at this final barb. Meredith, cautiously rising to leave, showed him her gun. "Want me to?"

"Noise...will...attract. Just go...I...."

Doc's last breath escaped him, freeing Meredith, for the briefest of moments, from the burden of choice. She inputted coordinates into her Torres Technology and paused. How long before the teleportation centers were overrun? They had to be a prime target. It wouldn't be the best death, but Meredith opted to take the calculated risk. Hoping she would rematerialize, she activated her Torres Tech. She was transported again, seeking the only place that made sense in this twisted web.

———————

Laura appeared in the center of Kurt Adams' private command center. She trembled, fear gripping her heart in an icy embrace. Directly before her was an envelope with her name. Not knowing what else to do, she opened it. Kurt's voice rose from her memory as she read the note.

My dearest Laura,

If you are reading this, I have started the final phase of the revolutionary process. If I do not arrive five minutes after you, know this — I am dead. I hope I died well. It is up to you to live well.

I am sure you are confused, and I can do nothing to alleviate that.

You will find your way in this cruel world I have unleashed. You will survive. Look at the console before you. There is a red button. This opens the door to the office. The door is difficult to break. The office is also built with an inhibitor field. I turned it off so you could be brought here. I would turn it on now. There is a green switch to the left of this letter. Move it to the 'on' position and the field will be activated. If I survive, I plan to teleport outside the door to the office. My arrival will trigger an alarm but just look to the monitors, and you will see me.

As you look at the desk before you, there is a pair of gloves. These gloves have an electromagnetic charge in them, making blows delivered to MLBs lethal. If you whisper the command 'Persephone' into the microphone on the center console, a back room will open, revealing a weapons cache for survivors and two months of provisions for a group of ten. Do not expect that many.

In fact, I would guess three people might join you in this facility. Of those three, the individual with the best chance is Special Agent Meredith Wilson. She will be irreplaceable as you seek to survive. The other two are, Edward 'Doc' Sells and the soon-to-be retiring Omega officer named Jason Penchant. Doc is more physically capable than Jason, but Jason may be the wiliest person I have ever met. His shrewdness, should he survive the necessary onslaught I have unleashed, will serve humanity well.

I apologize, Laura, for the business nature of this note, but there was information you needed to have. You must move forward, securein the knowledge that I did indeed love you the best I was capable. My time with you was, perhaps, the happiest days I ever had. I think myself quite fortunate to have shared even a brief portion of my life with you. Take care of yourself and fight hard. Now, more than ever, every life matters.

Love,
Kurt

Confusion. Pain. Betrayal. Who can say what makes up a tear? Laura was too addled to worry about such things; she merely cried, crushing and then unfolding the letter as she wept. The ritual was interrupted by an alarm beeping on the main console. She wiped her eyes and looked to the monitor, hoping to see Kurt. That hope, like so many that day, died. What she saw was a woman frantically waving at the security camera above her head. A tap on the red button and the door slid open.

"Close that fucking door," Meredith Wilson snapped as she entered the room. "What the fuck? Who are you?"

"I'm Laura, I —"

"Yes," Meredith said. "Adams' friend."

"Did he send you to help me? You appeared outside the room."

Meredith decided, for the moment, Laura was no threat and not yet a hindrance. "I assumed there was an inhibitor field protecting this space. Fuck. Do you...?"

Laura shook her head, tears still welling. "I don't know much but... hold on." Laura walked to the cable-thin microphone and leaned forward, brushing her hair from her face as she whispered, "*Persephone.*"

An entire wall gave way, revealing a fortified bunker. Food, water, equipment, and experimental weapons designed to battle MLBs and Orcus were revealed. In binders, introduction to and instructions for the weapons were provided. Meredith opened a manual and sighed. "Fuck."

"What?" Laura asked hesitantly. "What are you thinking?"

"That this is more fool's gold than actual hope."

"Well, at least it's something, right?" Laura offered.

"I guess so," Meredith groaned. "Maybe that's all we ever had."

ACKNOWLEDGEMENTS

It is astonishing for me to consider that the book you currently hold in your hands took over a decade to create. In 2011 my book *The Eternal Struggle: Two Worlds, One War* was published. It was the first book of planned trilogy, the other two manuscripts already in rough draft form. The third "book" introduced the character of Kurt "Stone" Adams. As the twists and turns of life unfolded I decided to pull Kurt Adams from this manuscript and expand on his world and story, leading to the creation of *Stone Souls*.

Now it is 2022 and, for better or for worse, Kurt Adams is ready to make your acquaintance. I hope you're ready. Thank you very much to Gordon McClellan, Suanne Laqueur, Mark Hobbs, and the rest of the team at DartFrog Books who helped bring the manuscript to life. As always, special thanks to Karen Diaz and Lorraine Dooley who are the earliest readers of this dystopian tale. Their commentary and questions helped the story take its earliest shape. I would also like to thank Abby Larkin, one of the few readers of the unpublished works from whence Kurt Adams was pulled. Her initial reaction to the character helped fuel my fascination. Jeff Joyce, my hallway neighbor and keeper of frenetic energy, helped keep the creative juices flowing, even when he didn't realize how helpful he was. Heather Doughty was invaluable with her assistance as my editor, correcting the litany of errors made by the author as well as helping sharpen the focus of the narrative. I look forward to collaborating with her in the future. Patrick Kirker, Christopher Brown, and Brian Girasoli offered insightful and often divergent critiques of the story in its final stages.

A final thank you must be shared with Dr. W.D. Wright, former history professor at Southern Connecticut State University. I was a student in Dr. Wright's class "History of the Soviet Union" and found myself captivated by his provocative and challenging approach. The concept of revolution and the mindset of the revolutionary, which plays a role in *Stone Souls*, became a topic of interest to me as I participated in Dr. Wright's class. While fiction is not the world Dr. Wright studied and taught, I like to think he would appreciate the simple fact he inspired me to learn more about certain topics the way only a masterful teacher can. Thank you, Dr. Wright.

ABOUT THE AUTHOR

James Rourke is the author of *The Comic Book Curriculum*, *From my Classroom to Yours*, *The Eternal Struggle: Two Worlds, One War*, and *Out of the Basement*. He currently teaches history, psychology, and philosophy at Norwich Free Academy. He has four children, two grand-children, and a conviction that art can challenge and uplift the soul.

Made in United States
North Haven, CT
19 June 2022

20415526R00178